THE
COLOR
INSIDE
A
MELON

THE
COLOR
INSIDE
A
MELON

a novel

John Domini

DZANC
BOOKS

5220 Dexter Ann Arbor Rd.
Ann Arbor, MI 48103
www.dzancbooks.org

Library of Congress Cataloging-in-Publication Data

First US Edition: June 2019
Cover design: Original artwork by Frank Hansen (Moberg Gallery, Des Moines, IA), and design by Steven Seighman
Interior design by Michelle Dotter

Printed in the United States of America

10   9   8   7   6   5   4   3   2   1

For Michelle Dotter —
& all the immigrants.

If in Naples, I should report this now, would they believe me,
if I should say I saw such islanders?

— *The Tempest*

ONE

YOU REACH A CERTAIN CORNER of the city, a certain hour, when you've taken a hit and there's a man in your face, and it's something else altogether. It's not at all the town you know. You've learned to work its angles, even a street market in midsummer, the stink and caterwaul and the need to squint as a fishmonger raises a hose over his stall and casts a halo over the day's catch. You've learned the code in the echo off the stones at 3 a.m. Could be some lonesome soul out trolling for company, could be you need to double-check the lock. You've grown accustomed to the compromises, lurching after aspiration and against the short leash of everything else. Yet you reach the right urban cranny, or rather the wrong one, where your head's burning from someone else's knuckles, where the guy's actually got a knife out—then whatever you think you know, it's a fairytale. What *were* you thinking, anyway? Sodom, Xanadu? If you've got a view, a terrazzo, a rooftop—if the attack left you facing away from the party and out over the city—everything you see appears rimed or studded with gold, that's the pain, and even after the hallucination fades you're left with something else entirely. Five stories below (or is it fifteen, for a woozy moment?), the hubs and spokes wink in and out of sight. You can't rely on the streetlights. It's no longer Naples, the place a native Italian would call your "adopted home." That city's disappeared. It's gone to join the one you were born in: Mogadishu, another place that people were foolish enough to think they knew.

All of a sudden, all over again, you're the alien. No clue.

⌗

Risto swayed at the rooftop wall, wondering if he'd have to fly.

It wasn't as if he could call a cop. The man who'd swatted him was a cop, or as close to it as you were going to find up here. Here at the top of an abandoned palazzo, they'd set up a club for the night. Risto's assailant was one of the bouncers. Up here, at penthouse level, the building had only two apartments, and now Risto found himself pinned against the railing of a terrazzo, and the rawboned creep who held him, just five, ten minutes earlier, had stood collecting the cover charge outside the apartment door. The place still had a door. There were doors enough, up here, that in one of the rooms they must've kept a whore. They must've had a card game going too, the crew that ran this dance-and-drinks arrangement, this party that floated from one condemned property to another. Whores and cards, that's what brought in the real money. The take would be paltry at both the gate and the bar. What passed for a bar, and for a gate. Never mind that tonight they had a sweet setup, La Fenestrella. The penthouse had a real terrazzo, more than big enough for pushing and shoving and throwing a punch.

There could've been a whole garden up here, back before the spring earthquake. Could've been a grape arbor. Even with his back to the dance floor, Risto had a feel for its extent, the long way the DJ's vibrations had to travel. Still, the drinks and cover wouldn't bring in enough to keep the cops looking the other way. The club was asking five Euros, but Risto had seen a couple of girls pay no more than a smile. Himself, he'd glided in on the say-so of a couple of friends, veterans of the scene, Eftah and Giussi. As for this bouncer, he might've been paid in Ecstasy. La Fenestrella floated on the fringes and paid in crumbs, and that Risto should find himself in such a place was itself a wild hair.

Yet this free-handed "security" had gone wilder. As the man muscled Risto to the rail, he'd kept grinding against Risto's butt. Looking to tweak his high?

Risto himself may have started tweaking. He was cold sober and hetero and yet he'd choked out a wisecrack, *You should try this on my friends*. If the tough guy wanted to cop a feel, he should try Giussi especially, always quick to work the dancers. By the time Risto got smacked, Giussi had already made a pickup. Still, the bouncer could've tried his moves on Risto's so-called "cousin," Eftah. Eftah would've welcomed the attention, because the men who liked men tended to prefer his boyfriend. The cousin had got himself a willowy hothouse flower, Moroccan, while the crowd here was mostly mushroom-shaped. Out of the sub-Sahara, like Risto.

Not that he had the chance to make suggestions. His little quip was squelched and he'd wound up head and shoulders over the rail. At his back, the bouncer held one arm bent and pinned.

Below, the hubs and spokes winked and reeled. Was that the fish market where they gave good weight? Or over there, was that the dome of the Galleria? Ground Zero for folks with real money, the Galleria and its piazzas were safe; you could walk those blocks till deep in the night, and with that thought Risto found he could straighten up. He could brace his free hand on the rail and stand, facing out rather than down. After that, he took a moment to paw his head.

He'd made an easy target, no question. At his first job in Naples, he'd been the smallest brother on the docks, and tonight, years later, he was a doughboy compared to most of the crowd. Clubgoers here picked the local tomatoes and mucked out the buffalo barns; they did the heavy lifting for cut-rate construction. Risto might be as dark as any of them, but he had the fingers of a keyboard jockey. On his job, what he needed most was a good eye.

Tonight, he ought to be the last person to raise difficult questions. Now that he had, though, and now that he'd regathered maybe half a brain, *per carità,* he ought to try and find some help. Try and find the friends who'd brought him. Working against his pinned wrist, Risto wormed this way and that against the rail. There, yes, Eftah. He gave a yell. Eftah might not be a cousin exactly, but up here he was family, and such a slab of immigrant beef he could've worked as a bouncer himself. He wore a party scent, flirtatious, citrus, but as he approached, the man at Risto's back let go.

Everyone got some breathing room.

Risto sized up his adversary: a stretch of tarred rope, a Tutsi, taller. His sharp corners were brought out by his jacket, a narrow-waisted, canary-yellow disco affair worn with the cuffs rolled. Plus a V-cut Afro, another throwback. But then, this "Papers" wanted people to look. He wanted customers, Papers, because he ran a business out of a pocket inside the back of his coat. That's where the trouble had started.

Could've been worse. Papers had moves that suggested he'd done time in the military, a backhand blow that smarted as if his knuckle were a deadbolt. Also Risto wasn't just the softie in this crowd; he was the newbie. Down in his art gallery, at the desk where he keyed in his checks and deposits, he might be Citizen Aristofano, a legitimate Italian. Tonight, in a club off the books, mostly for folks off the books, he was nobody. Most of the men and women here, like Risto, revealed a lot of melanin in the epidermis, but no one else had been so dimwitted as to pester an enforcer. No one would be impressed by Risto's I.D. These two to either side, boxing him against the rail, they knew the drill. Tonight probably wasn't the first time they'd gotten out the knives.

Workaday knives, and neither man put the weapon on display. Both kept it down at hip-level. A minute ago, a minute and a half, the bouncer had flourished his in Risto's face, menacing, deliberate, but now Papers and Eftah might've been back in a pig farm outside Mogadishu. Might've been closing in on tonight's butcherwork. Also both blades were serrated. Eftah's was the classic, the handyman tool, and Risto's cousin liked to boast that the make was Finnish. Papers held a switchblade, something that once must've been a showpiece, tiger-striped. By now, though, the handle was smudged, the plating nicked. Along the blade, serrations made you think of melon wedges.

Anyway, how could anything be a showpiece, in this broken-down venue? Show and art—what did they have to do with this brute corner and hour?

Risto knew the neighborhood. It sprawled across one of the Naples highlands, the outcroppings that hemmed in the old center and the bay. Not a bad neighborhood, for this city, though you couldn't rely on the streetlights. Repairs were still catching up since the quake. Fifteen weeks ago, back in springtime, tremors had wracked the metro area. Italian authorities had rushed in, plus international agencies, NATO, the UN. They'd all rushed in. Since the last big quake, in 1980, they'd had plans in place, "contingencies," and yet even now there remained pockets of wreckage. Even fifteen weeks past the Event, the sulfur lingered on the air, as if Vesuvius were a cookie cracked open just to drink in the smell. Tonight, down outside this palazzo, the most visible evidence of repair work had been the barricade at street level. Inspectors, post-quake, had declared the building too dangerous. But, follow-up? Infrastructure? PVC pipe blocked the front doors with a rig that suggested a jungle gym, and the crossbars were X'd with orange tape.

That was it. Naples had organized repair teams, Rome had sent emergency response units, NATO had trucked in uniforms, and the UN had whipped up fundraising. Still, five stories below, all you had was a ramshackle Do-Not-Cross. If there'd been a chain, a lock, anything, it was gone now. The warning tape flapped on the summer night. Strips of hard orange, kaboom: their flutter caught the light from a rewired block nearby. Risto thought of his gallery, of Chagall and his fireworks.

His gallery, his business, the whole-cloth construction called law and order—in tatters against the dark.

Risto drew to full height, though some ratchet in his spine seemed to skip a gear. He winced too at the mix of cheap perfume and rooftop tar, but he wouldn't let the party distract him. Citizen Aristofano, gallery owner, he palmed his shaved head and eyed his big semi-relation. *We cool?* Then he took in the man who'd just about thrown him off the roof. Him with the bat-wing shoulders and the black-market sideline.

He made sure he had Papers' eye. "A new world, eh? That's what you promised: a *new world.*"

The bouncer had made a sales pitch, a presentation. Three minutes ago? Five? Heavy-knuckled though he was, Papers had shown a light touch, jogging a manila folder just enough to allow contraband documents to peep out.

"But look what you show me. I could be back with the thugs in 'Dishu."

Now those documents were once more tucked out of sight, in the back of the dealer's flashy coat. The man himself was wary, glancing around.

"The promises you made," Risto went on, "I was right to push you a little. Find out what kind of a person I was dealing with."

Any other situation, his toughneck pretense would've made him laugh. But Papers shifted to the defensive. When you glanced where he kept glancing, you saw he'd come a long way from his post at the doorway.

"What kind of a person I'm dealing with, that's what I've got to find out—"

"He's with you?" Papers turned to Eftah, frowning.

The so-called cousin replied with a smile. He could count on the impact, teeth like his in a club so far outside the Italian dental plan.

"Ef-tah, right? The brother who charges a white man's rent."

"The Black Lord," said Eftah, "of No-Account Real Estate."

"And this type here, he came with you?"

Even as the bouncer asked, he was thinking about his job. Papers kept casting glances across the dance floor, though no one appeared to have taken an interest. The club was called La Fenestrella, "The Little Window"—never open on the same street twice—and they kept a doorman in reserve. The new guy carried more flab than Papers, and his brightly colored T-shirt made him look even fatter, but around him the party went on undiminished. So what if there was a tussle at the roof's edge? So what if the knives came out? Most of these brothers and sisters were carrying some weapon or other. Most of them hadn't needed September 11th to remind them what you can accomplish with a box cutter.

Anyway this was Sunday, at least till midnight. The main attraction so far was the breeze up here, a relief so late in July. The primary action remained clustered along the bar, crates-&-coolers, though a few couples had begun to bop. Everyone had better things to do than worry about some squabble in the corner. Or everyone except the lone white couple, kids hardly out of their teens, all of a sudden nowhere to be seen. Risto thought about that a moment (why not dial things down, a moment?), and recalled that the two rabbits had seemed almost to glow in the dark. They'd been done up in hipster black, going Goth for La Fenestrella. Black leather jackets and pale babyfat faces—they'd had enough of this scene. More than likely the ten Euros meant nothing to them. Among the Africans, meanwhile, Risto noticed only one paying special attention. Another rawboned type, this one had wrists and elbows scuffed with labor, chalky. The guy had been dancing, and the girl with him looked ready to party. She'd given some thought to that tube top. But all of a sudden, her partner had quit his boogie and turned to study the confrontation.

You could see this man had put in years in the field, scowling at the weather. You had to figure that a *nero* dealing in contraband, like Papers, was going to have backup.

Now the dealer spoke: "You want to make an arrangement, truly?"

The crook's Italian had that street formality.

"You came to me," Risto reminded him. "You figured I had the money."

"I did see you have the money. I did see you were—looking. A man who came looking, you know? What if I told you I wondered if you were police?"

Eftah gave a snort.

"In fact. For a person such as you to be police, how does that make sense? Doesn't make any sense at all. The police wouldn't go to the trouble, and they'd never send a houseboy such as you."

The dealer gave a sneer and his backup closed in. This new arrival, the guy scuffed with hard labor, wanted everyone to notice. He got his sandals flopping, punctuating the DJ's thrum. If the accomplice had a weapon, he kept it out of sight, but when he and Papers stood together, there was no mistaking that they'd made their way across the Mediterranean by tooth and claw.

So it was two against two, and Risto had no better option than to keep up the act. "Then how," he asked, "did you and I ever set off a comedy like this? Two reasonable people, trying to do a bit of business."

"Signore, are you forgetting? You put your hands on me."

"You wouldn't give me a straight answer. I was trying to ask about our poor murdered brother, and all you had to say…"

"Again with that faggot. Again the *murdered brother.*"

"How else am I to know who I'm dealing with? How else?"

"Houseboy, what? First you need a debate, 'New blacks in old Europe'?"

Risto's line had always been a lame excuse, and Papers had kicked away its cane. But Eftah, the way he smiled, you'd think he'd welcome a debate.

"Blacks like that boy," the dealer went on, "what can I tell you? What, another pair of working arms? Another one who'd never find the way out, the new world? But then there's you, a man who came here looking."

※

Aristofano: philosopher of happiness. Giussi liked to explain, he liked any opportunity to show off his book learning, and the gallery owner these days would've taken himself for a happy man. Granted, his name had gotten its start as a convenience. Back when he'd owned little more than the shirt on his back, a teenager new to the Naples accent, he'd accepted this hey-you with a shrug. "Aristofano" was the best that the locals could do, especially the Chinese who ran the docks. Anyway his actual name had always had a dubious feel, as one of the possible titles for a lizard god out of the Bakool Hills. A bush word, it posed a challenge for everyone, Risto included. His parents raised him with the colonial languages. Time and again they'd been forced into exile, yet Maman and Papà had never let go of their dream, Mogadishu the Jewel in the Horn of Africa. At home Risto had spoken French and Italian, and he'd attended the last of the schools run by the Dominican friars. His brother too.

These days, sure he was happy. He was happy in his marriage and his children, a boy and girl who dawdled just now in that agreeable parenthesis between infant demands and adolescent rancor. He had an Italian passport and, around his adopted city, a winner's reputation. Yet tonight—or was it already Monday morning?—he'd taken that reputation well past the breaking point.

Didn't make sense at all. But then, neither did bloody murder, and since learning of Friday night's homicidal insanity. Risto had suffered a sympathetic madness. The frenzy had brought him here, believing this

the likeliest place to begin looking for answers, to "find that butcher."
Yet look what he'd found first: a couple of blades catching the glare.
And for reassurance, all he had were these tagalongs, the men with
whom he'd shared his crazy notion. Granted, Giussi and Eftah had
agreed with him at once, and later Eftah's boyfriend. Granted, they
hadn't come up here just for the dancing. But it wasn't as if they ob-
jected to the dancing. The harlequin at the door, in his vampire 'do,
had speedily waved them in: all regulars, other than Risto. All among
the first to learn tonight's location. Wherever La Fenestrella set up, the
warlords who ran the joint sent word via text. A cryptic notice, and
never a tweet or an email. As Giussi put it, all of a sudden a child of the
South Bronx: "Bes' keep it on de downlow." That was the rule, and if
a newcomer expected to get any answers, he needed to play ball. The
least whiff of the law could—this came from Eftah's boyfriend—"open
up a second mouth for you, *compris?*"

Nevertheless, they'd all agreed to visit La Fenestrella that very
night. Just putting out feelers across the dance floor was more than
anyone could expect of the police.

What did the police care about a brother cut to ribbons? A *clandestino?*

The cops would note the fine bottle-black of the victim's Shabeeleh
Valley skin, and they would ascertain that he'd gone by the name La
Cia. They would determine that he too had been a kind of dealer,
hustling his own flesh when he didn't have better work, and they might
even have learned that the name had nothing to do with the cha-cha.
With that, the authorities would have a report, a fine clean printout,
along with a list of the evidence found at the scene. Throw in a few
turn-your-stomach snapshots, and they'd have a file. They'd label it in
block letters and assign it to a drawer.

Tonight, on the littered and rancid stairs leading up to the club,
Eftah had put it this way: "I've lived in Naples too long to have illu-
sions about the law."

Eftah admitted to forty-five, though like Giussi he preferred a nattering game of Pin the Age on the Clubhound. Then too, like La Cia,
both Giussi and the cousin had tenuous standing under Italian law. Ef-

tah appeared to have set down an anchor in this country, holding title on three apartment buildings. Yet whatever claim the man held to these properties could only be partial; the mortgage must list some silent partner. Eftah still hadn't earned his citizenship. He had never so much as gone down to the courthouse, not even when Citizen Aristofano had offered to stand as his sponsor. Then there was Giussi, almost as much a *clandestino* as the victim. The Ethiopian might be well read, but he scratched for a living, mostly in film and performance. Every year brought some fresh wrangle about his visa, and these supplied Giussi's stage shows with some of their wittiest disdain. After all, a low opinion of the authorities was hardly limited to folks with his or Eftah's skin tone. White Italians too, the savvy ones like Aristofano's wife, could see that the homicide had already become a political football.

Ordinarily a murder in the underclass, and smeared with the warpaint of perversion, would've been beneath the attention of the mayor and the governor. Yet though the body had turned up only night before last, already both these ranking local politicians had given the case lip service. They'd thrown around expressions like "the new Europe." The city's mayor complained in particular about where the killing had taken place. The scene of the crime had been another "irregular" dance club, like tonight's venue. La Cia had bled to death in the former back office of a clothing factory, the doors to which bore another of those warning notices in Halloween colors. The *Regione di Campania* had declared the building unsafe, and yet if you asked the governor of the *Regione*, he'd say the setting was incidental. The blame, insisted the governor, lay instead with a federal agency, the Office of Immigration. If that office had been doing its job, this illegal would've been on a boat back to Africa long ago. It wasn't the local authorities with blood on their hands, but rather the suits-&-ties up in Rome, where the party in power was that of the mayor—the opposition to the governor. Back and forth these two tossed the ball, to the tune of high-sounding rhetoric. Aristofano's wife had hit the mute button.

You think a white girl doesn't know bullshit when she hears it? Paola asked.

Born in Naples, his wife had the local cynicism, tangy, as much juice as rind.

You think I can't tell when they're striking poses? she asked. *Telling stories? There's blood on the floor, and these two, all they care about is their shoes.*

Actually, Risto had come to admire the mayor. In this country, she seemed exotic, a woman in office. After the quake, she'd run all over the greater metro area, laying out cash and posting uniforms. She'd arranged for the "Earthquake I.D.," a document essential for a lot of the homeless. But when La Cia went to pieces, so did whatever benefit of the doubt Risto was willing to give Madame Mayor or anyone else. The victim hadn't been a friend, but he'd been a friend of friends. He'd been among the circle that came through the gallery. So Saturday morning, after Risto put his RAI web broadcast up on the widescreen, after Paola saw what had him devouring the Internet, he was glad to hear her cry bullshit. He tried to match her grin, though this felt like a mask slipping into place. Beneath, taking shape, was something else entirely.

There'd been no need for furtive texts. He knew that come Sunday dinner, Giussi would be joining them. The gallery owner made sure they had an extra bottle on the table, next to the linguine and octopus. Good country Falanghina, and after three glasses and then some, he hadn't lifted a finger when Paola began to clear. He'd taken Giussi out on the balcony.

"I'm going to make some inquiries." Quiet as Risto was, he nonetheless made it an announcement. "I'm going to find out who killed La Cia."

Giussi's smile too suggested a mask, but on him this was nothing out of the ordinary. He kept it on the downlow. "*Inquiries*, brother, hmm."

Risto settled against the balcony rail.

"*Inquiries*, oh la, one thinks of a senator on trial. One thinks of a case that could drag on into infinity. I'd advise against ongoing inquiries."

The husband looked back through the doors, but Paola was in the kitchen. She enjoyed the hostess do-si-do.

"The better part of wisdom suggests, rather, a brief exploration only."

"But, naturally it needs to happen fast." Risto's nod was agitated. "An investigation like this, eh."

"We have, what is it, sixty hours? Isn't that the figure, sixty hours, otherwise the birds will have eaten all the breadcrumbs and you'll never find your way home? I've seen enough *noir* to know..."

"No, no." Now shaking his head. "I don't want to hear it."

Giussi's smile had grown almost paternal. The man's cadaverous build might be typical for an Ethiopian, but in his case the speedy metabolism seemed connected with a knack for swapping out one face for another. In centuries past he would've come to town among a troupe of Players, up on stilts and tooting a fife. He would've had a quip about the tube between his lips.

"Giussi, this is no movie. No movie, no fairytale—whatever we find, we take to the police. I'm not looking to wind up with a knife at my throat."

"Then, for a deadline, shall we say the *Expo in Città*?"

"*Expo in Città*, Friday. Sounds reasonable."

"Oh la, my brother, reasonable..."

"The opening celebration. If we get this butcher, we can celebrate."

"Actually, we'd have to finish our business by Thursday night. The celebration, just as you say, that's the next morning. All the events start gearing up—your opening, my own performance."

"Sure. Your show too, down by the Galleria. Look how it all comes together. We hand this bastard over to the police and then go out and enjoy the party."

"Why, he's thought it all through, our *Aristofano filosofo*."

Risto, massaging his eyes, spoke to the fire-pink creases between his fingers. "It's just, the boy deserves better. La Cia. He was one of us. One of the millions, trying... "

"*America I'm putting my queer shoulder to the wheel.*"

Okay, uncover the eyes. Giussi was dropping into a chair. "A sweetheart out of New York," he said blithely. "Also one of us, you might say, if by *us* you meant the queer. A poet, a sweetheart, a name you'd know."

The gallery owner had been working himself up to this for a day and half.

"Giussi, you don't understand. The Expo, you think that matters? What matters is Paola. My *wife*—she sets the deadline."

His guest cocked his narrow head.

"Paola's out of the picture this week. Morning after tomorrow, she leaves to join the kids, and she's staying away till the Expo."

"Eftah," Giussi said. "For this adventure, we need Eftah. You know he's game."

Adventure?

"You know our Black Lord of the No-Account."

Risto, nodding, fingered sweat from his eye sockets. "Eftah, sure. So long as you both understand—I'm not playing."

❊

There'd been more to consider, naturally. They could've raised a thousand questions, but Risto and his visitor stuck to essentials, in shorthand. Giussi, his whisper edged with cold glee, confessed he'd been one of the victim's lovers. Also he'd been among the crowd in that repurposed warehouse, the site of the murder, and today, before he'd finished his pasta, he'd received the text about tonight's Little Window. No greater gap necessary, for a flexible animal.

They did need to be flexible, Risto and Giussi, Eftah and his boyfriend. Once they arrived at tonight's condemned property, there was no way through the tumbledown street-level barricade other than to wriggle. Risto was startled by the bawl of pipe against pipe, a noise that recalled the mew of his daughter's stuffed kitten. Rosa loved to torture that toy. There were times she ordered Tonino to get his sword, an accessory out of *Gladiator*, and cut off the kitty's head. They had all the toys they wanted, his little natural-born citizens. They got to spend the last six weeks of summer in a three-hundred-year-old home above the harbor at Agropoli. Their last name might be Al'Kair, but their grandfather was a heart specialist, a surgeon who'd scrubbed his hands so hard and often they glowed a Paris white. Nonno liked to joke that he preferred the body's innards; he couldn't care less about the color of its integument.

Integument! Such cultivated chatter allowed Risto to entertain the notion, tonight, that if his family knew what he was trying to accomplish, they'd see the justice in it. They'd cheer him on, and Paola the loudest.

As for tonight's alibi, he'd left that to Giussi. The performer had such a silver tongue, the Marxist-Leninists had contracted him for a couple of rap numbers. Besides, even if the white girl knew bullshit when she heard it, this time she'd greeted it with a smile. You'd think she expected her husband to end up in a bad fix.

A three-way fix: not only did Risto have a five-story drop behind him and maybe two, maybe three knives out front, but also he felt soft spots in the club floor. Would it give way if they grappled again? Beyond Papers and his scuffed and rangy friend, he had the replacement doorman to worry about. A buffalo-headed lug, the man stood only a few strides off, and he kept glancing this way. His look suggested a janitor's, as if the only objection La Fenestrella had to a corpse was the mess it made. And that T-shirt! Decorated in butterflies and flowers, lavender and lime—the bouncer could've mixed up his clothes and those of a preschool daughter.

Come to think, wasn't this a children's party? A midnight recess? You reach a certain corner, a certain hour. Risto recalled that at the bar, a guy in a djellaba had stroked Giussi's narrow buttock. He'd hissed the sort of welcome one fifteen-year-old might give another, after they'd broken into the parents' booze: *Jewws*-see.

The gallery owner had watched from a step or two behind, just the place to see your friend get fondled. Just the place to take your own measure, on a spongy rooftop full of illegals. Transplantation to the North was built from scratch, from instinct and imagination; the hallowed virtues, the sweat of your brow, mattered less than quick thinking and dreaming without letup. Risto knew about the sweat, sure. He'd worked his goalie's hands, the kind of grip that came in handy when hoisting a piece or sighting where it should hang. But only in the art crowd could he be considered large. His build suggested the broken stub of a brick-brown aqueduct glimpsed out a train window. Still, he'd made himself over as a fireplug designed by Sister Mary Corita. With a shaved head, gold earring, and the right gaudy shirt, he helped create a buzz. No suit and tie for Gallery Wind & Confusion!

Also his appearance owed something to the larger model beside him, larger and older and, for all Risto knew, the last man standing out of what once had been his family. By now the gallery owner had spent nearly fifteen years in Naples, and he'd never seen Eftah go a day without shaving his head. He'd never seen the Black Lord without an earring, either, though this prompted nervous jokes about Somali pirates. In fact, at a moment like this, the man's greatest contribution might be his playfulness. Eftah always had some game going, some "experiment." Tonight he too was decked out in a dazzling East Africa wrap, with a yawning V that showed off his pecs, scrawled with curls. The body hair showed some gray, but even this was impressive against the top, its own colors almost as childish as the Buffalo's T.

That's who had Risto's back: players, all of them. Yet even Eftah's boyfriend proved a help. The kid had presence; at the bar he got them served quickly. Then, after their first cooling swallow of Nastro Azzuro, Eftah's lover declared that Risto had the right idea. To find this killer, declared the pretty young thing, you needed to go around the law. "The police don't waste time with a child of Sodom."

A smart mouth, on this golden Moroccan. He liked to be called Mepris, and he'd never bothered to explain the pseudonym. As slender as Giussi, he could fold up comfortably in the back of Eftah's Smartcar.

The performer preferred a vodka pop. "*Les flics*," he said, "oh la, how could they ignore such a bloody spectacle? Why aren't they howling about terrorists? This was practically another video of a beheading."

"Giussi," said Risto. "It's bad enough without dragging in ISIS."

Unlike the fundamentalists, La Cia's killers had first suggested a round of sex play. Bondage and discipline.

"A spectacle nevertheless," said Giussi. "Had it been ISIS, had it been Al Queda, they'd have people out selling the movie. The boy would be well-nigh a legend."

The gallery owner knuckled his scalp.

"Or perhaps La Cia's already a legend," Giussi went on. "A poor credulous monster, shut in a box now, in a cloven pine. He awaits his wizard."

This had to be *The Tempest*. Risto hadn't read the Shakespeare, but he'd seen his friend onstage often enough to know. Every performance, he worked in tidbits of the marooned. But now Giussi saw some correlation to this ugliness? The victim had been found naked. His clothes lay folded against one wall, as if at first he'd gone along with the arrangements. He'd put his hands behind his back for the cuffs and he'd dipped his head so they could strap on the ball gag. The rig barely fit over his shaggy 'do, a touch of Superfly. La Cia had loved the blaxploitation stuff, and he'd first come to Italy with a university film program. Whatever he'd been risking, there on his naked knees in an unlit room, he'd done it for the sake of a dream.

Naples homicide, however, would never have pictured La Cia in Hollywood. Questions of motive left the cops stumped; the killer hadn't taken the kid's student visa. His semester at *l'Università* was long over, but any African could tell you, the document might still spring you from a roundup or get you past a landlord. The I.D. was the first thing anyone in tonight's crowd would've snatched, or anyone other than this guy in Risto's face, him with the V-cut and the switchblade. The murderer, that is, must've been a man like Papers: a man with papers. Like Papers, he might even have had a stash. But Italy's media concentrated on other details. There'd been no signs of rape, the weapon appeared to be a serrated blade, and the couple who'd stumbled across the remains had been white and hetero. They'd been citizens, scenesters, like the two kids tonight, out for a thrill. In the lightless back of the club, in search of a private nook, they'd ignored the smell and splashed into what felt, underfoot, like seeping mud.

It was all online. Risto had put in the time, tracking down the statement out of Homicide, then turning up a couple of dodgy websites. Odd how wound up some people got. There was a racist site of course, gleeful at seeing one of the *neri* cut down, and another claimed to have a scan of the coroner's report. To Risto, what looked most convincing about the reproduction were the quirks in the handwriting. He'd never seen so many exclamation marks on a government form. Then once you you saw the nature of the wounds, it raised a new question. Whoever did this must've ended up covered in blood, and how could such a horror show have slipped away unnoticed?

That mystery, at least, looked easy to solve. La Fenestrella kept the lighting minimal, and Friday the party had been indoors. In the back rooms, a guy could get naked. Also Risto saw plenty of bruises and smears among the crowd. If you got your butt fondled, better check a mirror and see if your friend had left stains.

Still, Friday night left a mess. The killer had gone first for the carotid, disabling his victim, before tearing away the other pieces. The coroner, once he'd cleaned out the gutted eye sockets, had turned up the telltale ragged cuts. Serrated blade, fisherman's tool, handyman's. It'd also torn away a swath of cheek—but the right thumb, taking off the thumb, that would've been deliberate. It would've been no easy task, sawing away at the base of the thick digit, so much time and effort that you wondered why the murderer hadn't wanted the trophy. You wondered about a lot of things, like why he hadn't taken the scalp or the genitals. Scalp and genitals, either or both, were generally on the menu when a sociopath got out the knife. But this one had preferred a different pound of flesh, and then he'd left it behind. The police had found both the eyes—two deflated glue-sacks—and the thumb. The butcher had revealed a certain tidiness, nestling these scraps against the shrunken belly of the victim. La Cia had known how important it was, in the Industry, to keep the weight down.

⚔

Sunday night appeared to be Ladies' Night, here at penthouse level. Citizen Aristofano, as far outside the law as he'd been in all the fifteen years since he'd caught the boat from Misrata, found himself noticing. Long before he spotted the accomplice—the dealer's farmhand accomplice, now facing him dead-eyed—Risto had taken a moment for the guy's dance partner. The DJ was into a slow jam, just getting warm, and this woman in her tube top, she might've been serving up two scoops. Around her too, what passed for a dance floor was all about the girls and their gladrags.

Risto understood that these were sisters with jobs, decent jobs. Whores would be at work, most of them somewhere with Wi-Fi, hooking their clients online. Even for refugees, that'd become the norm, posting pictures and a number to call. Of course there'd always be those out on the roadside, like the cluster he'd spotted during the drive over.

All African, the women loitered around a bonfire of construction materials. They didn't need the heat, in July; they wanted the backlighting. But La Fenestrella got the women who vacuumed the rugs in a B'n'B or scrubbed the pans in a pizzeria. Risto could follow the money, even in a space that relied on clamp-lamps and moonlight. Also, while these girls might've arranged a late shift tomorrow, most of them were in for a full day's hangover. Most were going at it two-fisted, with a vodka-pop in one hand and a hash-and-tobacco twist in the other. Already, most had one arm slung around a man. For once they had the advantage on the lone white girl.

Not a bad-looking girl: a peroxide bombshell, with money to tart up her babyfat. She too had the cleavage working, in that black leather vest, but every brother in the place could tell she was on edge. She kept her bare arm hooked tight around her boyfriend's zippered sleeve. Even a newbie could've told her nobody was going to touch her. This crowd knew designer goods when they saw them, and the ofays had brought their own beer, too, a ruddy Irish import. Nobody was about to mess with a daddy's boy and his punk Britney, not with thirty witnesses on hand. Yet the white kids huddled at the far side of the bar, opposite the DJ. They kept their distance as well from the other penthouse apartment, the one that still had a door.

Risto's sense of the layout remained hazy. Before the quake, both of the top-story suites must've had their own entrances and roof access. Tonight, in one of the apartments, the one that offered sex and cards, the club owners would try to provide a few amenities. They'd have set up a generator. Out here on the roof, underfoot, ran two fat extension cords, industrial orange. Party orange, come to think, and overhead were strung two corkscrews of pink crepe. The paper looped in a sloppy X through the night, and only the DJ's setup appeared fully equipped. The man himself wore dreadlocks under a puffy Jamaican cap, but he was white, or white enough. Neapolitan Drab. You'd think the wannabe Rasta had agreed to work the turntables in exchange for a fat spliff or two, except he had a hookah going, thick-hosed, hip-high. When Risto caught a whiff of the bowl, it was nothing like hashish. Leafy, it might've tasted of apple.

A strange hire, this spinmaster, and under his hands the records sent out ripples of light. There was a halo, winking, the flashiest item on the roof. Risto scrubbed his face and once more turned to the greater ramshackle. Beside him, Eftah stood raising beer: a toast to their "lead detective." The gallery owner had to frown. He waved the three friends closer and suggested they each work the room on their own.

"That's best," he said, "discreet."

"Well," said Mepris, "I can't promise I won't act up a bit if I find myself face to face with, ah, you know who."

"Oh, Mepris," Eftah said, "always the drama."

"Oh, what? Daddy, with all the games you play, especially when it comes to telling the truth, who are you to tell *me* about drama?"

Eftah hiked his chest and chin, Mussolini on the balcony, but he kept things light. "These inquiries, dear boy, they're only an experiment. We're only trying it out a few days. My kinsman here, he's not looking to make a career change."

"Your cousin, so called," muttered the boyfriend.

"Honeychild," put in Giussi, "are you saying our fearless leader doesn't know what he's doing? Oh la. He knew enough not to tell the *wife*."

Giussi. Rarely did he open his mouth without leaving some sort of wound. But he was right to jump in, nobody needed a lovers' quarrel, especially not on top of the bickering during the ride out. Eftah and Mepris gave it one more scowl, Mussolini vs. Vogue, but then turned and made their separate ways. Giussi found a third direction, and Risto, just watching, could tell that these men's hormones carried a different tune from the rest of the crowd's. Toward dawn, maybe, you'd stumble across man-on-man couples. You'd find a pair such as featured in the lead photo for Risto's upcoming gallery show. A shot worthy of Mapplethorpe. One man's hand stood out black as a cuttlefish against the other's underpants.

The photographer was Tuttavia, his star, the natural choice for *Expo in Città*. Her latest set featured a party-pit like this, and no sooner did Risto think of one than they all flickered across tonight's scene. Every shot bristled with scavenger glamour.

Two used an effect like nothing the gallery owner had seen before, a dollop of yellow, a corona that framed a man's head. The compositions emphasized the head to begin with, the same young man
in each case. Yet he wore this golden cowl. Photoshop? Old-school
darkroom tricks? Any other Sunday, Risto would've been back in the
gallery, taking another look. Instead he'd come to the sort of place
where Tuttavia found her material, rickety and dangerous, and he
was looking for Lovers' Lane. Perhaps the orange cable lit the way,
trailing across the tarred rooftop to one of the remaining doors. In
the skyboxes of Naples, the depth of shadow took you back to when
Caravaggio was in town, if not further. You could go all the way
back to when Christ was a carpenter. Still, behind the door might be
chiaroscuro, but it didn't take an art historian to know what you'd
find there. You'd have the opportunity, if you were of a mind, to
cut a man's throat. If you carried a knife, you'd have the means. The
motive, eh. The motive must've been some unlikely shit indeed—as
unlikely as a file folder in La Fenestrella.

Risto was to remember later, with his back to the rooftop rail, how
quickly Papers had gotten his attention.

Who was this guy? Most *clandestini* came looking to score a stick of
hash and a sister to smoke it with. The brother in dandelion, however,
apparently dealt in office supplies. He could peg a potential customer
too. Risto had only started trolling around, looking for someone to
ask, when this dandy locked eyes. He whipped out his file folder. God
knows where the man had gotten it, but just like that, the thing was
out under his chin. The folder could've been a mirror, throwing light
into Risto's face. Or no, that was the necklace, silver, flashing in the
light of the DJ's clamp-lamp.

The stranger drew closer. His features proved drawn and weathered, no match for the clubland accessories. With his file, he gestured
across the rooftop and beyond, taking in the glimmer of better-lit
neighborhoods.

"We chose this, eh brother? This city, this North?"

He had salesmanship, give him credit. An instant familiarity. Risto
tried his rusty Arabic: "*A'salam alekom.*"

"*Masa'a alkair.* Good evening." His friend remained louder than the music required. "But, shouldn't we use the language of this city? This North?"

Again he waved the folder, this time indicating the hemisphere. Risto figured: first opportunity.

"Eh, brother," he said. "For men like you and me, even a *terribilità* like Friday night is nothing compared to what we've left behind."

"Such *terribilità*." Whatever this guy was selling, his calculation included an assessment of Risto's Italian. "It makes us men, no?"

"Most prefer not to think of it. The mutilation, the cold-blooded murder."

"The hardship. It makes us strong."

"Perhaps. Friday night, a brother cut to ribbons..."

"Many suffer, yes. Others. But you and I grow strong in the struggle. Men such as you and I, we seize our destiny."

Between them the Tutsi made a fist, and with the jacket sleeve folded back you noticed his arm, its ropy lap of muscle. Risto, not quite smiling, cast around for the others. The doorman knew he hadn't come alone. Giussi, however, was nowhere to be seen—most likely he'd found prey of his own—and Eftah and Mepris had fallen into a fresh squabble.

"We cross oceans and deserts and seize our destiny. We construct our own city."

Eftah was glaring, and the Moroccan showing teeth. Give Mepris credit, he'd lasted longer than most boyfriends.

"Things—" Risto stopped trying to smile. "—are in place for me."

"But certainly. You have some schooling in that head of yours. You put good food on your table, besides. Anyone can tell that at once."

Risto drew up his chest, trying for his own Mussolini.

"And it's this that makes me come to you. A man like you, you're like me. You ask, is this place what I chose?"

The line had a streetwise formality, it wasn't a linguistic misfire, and Risto began to wonder about this gaudy creature. His necklace bore a snake design, ersatz Mayan or Aztec, the same as Risto saw on his star photographer. She preferred bracelets, but the same style, pseudo Central America. Also the club security wore a feminine scent, incongruous with the distressed leather of his face. Jasmine?

"A person," Risto tried, "who likes women. I have a woman, ah, ah, a lover."

"Of course." The gaze revealed some amusement. "A man of your quality."

So much for that idea.

"Brother," the stranger went on, "call me Papers. Let us understand each other. It helps to have a name, doesn't it, when a man steps up out of nowhere, and he asks that you make a choice? For you and for your woman? You say you make your way, here. Yet these streets were laid out for others, men unlike us."

Again this Papers was waving toward what you could see of Naples. Meantime, he slipped a finger into his folder, up to the baggy second knuckle. He exposed a fragment of ivory paper, a bond that looked rare, heavyweight. There might've been a letterhead.

"Just look at this city. This idea of the North's, so out of date in our time."

A letterhead, yes, black against the ivory.

"This whole idea of *walking distance*. Why can't a man construct his city anywhere he wants? Why can't he construct an entire new world? A man of good schooling, you give him a computer and he'll build his own city."

Risto knuckled the top of his head.

"A computer, a bit of money, a Kalashnikov: for a man of destiny, it's a world."

"But then, suppose a man finds himself in the wrong dark corner... Suppose you're an unlucky man like La Cia, just the night before last. You heard?"

"Everyone heard, my brother. A man like that, a skinny leech, everyone knows, and this only proves what I'm saying. A man such as you, he makes a better choice."

Papers jigged the file folder, its innards flashing. The gesture brought out his height advantage, a mantis over a beetle. But as the salesman kept on, "Here in my hand I hold," something like that, Risto broke the code. It didn't matter what had clued him, which detail of the stationery. Documents like these had become easy to recognize. The guy had Earthquake I.D.

Papers jerked his head toward the doorway behind him, his necklace flashing. This too was easy to translate, and couldn't help but recall the murder, but Risto ignored the invitation. He looked instead over the document, the inch or so that peeked over the top of the folder. This revealed not one but two letterheads: first the seal of a United Nations agency, the umbrella organization for all the quake-recovery efforts, and then beside it the imprimatur of the local NATO base, a compound out in the mozzarella ranchlands. Earthquake I.D., citizenship for sale. In a crowd like tonight's, it didn't matter that the documents were temporary.

Following the *terremoto*, authorities had needed some stopgap certification for the newly homeless and shirtless. Three thousand folks? Five? They claimed to be citizens but could no longer produce government identification. They'd had their information zapped by the electromagnetic pulse, or they'd lost their paperwork the old-fashioned way, crushed or soaked or torn to bits. Authorities in hurricane-stricken New Orleans, or following the tsunami in Indonesia, had run into the same. First responders had taken names and drawn up lists, just as they did here between Vesuvius and the Burning Fields. Up in Parliament, they went hoarse asserting that Italy wasn't some benighted territory like ghetto Louisiana. In this country, they had more than enough supporting documentation—somewhere or other. Everyone would get back on the books. Meanwhile the Naples mayor, in one of the moves for which Risto admired her, worked out an agreement with the UN and NATO. They'd printed up these provisional papers, the same as he now saw brandished in an illegal club by a lying crook.

❋

Only a magistrate could issue the I.D., and only if there were a witness, plus other corroboration. The *Regione* was taking a new census, as well. The official line was, by fall everyone would be back to the same certificates and licenses as ever: the paper trail they'd never thought twice about.

Sure, this fall. *Insh'alla.* Here and now, I.D. like this might be worth triple the biggest poker pot on the table behind the door.

Still, Risto had his doubts. "Those can't be the good ones."

"Who says they can't?"

The gallery owner leaned in, never mind the man's perfume. "The good paper, from NATO? Truly?"

"There's the Signore. Thinking like a rich man."

"Eh. I can see how they'd be useful."

"There's the good word. With a head like yours and papers like these, what's to stop you from ending up like Berlusconi?"

Some number of the I.D. forms—some unknown number—had made it to the black market printed on NATO watermark. Who knows where they'd come from? One story had it that an American spider-woman had gotten her claws into the passcode of a NATO colonel. Another rumor was that a couple of amateurs had the good luck to take down a key liaison and snatch his briefcase. In any case, if you were looking for legal status in this country and you got your hands on one of these, you'd hit the jackpot. You had full vestiture in the very grain of the stationery. As for the signatures, anyone could forge those, and who could say how long it might take before some bureaucrat took note of the discrepancy? Who could say how much longer before the cops got involved?

Now, suppose a person had dangled contraband like that in front of La Cia.

"But with a head like yours, my friend, *Il Signore*, you understand. Materials such as these, how could I ever reveal how I came into their possession?"

Risto might've been studying another of those murder websites. He thought of the Camorra, then thought again. The mob didn't necessarily have a piece of this action, the templates run off at the American facility. The quake had set a lot of loose cannons rolling across the city's decks. Anyone could've lucked onto the good paper.

"Just step inside with me now, get your hands on one. I.D. like this, the Americans kept it under guard round the clock."

Round the clock, a fine fairytale. Why not, when customers couldn't tell the genuine paper stock from an imitation? Risto himself didn't know what to look for. He could've used better light and a magnifying glass. He could've done without the music, and what he would've really liked was to wipe the smile off this con man's face.

"A fellow with a head like yours," Papers went on, "you'll realize. With these and a computer, you'll have a new world."

When had he finished his beer? And where was his backup? Mepris had slipped away and Eftah was dancing with the white girl, a laughable match. The girl could shimmy, boneless in her leather, and beside her Risto's cousin looked solid as a peg. Laughable at first, then infuriating.

Again the dealer jerked his head toward the door behind him. "Don't you want a look?" he asked. "Some place where there's no one in the way—"

"Some place where you'll have no *witnesses?*"

Risto's voice might've been a noisy thing hung on a wall.

"Some place," he went on, "where you could cut me to *ribbons?*"

The crook showed military training, coming to attention. Risto held his gaze, letting him see just how great this felt, how satisfying.

"What are you," asked Papers, "some kind of schoolboy? Schoolboy waving his hand in the air?"

The gallery owner got his hands around his empty, still wet and cool. It occurred to him that he'd sounded like a white man. Like an utter clod of a white man, he'd let a stranger know exactly what he was thinking.

"Waving your hand in the air. Down South, you know, maybe what I used to do was, I used to chop off a nosy boy's hand."

Still Risto couldn't lower his voice. "Friday night, Papers. Just Friday night, a boy got himself *killed.*" It felt delicious, an outburst that undid his head and shoulders. It felt as if earlier today, out on his balcony, he shouldn't have worried who overheard.

"Again about that mutilated faggot?" Papers too sounded closer to honesty. "Don't try to tell me you're police."

"Police? My guess is, you're the one with friends on the police."

The other glowered but moved in time with the music, opening his coat. The pimp jacket proved to be a custom job, with a wide pocket in the back.

"That faggot?" said Risto. "He had a name, you know."

"What are you, the Gay Avenger?" The man's narrow smile matched his V-cut. "You know, I recognized a couple of those queens you came in with."

"So you're a regular, in places like this. You knew La Cia."

"Everyone knew La Freccia."

The name had nothing to do with the cha-cha. Rather, the boy had chosen the Italian word for "arrow."

The dealer was turning away. "The asshole liked to think he headed for Hollywood, but the only time he got to the movies was when someone paid him to—"

Risto didn't realize he'd grabbed the man until Papers came round with his worst face yet.

"Faggot. Putting your *hands* on me?"

He had the sense of losing connection, logic at the end of its rope.

"Schoolboy. Smart as you are, you couldn't see that piece of shit was in for it?"

"So you know something about it, how he died?"

"Everyone knows. That piece of shit was looking for trouble from—"

"Don't *call* him that."

He lost connection; he went into a show on flip cards, a flicker of ragged dancers and dangling bulbs, and among these a Risto-card, a tough guy who grabbed the crook's bright lapel and yanked him down face to face. The scene took on dimension and stink only when he wound up facing a knife. Papers had a lot of tricks up those sleeves. Punching away Risto's bottle, slipping the contraband into its pocket, whipping out this tiger-stripe—all of it seemed a single move. Not that the owner of Gallery Wind & Confusion knew anything about fighting hand to hand. Not that he could do anything about his dread flashback, either. The blade in Risto's face called to mind a nightmare from long ago, a head split by machete, but this was only was a flicker of the Joker. His head might've split already, erupting with a bizarre thrill: *Now we're getting somewhere.* He needed to concentrate just to drop his hand from the other's lapel. He could barely understand that the man was saying something more about the police, or rather the absence of police.

"The Avenger," growled the dealer. "Maybe tomorrow night, you'll be the one who needs the Avenger."

Difficult bringing the blade into focus, the serration, the chipping.

"You think I wouldn't? You think your money makes a bit of difference?"

Aristofano filosofo—this is the first person you've met. The first half hour of the investigation. As for the guy's bloody talk, only a rookie would pay any mind. Friday night the same as tonight, Papers would've shown up on business. He would've come looking to move inventory. Risto, Wind & Confusion is your gallery, not your head. "What I think is, you came here to make an arrangement."

"An *arrangement?*"

Risto had a response, another question about the I.D., but in the next moment he was thoughtless with pain. Had he been stabbed? Was that the knife, or the knuckles around the knife? Papers had the moves, and he wasted no time yanking his opponent's arm half out of its socket. Risto was at the railing before he got the picture: clouted, bent over, one hand pinned. Plus there was the grind at his butt, as if someone were trying to tweak his high, and his choked attempt at a joke.

...try this on my friends?

But what friends, where? The white girl's dance partner, the tent peg, had disappeared. Eftah could've run off with her, with both the tourist rabbits, and the rest of the crowd couldn't care less. The dancers eased away no more than a step, their brains between their hips. Over at the music stand, the kid flipped through LPs as if seeking the best soundtrack, a groove to suit the city's hubs and spokes, reeling now beneath the man at the rail.

But there, yes, a friend—Eftah. Risto's biggest friend, he displayed his handyman's favorite, its blade unfolded. A minute later the dealer's accomplice squared the triangle. Then:

"You wouldn't give me a straight answer. I was trying to ask about our poor murdered brother, and all you had to say…"

"Again with that faggot. Again the *murdered brother*."

"But how else am I to know who I'm dealing with? How else?"

"Houseboy, what? First you need a debate, 'New blacks in old Europe?'"

※

The glint off the knives seemed to pierce to the back of Risto's neck. For this he'd spent the last decade and a half putting blood and animality behind him? At least the circulation was returning to his arm, and he was beginning again to think. He found himself wondering what the cops might give him for this guy.

An exchange of favors: maybe the best idea he'd had all weekend. The police would be grateful, getting their hands on an illegal alien peddling contraband I.D. And if Papers turned out to have the good I.D., the watermark bond from NATO, *per carità*! The police would be grateful. Risto would need only the right man on the force, an officer who recognized the gallery owner from *Il Mattino* or the webcasts— and more importantly, a cop versed in the exchange of favors, the Neapolitan S.O.P. The right police contact would grant his informant special consideration. Better access to the murder, maybe even a peek in the evidence bag.

Could he have expected any better, tonight? Up where the very tar underfoot might give way? Massaging the tendons of his neck, he let Eftah do the talking.

"Papers, my man beside me here, this is his first time. Didn't you just say you'd never seen him in La Fenestrella? It's his first time, only an experiment, and for this you've got your knife out?"

The dealer's backup cracked a smile, shifting left, shifting right.

"Whether I've seen him or not," Papers asked, "don't you think I can tell a thing or two about him?" The way he swung from Risto to Eftah, his blade by his pants pocket, suggested something obscene. "Don't you think I can tell he likes a taste of cock?"

Obscene and grinning. But what had Risto expected tonight? Could he have done any better?

"Papers, honestly, if you could see the woman he's got at home..."

"Of course he's got a good thing at home. A smart boy like this."

Tonight's business would get the attention of the police, wasn't that enough? Besides, hadn't he handled a pushy bastard like this before? Plenty of artists tried to play hardball, strutting in with samples on a flash drive. All Risto needed to do now was keep up the front, playing the customer. If only his head and shoulders would undo. If only the talk didn't stick so in his craw.

"House-boy, lis-ten." Papers was looming again, the mantis. "You know I could cut your faggot throat before either of you laid a finger on me?"

Eftah squared his stance, showing off more of the steel in his hand.

"Cut you just like we did back in the hills."

As Papers spoke, you noticed his other metal, the snake at his neck. Beside him, his accomplice was up on the balls of his feet, and one glance across the rooftop revealed that most of the others had left off dancing. They'd turned to watch.

If only his head would *undo*.

"Boys, boys!" called a woman somewhere.

"Boys!" Again. "Look at yourselves, where's the justice?" The voice didn't sound African, but it did have an accent. "Where is the *justice*? You've got your knife out for the wrong man."

Tuttavia came out of the dark, toward her gallery owner. The way she gestured, her bracelets gave off sparks.

"Him—" She waved at Eftah, and maybe the sparks were from the white of her arm. "—you'd do us all a favor if you stuck a knife in *him*. A traitor to his people."

The big relative broke into a wide smile, a berserk shift of mood. Risto could swear the flash of the photographer's silver put a gleam in Eftah's eye. Her bracelets were only more street-market snakes, imitation Before Columbus. Yet they acted like magic. The Black Lord took such pleasure in this Snow Queen, her Italian flat around the edges and her distaste for him unrelenting.

"If you stick a knife in that money-grubbing creature," Tuttavia continued, "brothers all over Naples, they'll thank you."

"That's enough." Risto put his back to the dealer's weapon, facing the woman. He'd warned her about this. If Tuttavia found his only living family so unconscionable, she could get herself another gallery. He'd put it to her that bluntly, though they both knew she'd have no trouble finding someone. But she'd done as he asked, and tonight too she lost some of her hauteur.

The photographer had lips of a High Renaissance delicacy, while her black-eyed focus recalled the way her ancestors had searched the Baltic for signs of thaw. Whenever she had a show, one or two of the men at the reception would ask Risto whether she were under thirty. He'd duck the question, allowing a white girl her secrets. He'd remind these guys that her name—her chosen name, the one in the interviews and the gallery window—meant "whatever."

Here in La Fenestrella, though, it was Risto who had a secret and Tuttavia who knew. Just watching her arm drop and mouth button, he could tell. Giussi must've passed the word along. He liked to call Tuttavia "the Missus," and back at Sunday dinner, Risto had expected the Ethiopian to ask about her. Why wasn't the photographer at the table? But then, both Risto and his guest had left a fair amount unspoken. Later, somewhere between Risto's balcony and this one, the performance artist must've told her. After all, why shouldn't Tuttavia hitch a ride on tonight's trial balloon? Hadn't she known La Cia? At dinner Giussi had mentioned the connection: *She knew that wild boy.*

Now as Tuttavia drew herself up to full skinny-bitch height, she looked to be on firmer moral ground than any of them. She took the men's measure with a squinting draw on her Lucky Strike, then raised her handheld and took a shot of her gallery owner.

A flash: just the thing, for a surprise guest.

"This man," she declared, "listen, he's my man. He's my friend."

Gesturing with her handheld, she called attention to her lack of any bag or holder.

"You—" she turned to Papers—"I bet you've never seen him before, but did you ask yourself why not?"

"Anyone can tell he's got a good thing at home."

Risto, blinking, didn't miss the dealer's new uncertainty.

THE COLOR INSIDE A MELON   39

"And what do you suppose that means?" Tuttavia had barely gotten there, and already she'd grasped the situation. "He's my man, serious, a man with soul. With a serious job. Can't you see he's got money?"

"I could see he has money." The yellowjacket had let his knife sag.

"Can't you see he's got serious friends?"

Risto had heard this sort of talk at Wind & Confusion. *Serious, soul,* her preferred compliments. Tonight was an act of course, declamatory, outsize. She always had some ticking bomb in the sensibility, and Giussi had asked her to join him onstage. Still, the *clandestini*, the Fenestrella crowd, had come to trust Tuttavia. She'd been allowed into corners rarely shared with an ofay.

"And me," she continued, "you've seen me before, haven't you?"

Papers shared a look with his sidekick. "I've seen you before."

She gave a bit of a bow, calling attention to her outfit, possibly the most sober on the rooftop. Forever in black and white, tonight Tuttavia had broken out East Village jeans and a starched shirt, the wrists undone.

"But you," she went on, "tough guy, you won't let a girl get a picture."

Apparently tonight's act included The Coquette. The only date Risto had ever seen this woman with was Giussi, but tonight she was flirting, and she made it work. In another minute everyone was putting their weapons away. Risto's big cousin took his sweet time, naturally, first fitting the blade in its holster, and Papers matched him move for move. He worked with hands together before his heart. A kind of prayer—or was Risto the one praying? His eyes half-closed, a moist palm on top of his head?

Tuttavia stayed in character. "Tough guy, just look at you, the hair alone."

And wasn't Risto a tough guy? Didn't he have a role to play? He dropped his hand and stepped between Papers and the photographer. "You came to me," he reminded the dealer. "You could see I had the money."

Papers drew to attention. For the gallery owner, every word took heavy lifting.

"Look, this woman's been here before. She's seen you here before, and that means I know who I'm dealing with."

Papers tugged at his jacket. "And that was all the Signore wished to know."

"Eh." It was all he'd come up with, the Detective on a Wing and a Prayer. A crook like this would interest the police, and once the police got into the man's trick pocket, they'd be grateful. They'd offer something in return. Naturally there remained a thousand questions, a thousand five hundred, but Risto knew he'd get a day or two to take what he knew to the cops. Nobody was closing any deals tonight. Nobody, not even a houseboy, showed up at La Fenestrella with cash enough for the good NATO I.D.

Papers checked his sidekick. Without facing Risto again, just thinking aloud, he wondered if tomorrow or the next day looked busy.

"I'll make time," Risto said.

Across the roof, traffic had picked up. You'd think the dub-step allowed the city's nightcrawlers to feel their way.

Papers didn't make it easy. He insisted he had no phone, no pager. Risto wished he could pat the man down.

"Look, you say it's got to be by Tuesday…"

"You found this dark corner, didn't you? Signore, you're a player."

TWO

How much later was it that he woke to the light from his own little window? From the balcony, the morning light, supernatural in the way it came around corners and into the bedroom. The sunglow rimmed the half-open door, and this sent him for a moment back into a dream, a glimpse of Tuttavia's latest, the two golden headsets. But only for a moment, as his wife set the milk growling in its pitcher and the fertile scent of Naples coffee reached the bedroom. Squinting at the clock, the arithmetic creaking between his ears, Risto calculated half a night's sleep. Still, he didn't dawdle. With the kids down at her sister's, Paola would set up on the balcony. The light came on so strong because (more creaking between his ears) the blinds stood open, and so today called for high-end breakfast clothes. The djellaba she'd found him on the "black blocks"—a birthday present from the children, officially—set his wife cooing. She kissed him, and really, no way he could dawdle. Tonino and Rosa were down in Agropoli, starting their August early, and tomorrow morning this woman would be boarding a train to join them.

Nor could any hangover stand up to his view of the Gulf. Sightlines weren't unbroken, not with the hotels along the waterfront, and the light that'd woken him was glare. The sun rose over the city to Risto's back; it caught in the windows before him. Nonetheless, the morning Tyrrhenian was a carpet of blue leaves, their edges tongued up here and there by the breeze. The wakes of the fishing boats recalled the spring caterpillars in the Horn of Africa, a rare happy memory.

It took him a while, a few greedy sips of eye-opener, to realize that Paola had her eyes on him. He met her gaze, the good husband, but she pointed out only that he smelled of smoke. Monday morning, she said, he didn't want to show up stinking. Not when he hadn't put in his usual weekend hours. Otherwise, Paola seemed primarily concerned with Eftah and the boyfriend. Those two had enjoyed some good times in her house. The night they'd come over and whipped up one of their vegetarian workouts, the smell of saffron alone! In recent weeks, though, she'd seen nothing of her hefty sort-of in-law. She'd had to rely on Risto for news, and she couldn't help but wonder. Was the Black Lord of No-Account Real Estate about to wind up single again?

Riso boosted his recollection with a bit more coffee and went with the story of the ride home. The plan had been to drop back into Eftah's Smartcar, with Mepris in the back. By then Giussi had rejoined them, having sensed Tuttavia's arrival like a disturbance in the Force. The performer had emerged from behind a door, tucking and straightening, and after that he'd preferred to stay with the Missus. By the time Risto had gotten down to the car, between the landlord who shouldn't be able to own property and the eye-candy who shared that property: "Paola, the party was over." The expression on the Moroccan's face, as the boy folded himself into the wallet of a backseat, guaranteed at least some screaming. And Eftah, as he put the machine in gear, started to talk about what a long drive he was facing, first down to Risto's and then up to Materdei.

"Paola, it got so bad so fast. The best I could do was play along with Eftah and tell him to find me a taxi."

Paola worked up an appropriate sigh. The Moroccan, she said, had seemed different. "A boyfriend of quality, real spirit there, real wit and smarts." She trailed the back of a finger over the emerging stubble alongside one of Risto's ears. A stroke he'd loved even when he was still letting his hair grow.

"Last night," he revealed, "I could've used some of the kid's wit myself. I could've used a sharp comeback."

"Really? Something happened? Some sort of confrontation?"

"That's what I'm telling you."

"But, Risto... What are you telling me? Someone gave you trouble?"

"Yes. The cab driver."

After Eftah had found a taxi stand with a car waiting, the cabbie at first refused to accept the ride. He'd insisted on seeing the African's cash. The insult had made little impact on Risto—he'd had Papers and the police to think of—but it set his wife bubbling with vitriol. Paola gestured so angrily that he got a flash of nipple.

"A Neanderthal," she said. "A caveman. Risto, lover, you're lucky he didn't pat you down for a *knife*."

He didn't want her to catch him looking. He busied himself with his foam mustache and studied the coffee pitcher, Vietri ceramic with a rooster decoration, all beak and claw. That seemed like enough trouble for this morning: the angry bird, the troubled lovers, the racist driver. In fact, the cab's peace and quiet had allowed Risto to think of a likely contact on the force, a connection that still looked promising over breakfast. As for husband and wife, here, what else did they need? Wasn't it time for their laptops? Risto didn't care for handheld devices, not with his big picture-hanging paws. Inside, unplugging the two fold-ups, he saw the modem's LEDs as a DJ's soundboard, but he wasn't going to sneak in any murder websites now. His "experiment" could wait while he checked the arts blogs, the buzz for the show.

A lot of the chatter about Tuttavia and the *Expo* turned up on an anti-immigrant blog. They'd posted a rant. *Terrorist whore... For 3000 years our artistic patrimony has stood unrivaled, and now this "Expo" celebrates a traitor to that heritage...glorifying the vermin out of Africa, the virus that could bring down all of Europe... A whore from the North, is it any wonder no one talks about her past?*

Quite the diatribe, though nothing the gallery owner hadn't seen before. He knew his Warhol, too: don't read the words, measure the inches. Attention like this was a gift, especially on the verge of vacation season; the money leaving town in August had everything to do with the timing for the *Expo*. Besides, for the Fascists' blog, the visual was one of the photographer's more innocuous pieces. They used the promotional postcard for the upcoming show, a dance shot that brought out the couple's different skin tones. The woman's grimace smeared black on black, but the crown of the man's head was burnished almost to gold. Not the actual halo; this photo wasn't one of those. The most mysterious pieces, the most arresting, Risto preferred to save for the show.

Paola, across the table, was searching the same combinations. With both keyboards going, out on the balcony it sounded like rain. The wife browsed *Il Manifesto*; the Communists had the best writing on the arts. The Monday columnists again proved friendly, as Paola posted an item from her lap to his. Only a tweet, but it used the word "visionary." Then at some point the wife changed the subject. All she did was tongue something off her thumb and finger, slowly, and Risto met her gaze, waiting. She announced that she could wait till after lunch, when he'd be back for *riposo*. Her husband might be the immigrant success story, but he was no Superman.

"You know," Paola added, "I have to wonder, how late can you go? Can you make it to 15:00? And what good will you be?"

Risto found her round face a relief, after the cagelike lines on the screen.

"Paola Paolissima. You know that with the touch of a finger, you…"

"A finger? *My* finger? But, Risto-ri, that's not the digit I'm worried about."

Not quite grinning, he raised his chin. "You always say you like my snoring."

Laughing, she flashed more breast. "The snoring, Risto, that comes after."

He ought to be grinning. In the djellaba, every breeze could raise a tickle. But the Bay had caught his eye, and now the water bore a dark overlay. There were shadows cast by the city, rectangles and spires, the shapes of graves.

✖

In the shower, he took Paola's advice, putting in extra work with the loofah. Hashish clung to the skin more fiercely than tobacco. Likewise Risto lathered his head with extra gel, aromatherapy. He arrayed himself in a winning outfit before he put in the call to one of his buyers, a regular, old money. The man's extended family included someone with…was it the carabinieri? Was it city police? Either way, the buyer's *raccomandazione* would make a difference. A word from the rich and connected, no end to how it could help. At the least, should the situation get sticky again, the gallery owner would have another card to play.

Not that he made any mention of this over the phone. His call had woken the guy, and negotiations proved a struggle. First the self-styled "collector" agreed to come in and then he grumbled that he couldn't.

By the time the man confirmed that he'd drop by, Risto had grown more appreciative of the conversational shorthand he'd fallen into with Paola. Yesterday before lunch, for instance, they'd made swift work of Tuttavia, the fact that she wasn't invited. Paola had let the octopus do most of the talking. The smallness of the creature, laid out on the cutting board, underscored how she intended to cook for no one besides herself, her husband, and the finicky Ethiopian. Risto hadn't pestered her about it. He hadn't missed what his wife did with her smile, putting it through a retrofit, as soon as she announced that the photographer wouldn't be joining them. Husband, let it drop. You can always circle back, who knows, sometime on the beach.

This morning, with his phone in a fist and his buyer wavering, Risto paced inside the balcony doors. His wife, meantime, couldn't have looked more relaxed. Sometimes when she showed a lot of flesh like this, she set him thinking of white things luscious to the touch, of orchids and silk. Yet she wasn't so white, not nearly, rather *Napoli D.O.C.*, dusky even in midwinter. Her hair suggested an olive thicket. But in her the shadow and kink rounded off into bells and curves, lovely. A dollop of ricotta.

When he turned to her for goodbyes, her kiss was a thinking woman's. Risto found himself fishing for approval of his outfit. He'd gone with another mashup, the rainforest over Soho, working down from a golden earring. He'd tied on a Senegal wrap, lime, banana, and plum, over black jeans fashionable enough for Tuttavia.

Paola assured him he'd done a good job.

How about with his head, his shaving? Risto could've sworn he'd missed something, a spot that kept itching.

"You're fine," she said.

Besides, if the gallery owner did have a patch of gristle up top, that could be useful. Around the shop, you wanted a certain intensity. For Risto all it took was a hard stare, since his possessed something volcanic, almost crackling flinders. Could be this made him a cliché, a naked black head and a fiery gaze. Could be the Europeans got a perverse kick out of dealing with a Mau-Mau. Risto of course kept it clean: teeth and fingernails, collar and cuffs. Nonetheless, this morning as he walked to work, he couldn't help but reconsider the man reflected in the storefronts. The windows had gotten their sponge-down, and when he glimpsed himself amid the rainbow stipple, his head could've been a dum-dum bullet, with a notch at the earring.

He'd developed some palaver about his look. White folks tended to ask about the shirts, the wraps, and he would offer a geography lesson. His homeland, he would explain, was on one coast of the southern continent, while tops like these came from the other. From a country like Senegal, you know? The give and take struck Risto as dubious, in the marketplace you never stopped playing Charades, yet he couldn't deny the payoff. The ultimate question, now that he knew his gimmicks worked, was *why?* All right, he'd learned to play these folks up North, but then you had to consider the game itself. In the arts, you never wanted to abandon the Mau-Mau entirely. Roughage clung to winning work, like a notch hacked in a bullet, a grit that resisted the sleek functions of supply and demand. The gallery owner knew those functions, all the knobs and levers for closing a sale, but he had another touch as well, one sensitive to the scruffy baseline of any piece he chose for his walls.

So which of these drove his vocation? Was his a story about playing Naples or knowing the arts?

He descended into the raw odors off the Bay. The walk cleared away flashbacks to last night and, behind them, bad glimpses from fifteen years earlier. He even seemed to lose his midlife avoirdupois. For a block or two, he might've drifted in midair, a pollinating angel in a blossoming stone arbor. He passed more homes than shops, and their iron gates seemed delicate as rose stems, their stucco fronts the pastels of sunrise. Even the paneled doorways, dark as jerky, were punctuated by blossoms of stained glass. This was the richest neighborhood in the city, the Chiaia. The word used to set Risto thinking of American cowboys and Indians, the Wild West: *kee-YI-yahh*. A war cry or a cattle call: Risto and his brother could rely on tuning in a Western no matter where the family's exile took them. Even the difficult year in Casablanca, when the father's paychecks took forever to reach the medina, there always seemed to be a channel that featured the American desert and its gun-toting Quixotes.

These days, though, Aristofano Al'Kair made his home in the Chiaia. He knew which palazzi claimed the most impressive owners and which had once given Caravaggio a commission. The edifices stood gleaming still, their baroque filigree hosed down and polished. The cleaning crews were white, Russians, Latvians. Brothers from the South weren't even fit to wash the stoops on these blocks, and yet one of them floated through like a baron.

Inside his shop, sunlight spilled along the walls: golden coffee dolloped over a gelato. The kitchen feel persisted in the office nook, its corners rounded, its white more porcelain than plastic. The gallery owner took no more than a moment to bask, though. He'd arrived with his strategy in place, what to ask the buyer and how. The biggest chore would be fetching up the photos in storage, underfoot. The trapdoor and stepladder could leave him feeling sixty years old and arthritic. Still, once he got down there, he rather liked the cellar. The pick-and-shovel marks called to mind the scruff of artwork, its knuckly vivacity, and anyway underground was a very Italian space. A catacomb. It suggested that Risto's venture had the blessing of the ancestors, the Greeks and the Romans, though he knew the basement was a far more recent job. It was a bomb shelter, put in during the last big European war. On one of his first visits, he'd discovered a nasty graffito in street Neapolitan, plainly twentieth century.

Scratched into the stone: *Homeboy, that your baby? That kinky hair!?*

The cave had seen its share of Neanderthals. Nevertheless, some kind of ancient magic must've dwelt beneath the gallery, and not just because Risto and his wife had managed thirty mortgage payments. More's the miracle, the two of them had discovered the storefront during an evening *passagiata*. They'd simply stumbled across it, in a city often described as "the most densely populated in Europe." Madame Mayor and others were forever talking about Naples in bleak extremes, "the worst," "the hardest hit." But Risto's Chiaia location constituted a significant improvement over his original shop. That earlier *Confuso e Vento* had been a going-away gift from his mentor, the American. The American had retired to a millionaire's hideaway on the heights of Capri, and the African had found himself with the Camorra as a partner. The System laundered its money through local businesses, back on the blocks where he'd first set up shop. Three times in fifteen months, in the gallery lockbox, the owner had set aside far more ready cash than usual. Overnight, this had been replaced with a bundle that showed a lot more wear and tear, even the occasional crust of maroon. At each swap, too, the *malavita* took a considerable percentage.

Here in the Chiaia, the mortgage was co-signed by Paola's father, "with associates." Whoever those might be, they'd put up the real money and ended the shakedowns. Then the gallery had hit a new benchmark with its first show. A Tuttavia show—still her greatest single moneymaker, and the long appreciation in *Il Manifesto* had spurred a write-up in other papers and websites. For the local reviewer, Gallery Wind & Confusion had triggered visions of a new heaven and earth. "The space presents a radical city," *Il Mattino* had rhapsodized, "transgress-iterranean."

After that, Risto had brought in Yebleh, born in Benghazi. The painter had yet to turn thirty, but his oils of Saharan simooms had people talking about both Georgia O'Keefe and suicide bombers. Not that Yebleh didn't prove to be, every now and again, a handful. The boy's fondness for pills, alone, made Risto's next discovery feel like a relief. A couple, these two worked under the name Cops & Robbers. They did installations, with a wickedness that set you grinning: an unholy alliance of the zombie apocalypse, the pornographic comic book, and the Neapolitan crèche. Yet the things were put together of household materials and small enough to hang in the kitchen. The artists knew their way around a kitchen; they'd gotten married in a church and remained diligent about their kids. Cops & Robbers were a relief, for a gallery owner. With them he never had to worry, as with Tuttavia, that he might blunder into some personal shibboleth. For her everything was black or white, pariah or beloved, and in the arts, such people might be the norm. A bristling handful might be the norm. Still, Risto could think of exceptions. Degas for one: he'd enjoyed family vacations somewhere in this very neighborhood. Degas, at play among dancers and horses. It wasn't as if that made him a sham.

※

Up from the cellar, with Tuttavia's portfolio on the table, Risto took a moment off his feet. He wanted another look at the flash drive from Eftah, and at his desk, he unlocked the drawer.

A week back the big relative had stopped in without so much as a text in advance. He'd said yes to an espresso, and the cup in his spatulate fingers suggested a baby chick in the grip of a farmer. But his conversation had been all bitching and moaning. The older relative felt down at the mouth about how rarely he and Risto got together. Oh, they used to be so close! Happy as Eftah was for the success of his "nephew," there were days he would've preferred the kid who'd come to him helpless and clueless. Then between one tsk-tsk and the next, Eftah slipped the drive from his pocket. Its plastic casing purple with pink polka dots, in his hand it looked even more incongruous than the espresso cup.

The data was encrypted, he added. "It's just something, let's say— you might want this sometime but you don't need it yet."

The two Somalis fell silent for a long moment, one seated, one standing. Eftah held title on three buildings, including his own, and now out of the blue he needed to keep a backup down at Wind & Confusion? Encrypted, besides? Risto massaged his head, but after another moment took the spotted stick and tossed it into a drawer. This had nothing to do with the older man's guilt trip. Those debts were either long since settled or forever impossible to repay, and in any case it was easy to guess what his relative had here. The secrets of No-Account Real Estate, what else? More than likely, it concerned the property Eftah called home, up in Materdei.

Later on, sure, Risto had tried to get a peek. All he'd found was an icon from which even the nature of the file, Excel or whatever, had been removed. The title was grade-school arithmetic, "3X5," and this morning too, he got no further. When it came to the password, his guess must've been the most educated on two continents, but his thumb switched uselessly across the touchpad.

"Comrade!" The door swung open but the buyer remained half-in, half-out.

"Comrade." Risto had expected such an arrival, noisy and a burden on the air conditioning. Getting rid of Eftah's plug-in, he made sure of his smile. "Comrade Fidel."

The collector insisted that "all his friends" call him by this name. Not that it suited him, not at all; the man was heir to a shipping fortune. Also he was more gooney bird than guerilla. First impressions always had to do with clumsiness. As he bent to kiss Risto's cheek, his saint's medallion swung into Risto's face. The piece was a heavy one, too, the martyr's body gold and his blood a pair of rubies.

Late-summer air, grown hotter since Risto had arrived, poured in around them.

"Aristofano, my brother in the struggle, what a *vivid* look you've got today." Fidel rocked a half step out onto the sidewalk, grinning. "But, such a shirt! Why, you might've brought it up from Somalia!"

Didn't take the bastard long, did it? In the time it took Fidel to toy with one of Risto's floppy sleeves, he'd pinned their status to the gallery wall. *I was born here, you're the wetback.* Yet he couldn't let Fidel rile him, and not just because of his investment portfolio. Also Risto had to bear in mind the fallacies this man lived by, the very idea that teasing a refugee about his lost home and family made him a cool cat. A laughable misconception, like his chin beard and shaggy hair. The man's florid features remained among the most Aryan that Risto had encountered in Naples. The fact was, the only thing about the buyer that resembled the real Fidel was the hefty head.

The gallery owner freed his sleeve and gestured at the display table. "Look, I've got the entire show. Tuttavia would be the first to agree, you've earned a preview."

Earned, hm, interesting, Risto. The buyer however broke into a grin. "Your Tuttavia and I, we've grown close, you know."

What? Risto couldn't recall the photographer saying a word about this guy.

"We're great friends, these days," Fidel went on, "that girl and I." He put the exclamation with a shuffle-step, a cloggers' dance in Doc Martens.

Risto's wife hadn't mentioned anything either. She might've left Tuttavia off the list for Sunday dinner, but she remained the woman's closest confidant.

Fidel had at last come in, but he lingered by the door as if he'd guessed Risto's agenda: first item, get the man's money; second item, get his contact on the police. The gallery owner even had the wine out. Falanghina again. Down the bottle's inkwell green trailed glistening slicks of condensation. Not that Fidel was desperate for a drink, at this hour. At receptions, or at the rare get-together where he and the Al'Kairs crossed paths, he rarely finished more than a flute of champagne. Rather, he wore you out with stories of his sexual conquests. He'd brag in schoolboy euphemisms that Paola had to translate, but when it came to wine, he had his limits. As did Risto—even a murdered *clandestino* wouldn't make him set out a bottle for an alcoholic.

Fidel's true weakness resided in his fear of seeming ordinary. The collector wanted so much to be counted among the hipster elect that Risto had an array of buttons to push. He reiterated that these photos were the first of a small print run, signed and limited. He made a big deal of turning out the *Chiuso* sign, and he raised a toast or two, though whenever the big maladroit wanted a closer look, Risto took the man's glass. He kept the pictures out of harm's way. Over his favorites, Fidel would fold back the picture's protective sheet with one hand and with the other, with the whole arm, he'd create his own blinders, looping his face in a three-quarter frame. The way the man wrapped his head set Risto thinking of Tuttavia's inexplicable haloes. He'd check them again after his visitor was gone.

Fidel, meantime, was already worked up over one of the photos. A happy thrum emerged from the middle of his chest: *rr-nn*.

Risto played to the fantasy. "You and Tuttavia being such friends," he remarked, "I imagine you've heard. She's talking about joining Giussi onstage."

Fidel confined himself to a nodding pout, showing off aristocratic lips.

"Tuttavia onstage!" Risto went on. "*Per carità*, I would've thought she'd hide behind that camera forever."

The buyer had a fallback: an artist needs take chances.

"*Complimenti*, Comrade Fidel. You understand the sensibility."

"I understand the woman."

Risto had raised his Falanghina in toast, but he allowed himself no more than a drop. The smell brought back how much he'd had yesterday, and meantime Fidel moved swiftly from Giussi and Tuttavia to himself and his wife. Fidel started complaining again, though there were plenty of men who wished they were in his Docs. The shipping heir had got himself a dreamboat, Ukrainian, considerably younger. Zelusa had so much going on, with those green Siamese eyes, that flaxen Cossack hair, that midsection worthy of a ballerina, it could take a while to realize how little the girl was saying. She'd linger throughout an entire three-hour reception, and the most you'd get out of her was what your nose told you. Her preferred fragrance was Obsession. As for her designer, the name behind those miniskirts and heels, eh, just ask Fidel. No one could fail to notice the pleasure the husband took when others ogled his sultry pet. So too, this Lurch did nothing to quash the rumors about his and his wife's escapades. The gossip was what you'd expect, an occasional romp with another woman.

Anything you say, white boy. But if Fidel had started to swing, it was giving him vertigo. Today again he whined about his new credit cards, "starting to breed" in his billfold. His child bride, he claimed, thought she lived in Disneyland.

"I love my baby," he went on, "but I ask you, how can Naples be Disneyland?"

Risto wished he wouldn't wave his drink that way.

"How can I keep it up, day after day, another costume and another wild ride?"

"Try telling her what the Fascists say. Italy isn't turning into America, it's turning into Africa."

Fidel attempted a cynical smile. "Politics, I'll tell you. That was my father's advice, go into politics. 'You'll never have to worry again,' he'd say—and that was before I even *met* Zelusa."

The name, Risto figured, was another Italian reconfiguration. The word contained both "deluxe" and "zealot," which seemed about right. But he only gave a frown, sympathetic, patient. The buyer, even as he did his grumbling, had gotten down to a few favorites. He kept corralling his face and bending close. Best of show, if you asked Risto, were the two in which the photographer had graced her central figure with that new special effect. Rather a macabre effect: a glowing sickle, poised above the head. But then, Tuttavia often set you squirming, and this wouldn't be the first time she'd called attention to the winners in a set. In any case, as Fidel settled on a couple of choices, neither photo included the bright new fillip.

So much, thought Risto, for the woman's great friend.

"Rr-nn," thrummed the buyer. "Splendid. The stuff of the Old Masters."

"A limited run. Thirty only, each one signed and stamped."

As Risto began to stack the rejects, Fidel kept nattering. About Tuttavia's new digital camera: "The technology may be the latest generation, but the result, it's the Old Masters. It's classic. You see how she varies the pixel count?"

"*Complimenti, amico.* You don't need me to tell you."

"Well, I've seen her camera."

Him and about three hundred other "friends."

"But the camera, the technology, what did I just say? People make the most ridiculous claims for the technology. As if it all came down to *money!*"

Risto could give a guy the benefit of the doubt. The buyer had seen Tuttavia at work, after all. La Fenestrella and her other stomping grounds, fly-by-night, also offered Fidel an excellent opportunity for showing off his kewpie doll.

"Comrade," the visitor went on, "let me—let me put my cards on the table."

Had he averted his eyes? *Il Grande Sex Machine?* Risto pantomimed another sip.

"It's time I told you. I wouldn't have come, you know, if I hadn't felt the time was ripe. The time to tell you, my friend and comrade: I'm taking pictures." He squeezed his cup against his chest, spotting his black T. "Taking pictures, yes, myself. Yes, even a man such as I—can't I choose another way? Make myself over?"

The gallery owner couldn't just stand there knuckling his head.

"I mean, this shop, that's what I adore about it. The romance in the very name! The romance of another way, another life, even for a man such as I."

As far as the gallery's name was concerned, Fidel didn't have a clue. But then, Risto was glad for anything that brought them back to business. Stepping over to the buyer's selections, he lost no time picking the one that would fetch the highest price.

"My friend," he said, "first." He pointed with his chin. "Haunting, eh?"

"*Rr*-nn."

The shot pulled off one of the photographer's signature tricks, capturing a crowd's jostle and flow while also isolating one figure. Composition was Tuttavia's secret weapon, the way she sculpted what would otherwise come across as merely documentary. Tensions ran in all directions, and yet at the two-thirds mark, center-right, a gaunt young man emerged powerfully. "Haunting," Risto repeated.

"Dear boy, give me some credit, please. Don't I always pick the good work? Haven't you and I stood shoulder to shoulder fighting for the good work?"

The dear boy hoped his visitor wasn't hinting at anything.

"Risto. Now that I've told you, well, next. Isn't it time I showed you?"

He hoped Fidel's blush was just the drink.

"I've been taking so many pictures. And I'm under so much pressure." That blush was impossible to miss. "But now that I've told you, the time is ripe, for you and me. Shoulder to shoulder. Comrade, it's time—you should see my work. You should consider it for Wind & Confusion."

At last he met Risto's gaze, and at that gave a start. A start, or the doofus equivalent, topheavy, and after that he drained what was left of his wine.

"Oh, and this piece here, yes of course." Straightening up, Fidel showed a pink Adam's apple. "I've got the checkbook, Old School, and first things first. First I pay and then we talk."

When had Fidel begun to take up so much space? But then, across the street would've felt too close, now that Risto had gotten yoked into that weary old story, *Delusions of a Dilettante*. The loser was so convinced of his genius, he was blind to practical considerations. Somehow he'd come to think that the one place to show his stuff was the shop where he had the worst conflict of interest.

The gallery owner kept up the sweet talk: "That photograph could've been the feature. Another month, and I'd have picked it for the website and the card."

But when he named a price, it unsettled him worse. The highest figure he'd ever set for a single item, and his tone had been all wrong, almost waspish. You'd think he didn't want the sale. He was left pawing his face as Fidel fished the checkbook from a slim over-the-shoulder bag, both sheathed in black leather. Risto could see them between his fingers, all the bastard's accessories, the fucking ultra-hip…

As the buyer bent to write, the owner excused himself, making for the lav.

※

"Wind & Confusion" was out of the Old Testament, Isaiah. In all the time Risto had been running the place, in either location, a single lone walk-in had known the source. Even the American never got it: the prophet's vision of kingdoms swept away, of power on earth vanished into thin air. For Risto the verse was a lifelong companion, lodged in him since the final morning at the Dominican school. One of the friars had quoted the passage, over Risto's head and his brother's. The two teenagers had arrived for Assembly with stomachs growling, the neighborhood had been hit by a new wave of shortages, but all of a sudden they forgot about their UNESCO milk and biscuits. Instead they'd stared up at the school entryway, filling with the soldiers of the Shabab. The machine guns, it had seemed to Risto, were the shape of locusts. But the creature that gnawed away at the apparent world, forever afterward, was his teacher's recitation.

A single lone visitor had known the original. Nobody special, a scrambling academic—but then, who did Risto think he was? Back at his desk there stood an overgrown frat boy with a pathetic faith in what a big check could do for him. Fidel believed the money would make him a rock star, and seeing that left Risto shaken as badly as he'd been last night. In his gallery's undersized lavatory, he kept his pants up and stared, where else, into the mirror. No ordinary tack-up, this had a ceramic triangle frame studded, all cockamamie, with broken Fiestaware. A bathroom mirror put together by some local Schnabel, *Giuliano* Schnabel, the piece had been Risto's concept. He'd earned this place, earned his certificates, one at the university and the other at the conservatory. Then yesterday after dinner he'd announced, in quasi-code to a near-illegal, that he intended to solve the murder of a man he'd never met.

In the mirror, what you had was the cliché, the bullet head and gunbarrel gaze.

Once before, Risto had pursued a similar madness. He'd chased an ephemeron all the way from Mogadishu to Naples. He'd had little more to go on than the name of a man people called a cousin, a passport made of sighs: *Eff-tahh.* Yet this phantom had landed him finally on an unlicensed ferry out of Libya, and before that, briefly, it'd borne up his brother Ti'aba as well. The two boys had flown together, between wings labeled *Eftah* and *Naples.*

While one troop of "New Police" closed the school, others rounded up their father at the law office. By sundown, their mother was reminding Ti'aba and Risto of trustworthy contacts on either side of the Mediterranean. To the North there was that notorious Eftah, a scandal for some in the family, but a cat who always landed on his feet. The relation was second-tier, by marriage, but the man was a generous soul, you heard story after story, and the boys could count on better help from him than from the family in Alexandria. Also closer by, in the uplands above the city, Maman had country cousins, farm folk, good-hearted. Finally she handed Ti'aba a cloth bag, not quite a shopping bag, lumpy with a baggie of cash and what she called "portable valuables."

A few of those valuables, under ordinary circumstances, would've accessorized the outfit she'd put together for visiting the new "administrator in chief." But, ordinary circumstances? Few and far between, around Mogadishu, and the only thing rarer was the vision that drove Maman and Papà: the hallucinatory sheen of Paradise 'Dishu, glowing more fiercely every time the family went into exile. Maman and Papà saw the Jewel in the Horn, a place they claimed to recall from childhood, sophisticated as the Manhattan of Jackson Pollock. By the time Risto reached his teens, he'd learned that this golden era dated back further yet, to his parents' parents. He'd begun to understand the impact that could have, the happy recollections of forefathers gone too soon, before the night his mother handed over her cash and jewels and strode out into a ghost town run by thugs with guns.

She'd put thought into her ensemble—unseasonable clothes, green and gold of wintry seriousness. The design was her own, the piecework handled by a shop in Villaggio Arabo. She had an eye, Maman, and you noticed even when she'd covered her head and put on plastic at wrist and neck.

The magic of *Eftah* and *Naples* at first seemed to hoist her two sons to a bird's-eye view. They could look down at their father, rounded up with other lawyers and lawmakers in the first hours of the crackdown. In his holding pen, Papà stood proud and unafraid, and the boys could see their mother as well, shaming the guards into setting her husband free. Meantime Risto and Ti'aba reached the first sanctuary outside the city, just as Maman had described it, a farmworkers' shantytown. The camp had water, one of the wider creeks feeding the Shabeelah, and the longtime hands claimed that, back in the nineties, the grounds had housed a troop of American Rangers. There the brothers hesitated, sitting through first one night (so sudden, that equatorial twilight) and then a second. They weren't so young, well into their teens, and they could handle complex math and get by in five languages. They knew where they'd find the next safehouse, upstream along this same creek, and all their lives they'd been riding some shuttle or other, 'Dishu to Algiers, 'Dishu to Beirut to Alexandria. Lately they'd even been cadging rides off the friars, practicing their Italian on the way to and from school. Still they hesitated, sleeping on a collapsed appliance box. Ti'aba appeared to be waiting for someone to give him the go-ahead, and surely that person wasn't his little brother. Surely some course of action would reveal itself. So the squat became a surrogate for the school or the household, with the kids on idle before the bell rang for class, or before Maman called them to dinner. They had Papà's Parisian watch, heavy and Gothic, and in the camp the older boy did nothing so often as check the time.

Whatever he was waiting for, it couldn't have been the squad of irregulars who thumped to the foot of the access road. They arrived the third morning in a Fiat van missing its side door. Five armed men, none with any uniform beyond a bandana.

For cover, the younger brother found a sacred space. He crouched behind a hunk of freestanding oak, a big piece for that country, carved in a totem of the lizard god after whom he'd been named. The icon stood in the brush behind the shedding, overlooking the creek, and according to legend this divinity could assume nine hundred forms. You'd think he had one to drive off the locusts, the Kalashnikovs. But what could any god do about a machete? A colorless swag of metal, a bottom line of a weapon, the blade hung from the fist of the largest yokel trooper. As he made some prideful adjustment in his mufti, his eyes enflamed with khat though it wasn't yet half past seven, his machete zigzagged before the faces of two or three squatters who hadn't ducked into the scrub. Could they have expected these "Police?" Given up the location? Anyway Ti'aba blocked the younger boy's view, hustling crablike between him and the threat.

Ti'aba stuffed his brother's pockets with all but one of their hand-me-down valuables. *You know*, he whispered. *Where you belong, you know. You belong upstream and then north, north.* The older sent the younger ducking toward the creek, hustling him along with continued whispers: *You know. Down here is the last place we should be. North,*

north, up in Naples, that's where we belong. New family and a whole new world. In the meantime, stiffarm, out where it was sure to be seen, Ti'aba held the watch. It glittered across one open hand, white-faced, its digits cathedralesque. He was always the slender, showy one. He'd inherited the walk, the bones of their mother, and now he flaunted a gift from the father. He might've struck a pose, something camp, limp-wristed.

Risto, not yet Risto, was left with those whispers to keep him company. Or did he, rather, murmur the brand name of the watch? The name of the man in Naples, the chameleon totem, the God of Isaiah?

Whatever, he turtled away, clawing as much as swimming as he went from root to rock to mudbank against the current. If the machinery of the guns shifted into gear behind him, the noise was another name grunted and gone. In his ears was the river and in his mind's eye, if anything, this place toward which his entire family had pointed him: this *North*, where they belonged. Where his honorable father served as Chief Justice! Where Mogadishu was the crown of the Continent and the family danced on the grave of a goon of an Imam! Dreams out of a few stitches of brainstem, dreams anyone might have, and meanwhile his paws and claws mattered more, windmilling through the water. The goods in his pockets, given him for safekeeping till the rightful owners joined the *new family*, those mattered more. The going was on impulse, the grunting nothing like prayer.

Yet come nightfall the boy found safety. He arrived at the place his mother had spoken of, the hut of two elderly orchard and goat-keepers. They knew the Dominicans as well, it turned out; the brothers came to them for honey. The couple had no trouble with a hungry teen who first set off the herd dog and then loomed up, all slop and rags, against the crimson and smoke of the southern sky. With those hands that big, he might've burrowed here. But these farm folk had seen worse, out of the lowlands.

Likewise they had no problem with his insistence on sleeping outdoors, in the goat run, where he'd be sure to catch his brother. The stock could always use the warmth of a fellow creature, the salt lick of his face.

�֎

In the hills, strays were everywhere. The animals made natural companions for a boy who meandered with eyes on the horizon. In a week he could play herdsman. By then he had the right footwear, home-stitched sandals.

Downstream, he found an overlook from which he could scout the grounds where he'd last seen Ti'aba. Even at that distance, it was something else entirely. A harvest of char and gristle. The lone remaining upright was the totem of the chameleon, and you noticed the skull in every one of its faces. The air carried a slimy residue, offal and gasoline, and at the base of the access road there rose a blackened heap, slag at the base and jutting bones up top. In the mind's eye, these Northern days, the remnants of the bonfire sometimes overlapped the domes of Naples. Even the Galleria, the shopper's Duomo, suffered the overlap, and turned into the Galleria after a bombing, its dome reduced to smoking struts and broken glass.

Back above 'Dishu, the stinking mound had included a head or two. Risto got to see what a skull looked like several days after the machete split it. First the machete and then a gas-fed fire—these made quick work of any cry to heaven or attempt to bargain, even the offer of a fine Parisian watch. No doubt the prayers and howls had felt full of heart and inspiration, but they came out of an animal matter as easy to cook as any other, a meat he saw now in varying shades of holocaust, including the tripe formerly coiled inside the heads split by machete, and he knew the truth in those scorched remainders, knew that if they included some nuggets of Ti'aba, some button or tooth — eh. Feed it to the goats. So too, if Ti'aba wasn't some scrap of jerky in this bombed-out Duomo, the last thing he'd want would be for his little brother to go on seeking him, taking the herd of strays down the access road toward the city. For miles and miles around this devastation, brother would find nothing to do with brother, nothing of the boy who smirked and showed off his flat stomach, who knew the first seven-eight lines of the *Aeneid* by heart but who thought the *Odyssey* was way way cooler, who was sick of the Dominicans' blather about our Madonna in Heaven but remained a firm believer in one day meeting our Madonna at the Top of the Pops. She had a kid or two from Africa, didn't she? And didn't the brother live yet, a long way from this stink and grue, in his incorruptible final advice? *Where you belong, you know.*

After that morning, Risto had a year and more left on the continent, and there'd been days when his greatest accomplishment had been to shake off another prolonged family reverie. He could lose an hour or more just thinking of how his mother used to stroke his face. Some evenings she'd sing in French, others in Italian. Also different fantasies nagged the runaway, revenge fantasies, and the violence of those set him sketching his first fake recollections of Ti'aba and the machete. For a while there, Risto could swear he'd seen the blade take his brother's head off, and one evening in Alexandria, a rare night of European wine in a Muslim city, he claimed he'd witnessed a Shabab video. He'd seen Ti'aba forced to his knees and beheaded. A doozy, a whopper, the "memory" clearly needed work, and Risto had a far more plausible version by the time he shared it with the white girl he would marry. Even so, the story remained an illegal alien, trying to pass, lacking papers.

But while he was still on the wrong side of the Mediterranean, and still a rickety construct, the whirlwind of Alexandria nearly left him in smithereens. Maman's relatives were scraping by, out of the apartment at sunup to chase after a few piasters. The family labored under the same burdens as, down in Cairo, brought the protestors out into Tahrir Square, and you'd think such hard times would've sobered the boy. You'd think that, after Beirut, after Casablanca, he could resist a city's blandishments. Yet Alexandria seemed at once a City of Desire, its El Geish waterfront no less than lip-smacking, and also a City of Memory, where any intersection might turn up Maman or Papà, dressed for business. *Per carità,* how they would rush off, disappearing before he got close, and Ti'aba as well, hurrying along with tea and ghorayeba cookies. The younger brother, now infatuated, now stunned, wound up spending too much. There came a day he found Euros at a decent rate, but all he could buy were a handful of bills, five exactly, middle denomination. This left Maman's jewels down to three pieces.

Not nearly enough for a reliable ferry out of Libya, and many nights Maman's people couldn't offer dinner unless Risto himself brought home the flatbread and chickpeas. But what had the ghosts in the streets been trying to tell him, if not that he needed to *hustle*? He needed to live on his *feet*. As for his Euros, best he stashed them between the layers of his sandals.

His energy was some part mania, naturally; he was seeing things. Nevertheless it helped to generate a cultivated line of talk, and the metropolis was getting tourists again. The regime in Cairo was keeping a lot of uniforms on the streets, and you saw more businessmen down from the North. Among these, a certain number traveled solo and enjoyed a bit of unstructured time; they preferred, rather than a guide or a concierge, more of a companion, an *escort*. A young man like Risto, with his fine chest and a cultivated line of talk. His learning came in handy even with the more personal services, the seduction, since this often began with a verse from Cavafy. Risto knew something of the poet—this alone set him apart from most of the rent boys along the El Geish—and with a bit of research he found out that the Greek had sailed South as an immigrant for love. The young Somali made sure to have pertinent verses ready in three languages. So too he tracked down a set of Alexandria novels, and memorized the quips of their central poet figure, fey and theatrical.

So—problem? Problem, if his business entailed, at the least, several long minutes of determined fondling? Alternatively, the escort might put on a one-handed show. If the money were right, he might even allow that evening's employer a taste, and for the young sub-Saharan, no, none of this raised concerns. On the contrary, negotiations never got complicated. With the buyers in town so briefly, the transaction remained limited and the pay went as high as the market allowed. Risto was chaff in the wake of a catastrophe, he knew that much, and the money was the glue and ballast he needed. Just for starters, he still lacked for a reliable name. As an escort, he left that up to the man paying. There were nights he got one name to his face and then, as his client slid down-body, heard another for the darker cluster between his legs. Yet whatever these guys called him, what they asked left him unfazed. He had no objection to a buttfuck, either, since the few men who could afford it had condoms, oils, and a comfortable room.

His best night in Alexandria, of course, couldn't begin to match the comforts he took for granted in Naples. The grief and edge of those days now yielded to adult understanding. The gallery owner recognized for instance the impact of his schooling, gender-segregated right through the onrush of hormones. He'd had classmates put a hand on him, and though he'd deflected their suggestions of a blowjob, he'd walked in on one or two. At home, meanwhile, Maman and Papà had remained proud sophisticates, entirely frank. Then once they were gone, how many options did a teenage refugee have? And didn't some of those young people emerge from their desperation with souls intact? Especially a boy like Risto—or whatever name he'd gone by—a very lucky boy. He'd never dated a con man or a sociopath. He'd never wound up with counterfeit paper or a knife at his gullet. For him it was just the hustle, living on his feet, and eventually he arranged a departure from one of the safer ports of debarkation, just across the El Alamein highlands. As for the ride there, he had an oilman out of the Crimea, with a bodyguard and a Mercedes. One more weekend as boytoy wouldn't interfere with Risto getting put back together. One more nightmare, featuring the Russian's straight razor, wouldn't keep him from Naples.

Since then, it wasn't as if he'd never been reminded. It wasn't as if he'd never spoken of the scorched earth, the scuffling. Most of what he'd told others was the truth. Still, in a decade and a half, nothing had so brought up the old trouble like Saturday morning at the laptop, as if his thumb on the touchpad was a scalpel slipping under a scar.

Then last night, Papers had his question. *We chose this...? This city...?*

A good hook, especially if you liked the place. The gallery owner couldn't help but believe he'd forged a decent bargain, at the end of his caravan routes. Hadn't he surrounded himself with others shaped by some *terribilità*? Didn't that include Paola? His wife's story was complicated, granted, but when it came to kicking over old gods, she was eager to get a foot in. With help like hers, no wonder they'd arrived at—well, what could he call it, if not immigrant success? You reach a certain corner of the city, and you can take a certain pride. Maybe the impact of an art gallery run by an African wasn't so grand, on a scale of tectonic shifts and peoples crossing oceans. Still, it wasn't just another of the nine hundred forms of the shuck and jive.

Yet this weekend, what had he come to?

※

Out of the lav, Risto went for the Falanghina. He put the cork in and, ignoring his own cup, all but full, he took the measure of Fidel's smile. Looking pretty looped, white boy. Also he noted how his bad memories no longer took up much time; he'd hardly kept the man waiting five minutes. Finally, a sobering question.

"The price, Comrade—what do you think, it's fair?"

The larger man drew upright, his pen hand on his checkbook. Old School, he'd filled in the figure but hadn't yet signed.

"My dear brother in the struggle," Fidel said slowly. "You do make a fellow wonder. You, now, you wouldn't have another bid in for this piece?"

Risto pawed his face. Even a man with his conscience bothering him should be able to come across more clearly than this.

"You do make a fellow ask himself, 'Is he toying with me, my African friend?' I have enough people trying to sweet talk me out of my money as it is. And sometimes, so I've heard, a check from one buyer will make another spring for more."

"Comrade, no. Nothing like that, not at this gallery."

Fidel, changing his grip on his pen, called to mind Papers and his knife.

"Don't buy it, then," Risto snapped. "Enough of these games."

Sweet-talk? Not at this gallery, not any longer. "You're the one who wants me to carry your work," he went on. "You're the one who should care about my prices."

He allowed himself a swallow of wine. As for Fidel's police connection, who needed it? Couldn't he call the hotline like any other citizen? Meantime, even Tuttavia's photos seemed to chastise him; Risto needn't have dragged her into this.

"You've thought about it? My, my work, Comrade?" Fidel was saying. "You've thought about it for your space here?"

"Oh, *per carità*."

The visitor, his jaw agitated, couldn't have looked more like an overindulged crank. Then why indulge him further? "Fidel, never. Not going to happen."

Risto spelled it out for him. Even if, as owner of Wind & Confusion, he "fell in love with the photographs" (no harm allowing for the possibility), he could never consider the work of so regular a buyer. "Fidel, think. Much as that would damage our reputation, the real loser would be you." No one would ever take the man seriously, if his first exhibition came at the place where he spent the most money. The same unforgiving logic applied if Risto should call some other gallery.

"A call like that would be like a visit from the Camorra. Your photos might be good enough for MOMA, but if I make the recommendation we both wind up dead."

No harm allowing for the possibility. No need to point out how out of his league the man was, a Philistine to begin with and untrained to boot. Plenty of folks who came through Wind & Confusion would be only too glad to see this poser slapped down, but Risto could already taste how sour that would leave him feeling. Once he and the buyer were done, after all, he still had to nudge the somnolent police.

"Com-rade."

The gallery owner didn't miss how the word had cracked, almost a sob. He kept to the high road. He allowed that a faux pas like this was pretty common, for a beginner, and he acknowledged he was flattered to be asked. "The trust between us..." he began.

"How on *earth*," Fidel cut in, "could I have been so stupid, so deluded?"

Risto cast around for better. He pointed out that, while he couldn't put pressure on other local shops, he could certainly suggest a few names and places. He could think of people who might be receptive.

"Ho, ho, ho" said Fidel. "Our amazing African! There's always someone he can think of."

Risto held his tongue. The big Comrade felt uncomfortable enough just squinting at his checkbook, seeing his own name. A name in no way avant-garde, one of the most ordinary in Italy: Castelsabbia.

When the payment changed hands, the gallery owner was careful of his smile. Between them, the authentic thing remained the photo, and Risto hadn't gotten an undistracted look all morning. Now as he pocketed the check, he took the time, repeating himself: "Haunting."

Then he was looking more closely, his smile collapsing. Fidel began to respond, but Risto raised a finger.

The black-&-white brought off Tuttavia's usual magic, the off-center placement of its figure somehow heightening the ferocity of his stare. Otherwise his face was a mottle, the fox-like cheeks aglow but the rest fading to shadow. Alone and upright amid a blur of dancers, the man suggested a dark bust atop a pillar of bright marble. His shirt must've been glaring, a Miami yellow. But the photo did without color—no yellow, no gold—no halo. This slim *clandestino* wore nothing but a double-wide Afro.

"But how," Risto found himself asking, "how could she have..."

"Dear boy. I realize it's a masterpiece. You've got the proof right in your pocket."

The gallery owner forced up a chuckle. To his ear it rang hollow, but better that than a question that made no sense. He knew what he'd seen. Tuttavia had delivered these prints last week, and before this morning, each time Risto looked through the set, he'd seen it. This was the young man with the halo.

Fidel kept on: *....like letting go a part of yourself...*

Fetching the pieces from the cellar, Risto had been caught up in his game plan. Now, however, he recognized the photo, one of two. The companion shot had to be among Fidel's rejects, and the stack lay close at hand, but the gallery owner couldn't yet bring himself to look. He needed to think, or try to. Could both pictures have come upstairs changed, on a Monday morning? They'd shared the same nameless protagonist, yet could this young sun-king, in both his portraits, have been stripped of his crown? Forget Photoshop, forget tricks in a darkroom (assuming Tuttavia had even set up a darkroom). No photographer could've managed this, slipping on a golden hoodie and then taking it off over the weekend.

Dealing with Fidel, Risto had been the one playing tricks. Now he was getting his comeuppance, surprised by genuine magic. His Angel in an Afro had been stripped.

The woman's a wonder, Fidel was saying.

Risto went for the pile of rejects. As he flipped through, his first words came brainlessly: "Yes, and your great *friend*."

Brainless as a white man, he'd startled his buyer. He'd brought out the klutz in Fidel, so he dropped his pen and, after he'd bent to fetch the thing, whacked his head on the desktop.

"Com-rade. Are you all right?"

The other man grinned, blink-blink-blink.

"You're right of course," Risto said. "You don't need me to tell you."

Sweet nothings were all he could manage, because: behold. In the second photograph the *clandestino* wore the same ghostly shirt, heavy-gravity stare—and big, halo-free hair.

The buyer was trying to reply, but Risto cut him off. "Fidel, look at this. Look, the same man as in the one you bought."

A fresh blush spread across the gooney's face. He grumbled that he couldn't consider a second purchase.

Risto hoped his laugh sounded between-friends. He went for the wine, wetting his lips. "At this point," he declared, "that's the last thing I care about."

As for what he did care about, it almost set off another rabbitty outburst. The on-again, off-again gold, this was happening in his shop. It was a thrill, of all things, his own private mystery. It prickled the shaved back of his head and set him wondering whether, since he'd started dealing in the supernatural, it might send him a clue concerning La Cia. Though then again—Risto glimpsed the possibility as if he stood at a rooftop rail—it might be he'd gone crazy. It might be he was seeing things again, post-traumatic. But did people think a black boy didn't know psychosis when he suffered it? Did they think he didn't notice, for instance, the strict *limits* on today's madness? His Golden

Arches weren't popping up on every street corner. They weren't even in any other photos; he flipped though and couldn't find a one.

A thrill, and naturally a little frightening. No doubt Isaiah felt the same, before his visions. Or Jean-Paul Basquiat, imagining his heads aflame.

"Fidel," he said, "I'm not trying to sell you anything."

He laid the two shots side by side. "Just look, please. The figure in these, the way it dominates. If this were a Caravaggio, the boy would be a saint. Comrade, can you see him with a halo?"

"A halo?" Fidel ventured a smile. "Frankly, dear boy, I don't see it. That hair on the boy, that Afro, that's the blackest thing in the entire picture."

Risto let it pass, though he took hold of the wine bottle.

Fidel went on to assert that, in these two photos, a halo would be creepy. "Ho, ho, ho. Crr-eee-py. That black boy's dead."

Risto brought the bottle to his forehead, needing the cold and wet. "Dead? This one here, facing us?"

"But that's the one who was murdered, Risto. That boy, somebody took a knife, and they cut him to ribbons." Fidel switched two fingers up then down, nothing like a knife. "That's the one that's been in the news."

THREE

Fidel slumped sideways to make the phone call. His Droid at his ear, he practically spilled out of the chair. Still he spoke with curt *noblesse oblige*. In minutes he arranged an appointment for Risto with a relation on the *Guardia di Finanza,* the national money police. The officer had a name off the playground, Nardo, but in the *Guardia* he ranked well up there. For Risto's purposes, this mattered more than whichever tentacle Nardo had saddled, in order to ride the octopus of Italian law and order. The officers in Homicide would ask about rank.

Not that Risto had shared any of this with Fidel. The gallery owner revealed only that he had a line on some of the illegal I.D., the good paper. Insofar as possible, he let the Falanghina do the talking.

Besides, the call was on Fidel's turf. Within a cluster of privilege like his, boys began sorting out status before they reached communion class, and this contact on the *Guardia* (probably more of a blood relative than Eftah was to Risto) plainly counted as the nerd of the group. Nardo cut a shoulderless figure, in a raddled combover. His red hair made you wonder just which tribe, among the aboriginal Eurotrash, had launched the clan of the Castelsabbia. At the lone gallery opening to which the *finanziario* had been invited, he'd made Fidel appear suave and athletic. Nardo had even shown up wearing his office badge, and the first to point out the oversight had been his high-rolling relative. As the bean-counter unpinned the name tag, too, he couldn't keep his sheepish gaze off Fidel's Ukrainian kitten. Nardo got a snootful of Obsession.

This morning again, Fidel played the cosmopolitan. He threw in touches of English, "okay" and "earthquake." Afterward, fumbling to put the phone away, Fidel assured Risto he could visit the *Guardia* offices before lunch.

"Now especially," he said, "they need you, you people."

Risto stayed with the photos, stacking, making sure of the protective tissue.

"Tracking down the counterfeit, the bad, the false documents. This is citywide. The whole pop, pop, population must work together."

"Work together," said the gallery owner.

He'd arrived at the top of the stack, Fidel's purchase. On this piece and its twin, back when the boy in the photo was still alive, Risto had encountered a prodigy. The occult had visited the office—and the bright trace it'd left behind, what could he call that? What, except the mark of death?

"Work with the authorities," he said, "that's best."

He fought off a chill, he pawed his face, but the pale slouch at his desk noticed nothing. The only person keeping his eyes on him remained the ghost in Tuttavia's picture. Risto, staring back, could assure himself that the photo looked nothing like the ones on the news and murder sites. The regular media had gone with one of La Cia's lapsed documents, a snapshot in which the hair was trim, the gaze bored. One blogger linked to what he claimed was the shot from the morgue, an atrocity if so, and a second one for what the photo revealed: a collapsed rind with two greasy spider-holes. It could've been anyone.

Best cure for the shivers would be the Falanghina. The bottle had a couple of fingers remaining, and he'd kept it away from the art, over by the window. But then, shouldn't he leave the last splash for the gods? Wasn't it high time he did something for the gods? Risto had been a lot rougher on them than the other way around, and anyway what he needed was espresso. Today again he found himself a success; he'd wangled an appointment with The Man. He could only guess what it would require, signing a form or taking an oath, but then his whole career as a detective was like that—he could only guess. Still, at the moment, he had no knife at his throat. His biggest worry was Fidel.

Il Signore, once he heaved himself out of the chair, could've been a Calder mobile. Risto didn't want to think about him behind a steering wheel.

He mentioned the gelateria down the block. A double scoop of decadence to cap off the morning.

Risto sprang for them both, plus table service, and he took care not to wince at the man's choice of flavor: pistachio and English cream, threaded with caramel and marshmallow. Eh, they had it in the case. He himself kept it simple, lemon, plus of course the coffee. As they ate he suggested his buyer take more time in these high-end pedestrian zones. The Gucci store was only a couple of blocks away, and Ferragamo, Hermès. Zelusa would like that.

"For you," Risto said, "those places will bring out their latest."

The face Fidel made, you'd think the gelato had gotten to him, brain-freeze. "Comrade, offers of credit, that's what they'll bring out."

The gallery owner pointed out that his buyer had no pressing business. Not today, Risto imagined, and not for the rest of his life, but aloud he spoke of publicity. The promotion for *Expo in Città*, for Wind & Confusion, all that looming whoop-de-doo: Fidel could help. Hadn't Risto scanned his purchase and given him a printout? A nice, clean three-by-five, now in the Comrade's bag? The scan too had shown up without the death cowl, the Corona Fenestrella, but over the gelato Risto kept his tone hearty.

"Show the shot around," he urged. "A man like you, a mover and shaker, if you show it around, people will sit up and take notice."

He presented such an easy array of buttons. Cleaning up, using a second napkin, Fidel declared he'd start with Prada. Those people had called just this morning, nagging him about some problem with his account. "Comrade," he declared, "I'll show *them*."

As he ambled off, the man looked steady on his pins, and Risto brought out his phone. His assistant shouldn't mind covering for him, especially not after he told her about the sale. Risto himself could use the celebration, though he kept his voice down. Besides, sharing the morning's news allowed him a systems check. Was he sober? Did he need a second napkin?

Check, check, and when he got around to his request, the girl had no objection. Ippolita trusted him to keep track of her hours. Besides, it wasn't as if he was asking for a Saturday. Saturday, even for *Il Signore*, would be a real sacrifice.

"Ippolita. '*Il Signore*?'"

In her laugh, you heard how easy she had it, as one of the pampered lovelies of La Chiaia. "Boh, so long as it isn't exam week, you may count on me."

Risto meantime kept up the systems check. Could he afford this, really? If he got anywhere with Homicide, he'd need more time off, and like most Neapolitan businesses his gallery had taken a hit in the quake. This very morning, hadn't he asked a king's ransom for a photograph? Granted, money was hardly the only thing eating at Risto just now. Nevertheless, earlier in July he and Paola had needed to shuttle something out of savings. As for Ippolita, she certainly added to the ambience around the shop, but she tended to pull in guys looking for a date rather than people looking to buy.

It was Paola who'd urged him to take on the girl. Risto's wife insisted that Ippolita was just the thing for Wind & Confusion, right down to the accessories, the hair with its "Parisian Red" highlights and the arms with a rattle of bracelets. Weren't most of those bracelets the same Mexican snakes, Mexican or something, as worn by Tuttavia? And in Ippolita's case, didn't the silver complement the red? The girl had style, Paola had picked up on it at first meeting, when an old parish connection had made the introduction. She was the oldest daughter of somebody or other, Risto couldn't keep track, but he did see what such an *assistente* would bring to the party. You couldn't have a party, so Paola told him, without a pretty girl. As for Ippolita's effect on the husband, the temptation, so far as Risto could tell his wife never gave it a thought. The only woman who'd ever made her worry had been Tuttavia, and that was years ago.

This morning, in any case, Ippolita had no problem coming in. As for the photos, still up on in the gallery space, she'd let them be. After all, they'd be mounting the show in the next day or so, she and *Il Signore*...

Risto let it pass. "And meantime, Vittorio Emmanuele Castelsabbia is walking around downtown, showing off one of our best pieces."

Her tone soured. "Boh, him, I do hope he doesn't drop by. Not while I'm there alone. I'm so sure he'd like to make me his love slave."

"You're sure. You can look right into the man's heart."

"But, do I need to, really? Do I, when the girls in the shops, they're all friends of mine? The girls at Gucci, Prada, they tell me all about him and his love slave."

Risto nodded, forgetting that the *assistente* couldn't see him. Even now, the white folks knew this city a lot better than he did, and this girl wasn't the only one with informants all over the neighborhood. Paola had so many eyes on the street, it was no wonder she never worried about her husband.

⌖

Like most of the bureaucracy, the Finance Ministry had its local offices over in the Piazza Municipio. This area did without the pastels and curls of La Chiaia. The balconies amounted to a kind of public address system, all facing downhill, so that an officeholder could toss a beach ball out his window and, so long as the traffic gave him a break, watch it roll clear down into the bay. Down there, too, you had the ferries to the islands and beyond, docked under a snapshot-ready hulk, a castle from the fifteenth century. A lot of this waterfront remained inaccessible, behind walls of corrugated tin or ribbons of orange plastic—ribbons never left to flap broken, not in this neighborhood. The quake had played havoc here, though for the Expo the castle was supposed to reopen, and the ferries at its feet were back up to 90% of their schedule. For Risto, coming on foot from the Chiaia gelateria, this meant cutting inland through the city and past the shoppers' basilica, Galleria Umberto I.

A mall like no other on earth, the Galleria, even if you didn't imagine it a heap of charred corpses, with a dome of blistered bone struts. On better days it called to mind a vast and resonating Easter egg, rising three stories over an X of stops at floor level. Here for once the downtown shrugged off the heavy hand of the baroque, as well as all the earlier bullies of urban planning, Greek, Roman, or medieval. The Galleria ushered Naples into *La Belle Époque*. Underfoot, marble depictions of the Zodiac had the same mania for the curlicue as Guimard and his Metro signs. Overhead, the domed glass ceilings and arching steel girders suggested the opulent cavern of an Impressionist train station. The gallery owner, when he thought of Paris, thought of the Orsay, and the Galleria worked for him. He wasn't surprised to learn the place had figured in a novel or two, a movie or three, and while he did at times picture the building in ruins, it wasn't as if he liked the idea. Indeed, here in the waking world, waking and quaking, he'd hated to see how the spring's upheavals had damaged the dome. A number of the glass panes, thick and braced though they were, had cracked and fallen. Fittings had needed realignment, reinforcement. These repairs did appear to be complete, now, or just about. The city would have the place ready for its deadline.

Come Friday, the triangular piazza at the building's foot would serve as one of the sites for *Expo in Città*. The people behind the celebrations were thinking of Sontag in Sarajevo, a balm for a wounded city, and they couldn't very well exclude the Galleria. This stage would feature music and performance, including an hour slot for Giussi. Now as Risto came out of close and difficult blocks, crosshatched with support struts, he discovered more clutter around the mall itself. Planking, wiring, scaffolding: construction as tic-tac-toe. It was Monday morning for the stage crews as well.

Once you got away from such tourist places, of course, you found the garbage piling up. The crap overflowed its dumpsters, though at least it remained in bags, mostly. The rinds and bones didn't spill and cook the way they had during the crisis, several years back. In those days, the stink had finally penetrated to uppermost chambers of government. The State had hacked a few pathways through the thickets of Camorra contracts. Garbage removal had gotten better, recycling too, and this summer it was part of the PR, the claims of recovery. Still, there remained patches of slapdash cleanup, and out on the city's periphery people had no legal landfill. As for the conversion plants, they already had more garbage than they could handle.

Downtown, however, was largely walkable. Just because you had to step around a few trash bags, that didn't mean the Expo was a sham.

For Risto, far harder to take was the check-in at the Ministry. Under the Corinthian pillars of the entrance, the *Guardia di Finanza* had stationed a few of its own security. White guys in white leather gun belts, one held a semi-automatic, reeking of its morning rubdown, The gun's business end was trained on Risto's crotch as he posed, a Da Vinci man gone brown, bald, and squat. He suffered a groping, too. Once he got his I.D. back, he could hardly keep from running for the stairs.

But the bookkeepers up in their office—there's the scene that called to mind illegal aliens. Illegals and an "irregular venue," though the mole runs of Italian bureaucracy didn't allow much room for dancing. Extension cords and phone lines looped at ankle height; a chair served as a file cabinet, heaped with papers. At the top of each heap, the exposed sheets had weathered the same soulless gray as the furniture. As for the computers, these were smeared with fingerprints and festooned with externals. Disc readers or power packs stood on their sides, most of them bookends for the paperwork. A number of the computer cables ended in butterfly adaptors such as Risto had never seen, technology that went back generations. The air conditioner was likewise dated, a cacophonous unit that didn't fit its window, the gap stuffed with crumpled newspaper. You didn't want to think about the chemicals, the odor. You didn't want to speculate, either, about where the *Guardia di Finanza* kept your accounts. In this tatterdemalion, they must've been losing track of files long before the quake and its electro-magnetic pulse.

Risto found just three "officers" on duty, three striped ties and blue blazers. White guys of course. The youngest and most in trim, his blazer draped over the back of his chair, had hidden the dips and moguls of his desktop beneath the *Gazzetto del Sport*. The man sat sunk in his reading. Were there blood on the floor, were La Cia lying mutilated beside him, all he'd care about would be his shoes. Nardo, however, appeared to have actual work. He had one spreadsheet on a clipboard and another up on his monitor. Onscreen the columns of figures seemed to guarantee eyestrain, mud-yellow on sea-green.

Before the man extended a hand to his visitor, he moved the other to a corner of the computer tower, getting a grip on one of those butterfly plug-ins.

Oh, and the Signore's registration forms, he had them here a minute ago...

Still, Nardo approximated the businesslike. Unlike his relative in Doc Martens, this guy needed the job, and he'd developed better coordination. Nimbly the bean counter hopped among the desks and heaps, the surge protectors. He had on nightclub footwear, loafers with bandolier buckles. In these he sidled past the colleague busy with the sports, rounding up the third officer to witness the gallery owner's signature. An officer, or a Recording Angel. The third man had an angel's curls, profuse, luxuriant, ebony. Some not-too-distant ancestor had been African. Before Nardo came by, this *finanziario* had sat making notes in an immense tome, something like the ornamental atlas out of an Imperial court. The book collected a stack of printouts between covers of startling blue, fastened by brads of impossible length.

There was no swearing on the Bible or anything like that. The man over the scores never budged, and Risto hesitated only when jotting down his date of birth. The date seemed too far back, more than thirty-five years back, and for a moment he needed to double-check both the old date and the new title: "Civilian Informant." Even after the form was filled in and signed, the paperwork appeared to change nothing. Nardo went into another pirouette, heading off to file his copy, and the Angel settled back down to his celestial Directory.

"Look," said Risto, "am I in the right place?"

At least his contract found an actual drawer, with a label. The officer, slipping the sheet into an accordion file, made reassuring noises.

"But what I came here to talk about, isn't it different from what you do? Fidel told you, my information is about the Earthquake I.D."

This was the tricky part, the referral. Nardo, returning to his seat, appeared concerned only with his troublesome computer connection.

"Here, look—" Risto waved at the desk's swill. "—what you do, it's all about finance. The wrong name on a check or a credit card."

Plus there was the air conditioner, roaring, rattling.

"But my information, it's about a cash business. Cash, and possibly a murder."

Poor little accountant with a badge. Nardo's hand went to his combover and, as the screen beside him flickered, his eyes changed color. Blue-green, gold-blue. All right, let the man work through his personal bureaucracy. As Risto began his explanations, he was careful to paper over the worst details.

As for the officer, he didn't have a lot of questions, but these took time, the way he began to stutter. It took a while before Risto realized he hadn't heard of the murder.

"You never heard of it. The papers, the web, the politicians making speeches—you never heard a word?"

"A business suh, suh-huch as this, it's beyond my competence."

Risto knuckled his scalp.

"Your, your gallery, signore? Your su-uh, your suck, success? That's great for the future of your, your pee, your people in Italy. You set an ex, an exam, an example."

"*Okay.*" The English put a distance between them.

"But I, I'd never have known about that ee, ee-heether. Your gallery, I'd never have heard of it if it, if it w-whirr, weren't for Vito. Vittorio."

"Then it's like I was saying, I'm not in the right place. I need a referral."

"And this uh, ugly business. It's all rather, rather *dark*, isn't it? It's dark and un-huh-unhappy, all about people I, I'd n-never..."

Better avoid the man's eyes, too.

"I, this, it's quite beyond me. Whuh-who are these people? Nobody has a name, nor a family ee-hee-ther, and half of them can't even say whuh, what sex they are."

"They have families." Leave it at that, Aristofano.

"In the news, the paper, if, if I saw the story, I would turn the page."

※

Leave it. If you're going to accomplish anything here, you need to see things from the white boy's side of the desk. A sturdy desk, a haven amid butterflies. More than likely, the sinecure had been a hand-me-down from an uncle. Risto had to understand as well that Bernardo here surely had a colleague from Africa, these days, and he called this man a friend. He wouldn't have a clue about the colleague's homeland, or about his uncle, or whether he even had an uncle who remained in one piece and above ground. Still, every time Nardo met the African, he'd say it was a pleasure. He'd have a compliment handy, maybe a kind word for the guy's blazer, and he'd never feel the least counterfeit about the chitchat. The same disconnect allowed him to put on one face for this brown colleague and another, very different, for the young man cut to ribbons last weekend... oh, what was his name? La Fibonaccia?

Naturally the *finanziario* was more than happy to hand the mess over to someone else. Risto only had to mention City Homicide. At that the man suffered a whole-body stutter, touching hair, keyboard, and butterfly.

Then with a hand on his office phone, an old landline, Nardo locked up again. "You do ree-hee-lize," he said, "a deputy like myself, I, I have limits."

"To be sure. For the State to function, there must be limits."

So it worked, the idea that'd come to Risto while he'd had a knife in his face. The *finanziario* was so nervous about the call, he practically tied himself into a knot there between phone and computer, but the gallery owner saw this as a piece of art. A Michelangelo, the torso in a twist, and when Risto took the receiver, he smiled at the policeman's accent. The man spoke like a Florentine, plummy, making a production of the name: Del-la Fi-gu-ra-zi-o-ne. Later, as the Civilian Informant got into his story, the officer gave the same drawn-out treatment to "La Fenestrella." The club was familiar around the precinct, "of interest."

Really? Then why hadn't the cops shut it down?

Risto remained careful of his tone. "Don't you have evidence I could look at?"

Della Figurazione too could leave things unsaid. "Ah, now, old Nardo there, you tell him I'm grateful for the lead..."

"Excuse me, but I'm the one with the lead. Not old Nardo."

Here was a switch: he felt glad for the unmuffled air conditioner. He could talk freely, getting into details like the dealer's blade. "Serrated, Della Figurazione."

"Serrated?" It came to Risto that he should ignore the blasé pose: the detective was taking notes. "Where'd he keep something like that?"

"He had a costume, a jacket with a trick pocket. Look, the evidence from the crime scene? That's got to have something—some identifying mark."

"Ah."

The detective mentioned "channels," then added gently: "Signore Auk Yeer, what's in the evidence is disturbing stuff."

"Disturbing?" Risto hunkered down in a trough between papers. "I shouldn't have to remind you, I'm from Africa. Somalia, Della Figurazione. *Disturbing*, I know all about that. What if I told you I saw my brother get his head cut off?"

He put his lips to the mouthpiece. "My family got caught on the wrong side. My brother, they split his head like a melon."

Hadn't he shared this story before? Hadn't he told a couple of reporters, Italians, white boys, and after that read about it in the papers and on the web? His wife had seen the items, and her father, and from there it had rippled through circles of friends. Word had gotten out so thoroughly that, if Risto's two kids amounted to more than slices of fruit in a salad—*famiglia mista*, people called it—their substance owed something to this story. The make-believe lent muscle, somehow.

From the other end of the line, Risto heard condolences. "Horrible, signore. They cut his head off, and also they split it open?"

Anyway, hadn't he figured right, all morning long? First with Fidel and then here above Piazza Municipio? "I can handle it," he said finally. "Whatever's in the evidence."

Della Figurazione grew brusque. He sounded as if his work too required a good eye. The detective revealed he'd known something of Risto and his gallery; he read *Il Mattino*. "But this brings us to another question," he continued. "How did a man like you ever find old Nardo?"

Risto managed a chuckle. "Detective. Nardo had me sign something, you know. A contract that called me a Civilian Informant. For an informant to get a look at evidence, it's only reasonable."

"Reasonable." How sincere was that exhale?

"Look, you just said you'd read about me. You know I'm not one of these people who play games with the police."

"I said I know what you do. But I've also got to think about what I do."

Risto's phone ear was dripping sweat. "The story I told you about my brother, eh. Don't let it give you the wrong idea."

"Signore, this is no longer about your brother. It's about myself and my position."

Come to think, why had Risto rushed into his bloody little *favola*? Ti'aba's slaughter had no place here, especially in its made-up version. Today was different from telling Paola or Giussi. With them it was roughly the same as with a reporter, but today, what had Risto been thinking? He couldn't even see who he was talking to. Nevertheless, he'd blurted out the worst of his past—the lie that, small as it was, tainted his entire European run of luck and accomplishment. He'd shared it with three other folks in earshot, and he'd gone so far as to throw in the most extravagant of his fabrications, the thumb he put on the storytelling scale. Risto sank back down in the trough of spreadsheets. Could this be his worst case yet of talking like a white man? Wouldn't he do himself more good just listening? Della Figurazione, he noticed, had a bit of a wheeze. Naples city buildings didn't allow smoking, but this high-toned cop sounded as if he didn't believe the rule applied to him.

Regarding the murder, the detective revealed only that he was impressed. "It does appear that you and I ought to stay in touch," he said. "What you've given me does call for police action, perhaps an operation."

An operation? Risto kept his head down, muzzling himself.

"About that, signore, as I say, we'll stay in touch. But let me ask. Your man *Papers*—did he go in for jewelry?"

"Some."

"What? You're telling me, last night, you saw jewelry, like silver or gold?"

"Silver, around his neck. Also perfume."

"How about a silver bracelet, an American look, ah, South American? You know the type, a snake usually, all one piece, maybe Mexican."

Sure, he knew the type. Risto checked the finance officer, squinting at his screen, deaf to the African at his elbow, then went on to clarify: Papers had worn a necklace. Silver, yes, Central American. "Nothing on his wrist, though. If he'd had anything on his wrist, I would've seen it."

He didn't elaborate, and soon the two were swapping phone numbers. When Della Figurazione again mentioned the possibility of an operation, the last thing Risto wanted to do was bring up Tuttavia, her choice of bracelets.

⌗

The metropolis rose from the sea's edge in parallel boulevards, gently graded, a staircase down which a baby giant would clamber to its wading pool. Not that the piazzas had clean right angles or perfect circles. Anyone looking for plumb-bob geometry should try Bologna. But coming down or climbing up, you moved through a grid laid out by the Greeks, rough rectangles of east-west *decumani* and their connectors. The culture remained in business day to day and yet, with just a look around, it took you back three thousand years. No other downtown on the continent could claim such antiquity, almost so old as to rival the urban centers over in what used to be called Mesopotamia, or down in, what was the name, Abyssinia. Granted, those cities, South and East, had been reduced to rubble, and much of time the damage was done by barbarians out of the North. Still, a place like Ur, or Zeila on the Horn, they'd been the originals, in which tribes who'd formerly called each other devils came together in a space that wasn't inferno. Mixing races, they'd given rise to a royal line. The first king had been a kind of *clandestino*, the love child of Solomon and Sheba.

An unlikely thought for a European businessman on a weekday. But once Risto finished with the *Guardia*, he put his back to the water and began to climb, and up in his head the route was stranger. The hike took him above the quadrilaterals, up past the Museum with its high-quality rubble. Here the streets developed kinks, asymmetrical, prime territory for the Little Window. The layout followed what used to be footpaths. A hilltop like Materdei, forty-five minutes up from the island ferries, eschewed the lower city's logic. Granted, Materdei had its own office crowd, and its traffic included the new electrics. Nevertheless, when you came out on a penthouse balcony like Eftah's, no farther from the *centro* than a catapult might sling a cobblestone, you could see that, not so long ago: the land at your feet had been countryside, fertile with Vesuvian nutrients. Where there hadn't been vineyards or orchards, there must've been goats.

Then what advantage did Naples have over the cities put up by men Risto's color? Why hadn't Naples been left in shreds, turning back to weeds and scrub?

Paola, now, she'd say her husband had gotten past all that. She'd tell him he'd just had a rough morning, in which the worst out of his past had reared up from behind its grimy tombstone, not once but twice. With a fleshy shrug she'd remind him that together, they'd found a better way. Living well was the best *hommage*. Living well, he did honor to the wreckage he'd once called home, and at the same time he stuck his thick middle finger in the face of any smug European. He accomplished both, yes, and if anyone understood, it was Paola. He had no one so close, certainly not Eftah, though that's who was up in Materdei. Eftah had been no help with the hearings for citizenship, whereas Paola had sat right beside her husband, sorting through the entire paper trail, even the scraps out of Somalia. She'd sat there with Tonino squirming in her belly, a Buddha in a hormonal glow, opening the way to Nirvana. That went for the law as well. To marry an Italian made you Italian.

Getting that maroon and gold passport, of course, had required a lot more besides, including an armload of files and weeks' worth of evaluations. But the head doctors who evaluated him for citizenship added nothing to the bit of jargon Paola first taught him. "Survivor's guilt," those two words alone, seemed to contain more meaning than the entire seven and a half pages of psychological profile.

The naturalization process, like every other legal process, groaned under the weight of xenophobia. Up and down the local hills, too, the cops handed out their Get-Lost letters. Granted, a street vendor out of South Sudan or the Republic of the Congo wasn't worried about a letter. Sure, the document ordered the recipient out of the country in three days. But in what unimaginable city or state would there be a follow-up? In what wing of what agency? Chances were the greater metro did have a list somewhere, in some littered treehouse like the one Risto had just visited. Somewhere, after all, Naples maintained a warehouse for the goods seized off the streets. That was the real damage done, when the police busted one of the hawkers on the streets: they impounded his duffel bag. As for the Quit-Italy order, a brother could use that to wipe his dark ass. But if a salesman lost his inventory, he had to go to the mob. The Camorra never lacked for junkware, almost as if they could dip into the goods the city had confiscated. The crap for sale along Corso Umberto'Uno, the wind-up birds and octopi, the necklace knockoffs, the jackknives—God knows, it all looked the same, endlessly recycled.

You heard of Africans and Arabs fighting back. Every now and then, the Immigrant Council took on an appeal. The Council, however, wasn't much help with the application for citizenship. When Aristofano Al'Kair had submitted his petition, questions about his own *clandestino* days were resolved by the laying-on of white, Neapolitan hands. Every time he went before another magistrate, he could hear how little his paperwork amounted to, compared to Paola's maiden name.

Such *Italianità* as it was pronounced! So much tongue in the o's, the r's!

The documentation also needed to include whatever the petitioner could scare up about his former family. For this too Risto had depended on his Italian family, on Paola's father in particular. The man found a team of investigators based in Addis Ababa. Former military personnel, working through a translation service, somehow they'd owed a favor to a Neapolitan surgeon. And give them credit: the Ethiopians came up with remnants that Risto would never have believed existed. They emailed a scan of orders for execution, issued by some sort of chieftain-imam who'd controlled about half of the city for the better part of a year. One name on the list could well have been Risto's father's, the spelling a reasonable fit and followed by the Arabic shorthand for "lawyer." A symbol at the top of the page, the investigators explained, indicated that anyone listed beneath had been beheaded. As for Risto's mother, the crew in Addis Ababa provided another scan, a log in English out of a Red Cross hospital. A woman had been brought in dying, "*head trma & vaginal infect.*" The phonetic transcription of the name seemed like a match, as did her approximate age and height, and at the end this woman had raved in both French and Italian. She'd kept urging two boys to run north.

Years later, fifteen hundred miles to the north, Petitioner Al'Kair had remained stone-faced as he handed the printouts over to the citizenship tribunal. He'd recited the names with no more feeling than a hit man required to allocute. For that as for the rest, Paola was the one to thank. Once again he'd lied to her about Ti'aba, bearing false witness before his most intimate tribunal, settled over her swelling belly. He'd acted out the machete's chop, the storytelling caught in his throat, and for weeks afterward his dreams took him on a long swim back, first across the sea and then upstream—indeed, he might jerk awake wet-faced and choking—upstream, where he was powerless to prevent himself from reaching toward all-too-familiar creek stones, the skulls of brother, mother, and father. His big hands closed over those rounds, the bone nibbled hairless and white, and his fingers slipped into the cracks...

But his lying was all about the long ago and far away, as Paola would be the first to tell him. He was a European businessman on a weekday morning. One child was old enough to swim on his own, and the other scurried in and out of the low Tyrrhenian surf. As for citizenship, Risto's was so secure he could go down to post-Khadaffi Libya and come back with a watercolorist. All this the husband had managed without changing his skin color or turning his back on less-legal brothers like Eftah and Giussi.

Survivor's guilt, eh. The past couple of days, with their hard knocks and hallucinations—they didn't make him some sort of sham. Besides, Risto had a more glaring example of someone who'd never come to terms with the past. He had Tuttavia. Whatever dead that woman had left behind, the corpses appeared to be booby-trapped. For all the photos she'd brought to Risto, and for all the Sunday dinners they'd shared, she still had interior chambers he'd never cracked. He'd gotten no more than a glimpse of the odyssey that must've preceded her first visit to his shop. She'd mentioned a conservatory, but never a degree. Really, her gallery owner was left to surmise what he could from her unchanging project: the refugee. Everyone in her viewfinder preferred an alias. In migrant squats, in outlaw clubs, they appeared so comfortable with the photographer that Risto had to conclude her journey to Naples had been some Southbound variation of his own. As a fugitive, Tuttavia would've had her disadvantages. Your average road warrior could snap her like a twig. But then again, she was white, well-spoken, and well put together.

All the woman would say was that, as she'd crossed the Continent, she'd had "one rule: keep moving. Never get trapped." Risto hadn't pestered for more. Once, following a fresh set of raves ("Diane Arbus in the hellholes of the South"), he'd gone online with the serial number of her camera. A top-of-the-line Nikon, it had somehow survived the road. You thought of Marco Polo and the jewels he'd sewn into his coat. Online, the serial number brought up a man's name and an address in Vilnius, and these Risto shared with her. The response was pretty much what you'd expect. First the Ice Queen blushed hotly, and then she went as closemouthed as an African.

He didn't pester. Everywhere he looked, people were using an alias.

⌗

These Camorra places had so much chrome. Up in Materdei, if you took a table in the sun, the metal could singe your arm. Risto had wondered about that, the bar so bright and shiny, the clientele so shady. He'd asked about it once, during a night out with Eftah and Paola, trying the Arab place in Piazza Bellini. They'd laughed at him, though nicely. Risto was talking poetry, they said, metaphors, *per carit*à. The choice of chrome was a business decision. The System used the materials they could get the cheapest, and when they needed a front, they preferred a bar to a restaurant. A pizzeria required permits, contracts, and if the baker knew his way around an oven, the mob wound up with an actual going concern. A satisfied customer was nothing but fuss and bother to the *malavita*. They weren't about neighborhood development.

But any junky could make a cup of coffee, and up in Materdei, they seemed to have one behind the counter. If this place had been down by the docks, a pit stop for the mob whores, the kid would never have gotten away with such a watery brew. The hookers on the Camorra payroll could be as bloodthirsty as their gangster bosses. Risto forced down the coffee and asked for water, a bottle of Vera, please. He needed to rehydrate before he joined Eftah and a couple of scary pals, the three of them lounging amid the chrome.

Risto had learned to check at the café before he tackled the last steep block up to the cousin's palazzo. The hilltop piazza was a box of midday heat, with a cluttered baroque church to one side and, to the other, the featureless jiffy concrete of the recent sprawl. The best air conditioning was in the bar; a good unit somehow fit the *malavita* budget. Risto's big relation saw no reason not to take advantage, and at his table everyone got quick service. Guys like these fetched the barista with no more than a jerk of the chin, and a certain angle of wave brought them beer and a sandwich. Typically this was mozzarella and capicolla, delivered fresh-made from the deli on the far side of the piazza. You could see the deli's runner darting through the traffic, his apron up over his bag arm, and you noticed too the outfits on the men waiting, a mashup of gym clothes and dress shirts. This was their office, though one at least was always too large for an office. A no-neck behemoth, he'd flaunt his nickname, making sure that everyone knew it: a name out of a cartoon or a dumb movie.

"Jabba the Hut" was this afternoon's muscle. Just now, breakfast time for him, the Hut sat enjoying a laugh. The back of his immense head, with its bags and creases and curls, looked a lot scarier than his cud-chewer's face, all smiles.

"That f-faggot La Cia," he giggled. "If it was m-me who killed La Cia, first I'd have stuck my old sh-shotgun up his ass!"

Eftah rolled his eyes, a greeting for Risto. "My my my. Aren't *you* an angel? You'd have given him one last good time."

They laughed some more, the two killers and the crooked landlord. Social networking in a System town, where collusion was one of Eftah's favorite lecture subjects. *Risto, you should've seen it in 1980, after the last big quake.*

Actually, Eftah hadn't been here in 1980. He'd left Mogadishu among the first wave, following the coup of '91.

There was government money, UN money, money from America. 1980, oh my, it was everywhere. All the bad guys had to do was show up with a bucket.

The bad guys. This was the point of Eftah's lecture, or one of them: that he himself belonged in a different category. The Black Lord might charge market rent, market plus, but he honored his leases and kept up repairs. You had to admire the man's instinct for the lesser evil.

Could be that's what had prodded the gallery owner into his forced march up from Piazza Municipio: a yearning for the lesser evil. Could be he was just sick of the thug economics around here. From where Risto stood he could see the result, a real eyesore of a palazzo. Between its third and fifth story, the building's corners sprouted exposed wiring, red and wormlike. Risto thought of whatever was left of La Cia's thumb.

"Eftah, *abba*." Enough with the nightmares in broad daylight. "Could we talk?"

"Talk?" The Hut gave a full-body chortle, his chair yelping. "Talk, is that what you fags call it?"

Eftah blew the man a kiss. He hoisted his cup and made introductions.

"So what if he's your cousin?" Sneering. "Let me tell you, there's one cousin of mine, I'd do her in a minute."

"In your family, my friend, I imagine it wouldn't be the first time."

Now the other *Camorrista* was laughing, and Eftah gave Risto a wink. When things quieted, he added that he was waiting for Mepris.

"Mayy-pree?" barked the smaller gangster. "Is that your latest fuck buddy? What do you think we're running here, a gay bar?"

Mildly Eftah met his gaze. "A gay bar and a nigger place."

The laughter itself might've been made of chrome.

"Oh my, you don't see it coming, really?"

The murderers quieted, frowning.

"Don't you see it's simply a matter of time? It'll be the same here as everywhere. Everywhere, you'll have a gay bar, plus a nigger place." Eftah kept it mild. "At least, my people, we keep the expenses down. Thank God for small favors. My people, there's no need for electricity, is there?"

This coaxed fresh chuckles.

"The contract with the electric company? Forget about it. Then there's the furnishings—what, a couple of mattresses?"

Risto had heard this before. With Paola or someone of that caliber, Eftah cleaned up the language, but the idea was the same, a coon show.

"What do you need with *mattresses*, even, come to think? A little hay on the floor. A little hay, that's all, it's what these animals are used to."

The Black Lord's Third Millennial Coon Show.

"These people," he said, "if they want music, they use a stick and a log."

The routine worked for today's crowd, no question. "A st-stick and a log?" the Hut was saying. "A st-*stick*?"

Risto's wife put such stuff in a better light. *Honestly*, she would say, *you've got to admire him, the way he's kept his sense of humor*. She argued that trash talk like this was the least they could expect, after whatever the man had gone through to get his properties. If Paola were here now, she'd notice most what the act accomplished—how it distracted the toughs from her sweat-soaked husband.

Risto, however, had to turn away. Out in the piazza, he spotted Mepris.

The boyfriend picked his way between Smarts and Vespas, looking grim. He could've been a sketch figure of alarm, glaring, stiff-necked. Was that what Risto had looked like, when he'd first crossed the piazza?

Eftah got up grinning, but the Moroccan came in kicking the door wide. As the heat surged inside, the boy staggered his housemate with a slap.

"You wrinkled old queer," snapped Mepris. "You and your macho games!"

The second slap sounded worse than the first.

"You've gone so far wrong, so far. And it'd be so easy to do some *good!*"

The Cammoristi loved it. You'd think their chairs would collapse beneath their rocking, their howls, and the smaller hood went into a pantomime, slapping at his pal. Even the barista stood gaping over the sink, as if he were high off the steam.

"To do what's decent, it'd be *so easy*. It's had me stalking around all morning."

Risto, grimacing at the outburst's tinny echo, could only wonder.

"And *this* is where I find you! The sick old man of Europe, back at his macho games. Playing his own family!"

What, family? Eftah's expression offered nothing, and anyway who could think, the way the Hut was shrieking? *Best show in town...*

"Just to think of it makes me want to get a knife!" The Moroccan slashed a fist through the air. "I swear I want to cut your balls off!"

Per carità. How many suspects was Risto going to have?

Then again, he knew his so-called cousin. Risto had often played the Concerned Onlooker. The dialogue had never been so bloodthirsty, but when it came to tantrums, Eftah was a connoisseur. He might be fifty, might be older, but he rarely went a day without pouting and stamping his feet.

Mepris called his lover an "overgrown *enfant terrible*;" Risto would add that this *enfant* preferred his hookups be babies themselves. The young ones with the cocksucker faces, that's what Eftah liked. When Risto had shared the apartment, only once had he needed to fend off a murmur and a grope. Only once, and though it was his first month in Italy, he hadn't wound up on the street. His host had withdrawn his calloused hands, at first resistance, even as Risto was repeating, evenly, *No.* The younger man never heard an apology, exactly, but the next morning Eftah had a fresh box of creamy *cornuti* to go with the cappuccino. A rich breakfast, and as they ate he'd worked in a reminder, almost sheepish, that the two of them were barely blood relations.

In those days, Risto hardly knew *what* he was. His name remained under construction, his hustling in Alexandria under lock and key. He wouldn't share that story with Eftah for years; so long as he was living under the man's roof, he didn't need the complication. Even so, had Risto been more of a cutie, his rejection might've turned Eftah vindictive. The Black Lord had a terrible weakness for a *Vogue* bone structure.

Mepris, however, seemed to have broken the mold—a boyfriend of quality, as Paola said. The Moroccan might've had a few years on the others (Eftah could handle thirty, when it came in such a package), and he'd moved to the Materdei place with books enough to fill three shelves. There were English titles as well as Italian and French, and as one of the bookends, on the highest shelf, Mepris set a thick sheaf of manuscript. Risto had asked about that, and he never got a straight answer, but the Moroccan revealed some sensibility, no denying. In July the boy had celebrated his first anniversary in this aerie, a serious spike on Eftah's relationship graph.

Then there was today's spike, nothing so happy. Barely two weeks had passed since the anniversary celebration, but over that time it'd seemed ever more likely that one of these two was going to get hit. Now the older man's alligator-brown hide might conceal the blow, but if you knew him you could see the damage, a bruising of the spirit.

Mepris had stormed out. He wasn't going to stay and get laughed at, especially not with his lover keeping up a smug front for the goombahs. But before long the two Somalis quit the bar, and after they made it uphill to the Black Lord's palazzo and upstairs to his rooftop, Eftah set to work repairing his reputation. From this height, he could point out the substandard building projects in the surrounding blocks: three, no four, no five. He could take in his own place with a full-arm sweep, indicating the whole terrazzo from seaside to hillside, letting a guest see that everything was up to code. Eftah had never cut corners, not even when he'd set up the grape trellis, its vines deeply potted and now in full leaf.

"Up here," he said, "it's Tuscany, no? The villa of a rock star. Hollywood Italy!"

But on the next roof downhill, the greenery was tangled ailanthus, weed trees that sprouted through the tar. "Shame," said the man who'd been slapped, "shame, shame."

For a while Risto couldn't respond. The breeze took all his attention, air-drying his sweat-soaked wrap. That alone felt like it would absolve any sin. It felt like a feast, even as his host went back into the kitchen and re-emerged carrying a full tray. Lunch would be under the trellis; the repast would be part of the compensation, for the Concerned Onlooker. In the shade of the grape leaves Risto found the pickings at once light and overwhelming, cold grains and greens and garlic. These took him back to his first dinners in the North, when he thought he'd waded off the boat into paradise. Plus Eftah had a bottle of Ischian wine underway, a white so icy that Risto tightened his wraparound. After the two cleared their plates, they refilled their glasses.

"Yes," said Risto, "kill the bottle."

In time they were back at the railing, swaying in the breeze, cleansing the soul. Eftah reiterated that there were men in this city far wickeder than he.

"You saw that monster in the bar," he said.

Risto let his head loll. He checked the sky for flaws: a couple smudges of sulfur. Eftah muttered the phrase "the sick old man of Europe," but Risto didn't catch the context, and then the host had moved on to the history of his building. The palazzo had gone up in the eighteenth century, a home for the "morganatic wife" of a powerful baron. "Morganatic," Eftah said. "Nice. Very nice."

This wasn't the first time Risto had heard about the baron, though the tone had never been so gloomy. He straightened up. "Old stories."

The sort-of cousin eyed him differently.

"Unhappy old stories," Risto went on. "Listen, Eftah—my own old stories, from 'Dishu? This morning they came up twice." The philosopher of happiness sounded pretty gloomy himself. "I mean Ti'aba, all that. The worst."

"My my my." You'd think Eftah had a switch, Heavy/Light. "All that, truly, the utter worst? Plus, you say it just—came up?"

Risto ran a quick mental audit. Had his big relative heard the same embellished version of Ti'aba's last minutes as everyone else? He had, yes, and so the younger man went on to say only that most of the time, up here on this terrazzo was about as close as he got to the old country.

"You and your brother in the clan."

"The clan, eh. I couldn't even tell you their name."

"Best I can recall, it was something like...Hai-wai? Whatever. Just don't get the name wrong down there, oh my no, don't you dare use it in vain."

Eftah's crow's feet deepened, showing his age. "Everywhere there's shame, South as well as North, but I'll take the kind that allows me to stay in my skin."

The man had a switch, Heavy/Light, and he couldn't stop fiddling with it.

"I'll stay in my own *skin*, thank you, and I'll live the way I *like*!"

The best Risto could come up with: *As long as you use a condom...*

"Mepris," Eftah went on, "oh that boy, that firecracker. Mepris, he's up in his head too much, but I do appreciate how he knows the history. He knows what century would've been best for me. Down South, in Alexandria one century and Addis Ababa the next, he tells me when I could've lived as I like."

"In 'Dishu too," Risto put in. "I used to hear stories..."

"Yes, the old folks had their fairytales, the Jewel in the Horn. But that was another century. A good thirty years now—my one and only lifetime—the city's been no place for a man like me."

Eftah rarely came so close to eloquence, but Risto hadn't climbed all this way just to listen. "Look, I had to run away too."

"Down South, if I just looked at a man the wrong way, they'd tear out my eyes"

Risto gave a chop, flat-handed. "Today was very *hard*. I remembered everything, even Maman."

Again the switch was thrown. The man gave a grin. "Listen to you. 'Maman,' my, when did that start? At home, oh don't think I don't remember, she was Mamma."

"Home. You mean Beirut or Casablanca?"

"Just listen to you. Hard-boiled detective. But then, today, you remembered."

Risto managed his own smile. "You know the story."

"Know it? I heard it first, what, fifteen years ago? Still, there's today, isn't there—or should we say, more significantly, there was last night."

Risto reached for what was left of his wine. "Don't you think I've thought about that? Last night La Cia, this morning Ti'aba."

"The connection does come to mind."

"Oh, hear the elder. Elder of the clan."

He wound up leaving the drink alone, fingering his sweaty scalp while Eftah suggested he get specific.

"Eh." Risto told him about the outburst in the office of the *Guardia*.

"My my my." Eftah's face grew longer, the eyebrows arching. "What *are* these wild scenes? An office like that, a Monday morning, it's nothing but white men."

"But, the white men, Eftah, look. I have news."

He peered down the switchbacks to the *centro*.

"I came here with news. The man I was talking to, he was white, yes, but that's not all. He was police. As of this morning, I've got a man on the police."

The face went round again. Eftah could've been the brown Humpty Dumpty, and Risto started to pace as if he needed another hill to climb. Working with the cops, *per carità*. The thrill of just getting an officer to listen, a white man with a title—that couldn't be the only reason he'd come out with the bit about Ti'aba, not when he'd first screened the entire movie in his gallery lav. Still, that had to be part of it. Here on his big relative's terrazzo, Risto was struck by how he pronounced the police phrase "an operation." It had the knowing air he'd employ at an opening. *You see of course the classic proportions, two parts to one....*

Couldn't be the only reason, but: "You see why I needed to talk."

"My my my." Eftah had straightened up, Mussolini. "The immigrant success."

"Success, eh." Risto broke off pacing, taking stock. He'd had a homemade meal and a few swallows of pale, chilled medicine. If he

wanted more, if he was after the kind of reassurance he might get from
a father figure, first he'd need to find one. Daddy Bear was one role this
clansman had never played, no matter how he might look the part.

Just the opposite, Eftah went on preening. He declared that he and
Giussi and Risto had made a difference, "with our work last night."

Work? Risto couldn't quite nod.

"That conversation you had this morning, my boy, that would
never have happened before last night. Before we found something the
authorities wanted. Last night, we gave them a reason, when it came to
putting this butcher in cuffs."

"Sure." Come on, nod. "We gave them a reason, sure. But, *abba*,
now, something else. It's time you let me know what's going on with
Mepris."

The older man's laugh wasn't much, another pose.

"Look, Eftah, this isn't just about him, about your love life. Something else."

"My dear *cousin*, you of all people, you should remember that he's
hardly the first to threaten me with bloody murder."

"Okay, but look." First Risto made plain how highly he and Paola
thought of the Morrocan. No surprise, to judge from Eftah's gaze.
Beyond that, though, if Mepris were to go the way of all the other
boyfriends, it seemed to have something to do with Risto himself.
"Whenever I'm around, he really goes off. Last night at the club, today
in the bar. He went off like a bomb. He said you were playing me."

The accusation had something Risto trusted, something scruffy
and baseline. If not, why was Eftah trying to change the subject? Why
was he bringing up Tuttavia?

"A threat like that, bloody murder, I would've expected to hear it
from her. No love for me, God knows, in her heart. Her cold Baltic
heart."

"Well, it's about your loyalties. Your ultimate loyalties, who you
stand with."

"It's about the rent check. What I charge my African brothers, when
in one of my places, at least they can count on electricity and water."
He tried to chuckle. "For this that Viking calls me a robber baron."

"Eftah, I've spoken to her."

"Well, just last night, it wasn't as if she's put away her sword."

And Mepris? What would've happened if he'd come into the bar with a sword? "*Abba*," said Risto, "what's your boyfriend talking about?"

His host was shaking his head, glowering around the terrazzo. You'd think that, today, it was he who'd reached a certain corner of the city and found it not at all the place he knew. Then with a grumble he strode off into the dark of his penthouse. Risto hardly had time to wonder, to knuckle the sweat from his eyebrows, before his host emerged again with his open laptop PC. At the table under the trellis, he shoved aside dishes and silver and made sure the screen was visible, at an angle in the shade.

"Everyone's so righteous," the clansman asked. "Everyone thinks they know the Way of the Righteous—well, take a look at these. Maybe you can draw me a map."

※

"3X5" was small for a picture file. When Risto had first seen the size, on the flash drive Eftah had dropped off at Wind & Confusion, he wouldn't have guessed it was photographs. But the title turned out to be simple arithmetic, the number of pictures. So brief an album didn't take up many bytes, though someone had tweaked a few of the JPGs. They'd done simple enhancements, a touch of grain or saturation.

The "3" however may've had a second meaning, a reference to the participants.

Giussi was the easiest to recognize, his elastic expressiveness the same as he used onstage. Also, at the first good once-over, you had no trouble picking out Fidel's Ukrainian doll. Zelusa might've worn that particular combination of eye shadow and lip gloss, plum over cherry, the last time she'd floated around the gallery. The schoolgirl knee socks looked familiar as well. But as to the third in this ménage, the gallery owner resisted giving her a name, holding off until he noticed he was doing so. Of course, before this, he'd never seen Tuttavia naked. Still, he shouldn't kid himself, he'd done enough kidding himself the last couple of days, and his denials were a waste of breath. *No, lashes like that, no, she'd never*...A waste of breath. *Never, not in high heels*...But Risto needed to accept the evidence before him. He needed to shake off his clansman (*It's her, dear boy, truly...*) and lean over the keyboard. Interrupting the slideshow, he zoomed in on a shot or two.

The more he studied how Tuttavia put her fingers to use, the more the gestures proved stylized, especially in the difference between her hands and her mouth. In none of the shots did Tuttavia suck or munch or fully engage in a kiss, and the one time she stuck out her tongue made such a parody of arousal, it would ruin the show for any poor sap who'd paid to watch. Risto's star client left the toy alone too, the vibrator or whatever that was. She'd been game, she would if Giussi would, but it was the other woman who worked the get-together for optimum intensity. Zelusa revealed the authentic grimace, the Russian doll cracked open. You wondered about the noise she made, whether orgasm had an accent, and about whether she'd been primed with vodka or X. When the girl took up the dildo, she showed wholehearted determination, a stark contrast to Tuttavia's pretending. The expression "older and wiser" didn't apply, not in those lashes and heels, but if the session were some sort of practice run for Giussi bringing another player onstage, it looked as if he ought to consider the younger and cra- zier. Their two faces, the Eastern African and Eastern European, made a connection that excluded Tuttavia altogether. The man's erection too served as a piece of stagecraft. Giussi had never been cold to hetero pleasure. A few of his setpieces, in performance, acted out affairs with women, and in this simulation he demonstrated correct smut protocol. The sequence ended when he delivered the money shot. His climax was a phony, to be sure, though Zelusa never took her mouth off him, never let go of his narrow butt. Still, an extra moment with the picture was all it took to reveal the fakery, the trick of the camera angle and the faux rough grain.

These weren't the only signs of amateur work, either, and the sloppiness on his clansman's laptop irked Risto as much as anything else. It confirmed that the hand on the camera had been Fidel's, and all thumbs as ever. Fidel had seen Mapplethorpe, he'd seen Helmut Newton, but he hadn't learned a thing. He hadn't let the bodies speak for themselves. Giussi could've been fascinating, with his interplay of wrinkles and vigor. But Fidel had botched the focus. A threesome pictorial, for all the attention it lavished on the women, needed to honor the man, the moral of the story, the Omnipotent. To Risto's eye, moreover, it was obvious how the performance artist had messed with playing Massa. Giussi had brought off a bit of mugging here, a small gesture there, which cracked through the rinds of fantasy. The way the shots were framed, however, never allowed space for these disruptions. Fidel couldn't abide the least interference, the least pinch of the unexpected, when it came to his comfort zone. Throughout his triple-X charade, from the first murmurs in his babydoll's ear to the last fiddling with color and saturation, Signore Castelsabbia had seen little beyond his own reflection: the tales he'd tell at the next party — and tell himself, the next time he got his hand between his legs.

Risto sat back from the screen. His first words were an echo of something he'd heard elsewhere, not long ago. "Him and his love slave…"

"Exactly. An inelegant business such as this, honestly, where was I supposed to go with it? The attachment shows up in my email, and, I ask you."

Eftah swung a scuffed hand from the screen to the city view.

"Where's a fellow to wash away the sin? Tell me. Where's the cathedral?"

The question was welcome, a change of pace. When Risto checked the slideshow again, for a moment he wasn't faced with godawful erotica, but rather a battered city map, worn at the folds and flyspecked. The map revealed, for starters, the places Fidel would've taken his kitten in return for her purring and stretching on camera. Zelusa would've been rewarded with, say, a line of credit at Versace. She'd have given her Daddy (more Stalin than Guevara, comrade) another excuse to whine that she took advantage, that girl, she had him wrapped around her finger…

So too, Risto could spy on Giussi, in the laptop atlas. He could see why the performer had signed on for the show, the kick it gave him, indulging his fringe wizardry while skinning a rabbit. He would've insisted on cash, a fold of Euros as thick as a rabbit's pelt. Risto could understand Giussi.

But the third party, the woman—he couldn't find her, on his map. "Tuttavia," he repeated.

"The gallery's greatest star, and you her greatest champion, the astonishing Aristofano Al'Kair..."

Risto massaged his head. He'd worked with the woman for years, dropping in at both her Naples apartments, even helping with the move into the latest. A top-story space alongside a deconsecrated cathedral, her new rooms were as close to a quiet retreat as you could find in this city. But neither place, neither studio, had left room for an intimate life. He'd seen the narrow underside of the platform on which she slept. A feeble excuse for a bed. The stepladder was stashed behind her computer desk.

Risto continued to fumble. "I'm the only man in Italy who knows her age."

The clansman, thoughtful, pointed out that he knew a thing or two about the woman. He'd watched her from across the dance floor, and her pictures included a handful of men with whom he'd "had dealings." As soon as he'd opened this download, he'd known it would leave Risto flummoxed. "There's reason for concern," Eftah declared. "That woman, really, I wouldn't be surprised if she's remained celibate her entire time in Naples."

The gallery owner, shifting back from the screen, took in his countryman. "I wouldn't be surprised," he said.

"Yes, what do we know about Tuttavia, really? Mepris, that smart boy, he's got a different idea entirely. He says she's got to have lovers. The white girl who does without, if you ask my Mepris, that's just a black man's fantasy."

Today, Risto noticed, Eftah too was upsetting expectation. He'd done without the anomalous colors of a clubhound. In his ear he'd popped a simple stud and his jeans were all loops and pockets. He was the Handyman, not the Robber Baron—though this wouldn't make a bit of difference to Tuttavia. She'd gone so far, once, as to forbid Risto from selling Eftah any of her work. She'd actually used that word, "forbid," and her gallery owner had needed to call upon his deepest reserves of African restraint. He'd taken her down to the gelateria and spelled out a few rules.

The clansman kept on. "That Goth thing of hers, my my my, as if she wouldn't be fazed by a knife at her throat. But she never goes out without protection. Never without her man." Giussi, he continued, must've given her the heads-up about last night. "And have you heard the way she talks about him?"

Risto mentioned the dinners at his place.

Eftah had another setting in mind. "In a place like La Fenestrella, Risto, have you heard? The things she says about Giussi? You'd think she was just another fag hag." In the clubs Tuttavia would claim she'd been getting hit on since she was fifteen. She preferred a date who—"Risto, do you know the line, 'It's like I'm his sister'?"

"*Per carità*. She actually said that?"

"I swear by the prettiest face on the dance floor. And the woman was talking about Giussi! My brother the polymorphously perverse!"

Risto had turned back to the laptop, but he kept drawing blanks. "His sister, eh."

"Cousin, what I see there—it's only an experiment."

Risto zoomed in on his star client, stilted and not all there. "She did tell me she wanted to try performance."

"Yes, and like I say, Mepris believes she's already into performance. The nun act, he calls it, and he doesn't buy it."

Inside the penthouse, the shadows suggested the maw of a catacomb, still more mystery. Eftah meantime began pulling together the lunchware.

"So," said Risto, "you received this in an email."

The news would be easier to take if the clansman wouldn't chuckle. Still, Eftah strove to reassure. He claimed that Giussi's mailing didn't appear to have "caused any great uproar, among his core audience." It'd been a bit over week now, explained the Black Lord, and there didn't look to be any "complications."

"A week now, cousin, just think back to when I dropped off your copy."

"You received it in an email from Giussi."

"Exactly, and I was one of, ah, a select few." Eftah chuckled.

Risto pointed out that the photos must've come first from the man who took them.

"Yes, and that lily-white oaf, I expect he was hoping this would happen."

"Hoping the pictures would..."

"He knew Giussi has the best mailing list."

Risto was out of his chair, he felt so absurdly betrayed. Down at Wind & Confusion, Fidel had sounded as if he were trusting the gallery owner with his most precious secret—but in fact he'd been pitching his photography all over the demimonde. Risto could just see how Giussi would've taken it: buttoning his aristocratic lips, careful not to smile.

Absurd. "So, viral marketing."

"Precisely. Dear boy, you do realize, success like yours, the Flying Refugee, soaring from hobo to emperor—you do realize we all want the same? You're the primary inspiration, when Giussi fires his latest act off into cyberspace."

Risto put some distance between them. "The American," he said. "My old boss? A stunt like this—*exactly* his kind of stunt."

"Oh my my, just his sort of thing, yes."

"And it's nothing but consenting adults. Nothing against the law."

"What would the law have to do with it? Or the bad guys either?" The clansman gave a napkin a cleansing flap. "My friends from the bar take an interest only when someone cares to pay."

Risto had made it to the rail. His wineglass warm, his legs heavy, he turned and found Eftah plucking at his wattles.

"In any case, cousin, I ask you: considering what I had to confess, I ask you, where do I find a priest?"

With his hand at his neck, the clansman made Risto think of the knives last night. The Black Lord hadn't been up against anything so bad as that, once he opened Giussi's download, but his options hadn't looked promising either. What could he have done, except give this a lick and a prayer?

"Dear boy, myself, I rather enjoy a whiff of scandal. But then there's you. You, your gallery, your young family."

"*Abba*, I get it. Reason for concern."

Yet by the same logic, the older man went on, he hadn't wanted to "unpack the entire mess right then and there." The very idea set him plucking again. "My hard-working brother, imagine, you've got a show coming up with this woman."

Risto wished he could get some coffee. He wished he didn't find it so easy to follow Eftah's reasoning. Yet he wasn't sure he'd have handled the set of photos any differently; he couldn't even say if he'd have confided in Paola.

A fresh breeze stirred from inside the penthouse. No sooner had Risto realized someone must've opened a door than, out of the dark, emerged Mepris.

✳

The Hut and his cronies wouldn't have cared for the sequel. Eftah and Mepris kept their hands to themselves. When their glances met, there was a glitter as if the name-calling were about to start up again, but then the Moroccan spotted the machine on the table. He touched a key. Once the colors began to play over his delicate fingers, he allowed himself a smile.

"Our Father Eftah." He raised his eyes to Risto. "He's not good in all things, but every once in a while, why look—he's good in *small* things."

The clansman gave a mock grumble, but Mepris wasn't quite ready to retract his claws. Levelly the boyfriend announced that he was on the verge of finding another place. "This *amour fou*, it's got me at wit's end." Stalking back into the kitchen, he had more complaints, not quite audible over the kiss of the refrigerator door, echoing beneath the Borbon ceilings. The boy returned with a beer, a specialty brew he must've picked up in one of the city's Irish pubs. Neapolitan Eire had been the rage, before the quake. The bottle suggested a sculptor's mallet.

"My my my," murmured Eftah. "Lunch."

Mepris looked to Risto. "I expect that scene in the bar was the last thing you needed. Two more brothers beating up on each other."

"Oh listen, the morning I've had. I've had...something on my conscience."

"Your conscience?" The Moroccan's accent gave the word a melody. "And you came to see the Black Lord?"

Both these two stood taller than Risto, and he needed to shade his eyes.

"*Mon vieux*, you know better than most. Up here, it's hardly the City of God."

"Oh, and our angel Mepris, he's got the Google map for the City of God."

"Well, I can tell you what *won't* get you there. A half-measure like handing the poor man a file he can't even open!"

"Look," Risto said, "I'm not sure I'd have handled it differently."

"Oh, listen to this child, 'a half-measure.' But half-measures, compromises—how else do we get to live the way we like? Have you noticed I'm in work clothes?"

"What I notice is, the Black Lord refuses to see his own shadow. He stands there like Father Eftah."

Risto kneaded under his eyebrows. "Myself, when I see those pictures, all I can think is, we've got to talk. Giussi and me, Tuttavia and me."

Mepris got a long pull of beer, his hand a dandelion against the oak-dark bottle. Then: "Ab-ba Ef-tah. Dada, more like."

Eftah put his face so close to the boyfriend's, you'd think he was trying to call attention to the different shapes of their noses.

"Da-da, are you trying to threaten me?"

"My cherub, can we do without the halo, for a minute? Can we take a minute for someone other than you? For our visitor, for instance, the only family I've got?"

So Risto's clansman was the one to pass along his news: a contact on the police. Eftah made a dance of it, bowing toward Risto, wheeling towards Mepris. Eventually the Moroccan hoisted his bottle, his stare deep with appreciation.

"My compliments, Aristofano. Once more you astound us all."

Risto dumped the last of his sunburnt drink into one of the pots for the grapevines. "Look, anything I might do, any operation, eh. The detective said *perhaps*."

"Of course he did," replied Mepris. "What'd you expect, that he would invite you down to rummage through the evidence?"

Risto took a moment with the empty wineglass, the refractions across its belly. A labyrinth of rainbow, lovely but leading nowhere.

The Moroccan kept up the kind words: Last night, the work you had us doing...

Eftah cut in. "Baby, honestly, don't you hear what my clansman's saying?" He jabbed the lunch plates at his boyfriend. "He's got something on his conscience. What he did today, playing ball with the white man, it's a *compromise*."

Mepris laughed wetly. "Our Dada."

"Baby, you know, now that you mention it? Dada I mean? You know, those people, I don't believe any of them ever finished a novel either."

"Oh please. A drama that never ends, big boy, that's you, that's all you."

Whatever Risto had come here for, it wasn't bickering. Turning to Eftah, he took the plates. He made for the kitchen, the cool, reminding the others that he had Paola waiting. Between last night and this afternoon, he'd put a strain on her goodwill.

"A strain, cousin, honestly?" The Black Lord followed him in, his smile nothing you'd care to think about. "Is something up with Paola?"

"Eftah." Risto bent over the dishwasher, racking the lunchware. "Haven't you done enough messing around in my business? That flash drive, *per carità*! I might as well have taken it down to Via Caracciolo and thrown it off the rocks."

The boyfriend showed less malice. "Actually, I believe the device is waterproof."

Airlessly Risto laughed, still full of questions, doubtful that his wife could do him much good. The person he most needed to sit down with was Tuttavia.

The Materdei church bell tolled, its reverberations slow in the heat. Two, three.

※

Maybe it was the move indoors, maybe the change of subject, but
Mepris and Eftah came to a détente. Risto's marriage, it sounded like,
had brought them together. Eftah brought up the friendship between
Paola and the photographer. "Those two are so close, you know, maybe
you should leave it to them." The boyfriend agreed: "Shenanigans like
these, everyone sorts them out their own way."

Now who would ever go to these two for couples counseling?
Around Risto the kitchen breathed, the walls tufa, the ready-to-hand
building material you found in the older places. A moment ago he'd
enjoyed the drop in temperature, but now it set him shivering, and
when he glanced back toward the arbor, the outdoors was too bright.
Against the sky, his hosts resembled two blobs of oatmeal flung on a
blue wall. Two blobs running together: Mepris and Eftah may have
kissed. In a relationship like theirs, what was the point if you didn't get
to make up?

The other way, in the front room, the sunlight left a speckle across
the photos along the far wall. But as Risto eased into the dimness,
hands half extended, two of those far photos revealed a different sort
of glinting. They weren't reflection; they didn't blur. Within those two
frames, the glow was confined to neat crescents.

On shelves alongside the front door, Eftah kept the equivalent of a
family gallery. Rectangles and squares, ordinary portrait setups, by this
hour they ought to be beyond the sun's reach. Besides, his relative could
pay for glare-proof glass. Still, you couldn't miss them: two swipes of
glitter. You'd think the source lay within, somehow. Yet while Eftah had
brought his wiring into the twenty-first century, he'd hardly installed
lasers. If the trick wasn't in the photos and frames, then it had to be in
the observer, founder and part owner of Gallery Wind & Confusion.
A pair of sickle-shaped illuminations, the widest part of the blade up
top, the ends poking down.

Halos, could be, circling or half-circling his big clansman's head.

Both pics were recent: one a snapshot with Mepris, color, and the
other a studio portrait in black and white. The Black Lord liked to keep
those up to date. In each, the wide Hutu head wore a tiara. Or a sickle,
ready to chop—but whatever you called it, the thing didn't show up

in the older photos. A few of these stood along the shelves, including
a shot that had somehow made the sea crossing, the teenage Eftah arm
in arm with a priest. Like Risto and Ti'aba, he'd come through the
mission schools. But that picture was free of ghostwriting, like the one
with Eftah's first Italian construction crew and the one from his days
fixing up this palazzo. A photograph steals the soul, according to the
old bush magic, the griots and shamans, but to judge from these, after
a few years the spirit flew free again. Only two shots revealed the same
wrinkles as Eftah wore this afternoon, and those were the ones with the
angel's headgear.

Risto bent so close to the glass he could see his own pale reflection.
That had nothing to do with the Special Effects, either, the lumines-
cence like a moon behind a scrim of weather. Face it: this coiled fillip
was part of the photograph. It revealed the buckle of the heavy paper,
the grain of the focus.

He was startled by Eftah, all at once by his side, one hand extended
toward the pictures. "My brother, that man you see there, you don't
think of him as the devil?"

Risto managed a smile. A better possibility occurred to him, a sap
that rose up his spine. "No, my brother. No, just the opposite." He ran
his index finger in an arc, back and forth over the larger halo. "Look,
Eftah. Look, he's an angel."

The clansman switched on the overheads. He bent towards the
photos, guppy-mouth. "An angel...."

The sap dried away. Risto blinked against the light, picking up his
big relation's odor, wine and iron.

"Actually," said Mepris, "we don't see a lot of angels around here."

Outside the picture frames, Eftah wore workaday gold. The stud
in his ear was a tough guy's, ready to bust some balls, maybe rolling
with Camorra the Hut, maybe riding with the city police. Some of the
cops around here were practically colleagues, they'd served the Black
Lord with so many of those letters, Get Out in Three Days. Eftah liked
to joke that he'd mashed the papers into paste; it bonded beautifully
with the tufa. Risto could use some snark like that. He could use a
wake-up slap. Weren't his children learning the laws of the empirical

North? Hadn't the kids' African grandparents, despite their irrational belief in the promise of Mogadishu, rejected any other hoodoo? Yet the European Risto stood here seeing things. He stood faced with yellow lights—warning lights. Twice now they'd been made manifest, each time for him alone. On the second go-round, then, he'd better start to think like a detective. Before the weekend, the mystic goldflake had shown up on a man about to get his throat cut. Come Monday, why should the magic change its M.O.? Why, when the *abba* beside him had so many monsters in his life, black as well as white?

FOUR

How did Paola keep the heat out of the house? The marble floors, once Risto was out of his sandals, cooled even the stale sweat of his jungle top. And how did his wife know he couldn't handle much wine? Paola trickled it into one of the fingerling glasses they used for limoncello, and when she handed this to Risto she held on for an extra moment, as if to help him strike a balance between the warmth of her touch and the chill of the drink. That touch was half her conversation, too, and much of the rest was in her eyes, haloes of another kind, iris-blue shadows over moss-brown depths. She'd grown used to *Risto Silenzio*, after the quake left their summer littered with debris. The cash flow had slowed all over Naples, the Expo kept demanding another pound of flesh, and there'd been meetings with the Immigrant Council.

Up in Materdei, Eftah had called a cab, sparing Risto the indignity of proving he could pay. The whole way down he'd sat wordless. He might've been a conjure-puppet out of *kuragura*, the kind of "barbarism" that Papà had always insisted had no place in their family. And by what abracadabra did Paola convey him into the bedroom? How did she conjure his aches to thin air, his aches and grubbiness and even his worst fears?

Sex with a familiar white woman. The slap of her belly recalled her pregnancies, the bleats recalled the pleasures of splashing in a bath or wading pool with Tonino or Rosa, and yet this was something else entirely, these long minutes naked with his wife. Her face lost its corners, her smoker's bags smoothed away by the same touch of the witch, the same as took hold of Risto, reaching all the impossible way down so that his cock bulled up and clenched. Soon followed the elongated moist perversion of entering, a dialogue punctuated with body-long twitches. With that, when first Aristofano closed his eyes, he found himself in a stranger place: the steamy changing room at the Dominican school, and before him rose a pillar of filthy mist, streaked with red spray. A nasty apparition, but it only lasted the space of a shudder. Even as the husband broke into a groan, wildly different figures crowded his mind's eye, women and whatever, from fantasies he'd toyed with a thousand times to flares out of the slideshow he'd just seen on Eftah's rooftop, even off-limits Tuttavia. All these glimpses took him to fresh shudders, yet throughout, first thrust to last spasm, the core alchemical element remained Paola Paolissima. Somehow she'd drawn Risto's earlier unhappiness to his surface and cleansed it of toxins. The two of them became something else entirely, whinnying, bucking, a creature out of superstitions.

They didn't bother with a condom. They had nothing to worry about, thanks to her after-the-fact medicines, the black-and-teals kept out of the children's reach. The prescription was another of her father's arrangements. Also it came to Risto that Paola might be enjoying some extra kick out of the magazine open on the bedroom floor. This issue included a long section of lovers' confessions; in summer the press ran a lot of titillation. Yes, when you stopped to think, when you fell out of each other's clutch and managed again to think, the whole storm of sensation melted away into something adult. An adult has to concede a place, in that storm, to Risto's hard road of a morning, and to his wife's morning, whatever news she might have for him.

※

They lay spooning while Risto told Paola about his abbreviated nightmare. The locker room, the smoke demon, the red grease.

"Your brother," she said.

"Perhaps."

"Perhaps? Risto-ri. The two of us, by this time, don't we know better?"

He began to knead his head, but she stopped him.

"Lover, well, perhaps. Perhaps, by this time, a wife ought to be more sensitive? You know, when you arrived, I wasn't sure we ought to head for the bedroom."

Was this his beneficent witch? Uncertain of her spells?

"But what could be better than the body's own medicine?"

Sweet as their nestling felt, Risto discovered himself leaking tears. He had to get a hand over his eyes, to grope in the dark until he came up with a confession. Twice in one morning, he told her, he'd revisited Ti'aba's murder.

"And the second time, *per carità*, I just blurted it out—to a white man."

He swallowed and, like that, his tears had gone dry. Just like that, what on earth? He heard his wife starting to apologize, scolding herself for taking him into the bedroom, and all of a sudden he was the one making assurances. Paola, no way this does damage. Never, no way, the simple act of love, mutual affection...

"Now, no need to lecture, *amore*."

"Paola Paolissima, sometimes I think this is what I have instead of artwork."

She went up on an elbow, burying that hand in her wiry hair.

"This, love and marriage. It's my paint and canvas."

"Risto-ri. That's a lovely thought, truly, but a little unnerving. I mean, the two of us in bed—that's hardly something I want to see in a gallery."

Crying had passed like a blur, the single stroke of a brush. "Eh, a business model like that...I'm all done with that, after Alexandria."

Raising a hand, he stilled her comeback. He'd only meant that he was grateful; this had been good for him. "Lately," Risto went on, "I've had death on the brain. These last seven or eight weeks, it's all been hard, but lately—it's been worse."

She walked her fingertips alongside his ear.

"There's something I should tell you."

Still he was hesitating, clearing his throat. First he'd been fucking, then he'd been crying, then soothing and strong, and next thing you know, he couldn't trust his mouth. It took a swab of his scalp before Risto got it into words: the haloes.

"See, at first I thought it had to do with Tuttavia." When he shook his head, even this felt compromised, distorted by the pillow. He propped himself up, getting into the second set of golden headgear: the two up in Materdei.

"Well then, it's you, *amore*." After his own voice, Paola's sounded serene. "What you're seeing is in you."

"Paola, you don't think it's frightening? The first halo, I saw it on La Cia. On a stranger, really. Before this weekend, I barely knew the man's name." Then after the weekend, the gilding on the pictures of the *clandestino* had gone away, and now Risto had seen the same on Eftah.

"On Eftah," he repeated.

The wife was nodding, her hair tickling one of his nipples. Her next question went back to something he'd mentioned out in the living room. Today, Risto and Eftah had met at that Camorra bar? In the piazza? If so, Paola imagined, there must've been some nasty characters at the table.

"He's *not* my cousin," Risto said. "As for his friends, you know."

"Of course I know."

He had no call to bark like that, as if she were the man from Homicide.

"Risto-ri. Don't you think a white girl can imagine how our Eftah, at times, how he might look to you? Don't we all recognize the risks he's taking?"

No call to get aggravated, just because he knew where she was going.

"And what can we do except watch, while Eftah's out there, dancing at the edge of the abyss? Dancing with some very nasty characters? And while you're watching, if you're a man with death on the brain, well."

When at last Risto came up with a reply, *So it's on me, this is in me*, the words contained too little, even as he himself swelled up full. He swelled and broke, racked once more with tears. His wife adjusted to cradle him and offered tender talk. *Such a bloody thing, a terribilità...* Risto let her work, pulling him out of a snuffle and into a kiss, and this time he tasted the garlic. A calming jolt—was it from Eftah's lunch or hers? How many folks tossed some ingredient into a marriage's brew? The husband extricated himself, straightening against the headboard.

"Look," he said, "I know what you think. You think this is about Ti'aba."

"*Amore*, honestly, it does come to mind."

For a moment she changed her tune, bucking him up. Just look at all he'd accomplished! Going nonstop, too, just look! "And do I even need to mention the Immigrant Council?"

Each of her attaboys grew quieter, however. "But, Risto-ri," she said finally, "perhaps the time has come to talk with—"

"'To talk with someone.' Paola, please. Therapy, still more therapy after what the citizenship put me through? *Please.*"

He pointed out that Paola's own father had arranged for the psychiatrists.

"*Amore*, honestly, do you think I don't remember?" She'd sat up as well. "I remember down to the minute, forty-five minutes, every session. Most of them, well, I'd say your interview with the *Manifesto* was more therapeutic."

Risto's hands had dropped over his crotch, and Paola's arms were up across her breasts. She was only suggesting that a man in Risto's position "might try getting serious about the talking cure." He was only pointing out that he couldn't "go around haunted and guilty all the time."

With the "evaluators" for citizenship, he'd kept up his fairytale about Ti'aba, his white lie about the black machete. But so what? "Paola, it's like *The Shining*. A guy who's always dwelling on his murdered family, it's like he checked into the same hotel."

"Risto-ri." He'd fetched a smile, at least.

"I mean, I'm telling you, my wife, or I'm trying to. I'm seeing things."

"Well, are you just seeing them, or are you *believing* in them?"

"Believing, eh. I'm wondering."

"My husband wonders if he's being shown the Mark of Death? My husband and the father of my children. He wonders if the Fates have revealed their dangling thread?"

"*Okay.*" Careful; the English alone felt harsh. "Okay, this with La Cia, it's, it's stuck in my craw. But it's hardly my first nightmare in fifteen years. There's always the chance that I'll turn a corner in Naples and wind up back in Mogadishu."

"Well." Her arms relaxed. "Haven't I turned that corner with you? 'Dishu and Alexandria, Beirut too for that matter, by now I could draw you a map."

Risto gave a gesture, grateful he hoped. He acknowledged he'd thought about it, the talking cure. Still, it seemed to him he'd spent enough time in the Ghost Hotel. Regarding Ti'aba, he'd told his wife the same fib he'd told the therapists. But what did it matter? How often did the two of them get an afternoon alone?

❈

The husband had plenty else to talk about, even leaving out Naples Homicide. With another head massage, a smile he hoped was the right fit, he told Paola about the orgy. The simulated orgy, to be precise, and he didn't stint on details, both what he'd seen and what he hadn't, in Eftah's slideshow. As he talked he came to think this would help, cooling him, providing distance.

"In my position," he concluded, "I may not need to do anything."

Paola had laughed as she listened, her nipples playing peekaboo between louvered strips of sun. Still, her first substantial response was no-nonsense.

"The gallery's exposed, yes," Risto replied. "That thumbnail Eftah gave me, that stays encrypted."

"I should say so."

"And if I speak with anyone, it ought to be Giussi first."

"Well, who you talk to first, between those two partners in crime..."

"That's how it looks. Like each was egging the other on."

She indulged in more laughter and peekaboo, and Risto couldn't help grinning. He wouldn't have brought it up if he hadn't wanted to know what she thought, and Paola agreed with his clansman. The photos were "racy" at worst. "It's nothing so damaging as the hijinks Berlusconi had going on out at his villa." With a stroke to Risto's ear, his ear and the stubble alongside, she too spoke of "consenting adults." Consenting *Neapolitans*, what's more. Everyone involved was protected within the local pecking order. The performance artist might be a new-comer up North, but he was protected by the formidable old name Castelsabbia; meanwhile that man, with the formidable name but the flimsy talent, might risk a few sneers among the gallery-goers—"but then again, he's got Giussi there, the Pulcinello out of Ethiopia. With him in there, it's all a joke, and so Fidel's protected too. It might even look good for race relations."

When she got to Tuttavia, though, the wife lost her party spirit. Her hand dropped, her head dropped, and after a moment, speaking into his chest, she brought up his mentor, the American.

"The American, he'd turn this to his advantage, wouldn't he?"

Nothing like a whiff of scandal to put a gallery on the cutting edge, said Paola, her energy picking up once more. She pointed out that every non-essential venture in town, everyone in the arts—"you know," she said, "the toy department"—was looking for any help they could get, just now. Wasn't that the whole purpose of *Expo in Città*?

"A few of these photos on the right screens," she said, "and you've got, what did he call it? Your old boss? *Buzz*, that's it, you've got buzz."

"Buzz, eh. Next thing you know, you'll ask Ippolita to take her clothes off."

No call to bark, husband. This wasn't the first time she'd made that crack about the toy department. Risto turned sheepish, bringing up the wine at lunch. "The good island stuff."

She could snap as well. "*Amore*, you realize that if Ippolita ever cares to find out what it's like with a woman—there's some of us who'd be happy to oblige."

Between them, a labyrinth of crumpled sheets had opened. "The gallery's exposed," he repeated. "The next show is all Tuttavia."

"Well, Tuttavia…" Tentative again, she acknowledged that their Lithuanian friend had grown more difficult. Pricklier. "You noticed, yesterday, she wasn't invited."

Risto confined his questions to a shift in his grip.

"Still, honestly," she went on, "perversion as a performance—how could that reflect badly on her work? Isn't it straight to the heart of her work? Just think of the reviews: 'The artist goes naked, touring a world of shadows.'"

What mattered more, if you asked Paola, was that her husband's adopted country wasn't saddled with the kinds of politicians they had over in America. "Over there, the senators and the congressmen, aren't they always thumping on the Bible? Preaching out of Leviticus and wishing we'd all go back to living in tents? They'd probably take a torch to Wind & Confusion."

"Eh. I'd hate to think what they'd do if Caravaggio were still in town."

"Caravaggio? Wouldn't they call him a faggot with a knife? But all that, that's about reputation, what other people think." In Tuttavia's case, if there was a danger, it was in her. "With her, there are no 'other people,' there's only the intimate few."

At some point his wife had retaken his hand. "Risto, honestly, do you think you're the only one who knows a secret or two about her?"

He stitched up a smile.

"I suppose it's time I tell you. In the morning I'm off to Agropoli. After that, no sooner do I return than I'm playing the hostess, raising a toast to the woman."

Friday night, Paola would join them at the gallery. "Tell me?" he asked.

But she was a diva all of a sudden, louche and accustomed to having folks listen. Then what was he, a fanboy?

Louder: "Is this about the kids?" Rosa or Tonino, he said, would never catch a whisper of Tuttavia's act. "Porn, art, whatever, it's a fraud. The only way the kids'll find out is searching the web fifteen years from now. It'll be in a footnote somewhere."

His wife maintained her distance, a hand now at her throat.

"Rosa and Tonino?" he went on. "Those two face worse every time they move up a grade." He grabbed his cheek, getting a good fold of deep brown.

"In fact," said Paola, "they're a part of this, the children. Part of what I have to tell you. But Risto-ri, please, let me tell it in my own way."

A moment's more staring, and then a coming together: a kiss from a familiar white woman. The way Risto fell into it, his spine prickling, he might've been a teenager. He might've been about to burst into tears again. Insofar as he was thinking, his mind was still on the kids. Tonino had been an accident, a classic, a bucket of cold consequences dumped over a torrid interracial affair. Interracial and bisexual—in those days they'd each had a chip on their shoulder. They'd been only too happy to scandalize, to let folks know all the rules they'd broken. Paola got a real kick out of seeing the blood rise into the white faces at the University, when she introduced her boyfriend. She especially enjoyed his effect under her sister's grape arbor, and in their father's waiting room. She insisted the Somali receive the same attention as the most jewel-bedecked widow out of the Chiaia.

Risto, apprenticed to the American, found the man a mentor in this department as well. He'd never lacked for lady friends, Risto's boss, and back in New York he'd learned a lot about hookups freighted with politics. Already he'd urged the *assistente* to experiment with a gold earring and a West African wrap. The white folks liked that, just the right degree of menace, especially in a kid with such a busy vocabulary, and Risto could adapt the lesson to Paola. When she tried to shock him with revelations out of her past, he could take the cap off his own old wiring. He could shoot some high voltage himself. For he and this white girl, too, exposing their scary bits bore out how easily they let down their guard. Each admitted that they weren't used to lovemaking of such sustained enthusiasm. Here in the most densely populated city in Europe, they could go whole hog in the gallery closet. On top of that, though, they also had, what would you call it? Tranquility? Capaciousness? Every time, before seizing the moment, neither had to force the issue, and afterward neither needed to put the other in his or her place.

Had it made them careless? Letting down their guard, easing into something more adult, had that extended to the precautions each kept handy? *Settebello* sold their condoms all over the city, and Paola had her under-the-table prescriptions. Nevertheless, one evening she'd arrived with news. He'd moved on to his own gallery by then, the original space in the old centro. *Confuso & Vento* was three stories up, and at street level the shopkeepers were rattling down their grates, but Risto had picked up the sound of her approach, the special emphasis of her trot. She'd looked girlish, free of makeup. And the announcement that she was pregnant hadn't been Risto's biggest surprise.

"The kids," he found himself saying. "Such a surprise, at first—"

"*Amore*, yes, but haven't they turned out nicely? Both our children? When I look at those two, I think of the old saying: the color inside a melon."

"Paola. Are we even talking about Tuttavia anymore?"

"Tuttavia, of course—and I'm not the only one beating around the bush. I'm not the one who came home in a state, limp and bedraggled, talking about mystic visions. I have to ask myself if you can handle anything more demanding than a bedtime story."

She couldn't have looked friendlier, smiling in sweat-dappled nakedness.

"Then there was yesterday, closing the balcony door, staying out till all hours. Now you and I have our last chance to talk before the Expo, and Risto, we'll do it my way. Seems to me it's high time you heard about the color inside a melon,"

✳

Once there was a Neapolitan family with a pretty young daughter.

This girl had many suitors, and not just for the sweetness of her looks but also for the great-hearted nature of her kin, a family among the lights of the community. And with so many seeking the daughter's hand (almost a healing hand, she was such an angel) was it not bound to happen that, in the fullness of time, one man would emerge as champion? A man of respectable family himself, and with a dependable trade. But this same fine catch, well—he was quite dark. And with the swell of his lips, the knots in his hair, there were rumors of an African uncle...

Paola paused, dropping her head.

She'd been bringing it off, more than a little operatic. If he'd been kept dangling, he'd found the air up there enjoyable. Risto could recall nights when, having tucked the children into bed, he'd settled on the

floor outside their room, his head against the doorjamb, the better
to hear his wife doctor up some story from his past or hers. Now,
however, she'd fallen silent. She began to caress his nearest foot, as if
finger-painting the toes, adding highlights to the chocolate and cherry.
Eventually Paola wondered aloud whether her family had made it a
point to keep him from hearing this particular story.

He kept his foot where it was. "I can see what it's about."

Her father, she murmured, was the sort of man who would never
talk about such things. Babbo preferred to leave a disturbing subject
alone. Risto reached for her hair, sweeping it back. "Paolissima." Maybe
he'd wanted this sort of sharing; maybe he was weighing what he might
reveal. A moment outside the marriage's familiar: both a hesitation and
a seeking.

Paola went into her next gesture.

So, throughout the piazzas where the daughter's beauty was legend, there were as well legends of a less kindly nature, regarding this
otherwise splendid catch of a man. There were whispers of an African
uncle, of African grandparents. Only talk, this was, impossible to confirm—but the love between the two young people, that needed no
further witness or decree. To move the earth, it requires the hand of
God, and so too with this pretty girl and this dark boy: it was as if an
earthquake had marked them, stamped them the way in our own times
we designate currency or a passport.

In short order the girl and her beloved went into the church to
be wed, and they went off to the island for their honeymoon, and
they returned to the neighborhood expecting a child. Soon enough the
girl's parents were hosting another celebration for their daughter, more
specifically for their grandchild-to-be, an occasion for the bearing of
gifts. One guest brought a framed family portrait, doctored as if by
some miracle hand. Yet whatever the gift, from whichever soul around
the parish, these stalwarts repaid the largesse. They greeted their visitors
with a veritable groaning board, the viands delectably prepared and
arrayed, in particular some fresh honey melons out of the garden.

Most of the melons were at their succulent peak, to be sure. Most
split into halves that, as they rolled away from the knife, glistened like

snow. But a few turned out diseased, worm-eaten, and dark. There was no way to tell whether your melon was good or bad until you cut it open.

And so ubiquitous is the Evil One and his influence, some few of the guests proved likewise rotten. Some two or three proved shameless enough to take advantage of the family's hospitality, and of the young husband's restraint, there in the presence of his bride and her father. The dark *settebello* sat with folded hands while these ill-behaved few again bruited about the vicious old gossip.

Africans in the family, they whispered. Apes.

Finally one of these guests, full of wine—a wine, let us say, touched by the hand of Satan—put his swollen red face in the face of the girl's father and demanded to know just what he intended to do about this taint in his blood. At that, the host took up the heaviest knife in the household. A knife to cut muscle and bone at a single blow, it lent a terrible youth and strength to the arm of this grandfather-to-be, and as he whipped the mottled blade skyward, everyone fell back with a gasp. Yet when the man brought his weapon down, it was only to chop open another of the sweet, round fruits.

If the color inside a melon turns out white, the father declared, *then what's there to fight about?*

Afterward, Paola wouldn't listen to her husband's chiding.

"Oh, you, stubborn as a stump." She waggled a finger. "Do you mean to tell me you understand a Neapolitan proverb better than I do?"

Risto cocked his head and repeated, smiling, that his wife hadn't grasped what the old man in the fable was saying. She hadn't heard the threat.

"What if the melon had turned out dark?" he asked. "The melon, or the baby?"

"Oh, honestly, as if you were the only realist in Italy."

"But, just look at it, you've got the son sitting right there, steam coming out of his ears. Isn't the father saying, maybe they do have something to fight about?"

"Risto-ri, you know as well as I do, this is a story about what's *inside*. The gifts of the heart." By then she'd gotten some wine (all right, he'd take a glass), and her touch was wet with condensation. "The color of the skin, the bric-a-brac on the outside, that's not what this story's about."

She went on to say that "a real Neapolitan" would've had a much better argument against her interpretation. A real Neapolitan would know that the moral of the story also turned up in one of the city's songs.

Risto rolled his eyes. "Of course it's in a song. They're all in some song, all the old stories, and come to think of it, the old streets and piazzas too."

"*Amore*, honestly—isn't this your Brave New World?"

"It's a city that gets older but never gets anywhere. Everybody stays in the piazza. Everybody sits around the fire telling the old stories. And they say Africans are tribal."

Paola, delighted, insisted she was only talking about a certain melon in a certain ballad. The song wasn't famous, nothing like "'O Sole Mio." But anyone who'd grown up in Naples had heard it. "And in that version, you know, they're talking about an unhappy marriage."

His grin bent the other way. "A real Neapolitan, eh." If the alternative was a story of a bad marriage, he admitted, he preferred hers. "But, now."

Paola cradled her wine between her breasts, a fingernail ticking the glass.

⌗

Once there was a photographer of genuine talent but no particular home.

This artist was a woman still young, and herself pleasing to the eye, but those who noticed that noticed as well that this was an itinerant artisan, one who spent many a midnight awake and on the move. The woman's wandering had begun in a distant northern land, and she was pale as a ghost—a ghost with a necklace. That necklace was of course her camera, an accessory whose origin was itself a mystery, and without which this woman couldn't sustain her flickering simulacrum of a life. Only via that medium was this apparition restored to flesh and blood.

More's the miracle, our photographer found a merchant who possessed, himself, a kind of talent. Gifted with uncommon discernment for a thing well made, he could find these objects homes, the way a jeweler sets gems in gold. Better yet, he had a noble heart, so he could speak to this pretty nomad forthrightly and without foul intentions. Such was the benefactor who stood up for this pale young photographer, and for her shadow-forged product. He set her pictures round his shop and saw to it that the lordliest patrons out of the surrounding hills came down from their palaces to examine and purchase the work. On top of all that, this same stout fellow glimpsed the faulty connections surrounding this stranger's heart, and he promised the woman that, if she would only cease her wayfaring, here in his market city he would make such a name for her, fame itself would serve as her commodious and nourishing homeland.

The wanderer responded to his attentions with such a melting gaze, such halting attempts at his language, that it would seem she'd never encountered such disinterested mercies. So the wisp of a northern woman and the stolid shopkeeper of the south not only entered business together, but became friends as well. The man welcomed her at his hearth and his table, where she met his children, and also his wife.

"Paola, you know," he put in, "I always had some idea, the way it must've felt to you when she showed up."

"Oh, the man I married, he knows all my thorny spots."

"So many hours alone, with a woman like Tuttavia..."

"Not so many as she spent with me, Risto, in the end."

The merchant's wife, at first encounter with so gifted and comely a guest, suffered a spell of worry. An ineluctable worry, it would seem, and yet one that the wife eluded soon enough, as she came to understand her husband's affinity for this unearthly creature. The merchant himself had arrived from a faraway place, its ground furrowed with the graves of his loved ones; in his present country too he'd put in years as a ghost, never allowed a resting place. The wife remembered all this, as the photographer began to spend time in the company of herself and her husband—throughout which time, moreover, the merchant remained steadfast in his connubial obligations. Soon enough his spouse came to care for their mournful drop-by.

So precariously did this visitor cling to the ordinary, she seemed to prefer a photo's substance to that of actual skin and nerve. So other-worldly was her spirit, she made a natural companion for the children of the merchant and his wife, a lad and a girl. For wasn't the photographer, like the children, full of ringing assertions and yet unceasingly vulnerable? One moment wasn't she a cinch to see through, and the next, didn't she turn impenetrable?

"I was glad when you two became friendly," Risto said. "But this business, seeing her as a child, so sober a person, that never crossed my mind."

"That's why you need to hear this."

Just as the metropolis at large never saw this unmoored beauty without her camera, the children of the merchant never saw her with it. The fine-tooled wares came off her snow-white neck as soon as she entered the shopkeeper's house, and it remained no more than a paperweight, aluminum and plastic, until she was once more on her way. The mother did wonder, in time, how this otherwise insatiable maker of pictures should overlook her two little ones, as subjects. Much as the merchant's wife had lost her fear of this other woman, much as sympathy had replaced jealousy, the mother couldn't help but suffer a fresh perturbation at this seeming neglect. She knew full well that her children took a fetching photo, and what's more they had the briar curls and dirty gold skin you saw in many others captured by this wanderer and her flashing box. This boy and girl children might well be two more creatures of the night. But when the mother found a moment to query her most frequent, most artistic visitor, she received an answer stunning in its simplicity. Even the photographer's inelegant way with the language didn't lessen the blazing obviousness of what she had to say, so that the mother was left feeling as if she'd neglected to notice an earthquake.

"Tonino and Rosa, come on," Risto put in. "Our kids are too *happy* for Tuttavia."

"Exactly. Much too happy and heart-warming. Even mixed race, for someone like her, they just won't do."

"Come to think, a picture like that would be out of place around the gallery."

"You do call it Wind & Confusion, don't you, lover? Though I promise you, Risto, one day our children are going to make us millionaires."

"They're going be working for Benetton. For Diesel, one of those. Can't sell a pair of pants these days unless the model's mixed race."

"But as for Tuttavia, honestly, what was I thinking? She doesn't do fashion. Do you think Tuttavia would care if someone dangled a sack of Euros in her face?"

"A sack of Euros. Eh, Fidel, for his little project, that could've been the offer."

Paola allowed herself half a smile. "But what I asked the poor woman, after all she's been through—it was as if I'd asked her to sell her soul. A minute after I put the question, even as she was trying to explain, I realized. I'd been a perfect clod, me, the woman she must've thought of as her best friend in Italy."

Risto dropped his hands back over his genitals.

In truth an onlooker might make the claim that, quite the reverse of this stranger capturing the natural cheer of the shopkeeper's children on film, the children's goodwill had imprinted itself on her own grainy psychological stock. Every time this brooding artist visited with the children, before long it was as if she'd taken on a new identity, that of a sweet-tempered young nanny. She played Cowboys and Indians or Barbie versus Gladiator, pulling funny faces and striking ragdoll poses, and during one visit succeeded even in getting the girl to finish her salad. So great was the improvement in the woman's mood, during these visits, that the children's mother allowed herself to believe her guest would, over time, come into a greater and more durable well-being. The merchant's wife indulged the notion that she and her family would ease whatever disturbances this artist kept pent up within, so that the vagabond would no longer live condemned to her present fallen condition, wraithlike and contentious, severe in her black garb, white skin, and shocking red lips.

Then came a day when the mother had to step out of the house.

Risto palmed the crown of his head. "Oh, *bella*."

"Oh, *bello*, but you never saw how she could be with them."

"Don't tell me that. It's not like I don't know my own children."

Paola hid her wineglass.

"It's not like I didn't join in with Tuttavia, some Sundays. I left you and Giussi and I joined Tonino, boys versus girls."

"Aristofano, please, did you hear me calling you a bad father?"

Husband, please. Isn't this a partner, sitting here as naked as you?

"But do you think, whenever Tuttavia came over, I could stand on duty every minute? You think that's all I do around here? These wild and colorful shirts my husband insists on wearing, just for instance, require extra attention in the laundry room."

Once there came a day when the children's mother trusted her young ones to this woman of mystery. Confidently housewife abandoned house, with a bag inside a bag, the plastic net she used for food inside her well-supplied purse. She too had proven susceptible to the magic of children, the boisterousness that made an adult settle down, and so the mother took her usual sweet time with her purchases, having a standard to maintain in regard to the meals in her fortunate home. Then too, her new friend and babysitter remained rather the undernourished street person even with all her success, and so the mother hoped that she could be induced to enjoy a plateful of pasta before she left. The merchant's wife went so far as to splurge on a tasty country wine, though alas, the liquor never made it to anyone's lips. For after the mother returned to the apartment with no thought for anything other than how to juggle her purchases, the bag and the bottle, and after a moment's puzzled distraction at the hip-hop selection, loudly thumping through the wireless speakers—after that she was so shocked by what she discovered in the kitchen that she let the cold and dewy Falanghina slip from her hands and smash against the marble floor.

Not that the mother could give a thought to the stink or the mess or even the broken glass at her feet, because at the other end of the entryway she saw her precious firstborn, her son, down on hands and knees and scrambling away whimpering into the bedroom he shared with his sister. The mother couldn't be sure, but before her boy scooted out of sight she may even have seen his dun cheek burning red, a rare thing in him, a color that rose only in reaction to a blow. And behind and above the child there loomed the pale and incomprehensible visitor from the north. This woman's looks had contorted, her eyes slits and teeth bared, such as the Italians call "a black face," and in one bony fist she gripped a broad kitchen knife.

Risto was groaning, *Paola oh God.*

"Wait, Risto, please." Both his hands were up on his head, but she took one in her own. "You *know* me. Your Paola Paolissima, yes, and there's Tonino too. You're wonderful with those kids, don't ever worry about that, even my father says so. And this story I'm telling you now, Tony hasn't told it to you yet, has he?"

He mustered a thoughtful look.

"Our Tonino, don't you see, he doesn't think there's anything to tell."

"Paola, when you say she held a knife…."

"Now, yes, now you're getting it." She dropped her hand. "How many ways are there, when you're holding a knife? You think three hundred ways?"

Then, changing rhythm: "Even you, my Risto-ri, a good man. A good father. Still, two or three times now I think I've seen it, you've waved a knife around the kids."

"Paola. When you saw it you dropped the wine."

She echoed him: *yes, dropped the wine.* The stuff lay pooled on the marble so long, she added, she had to scrub with ammonia. "I didn't really get much of a look at Rosa, either, other than to see that she'd gone the other way out through the kitchen. With Rosa, I saw what I needed to see—she wasn't hurt."

"Just like that. At a glance."

"Risto, aren't you the one who knows all about this, a *terribilità?*"

How could she bristle and yet show remorse? "Aren't you the man who saw his own brother's head split open? In a moment I saw enough."

"You knew Tonino and Rosa were safe."

Neither of the kids, she replied, were in the room when she'd moved against Tuttavia. "Anyone watching, they'd say I jumped her, I suppose."

So there was a bottle smashed on the floor, Mama and Tuttavia grappling against the wall—and no one had said a word to Risto? Not even Tonino, not even on one of their man-to-man drives? Father and son would figure-eight around the city heights, from Capodimonte to Parca della Remembranza, in Sunday drives that always got the boy talking. "How long ago was this?"

"Risto, an uproar like this, it's not as if I'd hide it from you for long..."

"Take it easy. I'm just thinking about Fidel's attempt to crack the porn market. His ridiculous threesome. Eftah got the email only about a week ago."

Her head at that angle gave her jowls.

"Paola, see the timing? I'm thinking we can put that craziness together with this. This, what you're describing. Sounds like it was just before the kids left for Agropoli."

She nodded whole-body, so the bed waggled beneath them both.

"Yes," she added, "yes that's it, just before the kids left." She sounded surer with every word. "While I was getting them ready for my sister's, yes. Can't you see how it all happened at the same time? All at the same time, all the same crazy acting out, first here in our home and then off somewhere with Fidel."

The husband, nodding himself, noticed his own jowls. Neither he nor Paola was so young that they should seize on the easiest answer. "Acting out..."

"Well, *tesoro*, would you rather go back to the melon? Speaking in parables? Maybe we should try and guess the color inside Tuttavia."

In another minute she was complaining again about how busy they were. "When have you and I had a moment alone? This kind of alone? You can imagine how worried I was that Tonino and Rosa would say something."

He had the next line ready, the one about the kids not getting hurt.

"They weren't hurt at all. When I checked on them, in their room, Tonino was playing Ape Man. He was bouncing from his bed to Rosa's, and you should've heard how that girl squealed, rolling back and forth beneath."

She put her wineglass through a slow twiddle. "It was a while before I checked in on them."

It was a while, in a wrestler's embrace with this sudden stranger, in a spreading puddle of wine. Paola couldn't see much besides Tuttavia's face. She'd trusted a friend and now she confronted a black face. "I had wits enough about me, at least, to check if I smelled liquor on her breath." Just the opposite, the woman's grimace had made the mother think of someone far below drinking age.

"You know how a child looks—how can I put this—when it's discovered an emotion? Have you ever noticed, those times when Rosa or Tonino sit back and think to themselves, 'Oh, this is sadness?' Or, 'oh, this is my awe at the size of the universe?'"

"I remember," Risto said slowly, "the one about being awed by the universe."

"Yes, that one, doesn't it always knock you for a loop? The same in Somalia, I imagine, as in Italy. That's the expression I saw on our Tuttavia."

"So what are you saying? It was over just like that? You smacked the knife away and you got her in your arms—"

"I got hold of her and she came back to herself. Whatever had her in its grip, whatever had turned her into a child, she shook it off. As soon as I got her in my arms."

He couldn't keep from scowling.

"The poor woman went slack, and I let go, and she staggered over to—"

"What 'poor woman'? She was about to hack up our son!"

"Aristofano, I'm sorry about this, I am so sorry."

"You left them alone with her, and when you came back you had to wrestle with her. Just to keep our children safe!"

As Paola shrank around her glass, he noticed the goose bumps along her aureoles. "Didn't I insist that you and I get a decent moment together?" And hadn't she taken care of it, getting rid of the knife first, then the woman? It'd been a week now, more, and she hadn't allowed Tuttavia back. "Yesterday at lunch, you must've wondered, but you didn't ask. And don't you think she's called? Three times now, she's called and poured her heart out, just dying to explain."

Of course Tuttavia had some rationale, some lash that'd stung her out of the past. Risto wanted to hear about it, but first: "You set her straight. She's not welcome."

"No she's not."

Reassured, he put extra sweetness into saying so. His wife, however, showed him little besides the quivering swell of her hair; she gave him little besides the repeated word *sorry*. He wondered why the two of them didn't put their clothes on. Put their clothes on, make coffee, and talk like sensible people. But Paola Paolissima had lost her magic. This wasn't the woman who'd taken the toolbox down to the children's school as many as five days a week earlier this summer, helping with the quake repairs. She pitched in over at the church too, tutoring the homeless, the people who'd lost I.D. But all of a sudden she might've been some spoiled *sciantosa*, cosseted and dithery.

Risto settled against the headboard. "Paola, I need to hear this. Tuttavia's story."

✖

Once there lived a small family of small means in a far northern land.

In their icy and unforgiving capital, the economic rigging of a vast Iron Curtain had been torn away not long ago, and in this family the mother and father were pretty poorly buttressed and fastened themselves. Worse to relate, they weren't the kind of people to brim with ideas for making a living, and so their most valuable resource seemed to them to be their comely young daughter. At the Conservatory for the Visual Arts, this girlchild had demonstrated the earmarks of a rare aptitude, *as if touched by an angel,* so her workshop leader put it, and he'd gone on to gild her record further, seeing to it that the Conservatory awarded her a handsome stipend as she came out of adolescence and into womanhood. And what a womanhood, with a face and proportions so pleasing—an attractiveness, truth be told, that warmed the girls' parents far more than her creative flame. To them, a life in the arts seemed certain to exclude the girl from any more comfortable future, from some nice snug place in the bureaucracy, and it made little difference when notices of congratulation started to arrive at their mailbox. Invitations started to arrive, on formidable school stationery, as their daughter kept picking up Conservatory honors, and yet for each special occasion, the father and mother made do with the same suit and gown, ever more threadbare.

But in time these school nights unveiled, for the parents, a glimmering corona of opportunity. A certain high-ranking professor, a pillar of the institution, could be counted on to hover by his gifted pupil. The looks this master directed toward the young woman, intense and unwavering, and the way he could never speak two words to her without a tap on her shoulder or arm: these were signs that anyone might find easy to interpret.

"Wait a minute," Risto put in. "Wait, just so we understand."

"But, *bello*, what's there to understand? What could be simpler? A predator of the old school, shall we say, teaching at the old school."

"No, that's not it. Predators, I think I know more about them than you do."

She'd regained strength enough to fix him with a glare.

"Paola, we need to set some ground rules. We need to say, look, if Mogadishu is no excuse for me, then Vilnius is no excuse for her."

"But do I sound like I'm making excuses? And aren't I the one who saw her crying? Crying and crying and pouring her heart out..." The wife faltered again. "Risto, if I were so adept at making excuses, by now I'd have made them for myself. I was the one who'd left the kids with her. I was the one, and I couldn't stop scolding myself, not even as I stood there holding on to her."

Risto gave her more kindnesses, but what was really on his mind was Tuttavia in tears. The most talented woman he knew, also possibly the whitest, had broken down bawling in his kitchen. He couldn't shake the picture, a variant pornography: she crumpled like one of those buildings wired to implode, collapsing in slo-mo...

A fairytale marriage: the student princess and the king of the faculty. Then too, gamine and silky as she might be, decrepit and wrinkly as he might be, nevertheless the apprentice felt a certain inclination toward her master, if nothing to match the lubricity of his toward her. Rather the girl longed to acquire some portion of his aesthetic and his culture, since she was never one for the gilded rags of passing fashion, and so an insidious truth of their commingling was that she could never consider herself an entire innocent. From the first the *artiste* understood the rewards of the alliance, and so the seed of her own culpability, taking root in this rank soil, extended its tuberous grip across the mismatched twosome's life together. The girl wondered even whether it was her own fault when her husband, a man of more than sixty Baltic winters, demonstrated that his constant handling of her in the halls of the Conservatory was anything but an indication of verve in the bedroom.

Whenever the two of them were naked together, the man's capacity for the traditional manifestations of romance dwindled to nothing, a heap of rumpled flesh, and not simply from age but more likely due to long misuse, since it turned out the professor's notion of lovemaking had gnarled to the point of requiring, from his paramour, a quantum of abject degradation. This gentleman needed to bind his partner, and to spank her loudly with a leather strap, and at his most desperate he would cut his young wife, just lightly, with an ornamental knife. This weapon looked to be older than he, one of the few items in the neighborhood of which that could be said, with a tooled ivory handle weathered to the color of ash, and it sat on display over the scholar's desk. To the rest of the admiring world it looked like a sentimental article, an antique whose scalloped edge was kept stropped out of fond- ness, as if his dear father or grandfather were about to take it up and carve the Christmas ham.

"Paola, no way." Was he growling? "She told you what the knife looked like, the serrated blade and all?"

"But why not? Didn't I tell you she keeps calling? And this awful business, like something out of the Brothers Grimm, she's never had anyone to tell."

"I can't believe she'd have the, the trust." He was still tussling with the scene in his mind's eye, his star white girl broken and humiliated.

"Oh now Risto, again I have to wonder, who are you to talk? Hon- estly. Are you saying there's a correct way to reveal some horrible thing out of the past?"

※

Once there was a pretty young artist, newly wed, who understood the value of the occasional experiment.

She understood, that is, how a timeless thrill might be wrung from a novel combination, and so she gamely accepted the role of student when it came to the art and science of sexual pleasure; she acquiesced to whatever stipulations the old professor laid down, and in the process she didn't lack for the occasional pang of ecstasy. She learned and at times enjoyed her learning, a subtlety of spirit that complicated further the young woman's gnawing remorse over her part in this *amor fou*—all the more foolish at each new adventure in lovemaking, because the trussing and slicing and such failed, with greater and greater regularity, to have the intended effect. Man and wife would work through a session with cords and whips and more, and throughout the whole process from start to finish (that is, her start and her finish), he struggled with a miserable and floppy excuse for libido. Then wasn't it inevitable that, before this sorry cohabitation had gone on very long, the mister began craving to humiliate his missus further? In the room he liked to call "the Chamber of Higher Education," the aged pedagogue began to hint at greater atrocities against her, while out in the world he perpetrated his most vicious excesses, indulging to the fullest his yearning to debase the girl.

"Risto, now, you've heard she never finished school?"

"She's told me some man used to promise her that one day she'd come to Italy."

"Risto, a man like that, he'll promise all sorts of things."

He matched his wife's grim smile, recalling his gazillionaire buyer and Zelusa.

"That day you found her," he said, "that time with the knife. She must've seen something, that day."

"Must've seen something and—crack—it put her back in a world of pain."

"The old bastard back in Vilnius..." Risto was startled at his growling. "She must've left the bastard, run off. But still."

"Still, she gets the wrong reminder and, crack." Paola went on to explain how, later that evening, "after Tuttavia had pulled herself together and gotten out," Tonino had fished a plastic sword from a corner of the kitchen. "The short sword, you know, the old Roman thing. Now I wonder, a blade like that, waved in her face..."

Now judge of the influence this celebrated academic held, there by the northern sea! He could reverse the prevailing Conservatory winds with little more than a well-placed omission, a word unspoken at a critical moment; he could rely for his dirty work on the resentfulness in the human soul, since after all his young wife was an object of envy, to his colleagues for one reason and to her peers for another. Without the least display of rancor or manipulation he had the girl reduced to a stay-at-home, lacking the studio space and artist's supplies she had imagined would be hers free of charge for the rest of her life. The princess bride remembered that sweet fancy and all her other selfish considerations in consenting to this shared debacle. Yet much as shame might nag her, it wasn't enough to prevent the girl from acting upon her frustration. After the fourteenth door had slammed shut in her face, or was it the fifteenth, the wife erupted in fierce protest, threatening her former professor that she would reveal to a no-doubt-fascinated world what passed for intercourse between them. At which he went for the knife and opened her head to the bone.

"No," said Risto.

"Oh yes. And this is the woman we know, full of vinegar, a woman no one would dream of pushing around. From where we sit, it doesn't seem possible, does it?"

If you asked Risto, roughly three-quarters of what he'd seen today didn't seem possible. "The things people can do," he said. "You'd think every one of us was a walking, talking *trompe l'œil.*"

Paola, shifting, left a ghost image of her hip in the sheet. "Now who's sounding like a fairy tale?"

She seemed proud of him, a little; he might've been proud of himself.

"She showed me the scar, you know, Risto. From when she, what's that expression, when she 'knew the moment of her death'? It's under the hair."

The gallery owner had never gotten a look under his client's hair, and besides, she kept it subterranean black. Then there was how he'd

seen her today, in second-rate triple-X. The Tuttavia on Eftah's screen
didn't seem possible either.

"Paola," he said, "about the photos today. Fidel's awful photos." He
was frowning at the near wall; at this hour, the blinds gave the room
a tiger skin. "Look, it was Giussi who sent the email. He picked and
chose who got it. A select circle of friends—that's how Eftah puts it.
But it was Giussi, not Castelsabbia."

Risto shared a brief version of his visit from the goony bird. "I
mean, that man's trying to sell the stuff. He wouldn't be letting people
have a look for free." Besides, even if the *Signore* had wanted to share
his hackneyed notion of the cutting edge, he'd never send it to Risto's
clansman. "Fidel doesn't even know the email."

He knuckled his eye sockets, repeating: "Giussi."

"Now isn't that interesting?" She straightened up, kicking away a
sheet. "I mean, *amore*, weren't we just talking about betrayal? And here
Tuttavia's best friend in Naples is doing her as dirty as her old creep of
husband up north."

"Giussi—he's a performer. He's letting people know about a performance."

"People like Eftah?"

The Black Lord of No-Account Real Estate, Paola pointed out, was
little use to the Ethiopian's career. Come to think, Eftah couldn't do
much for Fidel's ambitions either, especially not when his artistic debut
was a hetero fantasy.

"A set of photos like that," she said, "coming from Giussi, it could
only be a joke. A dirty joke, boy stuff, you know?"

And, the wife went on, anyone who'd seen Giussi onstage knew
what color those boys had to be. In performance, he was always about
race, pigment and its discontents...

He cut in: "You're saying the butt of the joke is Tuttavia?"

"But, lover, isn't she?"

Risto mentioned the Ukrainian girl, but even as he did he saw her
role shrinking. Zelusa didn't have nearly as much at stake as the shining
star of Wind & Confusion. Paola finished the thought for him, unsmiling: this threesome pandered, in particular, to black male fantasy.

"Doesn't it, Risto? It's gangster rap. It's got everything but a Mercedes Benz."

"But he calls Tuttavia 'The Missus'. His wife."

"Yes, they're close, aren't they? And doesn't he know she can't stand Eftah? Doesn't he realize your clansman is the *last* person she'd want to see this?"

By now the shadows were no protection against Paola's logic. She would bet the family's parish-school tuition that everyone Giussi had sent the slideshow shared the performer's brown exterior.

""I wouldn't call it meanness plain and simple." The wife sounded regretful. "More a sort of retribution. Tuttavia, poor thing, she's just the vehicle."

Risto thought he sounded roughly fifteen, reiterating that he'd speak with both his friends in the slideshow.

"*Amore*, frankly, I doubt Giussi would listen to anyone else."

He sounded fifteen and naïve, the last guy who ought to play detective. Still, he brought up the reception at the end of the week. More than likely, the crowd at the gallery would include a few folks on Giussi's mailing list. "Tuttavia wants to go on stage, eh. She'll get her chance."

"She tells me—she told me—she puts on a front at every reception."

He nodded and found her eyes. "After all, it's not as if she killed anybody."

Paola got her arms up across her breasts again.

"What else did she tell you, Paola? After she'd brandished a knife at our kids?"

"Oh, 'brandished,' now you're exaggerating."

"Paola, maybe I'm the one who's been betrayed. I sponsored that woman for citizenship."

※

The gallery owner had looked over Tuttavia's paperwork. He might be the only man in Italy who knew her real age or actual name. A struggle in Cyrillic lettering, the name turned out to be Lucy—the saint of eyesight, of vision generally, and you'd think that would make good fit for talent like hers. But Tuttavia wanted no part of Lucy's martyrdom. *Took out her eyes, remember? When the one she should've cut was the nobleman, the guy with a mad crush.* Nowhere in the file she'd submitted for citizenship, however, had there been any record of violence. Then again, the photographer went before the court with no certificate of marriage either. On paper, she claimed no family besides her distant parents. Even now, Paola had to wonder aloud about the gaps in Tuttavia's paper trail. She'd been surprised at how smoothly the hearings had gone.

"When I think of that *magistrato*! Honestly! From the first moment he saw who she'd brought as a sponsor, Risto, he wouldn't even look you in the eye."

"Your father, Paola. He took an interest."

He'd sat down with the judge, Risto's in-law. The two old white men hadn't spent much time together, an aperitivo at a café in the Galleria, yet at the mention of the meeting, Paola was the one studying the walls.

The husband tried reminding her that she'd been in the middle of a story. The northern princess and her wicked keeper, remember? He tried for some mix of the loving partner and the man who knew bullshit when he heard it. Tuttavia's wretched early love life sounded about right, it might even help explain her recent turn as a porn star, but if at the end of the tale she was supposed to kill the old prof, that he could never believe. "Look, to begin with, the man had status, Grand Master of Lithuanian Arts or something. When a person like that falls victim to foul play, the police have to do their job."

Paola inclined her head. "I do love our Tuttavia."

"And here in our house, that day, you owed her this, a chance to explain."

"Well, what was the alternative, that I chase her out and scream bloody murder from the balcony?"

"The kids were safe, you'd made sure."

"Yes, I'd made sure, and after that I owed her the chance to explain. Risto, don't I know what it's like to have the old man over me, pulling strings?"

Yes: as she'd heard Tuttavia out, Paola had thought of her father. "It was intimate, an intimate moment, you understand?"

Risto had to wonder at the question, considering they sat in bed together, neither wearing a stitch of clothing. But he knew Paola, and her pillow talk usually came around to Oedipus. Her ill will over her father had turned up on their first date, and somehow it'd spurred his nascent affection. The two of them had made an appointment for coffee at the Café Mexico, then moved on to the art books under Port'Alba, and then to a Margherita with mushrooms deeper in the *centro*. By the time the pie arrived Risto had heard about it, the turmoil in his splendid night's company. Her father fronted for the Camorra. Between books and pizza, young Paola had broached the subject surf-like: first blurting out the facts coldly, as if to flatten any hint that she hadn't come to terms with Pop's dirty work, and then letting her sentences drain away unfinished, revealing the sea's litter.

This afternoon Paola turned over a familiar piece of detritus. She wished that Pop had simply told everyone the truth from the first. "If he'd simply let my sister and I know, as soon as we were old enough—that's where it comes from. The offices, Agropoli, it all depends on a percentage for the *malavita*."

Her family never had that kind of money. "We only had the name: nice old name, nice old connections all over the parish." This of course was exactly what the System needed. Paola's father gave them a signature above suspicion and a doctor whose outpatient business took him all over town.

"Some rough parts of the city," Risto agreed. "Secondigliano."

She hid behind her hair.

"Look," Risto said, "wherever he goes, he's still a doctor. In Secondigliano too, he's taking care of some decent folks."

"But can you imagine how it felt, growing up, to watch my father turn from a hero to a shit? To realize how everyone's looking at you? When I at least learned the truth, you know, it wasn't from him."

He agreed it must've been hard.

"Even that least show of integrity, just telling us *the truth*, even that..."

Risto pointed out she'd made her own way. "Do you want to get into that, Paola? What you did, setting yourself apart?"

Her glance was a flick of the blinds, amid the room's web of shadow. He left it at that. Whatever magic the two of them had was fragile.

As for Papà, the wife went on, these days he had less to say than ever. He'd even given up on the shaggy-dog stories for Tonino and Rosa with The Adventures of Grandpa Doc. "I guess he got uncomfortable with some of the questions the kids were asking. 'But Grandpa, why didn't that woman just come downtown? Why did that man need a doctor to deliver a package?'"

To Risto, the old man seemed to be showing a touch of the African, close about secrets. The gallery owner had done the same, laying a sturdy board over the one rotting patch in the floor of his success. Outside of Paola and Eftah, no one in the city knew how the in-law had helped with the move to the Chiaia, the silent partners he'd lined up for the shop's mortgage: "associates."

Now Risto mentioned the father's missionary year, down in the southern Sahara. "Down in the Sahel, Paola. They said they'd never had anyone of his caliber."

"And you may be sure that, the entire time he was away, there was a mule with the key code for his pharmacy cabinet."

The father never provided cocaine or X—the mob had people for that—but rather prescription goods. Morphine and penicillin always came in handy, plus for the women ortho tri-cyclen and pills for the morning after. Amphetamine too, since the Camorra construction crews worked fifteen-hour shifts. Risto once witnessed a pickup at the office himself, when he'd been waiting to get a wrenched thumb looked at. He was family, he was hurting, yet he'd sat waiting while the receptionist ushered in a woman who'd just come in. She'd worn a lot of makeup even for an Italian and toted a purse that looked as if it might break her back. One of those oat-buckets you saw in the pages of *Donna*.

"You tell me Papà's helped some people," Paola said. "But what about the lives he's helped to ruin? The junkies out in Secondigliano?"

He figured they ought to get back to Tuttavia. "She was what you wanted to talk about, right? Why you wanted this time today." Now that Risto thought about it, it seemed best that Paola had waited a while to share the story. "These last few days have been hard enough as it is."

"Especially with my husband either buried in his laptop or out till all hours."

"Paola Paolissima. I'm grateful, I'm saying. You worked it out so we could talk like adults. That'll carry over to when I sit down with Tuttavia."

"Oh Risto, honestly, do you think that's worth it?"

He fingered his scalp.

"Prying open that whole can of worms again, do you think that's best—when the woman's got no better friend than Giussi or I? You want to sit down and tell her we both betrayed her?"

They'd neglected to close the bedroom door. Beyond it Risto spied, of all things, a halo. This late in the day, the sun reached all the way from the balcony.

"Hearing that, God knows what she'd come out with, what wild accusations."

"Paola, she's got to grow up sometime. Got to get over the old hurts."

"Grow up? Do they, people, really grow up and change? Didn't you just say we're all stuck forever in the same old streets and piazzas?"

He risked a frown. "I believe I was talking about the old songs."

Then there was her frown, cockeyed.

"The old songs, there are some I'd be glad to have around forever. *Stay on the scene, like a sex machine...*"

He'd wanted to avoid a quarrel, but he hadn't expected a laugh. He'd never have thought Paola would let go the way she did, laughing hard enough to set the bed creaking. But then, that was their magic, rare as a song that got play in both Mogadishu and Naples. Rare as his ragged-ass journey to this naked moment. Risto didn't say anything more about meeting Tuttavia, he let it drop, but he had a good idea how to handle the photographer. The two of them shared a grief his wife could never know; they'd both had the sore spots out of their upbringing pummeled into numbness by life as a refugee. Tuttavia would've traveled with rough company, worse perhaps than his own, as a young woman who cleaned up nicely. She'd completed her journey without catching a "vaginal infect" or testing positive, by itself no small feat, and on top of that she'd brought off the Miracle of the Nikon. Along the access roads of a shadow Europe, the scummed tatters of the global marketplace, she'd safely shepherded the equivalent of Paola's dubious melon. As for the color inside, her first set of shots included a number that wound up on the walls of Wind & Confusion. Now her gallery owner knew how to handle her, formerly a scavenger going hand to mouth through ruined cities, now out of the blue arrived in paradise, a city of the arts in a land where it never snowed.

FIVE

THERE WAS A MOMENT TUESDAY afternoon, Tuesday late, back at the precinct house for the second meeting of the day with his man in Homicide, when it appeared that Risto was about to get slammed against a wall and frisked. He and Eftah both. Granted, they'd dressed down, dressed goofy, for tonight's operation. Both clansmen were needed for the trap that Detective Della Figurazione had set that morning, a bit of deceit that would work best if the Africans came on like Laurel'n'Hardy. Of course, in Risto and Eftah's case, no one could play the thin guy—they were more Hardy'n'Costello—but their "operation" could only be a comedy, a blackout sketch about refugee bisexuals throwing good money at bad I.D. The two arrived at the precinct house in low-rent Technicolor: a pair of squat bombs covered with graffiti. The gallery owner wore a recycled hospital scrub stenciled with crazy Senegalese geometry, while the larger man had gotten a long way from yesterday's workday gear, swaddling himself in a wraparound with a Rasta design. Across his back, in rust-green amid flapping banners of black and gold and coral, spread a six-fingered marijuana leaf.

In the reception area, the other civilians gave Risto and Eftah a wide berth. Meanwhile a couple of plainclothes came out of their cubicles, beyond the fortified glass. None of the police appeared to have taken a *riposo*. Each white face looked more frazzled than the last, and Risto only added to their aggravation by repeating himself: "Civilian Informants! Civilian Informants!"

For a moment, he and Eftah looked sure to end up spread-eagled, at gunpoint.

But the first plainclothes into the lobby turned out to be the same officer as had smoothed Risto's way that morning. Della Figurazione had anticipated the problem. Give the man credit, he apologized as soon as he had a chance. He and his two informants found a quiet space in a stairwell, the steel and sheetrock of city property. Compared to this morning, the precinct house was crammed, some sort of indoor five o'clock rush. But in the stairwell the officer found decent peace and quiet. He apologized, adding that since the *terremoto* tensions in the station had stretched near to snapping. Everyone was grateful for the extra funding from Madame Mayor, and for the support from Rome as well. Still, it wasn't enough, not when you're dealing with fifteen thousand new homeless. Many of those, continued Della Figurazione, came in the same dark shade as his two visitors, and even before the quake there'd been the threat of terrorism. The outlaw zones of Libya lay almost close enough for a Scud missile.

"*Signori*, I imagine I don't have to tell you. Wherever you've got the homeless, the desperate..."

Risto, already shaking his head, cut in. "Old story," he declared. "Old hurts and grievances. Tonight, the only way this can work is *tabula rasa.*"

"*Tabula rasa*," repeated the officer.

The words resonated in the stairwell, putting a burr on the detective's Sienese elocution. Della Figurazione might've impressed Risto, coming to the rescue, but one look at the man revealed his champagne taste. Just that watch! It showed two times at once, its dual diagonal faces in bank Gothic, one chocolate and one ebony. A Forzieri, perhaps? As for the cop's shirt, it was some higher order of bureaucrat's blue, a pinstripe with a delicate weave, crisply starched. The man's pants held their crease, and beneath their cuffs poked high-ticket loafers, the buckles a rain-wet gold. Plainclothes, eh.

But then, this was the guy who'd set the scheme in motion. The detective had laid it all out that morning, including a recommended dress code for his C.I. Should Risto return to the precinct, Della Figurazione had told him, he ought to dress "with some edge, ah. Color and edge." Besides, now that Risto's career in law enforcement was underway, surely fashion was the least of his concerns. Surely he'd tucked away the raw edges that'd emerged this morning, when he'd first found himself surrounded by white folks with badges and guns.

This badge in the stairwell, Risto had come to understand, wasn't some insignia of family privilege. Aristofano himself, some would say, had enjoyed far better luck. He'd gone from sleeping on cardboard to sleeping in La Chiaia, while his man in Homicide hadn't wound up particularly far from where he'd started. As for the accent, Della Figurazione must've done a semester or two up in Tuscany, the same as other local tyros. People understood the benefits of losing your Neapolitan slur. Still, you could see the city in him, the finicky hands, the fetching sneer. The filmmakers of *neorealismo*, if they'd still been trolling the streets for faces, would've pegged this guy as the delinquent with a conscience. They'd have been careful to keep him out of the sun, too. As soon as Della Figurazione put in some beach time next month, he'd darken up enough to run for Sheriff of Khartoum.

Now the detective kept things businesslike. The foot of the stairs was the War Room, and his two CIs were in uniform, and Risto too had been on task since his morning cappuccino on the balcony. He'd limited today's dealing with Tuttavia to a text message. Careful to keep today free, he'd suggested *Wed? Later?*

That delay hadn't been enough for his wife, though. "*Amore*," she'd said, "please, wait till I'm back in the city."

This entire week, Paola felt, they ought to tread carefully around the photographer. Risto didn't hide his exasperation. He didn't need any reminders of what his clients went through before a show, the witch's brew at the back of the brain. As for Tuttavia, she went into a kind of withdrawal, hiding out by taking to the streets. She too would troll for faces. Nevertheless, after the slideshow on Eftah's laptop—penny for your thoughts, white girl.

Breakfast on the terrazzo, however, was no place for a squabble. Risto sympathized about the pressure his wife was under, facing several nights alone with her sister. Each of Papa Doc's girls struggled with her own hoodoo. But the text from Homicide had come in early, though thank God after Paola had headed into the kitchen. Once he'd kissed her into a taxi, Risto didn't dawdle. Half an hour later he was in a meeting with a police detective.

For that visit, Della Figurazione had found a place to sit. The cubicle could've been an adjunct to the *Guardia di Finanza*, a slum of old phones and computer parts, and for a bad moment there it suggested the directionless clutter of the visitor's mind. *Per carit*à, Risto, what are you doing here? At least the detective had arranged a round of espresso; he'd had the local bar send a boy. A grown man, rather: the gofer in his smudged apron turned out to be the age of Risto's host, and this set him thinking. How had Della Figurazione put it, when he'd ordered the coffee? *An officer at my level can exercise a certain latitude?* Latitude, yes, you saw it in the GQ getup as well, and that's what Risto was counting on. He'd wanted a guy willing to risk a stretch.

The detective began to grill him about La Fenestrella as soon as the coffee boy was gone. The intensity spiked at one detail, something Risto hadn't given a second thought, namely Eftah's prior acquaintance with the dealer. The way Della Figurazione lit up at that, Risto's hackles would've raised if he hadn't kept them shaved. The officer actually slipped into dialect: " '*Na parola superchia*." Risto's Neapolitan still had some holes, but he knew the expression. It meant a password, powerful, one that could get a man in everywhere—which seemed a tad optimistic. Eftah might've stopped Papers from killing his younger clansman, Sunday night, but that was about the extent of the Black Lord's influence. Other than that, though, the detective's plan seemed solid. The precinct would set up the informant with a cell phone, the number innocuous yet linked to police computers (only a matter of signing the forms, said Della Figurazione), and then he'd go out and whisper the name "Papers" in all the oases of the *clandestini*.

Still, even if Risto mentioned his so-called cousin, if he claimed they both needed I.D., the dealer might not call his police-issue phone number. The spirit they hoped to summon was unpredictable; it had the jacket of a wasp and the head of a vampire. The detective acknowledged as much, saying that every operation was to some extent an "experiment." Nevertheless, there amid the clutter, Risto did as asked and checked if Eftah would be willing to take part. As if there were any doubt.

Then come lunchtime, when Papers took the bait, the clansman too got the news. Later still, past five o'clock, dressed for a pot party, he joined Risto at the station.

❋

Della Figurazione might call attention to his watch, pulling back a cuff to uncover both dials, but this was only to make sure that his two informants had the same time he did. As he sketched out the operation in the stairwell, he emphasized that Eftah and Risto would have "minimum exposure." Both Della Figurazione and the second officer (two pairs of walking fingers) would shadow the operation, circling toward the documents dealer (the mark in the air left by the detective's fist). The sting would never have gone forward if Papers hadn't asked to meet in a public place, indeed one of the most public in Naples. The dealer would be waiting at a park entrance, Capodimonte.

Della Figurazione himself would partner with a woman; couples often took in the sunset from up in Capodimonte. A former royal playground, the acreage now provided the city's most generous greenspace and the most fitting for a canoodle. Strollers went from one breathtaking panorama to another between the trees. The oaks were a special variety, the leaf complicated. The scent combined eucalyptus and cedar, camellia and myrtle. Up here, earthquake damage and construction rackets seemed as insignificant as a herd of goats on a hillside south of the Sahara. The palace on the grounds had been converted to a museum, where the must-see was Caravaggio's *Flagellation of Christ*. Another stray taking a pounding.

Out at the park's entrance, along with couples straight and gay, you found tourists down from their buses. The guide always held some sort of flag, up over a cluster of pasty faces, making Risto think of bundled lemons tied off with a tag. Far darker and freer to move were the vendors. Africans mostly, they sold off three-wheeled carts and out of duffel bags. A few simply extended bony arms, festooned with watches, rings, bracelets. Always some silver bracelets in that snake design, Olmec or whatever.

Papers too would be a vendor, hiding in plain sight. The park closed at sunset, and Risto was to show up an hour beforehand. As the day cooled, on top of everyone else you got the bikers, the joggers, the baby strollers. As the dealer put it, over the trick phone: *No one'll notice a couple of niggers passing papers.*

No one except the cops, sucker. Della Figurazione assured his CIs that they'd also have a backup on a mountain bike, and then finished up soberly: "It'll be good to get this oaf," he said. "A hooligan like this, we can use him."

There it was. Risto would never have used such language, hifalutin, but the idea was the same: the one that had set him running risks he'd never dreamed of. Today alone he'd worked up a racehorse sweat.

"And tonight, the operation remains entirely simple. You lure him in and we put him in cuffs. Ah, nothing for the storybooks."

Risto, fingering his crown, felt as if he'd never found a more delicious way to scratch an itch. During the morning meeting, the detective had even made encouraging noises about the evidence on La Cia. The way he put it, his CI brought an "intriguing perspective" to the murder. The upshot, by the afternoon visit, was that Risto felt like he could take care of everything. From Tuttavia to La Cia, everything, and as for the shop, he'd covered that with just one call. His *assistente* Ippolita, promised a sweetener in this month's salary, didn't ask him to explain.

Really, it was all coming together. It would be good to get this hooligan, a natural extension of yesterday's quieter efforts, peeling away the happy-face stickers plastered over Eftah's and Paola's deceit. Already it'd taught him a thing or two. Risto had known his share of off-the-books merchants, and the routes of their caravans, but he hadn't thought through the trade in contraband I.D. He hadn't considered the stakes.

His police contact was in Homicide, and yet he'd attached himself to tracking down some fake papers. Risto was glad for the connection, but he wondered if he'd stumbled into a movie, *The Brother from Bourne* or something. In a flick like that, the cop had always gone bad. He was after the loot! One big score! But what was that phrase the artists liked? *La vie est ailleurs*, life was elsewhere, yes. The *Bourne* life, you wouldn't find that here, where dealing in Earthquake I.D. had far more serious complications. If Papers had been selling counterfeit jewelry, or stolen antiquities, a man like Della Figurazione might possibly skim off a percentage. A handful of Euro lifted off a bad guy: that might count as "latitude." But with documents of identification, you got a scary spike in the risk. Risto, that morning, had had his eyes opened by a single question out of his new colleague:

"You realize that ISIS, Boko Haram, villains of that ilk, they all need I.D.?"

Risto sat back, eyes opened. "But, Naples..."

"Naples is the premier marketplace, according to our sources. Remember that the refugees around here, the vast majority are too poor to consider such a purchase."

He hadn't thought this through.

"Whereas a jihadi, visiting from Beirut? He can pay a king's ransom."

So much could go wrong, Risto realized, only a bottom-feeder like Papers would risk using the I.D. to pave his way to El Dorado. The potential payoff meant even less to a career cop like Della Figurazione. For him, the benefit lay in raising his profile. Around Homicide, even with the mayor and the governor striking poses across the slaughtered *clandestino,* Friday night's business remained little more than a nuisance. It was another folder in another drawer. But a hard case like Papers, perhaps enabling some terrorist to plant a bomb downtown—to put him in cuffs would add glitter to the resume.

For the man from 'Dishu, meantime, it was all coming together. Even his deadline fit the detective's plan.

"If we don't grab this guy tonight," said Della Figurazione, "the operation's over. It's tonight or it's over. Because tomorrow, ah..."

He extended an open hand toward Risto. "Sooner or later, even an outlaw is bound to catch wind of Signore Owl Keyer."

During the morning meeting, alone with the detective, Risto's worst hesitation had come as he signed the requisition for the police phone. At the line for date of birth, again the number bewildered him.

He felt like a teenager, and he needed to check his own phone, getting his bearings. Tuttavia had sent a non-response: *OK maybe.* Once he was out of the precinct house, too, he called Ippolita.

After that, his private cell was best left in the apartment. For going undercover, Risto needed only the phone the cops had given him, and for an outfit he chose the trash top, the hospital scrub as bad Kandinsky. This had been a gift, a joke, from Paola. Also he dug out old sandals, rough as chaw, and among his wife's jewelry found a cheap gilded hoop for one ear.

Hiking downtown for the second time in as many days, working up a laborer's stink, once more he swung past the Galleria. A number of shop windows remained X'd by scaffolding, though the crews appeared to have finished their renovations. They'd moved on to sponges and buckets, gussying up the place for the weekend. The only actual repair Risto could spot was far overhead, on the dome, where a worker picked his way along the catwalk. Still, the bulging emporium appeared about back to normal as he veered downslope, into the shade of a skin-of-the-teeth marketplace.

These two or three blocks of stalls and duffels also served as the business center for the city's transvestite whores. Naturally, they didn't get much action at mid-morning on a Tuesday. Still, if you knew what to look for, you'd see that cross-dressing in Naples was state of the art. The trannies had a reputation to uphold, a craft that went back to the party boys in the Greek tomb paintings, and Risto suffered the lameness of his own wardrobe. A hoop earring, really? Was he a teenager after all? His Alexandria days came to mind, puttering along El Geish in a come-hither sashay. Also the husband couldn't help thinking of his wife. In her twenties Paola had lived for a year with a musician named Serena, and the two women had spoken of moving to Berlin and getting married. She'd enjoyed another affair or two as well, and while that wasn't the same as hustling, it wasn't anything like the way she lived now. Years had gone by, to be sure, years spent almost entirely with her Risto-Ri. Still, every once in long while Paola felt moved to insist, *I could live with a woman. I could.*

Neither he nor his wife had brought this up yesterday, during their hours together. Nonetheless the way she felt about women had loomed between them, another fairytale, the one about the elephant in the room. You could see the big creature through the ill will about her father, and even more clearly behind everything she had to say about Tuttavia. The photographer's Goth androgyny, Southern Italy's own Girl with the Dragon Tattoo, practically invited lesbian fantasy. Back when she and Paola were getting to know each other, they'd shared the occasional touch or glance that left Risto unsettled. But he'd never raised the question, familiar as he was with the slum confusion between men and women. Yesterday, likewise, his wife's confession about her and the photographer had set him prickling with suspicion. No way that could be the whole story, two kids and a knife. Again, though, Risto left his misgivings unspoken. He only gave her an opening: *Do you want to get into that?*

She'd let this pass, and he'd confined himself to watching and listening. This morning too Risto needed to see past the obvious, among the merchants in the shadow of the Galleria. Their goods were mostly legitimate, if ticky-tack. The flash drives looked especially dubious, dangling like clusters of garlic. For truly illicit dealing, however, he had to find the *trasvestiti*. At this hour they were just getting up, coming out for coffee in T-shirts and jeans. But Risto knew what to look for, the hipshot posture, the ratted perm. This also had him noticing the range of hues in the current skin game. A couple young men were inky as La Cia, others khaki as Mepris. Players like that perked up at once when someone mentioned decent documents for sale; whatever these boys did for lunch, they'd be talking about Papers.

After that he had to prowl the Forcella. Fifteen minutes uphill, past the papier-mâché cave of the *Guardia di Finanzia*, these alleyways did business that never showed up in Nardo's books. Every cash box hid an envelope for the bad guys, and if you asked the finance officer, he'd say the Forcella was "d-dark"—avoiding the nastier slur, "Calcutta." Brothers and sisters out of the South had an ever-greater presence. A few even ran their own stalls, the awning design agitated, West African, and the wares packed tight as cornrows. Nowadays you got the quake reconstruction to boot, the dust and impedimentia. If Nardo saw the Forcella in the paper, he'd turn the page. Nonetheless, that cream puff too must've stopped in for a bargain, from time to time. The goods were always duty-free and you never had to show a boarding pass.

Risto took precautions. He kept a thumb in his wallet pocket and his questions in shorthand, and he knew better than to linger. Around inner Naples some of the worst blocks lay bang up against some of the best; from a UNESCO Heritage site to a Camorra stronghold, it was no more than a step across the street. Any downtowner knew these membranes, and where they were most permeable. You had to keep an eye out for a smash-&-grab, thieves riding two to a bike, but you could duck in and out of the marketplace without a problem. Someone like Risto didn't have to meander stall to stall, drawing more attention as he went. Instead he dropped the dealer's name in one corner of the Forcella, then circled round to the far side before he did it again. At each stop he found a quiet moment, isolated, to give out the number the cops had given him.

Only once did he worry he'd blown his cover. This came at one of the better intersections, a cathedral on the tourist itineraries. The place had catacombs, indicated by a spooky sign, a skull and bones. Alongside stood Risto's client Yebleh.

The young Libyan still looked as if he'd barely come off the boat. Actually he'd enjoyed a better crossing, in keeping with a better schooling. Conservatory training was rare enough, under Khadaffi, and working with a woman even rarer, but somehow this watercolorist had managed both. Later, after Risto had visited and Naples became a real possibility, Yebleh had dotted all the i's in the paperwork. He lined up work and study visas, and these had been renewed without a hitch not long before the quake. Nevertheless, slouched against the church wall, he suggested the old slur, *WOP*, "without papers." His straightened hair recalled the morning frazzle of the *trasvestiti*—if not some bebop-era throwback, a junkie on a Harlem street corner. His build was delicate, his hands birdlike. But they suffered extra-legal jitters.

Risto worked up a paternal smile. *"A'salam alekom."*

Yebleh's own look was puzzled, and he waggled a small hand uncertainly at the older man's getup. Risto had a story for that, a desire to go incognito: *eh, all weekend I'll be on stage.* Anyway he was more concerned about his client. Yebleh's gaze kept shifting, checking the streets that branched off from the church. From the tomb of a saint to the markets of the mob, it was just a step. Risto thought of the pills, baggies full, easy to find across the Forcella. Amphetamines were Yebleh's weakness, and for fifteen Euro he'd be set for days.

He had to ask, closing in.

"There's supposed to be a meeting," murmured Yebleh. "A meeting, you know, in the church. There's supposed to be a facilitator on the way."

The boy's eyes remained evasive, but his news left Risto almost bubbly. In another moment he'd offered to hang out a while, take a breather. As for Papers, if the dealer decided to call, it wasn't as if Risto wouldn't notice. He joined the painter against the wall, fending off a hard sell from the peddler on the sidewalk. A rangy Sudanese, proffering sunglasses: *Brother, c'mon. My brother.*

"Look at us," said Yebleh, as the salesman at last moved off. "Look what they've done to us. They've got us preying on each other."

Risto refitted his smile. "Should I switch back to Arabic? The wicked cities of Europe, may Allah smite them with fire and brimstone?"

The younger man remained glum. Risto gave his back a bear's scratch against the medieval stones. "Look, maybe I should tell you about when I worked on the docks."

His first job in the North. On the waterfront they could always use another pair of arms for the goods off the books. Home port Shanghai, home port Ningbo—"The Chinese pay the best," Risto said. "I imagine that's still the word on the street."

Yebleh, checking again for his facilitator, barely gave a nod.

"Like working in the Gulag," continued Risto. "You didn't even get gloves. And come evening, as soon as they handed you the cash? The mob had their girls out."

"'Girls,' that's one way to put it. Some of those Camorra hookers..."

"Some of them are killers, sure. If you don't have the Euro, they'll whip out the straight razor. But Yebleh, I knew better. You remember how I had to hustle."

"I remember." He frowned. "The inspiring narrative of the man who went from selling his body to selling fine art. Everyone at Wind & Confusion has heard it."

"Eh, wise guy. Look, it's not as if my troubles ended with the night boat north. Then there was Naples—*what they've done to us.*"

When Eftah first sent him down to the docks, a glimpse of thigh could set Risto poking up like a transmitter tower. For the first month or so he'd plowed through the girls, a man with something to prove. He hated to think of it now, but at least he'd had brains enough to raid his clansman's stash of condoms. Then as his need relented, on his slow way back and forth to Materdei, he'd begun to explore another world: the Naples museums and art houses. In the Nazionale he found the antiquities, at Capodimonte the baroque array. Once he learned about the contemporary shows at PAN or Mater Madre, he worked out ways to clean up and catch the openings.

"I liked it, that's all." The airy rooms, the endless looking....

"Besides," Yebleh put in, "a brother off the docks, he's not going to pass up free wine and hors d'oeuvres."

This was another of the Libyan's miracles, his familiarity with alcohol. He might've just downed a stiff drink, in fact; he'd turned playful, tossing back his bangs. Risto couldn't shift gears so fast. "Well, the galleries offered so much better. You know that on the docks, I saw a man die?'

Another worker lost a chunk of his head in a fall. Brain tissue, greasy, coiled, pale, spattered the indigo bay. Risto's first thought, once he could bring up a thought, had been of Jackson Pollock.

"Signore Aristofano, what is this, one terrible flashback after another!"

Risto knuckled what would've been his hairline.

"Really, now, are we going to live in flashback? I mean, let's have better, at least. Let's talk about all the pretty girls in those galleries."

Okay, oldtimer, join the party. "Some very interesting women, yes."

"And you, such a man of the world, telling stories out of Beirut and Tangier."

"Man of the world. I always thought of something from Brother Malcolm."

"Malcolm X helped you to pick up girls?"

"Yebleh, you know the line. The white man's worse nightmare."

The painter's smile sharpened. He knew the line: a nigger with a library card. He grasped as well how the young Aristofano had turned this to his advantage. Just as the locals were a darker shade of white, so this African's reading and culture brought on no more than a mild nightmare. The gallery-goers might be knocked back a bit, hearing a *clandestino* talk Cavafy and Caravaggio—but when they straightened up, they found their interest piqued. They followed up with questions, and one or two handed over a business card, and so provided the Risto with the first of the connections that would lead, eventually, to the gallery run by the American. Yebleh got all that, chuckling. In reply, though, he took another tack: "This Friday evening, you know, our photographer friend has got a nightmare all her own."

No problem finding Yebleh's eyes after that. No point getting offended, either, or pretending to be surprised. Risto spread a hand across his mouth, nodding. So this was what had lifted the young man's mood. Once the subject got around to the art scene, he'd recalled the photos. Naturally he was on Giussi's mailing list. The performance artist might even have enjoyed a tumble with Yebleh, one night when they'd split some X and begun to reminisce about Islamic school. The rumor remained unconfirmed, but regardless, anyone with half a brain could sort out the painter's feelings. "Our bright, shining star for *Expo in Città*—she's the one *exposed*."

Risto had already tried playing the buddy. Hoisting up his chest, he reminded Yebleh that the woman was with Wind & Confusion. "You and she, you work together."

The younger man pinched a wad of his cheek.

"Yes, and you and this white girl work *together*."

Just like that, Yebleh was in freefall, once more hiding his eyes.

"You chose this, my friend—this city, this North."

It felt right to echo Papers. To brandish his argument but not his blade, yes: Risto didn't want to hurt the younger man. Yebleh was almost a protégé. Just now, he only needed to dial down the schaden-freude, to sound more like a colleague, as he talked about the photographer's major Fail: "I can see what she intended, a performance, yielding power to the black man." Hearing that, Risto could go back to the Conservatory. He could use a word like "misconceived," an expression like "serious flaws in technique," a way of speaking that wouldn't be out of place in the upcoming A.A. meeting. Now that Risto thought about it, the lunch-hour therapy might itself have something to do with seeing Tuttavia in a garter belt and stockings. Giussi's erection couldn't have done Yebleh any good either.

Besides, didn't Risto need to talk about it? Couldn't he use another sort of sounding board, someone who wasn't his wife or (more or less) his cousin? A person in the business, even a mercurial watercolorist, gave him a chance to rehearse for Friday night. At the opening, he was bound to catch a whisper or two concerning his biggest client and her latest carrying-on. The gallery owner had to be sure of his tone.

"Anyone can see that the work's a failure," he declared. "But it's a natural extension of everything she's done, nonetheless."

Yebleh studied his hands, stroking the fingers of one with the thumb of the other.

"Look, it's not as if this makes her a fraud."

The painter's response was barely audible: "Our bright white star..."

Risto, bent close to hear, continued in a whisper. "Yebleh, you have no idea. *Per carita*, my first boss in this business? The American? Have you heard the kind of thing he put me through?"

If he weren't right on top of the man, Risto couldn't have seen his nod.

"Whatever you've heard, it's just one story out of fifteen. Then when at last I set up my own gallery, right away I got a visit from the Camorra."

The first *Confuso & Vento* had been just a couple of blocks from here, and the clans out of the Forcella took an interest. "They could use a—a cultural enterprise."

"Signore Aristofano..."

"They could *use* me. Swap out their dirty cash for clean."

This time, anyone could see Yebleh nodding. "*Abba*, please. I understand."

"You understand? They threatened to cut off my fingers, and still I kept moving. And now this is my city. It's got a *place* for me, for us *both*, that's the whole point..."

Risto broke off, turned around by a clack of iron on iron. He hadn't realized they'd edged so close to the church entrance. The studded doors were padlocked just now; tourist hours didn't start till Thursday. The same went for the little window beside the door, a grated window, smaller than Risto's hand and just above his head. In Naples you found these on all the older churches. A *fenestrella* of another kind, it allowed clergy to offer a few words of comfort and advice to needy souls below. These openings had doors as well, locked from within, but this morning someone inside had found the key. A voice called out, a woman's.

"What's all this shouting? Yebleh, is that you?"

The grate was sticky with filth, and from his angle Risto couldn't see much. Still, he'd say the face in the window was pretty, and Yebleh wasted no time calling back, ducking in front of his gallery owner.

"I said the other side," the woman told him, "the nuns' side. We were trying to have the moment of silence."

Risto took a long step back, checking behind him for any wares on the sidewalk. When he faced Yebleh again, the painter was giving him yet another sort of look, so young and unsure that all the older man could do was fall back on simple affirmations: *I'm glad we had this talk. A meeting, that's a great idea.*

But Yebleh had a last question. "What brings you down here anyway?"

Risto had a story for that, too: "Eh, I could always use better lighting."

Electronics were among the most reliable items on sale around the Forcella. For his original Wind & Confusion, he'd found a fixture ready to install, with wiring and safeguards up to code. It must've been intended for the NATO base at Aversa. Out there the Americans lived and worked in prefab boxes worthy of a gimcrack Texas metropolis, and Risto liked to imagine that, in one corner of one box, the cubicle monkeys lacked for proper illumination while his gallery glowed brightly downtown. The Empire had got its comeuppance, sort of, from a brown guy on the black market.

Meanwhile, he too had been put in his place. The Camorra had their own interpretation of what Risto and Paola had worked up for the gallery's mission statement: "Using the arts to enrich the community." Naturally the young Al'Kair had guessed that the System would take an interest, and his American mentor had brought up the possibility of money-laundering. But no shopkeeper was ever prepared for visitors like these two. Both the size of Eftah's friend the Hut, the bastards had pinned one hand to the wall and put a knife at the base of his thumb. To Risto this loomed up as large as a machete, a military model with the blade imprinted *Made in USA*. He didn't feel the cut, but he couldn't miss line of blood across his knuckle.

Whatcha need with ten fingers, hey, faggot? one or the other had asked. *Can't you work with five? How about three?*

No shopkeeper included something like that in his business plan. Risto, casting around for help, had noticed again his tall windows, turn-of-the-previous-century. His space was above the ground floor, but even so, a lot of it remained visible from on the street. Out there, chances were, some slow mover was a witness, but in this city people had long since learned to pick their battles. Besides, if there were a witness, more than likely he was white.

Afterwards he'd tried his most useful connections, the American mentor and the Neapolitan girlfriend—not yet a wife. Neither, however, offered more than a kindly touch. His former boss found a better bandage for his thumb and his lover stroked his head. Meantime, both tempered their sympathies with the reminder that even an immigrant with his papers in order shouldn't expect much from the police. The problem wasn't just the dirty cops, in cahoots. Maybe worse, if a witness didn't end up buried in lime, he'd disappear into state protection. He'd be sequestered in one anonymous motel after another till only the courthouse would feel like home. Really, was that any reason to come North? Also Paola had another story to share, a cranky parable about the bully down the block. You could run off to China, but you never escaped that bully down the block... Risto got it. Both his girl and his

guru viewed the shakedown as a rite of passage. Their outsider friend
had dreams of acting as a change agent, transforming the old city via
wind and confusion. Well then, how many fingers could he work with?

Years later, the gallery had moved up-market. In La Chiaia you didn't
get the goons bursting in; you only had those silent partners. "Men of
impeccable character," Paola's father had called them, and Risto had left
it at that, his ear tuned to the local hypocrisy. In the Forcella, however,
even a newcomer could spot the bad guys throwing their weight around.
Hard to mistake the bulge under a running jacket (and in this weather,
who wore a jacket?) or the black eye on a girl in a doorway. Today as
lunchtime came on, Risto grew sick of it.

Only once more could he stomach slipping in among the tight-
packed stalls. He found someone to ask about the fake I.D., and to
give his fake phone number, and after that headed back downslope. By
the docks you found the ragpicker markets, beneath the mob's attention. In them a Rwandan or Nigerian might think he'd passed though
some magic portal back to his home city and its souk. None of the
sellers had any idea who Risto was, but several greeted him with a soul
shake, hug-&-wrestle. More than once he whispered his undercover
pitch into another man's ear, dizzied at the odor. These days he rarely
encountered such a reek, made riper still by cologne. Bottles of scent
did a brisk business, here; one woman had a suitcase full of an odor
labeled *OBAMA*.

Eh, you wish it were so easy. Slap on the cologne, take over the
white Superpower—though there wasn't an *immigrato* in Naples who
didn't nurse some similar outsized dream. You'd never last if you didn't
put some sort of glow on the hardscrabble. If Aesop were alive today,
he'd have long since quit his hand-to-mouth island, and along with
it the old yarns about grasshoppers, grapes, and silly boys too lightly
clad. Aesop would've had a fable about a laptop and a Kalashnikov, like
Papers. The story made as much sense as anything else, here amid the
dockside flea markets. It made as much sense as Risto's own fairytale,
since his success might appear more ordinary, but his pilots had navi-
gated the back channels. That included the Immigrant Council, when
they'd lent a hand with his original gallery. In general the Council struck

Risto as futile, a multicolor Babel wrangling over scraps, but after the Camorra had put their blade to him, he'd been willing to try anything. He'd found a couple of sympathetic listeners, a pair of Afghanis. These leathery Pashtuns had connections of their own in the System, and starting that very month, they arranged for Wind & Confusion to take less of a hit each time its good money was exchanged for bad.

Risto could figure it out, the Afghan quid for the Mafia quo. His bearded new friends also showed up at the next few receptions, and they took a special interest in his more moneyed and dissolute patrons. Before long, they'd hooked up with an antiquities dealer based in Zurich. He could figure it out, and he could let it alone. He was only the gallery owner. Besides, not much later Paola had come to him pregnant, and he'd responded with an offer of marriage.

He had his own merchant caravan, on its own itinerary. Even the morning's undercover operation felt like just another round of barter. The sweat had turned his shirt to a swamp, and the vendors were breaking down for *riposo*, and all this felt familiar. He traveled as a changeling, but he'd come to know this city, a hive exhausted from millennial rounds of swarm and husk, and now he sensed again the gift he brought it: the vagabond energy of arts gone global. Granted, here the same as anywhere, creative life stood on wobbly pins. It depended on neglected building stock, where rents stayed low and landlords kept hands off. What's more, his own success had kindled up strangely, thanks to flint-strikes of good luck from all over the North. Nonetheless, as the lower markets quieted for lunch, it was as if the gulls overhead cried out the sort of affirmations he'd given Yebleh. *You're a hero. An inspiration. Even for the cops.*

Not that Risto was going to listen to any stupid birds. Especially not since he'd begun seeing things; the halos were more than enough craziness for one week. Anyway, if he'd had a mythic journey, the part that mattered had taken place after he came off the boat. This was what Paola and Eftah failed to grasp, with their theory about Post-Ti'aba Stress Disorder. They ignored the patient's *later* trauma. Risto would never suggest that Italy had been harder on him than Somalia, or Morocco, or Egypt—but over these last few days he hadn't been trying to resurrect his brother so much as reconstruct himself. What was that Eftah had said, about keeping everything in your own skin?

Certainly he needed putting together after the call came in.

Papers, on the other end, didn't fail to notice. You could hear his delight in rattling the houseboy, catching him when his mind was elsewhere. The Civilian Informant managed eventually to reiterate the instructions he'd gotten from the police: Capodimonte just before close. He'd had hours of practice, playing Pretend. By the time Risto rang off, however, the last thing on his mind was any immigrant success story. Rather he thought of his wife and kids. By this point they'd be sitting down in the breeze off Agropoli harbor. The sister would've held lunch, waiting for the train from what she called "the wicked city."

❊

In the stairwell, at the end of the afternoon, the detective moved on to the accomplice, the dealer's backup. "What can you tell me?"

What Risto recalled were the similarities: the bone structure, the farm-weathered skin, even the same necklace. "They could've come from the same clan," he said, and looked over at his own big relative. Risto was glad for such an undercover partner, done up boldly in Rasta and ganja. After getting the word from Papers, Risto had gone ahead and called Eftah. What did it matter if the police were listening? The Black Lord had been back in his castle, lounging with an ice-cold Fiano, but the news set him bubbling. He claimed this would help his love life.

"Won't it be *perfect* for Mepris?" he asked. "The Nelson Mandela of Naples, that's who he's got for a boyfriend, striking a blow for truth and reconciliation. A bad guy like this, a usurer—Tuttavia might even invite me to her next orgy."

He'd been so upbeat, the day's bright spot. Della Figurazione came across just the opposite, with one grim question after another.

"Guns?" Eftah sent an echo up the stairwell, echoing the officer, "Really, Detective, guns? You think this is L.A.?" One shooting, he declared, and La Fenestrella would be out of business.

"So you've seen them checking? Actually frisking people?"

When Eftah shook his head, you noticed how he'd oiled up after shaving. His scalp gleamed chestnut against the whitewashed sheetrock.

"You understand, contraband like this attracts some serious bad apples."

Risto scowled. "And anyone dark as us, they could be Boko Haram."

"Signore Oil Cur, ah, truly, I'm sorry about earlier..."

"Men like these," Eftah put in, "they prefer the knife, the primitive."

That's how Papers saw it, thought Risto. He saved the more advanced weapons for building a city. But Della Figurazione appeared satisfied, and as he pulled open the door he brought up the final piece of paperwork. The disclaimer, he said. One last signature, with—"ah, in case of complications"—a contact.

This time Risto suffered no hesitation; his contact was Tuttavia. The wife was out of town, no more than a thought, a blur.

Then came the cash, 100s and 500s, green and purple. The bills were a mess of course, part of the illusion, as was the woman on the job. This officer had hair the same gray as the pistol holstered at her back. She offered a frown, sympathetic, and dipped her head wordlessly. You'd think she'd spent time as a nun. Then Risto and Eftah were ushered out via an emergency exit, into an alley. They couldn't simply leave by the front door, after all, and Della Figurazione suggested they cab it up to the park. Illegals with money, right? At this hour, rush hour, the driver rarely got out of low gear, but Risto sat silent, smoothing one of the bills against the knee. He had no idea how the cops marked the stuff. Ritual scarring?

Bent over his knee, he realized too how little he'd had to eat. Back at breakfast, Paola, half joking, maybe less, had suggested he try a priest. She'd set down her coffee, brought up his "mysterious glowworms," then mentioned a certain "renegade Jesuit or something." The parish was up in the Vomero, and the man had a record of good works on behalf of the *clandestini*. Some people spoke of miracles. Still, it was after his wife had headed for the train station that Risto seemed to have stumbled into the Invisible World. He'd drifted across the lower city like a ghost, and now he carried cash no one could spend. He rode alongside a man who, in his most recent photo, wore the golden death's head.

Up in at the Capidimonte entrance, the first minute or so breezed by, unremarkable. Risto tried for a saunter as he made for the dealer, easy to spot even without his jacket. Papers remained one of the tallest in the crowd, and he still had the V-cut. He might've been showing it off as he nodded Risto and Eftah over. As for the commotion surrounding them, that was tailor-made: tourists bundled under plastic flags, joggers passing either way, mothers and nannies and strollers and grade schoolers. Not far off, a couple leaned into a kiss against a tree trunk, oak, scratchy you'd think. Closer by, vendors put extra body into their day's-end hawking. One was waving sun visors, wearing a vivid kid's T-shirt, Scrooge McDuck.

Even with all this, the dealer wouldn't pull out his contraband. He didn't like having Eftah in his face as well, two against one. Besides, the customer alone ought to be the one checking the watermarks and bond. This time Papers kept his goods protected, in a wide manila envelope. His bracelet flashed in the lowering sun, silver, but the design wasn't what Risto was looking for, more African than Mexican. Lacking the snake, the curves, it could've been a manacle. Papers had gone for pizzazz elsewhere, his necklace wet gold and his shirt warrior red, silken. Anyway, he posed no threat.

First Risto gave him a peek at the cash, a bundle in each pants pocket, and then the dealer used his envelope to indicate a hollow a few steps off the palace walk. At Capodimonte he didn't need a back room. A low cluster of myrtles would do fine. Eftah allowed the crook his space, but Risto took one more glance left-right. He believed he spotted the third policeman, square-built, cross-armed. He stood straddling a bike with off-road tires as big as Tonino's fist.

Papers headed for the trees. Risto, following, felt for a moment he was once more south of the Sahara, in the density of leaf and mulch. Then came the dealer's musk, heavy, amber. In the lovers' grove, Papers locked up Risto from behind, yoking him body on body from shoulder blades to butt. You reach a certain corner at a certain hour, and it's something else again. It's a gun at your ribs.

"You call this a city?" The growl at his ear sounded as if they were back on the phone. "Where a citizen like you can walk right into my hands?"

The only prop Papers had needed was the dusk. Now he had his prey at gunpoint, hooked up so tight that each time Risto flinched the stab in his ribs could've been a knife. Eftah appeared like a crucifix in a procession, advancing and retreating with arms spread wide. Risto himself, in his silly, sweaty costume, could've been a clown.

"Is this a city, when all of a sudden your white wife can't do you a bit of good? When I can knock everything to pieces, even a shop in Lah Kee-*yahh*-yah?"

The crook whipped the snout of the pistol up into Risto's armpit. Like that, everything had a halo, blinking fire-orange.

"I told you this city was dying. I told you I was your *destiny*."

Again the blow to the armpit. Risto bellowed as his knees caved. He could see the bruising, it seemed, see himself bruised and rough-housed backward, one arm twisted so badly that the fingers went cold, his legs so out of sync that his one of his sandals came off. Meantime the couple against the oak sank down with hands up, as if in salaam. The man with the bike popped off and on, his gestures incomprehensible. If the guy was a cop, he and the others were kept at bay: the accomplice, the dealer's man, had bulled out of the undergrowth and put a knife on the hostage. A knife, a dirty-steel fisherman's friend, a glint and jitter in the corner of one eye. Were those junkie shakes or simple fear? Had everyone turned to a tree? The one figure in motion appeared to be Eftah, still spread-winged but bopping, back on the dance floor in some Jamaican alarm-boogie.

Risto understood this was a kidnap before Papers rasped out the word, giving it the same serrated edge as "kee-*yahh*-yah." Swiftly the dealer had them out of sight in the brush. He had as firm a grip as night before last, and he kept on at Risto's ear, spraying tobacco and hash, and amid the tussle and ache still more became clear. Like, Papers didn't have a clue about the gallery business. He didn't realize that Wind & Confusion could really use the Expo, or any kind of August bump. The "associates" on the mortgage would be only too glad to have him go bankrupt.

All this came to Risto, the whorish compromise that was his success—the guts of another kill, here on the former hunting grounds.

For Papers of course the scene was something else entirely: his biggest payday. He'd let his lure drop, his envelope, back in the fog of iron and amber. And what was he saying? "A credit to the race. A pretty black face."

He and his man must've picked a getaway point. They could've stashed a vehicle.

"I'm not alone," Risto said. "Friends, eh."

"Faggot imbecile. You think I didn't know you'd bring friends?"

"Po-lice. I'm…"

But he was crabwalking, breathless, in brush so thick it put him up against every grade of weapon: fist, stick, knife, gun. The king who'd laid out Capodimonte liked a lot of cover. He liked small game and stolen kisses, and these woods must've seen a rape before. The woods and kidnapper both, made for the wham-bam. Now Risto had his foot on a root, his sandaled foot, and it could be a springboard—he could jump, break loose—but no way, houseboy. Another clout had his face in the dirt. He might've inhaled a worm. When he came up, choking, the knife was back in his eyes.

But then the *assistente* dropped away, scrabbling downhill ahead of his boss. The two had it all figured, sting the sting and reduce the C.I. to a shmoe. Reduce him to seeing things, like the murder of La Cia, the boy trussed up and bent over just as he was. But Papers would never waste time with the eyes or thumb. Risto had to focus: the beetle hump of an empty Nastro Azurro, the scummy splay of a condom. Then he was out of the woods, yanked into a clearing, and he caught the glare of a vehicle. Or was it just the steel-and-diesel smell? The iron jammed under his chin? And what was that, in the failing light—wildflowers? Fireworks over a Lilliputian city? All he could be sure of was the road, something for park maintenance.

He negotiated the ruts by feel, shoeless now, the weeds everywhere this late in summer. But the car, Risto: pay attention. The car was always a clue. Not that this Fiat appeared at all special, another stripped-down hybrid, and meantime Papers was barking orders in a bush language.

He too had to bark. "Fucking savage Neanderthal *ape*—"

The second kidnapper loomed up with a burlap sack.

※

The getaway baffled him all over again. They gunned it uphill, deeper into the park, farther from the city. Risto couldn't begin to make sense of it, not in his position, slung sideways across the back. The burlap was sweltering, prickling, and the stench could've been buffalo feed. Every jolt revived an injury, foot or rib or head.

Plus the things he'd screamed before they'd gotten the bag on him, ugly things, as if he were daring them to put a bullet behind his ear. He couldn't begin to make sense. He could barely understand how they'd tied him up, groping for the binding at his wrists. A belt, that was it. Maybe that would matter, once he got out of this.

Another jolt, humping across a rut, then the screech of the emergency brake. The getaway had lasted, what? Three minutes, five? The Fiat remained at a severe tilt, idling. As they dragged Risto out his bindings were wrenched loose, but the dealer had nothing to worry about. He could handle the hostage with just his grip and his gun. Risto was pummeled uphill and the car rumbled away and down.

Those ratty sandals he'd chosen for his costume! And that root he'd kicked! The toe throbbed angrily and Risto suffered a glimpse out of his past, the goatherds' cabin above Mogadishu. He'd reached that place likewise barefoot and helpless. Yes, but then he'd moved on, and where had he come to now? Under the hem of the bag, past the carnival colors of his top, Risto made out scrims of lichen, verdigris. Soon there was nothing underfoot but rock, and even burlap couldn't mask the tang of cave limestone. Naturally the park had caves. The site was all one big calcareous outcropping.

A few steps in, Papers flung him against a wall, but Risto kept his head down. As the kidnapper went through his pockets, he didn't resist. It wasn't his stuff.

Before long, alone again, it occurred to him that a wall was a kind of tool. This one, he discovered, wasn't all limestone. Some of this had to be the local tufa, hardened by exposure. Spurs poked up, and against these Risto had little trouble wrangling off the dealer's street-market belt. Once his hands were free, fuck you, burlap. Fuck you and the feeblemindedness you brought on. Risto spat out the taste and scrubbed his scalp two-handed. After that—the long, tough creature in the cave mouth.

Papers still had the gun. Till now Risto hadn't laid eyes on it, hadn't realized how small it was, all but swallowed whole in the dealer's hand. The sort of automatic made for a purse. Cradling the weapon as if it were a cigarette lighter, Papers appeared more concerned about what was in the other hand: the police-issue cell phone.

The first he spoke, frowning and head down, Risto couldn't catch it.

"The *book*," repeated Papers, "your book of numbers."

He extended the arm with the little device open, so Risto saw a descent to darkness: glowing screen, fading sky, closemouthed sneer.

"The most regular numbers. The book of the people you call."

"Papers. I know you heard me earlier, about the police."

"Heard you, faggot? I heard when you called me an ape."

Risto, down where it was darker still, wondered how much Papers could see.

"Called me a Neanderthal. A *savage*."

But even if the man could make out his look, some part apology, even so—

"You and the law, that dick, the *law*, you think an ape doesn't notice when a phone's got no book? Look, not even the number for the white girl with the camera."

Risto folded his hands, a good prisoner.

The dealer cackled. "Boh, why don't you give me a lecture? You the university savage, the most famous Al'Kair?"

At least Papers got his name right, the hiccup between syllables. It echoed down the cave hollow, correct the whole way. Risto found himself in a smile, or a quarter smile. His keeper too bared his teeth, but this was nothing like a smile, not the least fraction. Also he wasn't finished with "the white law" and their "pet ape." He let Risto know that for this morning's call, he too had used someone else's phone.

"And you see this place, houseboy? Let 'em try to find me, the police and their tracking device."

"Tracking device?" Risto put in. "You're talking science fiction."

"Faggot actually thinks I'm a Neanderthal. Thinks I don't remember, back home we used cell phones to track the Shabab."

What Risto remembered was La Fenestrella, where he'd thought the man had military training. "That takes a truck full of gear and half a day to set up. Besides, about this place you're right."

Was he bringing them any closer to actual conversation? The dealer didn't show it, his mouth shut again, a slash.

"Around Naples," Risto went on, "it's like where they hid Bin Laden. These hills and caves, they're no good for cell reception."

"Bin Laden?" More cackles. "And science fiction? Houseboy thinks he's Princess Leia. Thinks they're sending Luke and Hans and Seal Team 6."

Papers brought the gun up, and Risto flinched at the glint, but the weapon was only a counterbalance for the other arm. As if heaving a grenade, the wiry kidnapper slung the phone into the grotto below. The thing went to pieces with an enormous noise, echoing up and down, yet this came as a kind of relief. You realized the place had a floor. Risto settled back, one hand in the other armpit, fingering the sore spot. Along the wall opposite he discovered a telltale clutter. Another manila envelope, standard size, sat swollen—with documents, what else? Beside it stretched a lumpy duffel bag, perhaps at one time the bag of a sidewalk salesman. From one end poked a mat strapped into a tight roll, and folded over the other lay a dress jacket, canary yellow.

Office in the home. "Look," Risto tried, "I can see what you're expecting."

Papers too had relaxed, finding an angle of rock to sit against.

"I can see the kind of future you have in mind. Destiny, eh." How easily the talk came. "What's that you called me, the famous Al'Kair? You expect I'm the big score, the one that'll make you over into a whole different man. When you move back south, you'll be dealing in BMWs."

"The dick," growled Papers, "the *mediator*. Faggot thinks I'm going south."

Risto kept one arm around himself, as if that would hold it all in. The burlap was off, he reminded himself, and he hadn't gotten hit for a while now.

"Thinks I give a shit about the South." Papers was showing teeth again. "Houseboy, I couldn't give you a line of the Quran. What I know is, the Chinese pay the best. I know about Hollywood too. Hollywood, where they love a brother like me." He struck a pose, vulpine. "A sick old city like this, it's already a movie set."

Risto saw no reason not to bring up La Cia. "I hear that was his dream too, what the Americans call *Movieola*."

"Boh, again the Gay Avenger. Did you even know La Freccia?"

"Well, honestly…" But how could he have sounded so much like Paola?

"You know the boy and me, we *went* to the movies. Blowjob for a ticket."

"Look, Papers, honestly—this is what I've been thinking. There's no way you could be the murderer."

"The dick, the detective." Papers seemed to be brooding, sunk partly out of sight.

"There's no motive. An ugly business like that, it's not in your interest."

"That movie that night? I was going anyway."

Risto had already begun to ease away from the wall.

"A man's mouth," said the dealer, "a lot of times it's cleaner than a woman. Anyway, why should anyone make a fuss? Isn't it only nature's satisfaction? Up here in the North, they much such a fuss. People up North, they make it unclean, they make it crazy—and I get called the savage."

"*Per carità*. You were beating me up."

"Boh, the faggot never got beat up." The dealer glared around the outcropping. "Listen, how about I beat up old Europe? I smash it to bits, all the dying old cities? Then the men can start over, the *men* of destiny."

How could he fail to notice Risto's creeping?

"This Naples, the rabbits call it their oldest city. But how long would it take to smash it? Once the true brothers jump in—we are millions now. All we need is the axe. Seize the place, bust it all down, and to start over, just give me a good weapon and a working computer. Just give me the *money*. A fat payoff for a fake brother."

Risto tried to stay off his bad toe, his belly wallowing out of his shirt.

"La Cia, there was another fake. Holly-wood. What that boy did for me, to him it was all about the movie. Even the night they killed him, it was about the movie."

That stopped him. "The night they killed La Cia?"

"Faggot doesn't know. Word was all over the club, and he doesn't even know: in the back, they were making a movie."

"A movie? In the middle of the night, in a...?"

"Houseboy, that's close enough."

Risto lurched over onto hip and elbow.

"Close *enough*. You think I need you?"

Retreating, finding a perch, he let the kidnapper see him limp.

"Fake brother doesn't get it. Now that they can't play you, the law doesn't need you. And you think I need you, with everything I've got going on? A deal tonight, that'd be sweet. Get the money and get started. But you think I need it?"

Risto got back to Friday night, this business of a film set in the back room.

"Word was all over the club."

The dealer waved the gun, the metal catching a flash of sunset. "But when I make a movie, I'll go to Hollywood. Hollywood loves a true brother."

※

The first shouts from outside hardly raised an echo. Still, you couldn't miss them, and the next were louder, closer. Soon Risto picked up the accent, the Tuscan articulation. That brought him to his feet, or halfway, gasping, fighting the injury and tasting the lime. Papers didn't care, ignoring his hostage to peek out the cave mouth. He hollered in bush language. Or were those animal cries? A predator's screeching even as it shrinks into a corner? Anyway the kidnapper found what cover he could, to one side of the cave opening, and if he were calling the accomplice he didn't get any reply. Rather there was more of Della Figurazione—it had to be Della Figurazione, though God knows how. A quick deal with the sidekick? So quick,

it blew your mind? Risto doubted half an hour had gone by since
Papers grabbed him.

"Signore Allah Cur!"

And there was a second speaker, a woman. It blew your mind,
Star Wars, since it meant the cops had a car. Papers got the picture
too, he quit his jabber, and Risto couldn't help gimping a step or two
closer. Then some nugget on the floor dropped him into a squat. All
at once he was a swimmer set to dive, bristling with the memory of
another desperate dive, heading upstream, heading north. Yet here the
whole place was stone. Here, any 'Dishu troopers would've cut and
run at the police warning shot. Just one shot, but a terrible echo, it
left Papers grim as at last he sized up his prisoner. His eyes catching a
glimmer of moon or headlights, he could've been a butcher, calculating his best cut. Outside the cops resumed calling, but their math had
to be simple as well.

Papers began to pick his way downhill. Once more he ignored Risto,
using his gun as a cane, propping his crawl on that hand while with the
other he fished in a pants pocket. His explanation sounded polite.

"An ear, that's all. Didn't some crazy painter up north take off an ear?"

Out of the pocket came his knife, the tiger-stripe, another simple
equation.

"Toss out an ear, they'll come back with an offer."

The gallery owner had a thought about a finger, *isn't it usually a
finger*, and a thought about the approaching man's totter, not quite
in balance while descending into the dark. For a moment the fucking
savage was vulnerable. After that Risto wasn't thinking, he was nothing
but the pain in foot and ribs at takeoff, and in the impact at the crown
of his skull. A projectile fired out of his squat and into Papers, he nutted
the man between the eyes as once more things went two-dimensional.

Risto watched what was happening, both right now and years earlier, on the night boat out of Libya. On the boat, yes, he'd seen this, a
passenger who'd nagged the smugglers and then got a nutting, a whack
where it hurt the most with the bone that made the best weapon. And
here, yes, the gun was knocked loose and clattering away. The weapon
eluded both men, too small, too skittery, though Risto did manage to

swat it down into the dark as he clambered the other direction over the stunned kidnapper. The headlights filled the cave mouth with gold. The knife too glimmered in the mind's flatscreen, still in the bad man's grip. Risto couldn't think but he was talking, bellowing, his cries bursting straight out of his damaged chest and head, and somehow he kicked at the knife, or did he wish it away, meantime bear-crawling up into the woods air. He flattened everything and moved on.

Yet at the lip of the cave he stalled, grappling for a handhold. Papers had his leg.

The dealer yanked the smaller man down and straddled him. Risto whipped over, face up, swinging wildly. His hands were broad and strong, great for around the gallery, but his attacker's arms were longer. Papers sat on his hostage with his knife out of reach, drawing up for a killing blow, so that the cops' high-beams set his V-cut on fire. Flaming, leering, his head could've been a Basquiat—Risto couldn't help himself—and his switchblade, shimmering, scribbled graffiti against the cave ceiling. When the gun went off somewhere (not so loud this time: a pair of stones clapped together), it was still more of that '80s firecracker, young SAMO, burning junkie visions into the night.

Risto kept swatting, flailing, bucking. The creature above jerked with hunger, with triumph, leaking blood from its mouth as it preened before first bite. It was all on a screen, the ultimate hallucinations of a long, mad weekend, but then Papers jerked again, differently, slackening. The military man reverted to a worn-out fruit-picker, with a wheedling moan, and around it you could tune in a larger uproar and echo. There'd been another gunshot, hadn't there? There'd been movement in the weeds and more than one shot, and this *clandestino* who pictured himself as Hollywood chocolate cake, who in just these few days had taken roles in a crime story, a sex comedy, a wilderness drama, even a jet-set thriller —with a plot to bring down Europe—he'd been hit. He'd been caught in the chest, once at least, and now he slumped so badly that Risto had to get another grip on him. When had the guy lost his knife? Where better to catch hold than the wrist with the bracelet? You grab the man just to keep him from pitching face first into a jutting wedge of wall, an impulse like catching a drunk.

Then the outcry, the howls, each one louder than the one before. Risto shivered from hips to neck, and he couldn't stop even at the glint of the gun barrel close by, the policewoman beside him in a crouch.

"Signore. Signore, calm yourself! Let go."

He shivered and pinched the bracelet. He had Papers by the collar too, and beside his clenched hand, the disco red of the shirt had sunk into mud.

"*Calm* yourself. Look at me, signore. We've got him."

The stench caught up with Risto, a singed and rancid marinade.

"Look at me."

She had his shoulder, but he couldn't bear the idea of more hands on him. Wrenching left-right, rolling with a pain that looped from foot to head, he got out from under the body. Leave it to the police. Leave it and scuttle free, out of the cave onto the lichen and beyond.

He wound up at the feet of Della Figurazione, close enough to hear the squeak of his latex crime-scene gloves. The detective hadn't wanted any of this, you could see it in the way his fingers flexed, and this sent Risto first sinking to the dirt and then—at the first deep inhale, the air sweet enough almost to make you laugh, wine-ripe with late summer—lifting his gaze again. Up at the cave mouth, the dealer's corpse had been propped against a wall. The hair remained aglow, or was that the head itself, yielding some glimmer, some halo? Another trick of the headlights?

Della Figurazione cut off his line of sight, striding towards the cave. Risto found himself thinking that, while tonight's dead brother wasn't responsible for the one Friday, for the time being he could let the white folks sort it out. They had the gloves. They knew how to poke at a shooting victim, and if the air in one torn lung erupted noisily all of a sudden, a burble, a whistle, a keening, they didn't get hysterical. They just let the echo die. Soon enough they'd tell their CI how all this was possible. They'd even let him know why Eftah was here, in the car. The big clansman had his eyes on Risto, but he kept his door shut, his window up. Farther downhill there might be some sign of the cop on the bicycle. All of it seemed roughly as plausible as filming a movie in the back of an illegal dance club. But then, the man who'd told Risto about that hadn't been thinking straight either, not when he'd sat upright in the full glare of the high-beams, arms spread. Papers couldn't have made an easier target if he'd painted on a bull's eye.

Uphill and down, everything Risto laid eyes on seemed to beg for explanation. Still, he'd lost his shivers. He'd lost the need to shout, and he could leave the rest to Emergency Services. They knew the drill, when one of the boat people failed to make it to shore.

SIX

How light the sky was. Evenings this summer seemed to carry on as if midnight would never arrive. Maybe it had to do with the earthquake, the volcano's sulfuric exhale. Or maybe Risto ought to consider the eye of the beholder. To a man who's almost gotten himself killed, any sky might radiate like God.

After Eftah came out and hoisted him up, for a while Risto let his head loll back like a junkie on a nod. His clansman's cologne took him to twilight on the rooftop in Materdei. Here above the treetops, the sky seemed lush, loamy; he thought of Eftah lighting an after-dinner spliff. The way his feet ached, it could be from dancing.

But that last glimpse of Papers—that he should've avoided. What was left of the man had been laid out flat, a ripple of shadow and high-beam intensity. He was a desert escarpment, a landscape for the city he'd boasted of building.

Risto fell into sobs, though even bawling into Eftah's shirt, he couldn't fail to notice the kidnappers' Fiat. Its driver's door wide open, it stood nose to nose on the maintenance road with a larger vehicle. The cavalry had come in an Audi, it turned out. Della Figurazione was the one who showed him, steering his two civilians back downhill. They had a family vehicle with a bike rack, an actual backseat, and a first-aid kit. Risto found the blue ice and got it up into his armpit, and once they were off the bumpy maintenance road, his return became ordinary. Under the passing streetlights, he came back to himself enough to notice that Eftah had gone wordless, withdrawn, his forehead against the tinted window. Risto tried a simple question or two—hello?—but the only ear he caught was Della Figurazione's. The detective lifted his eyes to the rearview and,

right there at the wheel, got in some police work. He asked about the
I.D., the gun, the accomplice. Apparently the dealer's backup had simply
hightailed it, fleeing into the brush as soon as the cops loomed up on the
forest road. With the hostage so close, the police weren't going to waste
time on another footloose illegal.

Risto managed only half-answers, but they seemed like enough.
Della Figurazione looked instead to Eftah. Any ideas, he asked, where
the accomplice had gone?

"Ahh," continued the detective, after a while. "After all, it was you
who told us where they'd be hiding."

"It was you," said Risto. "You knew that neck of the woods."

"Your—your cousin made an educated guess."

The larger CI remained absent, his only response a thirsty pull
at his mouth. Around them, the edge-of-town gridlock had the Audi
inching along. Ordinarily Eftah would've taken this opportunity to
boast: *the Black Lord knows every strand in the Silk Road.* But it was
Risto who took up the slack; he wanted to hear about the detective's
watch. "Two-faced," he asked, "what's that about?"

"Signore." Della Figurazione made sure Risto saw he was frowning. "You think I'd fail to catch your inference?"

The piece was no Forzieri, he explained, rather a knockoff out of
the Forcella. "More than that," he went on, "it was a gift from my
former wife. Ahh, two-faced—now that I think about, that may fit the
case after all."

Anyway, the detective had another gadget on his mind. His CI's
cell phone, he admitted, had proven useless as a locator.

"Entirely useless, Signore El Queer. Our latest technology!"

Risto turned one hand over wearily. "I don't see why you believe
such tall tales."

"The phones work for the CIA, don't they? Out hunting down
terrorists?"

"Eh. I'd rather trust a man like Eftah here."

"Indeed. Our own Marco Polo."

But Eftah never joined in, his face to the traffic crawl. All the way
down from the park, Risto heard nothing but a murmur. Something

like "miserable holes"? Only at the uphill border of the *centro* did the clansman at last speak up.

"Anywhere here's fine." He sat up. "Thanks. I can manage."

He added that he'd keep his phone on, in case they needed him "at the precinct or whatever." Then with another pull at his mouth, Eftah at last began to sound like himself.

"Most nights," he said, "you know, my technology is old school. It's altogether astonishing. Some stranger whispers in my ear, some perfect stranger, and I'll let him take me to the ends of the earth."

"*Abba*." Risto grinned through his sore spots. "You were so lost in space, I didn't think you heard us."

The clansman didn't smile. "Outer space, oh my—you mean like where we sent that poor bastard's ghost? You saw it, Risto, didn't you? His ghost or soul or whatever."

He didn't appear at all concerned about the cop up front.

"As if a yellow handkerchief lifted off his face and floated away."

Della Figurazione made a big production of parking, muttering first out one window and then the other.

"Up at the hole, Risto, didn't you see it? Oh my, I certainly did, and I thought I was all done with that. Watching a man die, up in those miserable holes—tonight took me all the way back."

"Eftah."

"Watching a brother float away. Witness to the migration of the soul. The soul, the aura, whatever...."

Risto swabbed his face with the hand wet from blue ice. "*Abba*, it's on my conscience too."

"Conscience? Dear boy, the sins I carry, that poor bastard's the least of it. Our late friend up there, all things considered, he got what he deserved."

The officer was throwing an occasional glance in the rearview.

"But your clansman's conscience is nothing so pretty as yours. It's nothing nearly so pretty as what you saw tonight, either, that floating shred of yellow."

"Eftah." Two could play at this game, Ignore the White Man. "Whatever I saw, you sound as if you don't need me to tell you."

"Why should I, cousin, when it's in the DNA?"

Risto tried his cold fingers on his forehead, where he'd hit the dealer.

"It's something in the Hawaii or whatever we're called," Eftah went on. "In the sachems of the clan. They had a name for it, 'the Eye,' something like that."

"They could—they could see things?"

Eftah snorted. "Yes, I suppose that's what we'd call it, 'seeing things.' The whole notion has become a joke."

Out the window Risto saw dinner preparations, a woman trotting by with a bag of bread. Could it still be so early? "The clan and their *kuragura*," he tried, "we never wanted any part of..."

"Wanted? Did I say I *wanted* this, a glimpse of a brother as he departed his skin? You know there are millions of us now, over here, and every day who knows how many, who knows—every day, some go drifting off out of their African skin."

The detective had taken his parking performance as far as he could. "Signore Eftah," he said, "we are grateful for your help. I speak for the entire department."

"Cousin," Eftah went on, "the things in our brown skin, my my my."

"You have a safe walk home, Signore."

"But tonight I got a reminder, inside us there's this too—this heritage." His gaze had hardened. "And I thought I was all done with that."

Risto couldn't believe he was getting worked up again. "The Eye, they called it."

"Yes, cousin, and then I think of yesterday, when you were up in my front hall. When you couldn't take your eyes off my photos. Isn't that the real question?"

Thickset and gladrag'd, the two fell into such a staring silence that their driver began to scold. Such mumbo jumbo, *per carita!* The last thing anyone needed tonight!

"Just yesterday," said Eftah, "you were up there, and you couldn't get enough of those photos. What on earth did you see? Isn't that the larger question?"

Do I need to warn you, barked the detective, *about flashbacks? Night sweats?*

To Risto, it felt as if he at last had half a clue. Eftah's news had nothing to do with Friday night and La Cia, or with Tuttavia or bad porn or for that matter Paola. Nevertheless it felt like such a help. Insofar as Risto was the lead investigator on this case, at last he'd got a handle on the craziest part. As he and his clansman huddled, confirming they'd talk tomorrow, he found himself astonishingly worked up. Some of this had to be sheer giddiness, wrung out as he was...

Della Figurazione had lowered the windows and, swinging out of the car, stuck his head in Eftah's. *Enough!*

✖

The man from Homicide wasn't done yet. While Eftah headed off, the detective came around to his other CI's window. His tone didn't soften, though he raised a different warning. This kind of talk, about what they'd done this evening—it needed to end right here.

Risto kept his eyes on his clansman, disappearing, almost jogging.

"My friend," said the officer, "do we understand each other? That gallery of yours, the only item it's selling is the three monkeys."

Eh, as for evil, Risto had seen and heard enough for one night. Making assurances, putting away the blue ice, he claimed he didn't need an actual hospital. Why bother? At a full-service facility, the kind of place where Paola's father did his chest-cracking, there'd be no end of paperwork. Risto should be fine with one of the temporary care centers, the clinics set up post-quake by the Red Cross and the U.N.

Most of these were downtown, where it'd been easy to convert some abandoned palazzo. He'd be closer to home. What's more, he knew of one that would appeal to Della Figurazione. A place that specialized in psychological care, no doubt including flashbacks and night-sweats.

After Risto directed the officer to the clinic, however, he found his own worst damage was physical. He needed the other man's arm just to walk the final block, one of those old-city capillaries. He could've drowned in the urban marinade of sulfur, sweat, and olive oil on simmer. The good Eftah had done him floated away like a veil. Nevertheless, he liked the setup, the Cabinet of Dr. Caligari. This was where he'd

brought Yebleh. Fifteen months ago now, the watercolorist had first
gotten lost in the European candy store. His worst relapse had come
after the quake, the unstable tectonics somehow going straight to the
kid's head. For detox and a stretch of group work, the gallery owner
had preferred an option less visible than one of the hilltop sanatoriums.
This stopgap down by the waterfront looked nothing like a hospital,
a three-story palazzo that over the centuries had barnacled: a crooked
house for people who'd gotten bent.

Here Yebleh could work with others like himself—and Risto could
count on discretion. The doctor in charge was older, with a goatee
more salt than pepper and a well-worn saint's medallion; he was comfortable with private arrangements.

Tonight, after the detective handed him over, Risto seemed to slip
back up onto some viewing screen. He looked nothing like the arts
impresario who'd visited previously, making arrangements for a troubled client. Rather he was a flop-creature out of a cartoon, needing an
intern just to make it down the hall and out of his sticky clothes. After
that came the slapstick of getting up onto a padded table. As for the
intern with the strong hands, the lavender-scented sponge—could that
have been two interns, or an intern and a therapist? Who gave Risto
the fat ibuprofen, six hundred milligrams? Each time he came out of
doze, he stared up at a different smock. He couldn't be sure which
of them assured him his wounds didn't amount to much. Abrasions,
contusions, nothing more. The worst was up where he felt it, under
the left armpit, and as for his mottled forehead and torn eyebrow, one
doctor or whatever tried to make a joke. He said the patient "might
scare a few people."

At that Risto had his first clear thought: a lot of folks wouldn't
notice anything but the skin tone.

Also the clinic had a recliner of comfy vinyl built into a shower
closet, a rig designed for invalids. The disinfectant wash, the strokes
of the loofah, called to mind yesterday with his wife, and he either
got a brief erection or dreamed it. He couldn't say what became of his
carnival-colored pullover. The new shirt they gave him, the clean white
button-down, felt feathery against his ribs and just his size.

Dumbfounded, he stared at the intern who'd helped him put it on. She was another bewilderment, a good-looking young American who'd probably seen him naked. Had she been the one with the loofah? Risto was grateful she felt chatty, explaining in excellent Italian that the earthquake had brought her to town. She was part of the international relief effort, from one of those states that sounded Arab, Al'a- or Ak'a-something. Next thing he knew, she had him back on the table, getting a foot massage. She had him zoning out again, and when he came to they'd been joined by a third, a man. He too came from out of town, Venice it sounded like, and the doctor on duty, *il medico*. Okay, but was he here to examine the girl? Risto's wear and tear didn't prevent him from noticing how often the doc gave the American a touch: her arm, her shoulder, even her waist. Not that he didn't also take time with the patient. The way he laid hands on the African's head, you'd think he could read the stubble like Braille.

The Venetian went so far as to use the word "miracle." Risto understood that this was another play for the girl, lending intensity to their time together. Still, he was in no position to argue, *Aristofano fortunato*.

Later, when Tuttavia came to collect him, she too showed a kindness. She didn't ask why he'd given the cops her number. She waited till he came out of his latest snooze and, while he still lay yawning and goofy, asked if he wanted more painkiller.

To swing upright set off a drip in the back of his mouth. Elsewhere too, soreness jutted through his new wellbeing. All right, Tuttavia, another six hundred milligrams, thanks. The woman cracked a grin, assuring him he'd "sleep like a boss." As for footwear, the clinic kept a couple of boxes handy, sneakers, slip-ons. The design dated back to the last round of Death Chic, white skulls on black canvas, and as Risto searched for a pair that fit over his bandaged toe, he saw the brand was American by way of Korea. They'd made a donation off the Discontinued shelves, doing what they could for the shattered metropolis—just as a few folks in town expected of his star client, here. There were movers and shakers in town who claimed Tuttavia was the essential player in the *Expo*. At Wind & Confusion, if they enjoyed a comeback fall, she'd have everything to do with it. Now Risto had got her alone, playing nurse. His best chance to talk.

As she and Risto left the downtown clinic, Tuttavia got a good stretch beneath a streetlight. Her long skier's body recalled a shot of her in heels and stockings.

Once they'd settled into her SmartCar, he tried a small joke: "Tuttavia drives!"

She gestured as if to shoo a fly, bracelets rattling.

"A hybrid, too," he went on. "So bourgeois."

"But, what, *Il Signore* objects? I came to you on a mission of mercy. A hybrid was the best they could give me."

The city's car-sharing service had trouble holding onto their fleet. As fast as they put in new security, the hotwire types figured ways around it.

"I see they gave it to you freshly charged," he said. "The gas gauge is flat."

"A small consolation."

Hating to drive went along with the other clichés of The Temperament. *Mercurial, high-strung*—she checked all the boxes. Even the scar under her hair. Come to think, an Italian driver's license threw her so off balance, the woman would probably jump at the chance of cutting short tonight's trip, and there was the gelateria just down the block from the gallery.

Without a watch or phone, he had to check the dashboard clock. He had to make it sound like part of the treatment, "something sweet, an indulgence," meanwhile calculating that it'd be best to sit outdoors. The chatter and traffic would prevent folks from overhearing, and prevent Tuttavia from going all Shiva the Destroyer.

"*Ragazzo*," she told him, "it's all right. You and I need to talk anyway."

※

Inside the shop, the rectangular buckets of gelato called to mind a colorful array of paddles, just the thing for a man about to deliver a spanking. But she had to pay—the only money he'd had on him since lunch was police-issue. Nonetheless he lingered before the cashier, discomfited, till Tuttavia suggested he find them a table. The lights in here, she said, were so damn *bright*. Risto got the point, the others here saw nothing but Black, and outside he put himself through a fresh medical exam. Should he rethink this sitdown? After the trauma and the shock—rethink? He'd already been warned about keeping his mouth shut.

Still, he had the breeze off the waterfront and the pick-me-up of a fresh *limone*. The first spoonful set off sparklers, and he almost missed Tuttavia's first question.

"Tomorrow," he managed. "Tomorrow, Ippolita and I put the show up."

Opening his eyes, he confronted the same as before: Florence Nightingale on the Lower East Side. For a minute she stuck to business, the promotional postcard and the guest list. Then Tuttavia fingered up a Lucky and told him something surprising.

"My man, honestly: this feels like my last set of photographs."

"What?"

"My last show in flat work. It's...I've felt this before. Everything starts to shift."

She touched her fingertips to the V of her collar. "I know it when I feel it, the fresh energy arriving, and I've got to respect it."

"You can feel it," he said. "Everything starts to shift."

"That's my man. It's like I'm his sister. He's all about the fresh energy."

Risto's frown took effort.

"*Amico*, okay, maybe I should've saved this. I wondered about that, you know, the timing. You do look like could use a week on the beach."

He spooned up more ice and reminded her he had a lido reserved in Agropoli. "But that's after the opening. Tonight, you're right to let me know."

She nodded. "Yes exactly, because, besides, think, if I'm feeling the energy shift, isn't it a sympathetic vibration? You know what I mean—a shift across all of Europe, old and sick Europe? People everywhere can feel the tremors."

She was sounding so much like Papers, Risto was glad the only thing in her hand was the Lucky Strike.

"But you and my Wind & Confusion family, you and all my brothers, we're at Ground Zero."

Risto had to remind himself that he'd heard this kind of talk long before he'd been a hostage in a cave. He'd heard it often: an artist with maybe fifteen friends, with one gallery and half a degree, would make claims for the future of the world. Painter, photographer, whatever, this person would see their work as a watershed. The next pieces to emerge from their studio would upend the culture of the Continent. Or why stop there? Why, just because they only spoke one language, or maybe one-point-five? The artist was forging fresh embodiments for whatever was noblest across all Europe and America. Yes, and in the former colonies to boot. In the Gobi Desert of contemporary culture, his was the richest caravan—the lifesaver.

Visions of grandeur, a shrink might say, but no problem for a gallery owner. Risto could handle the mythmaking, harmless by and large. Nine times out of ten, these "creatives" saw their efforts come to nothing, so why not let them talk?

All right: Tuttavia's fairytale.

Our heroine, having burst into flame, illuminated others who could no longer be confined to screens and boxes. The commodity that hangs on a wall was no shape for this hour of the world. These days, rather, the impulse sweeping across oceans and mountains was toward installation and performance. In far-off lower Manhattan, there'd sprung up like-minded irregulars, the musicians of No Wave and the Ontological-Hysteric Theater. These had won fame and even profit, as had other master hands in this developing medium, in the abandoned Soviet factories of Berlin, in the deconsecrated nunneries of Paris, and in all the webbed corners of cyberspace.

And didn't this bode well for a revolution along the ancient Mediterranean? Here in Naples, if a woman of great gifts broke free of two dimensions, of black-&-white, wouldn't she erupt as a catalyst for the New Order? Here the movement would establish its appeal amid the ruin of an earthquake, bringing the lordliest patrons down from their palaces and into an Old City perhaps three-fifths ruin to begin with. Here, to reverse the crumbling was to breathe life into a radical dream. It was to forge a stronghold out of wind and confusion.

Tuttavia, waggling her cigarette, added that she and Risto made perfect leaders for the new movement. "Perfect for the new art, in a new millennium, in a *Nea Polis*."

Actually, thought Risto, the millennium's not so new anymore.

"We're two outsiders," she went on, "two refugees, on the run from oppression."

Risto sucked on his spoon. "Oppression, eh." Maybe it was time to risk mention of her past. "Look, what you're going through, what do you call it, it's a sea change. But, another time, you've told me, you went from painting to photography." And hadn't she mentioned some mentor up at the Conservatory...?

Briefly Tuttavia had trouble sorting her gelato from her smoke.

"But what's that *disgusting* old man got to do with this? Whatever I told you, Risto, truly I don't remember. To me he's just another dead white male."

"You—you know he's dead?"

"He deserves to be." A wrist rattle. "But, I ask you, what's he got to do with *this*? Risto, *I'm* alive, isn't that what matters?"

The question raised an unexpected chill: the cold of the cave up in Capodimonte. What'd it been, three hours? And he'd taken himself out on a gelato run?

No backing out now, though, not with Tuttavia in top gear. "*Tomb* frescoes," she barked. "Is that what you want for Wind & Confusion? The real question is whether the *gallery's* alive."

Risto checked the tables nearby, needing no magic to read minds: Mandingo & the Maiden! Al Qaeda in La Chiaia! Laughable stuff, but it kept him on task, trying to pick his way between what Paola had told him and Eftah had shown him. Already he'd seen how the mention of Tuttavia's former Master brought out her claws.

"Risto." She exhaled noisily but spoke more quietly. "All I'm saying is, my camera and computer, they're like boxes that make boxes. They're too confining."

He nodded, scraping up the last of his *dolce*.

"Have you noticed my show features a dead man?"

He nodded.

"Yes, and I mean, isn't it a sign? To capture La Cia in my box, and then the next thing I know, to see him laid out in a box? I couldn't have asked for a better sign that my old line of work was over and done with. It's up in the sky and written in *gold!* It's the epitaph: 'R.I.P., the culture of documentary commodity.'"

She stubbed out her Lucky so it remained upright, a tombstone. Risto figured, okay, she'd brought it up. He might as well corroborate the latest he'd heard, and he asked about the movie. Friday night, in the back of the club somewhere?

"I imagine," he said, "it was some sort of sex show."

"My man. My *Renaissance* Man. Who told you that?"

Oh, a guy who had about ninety seconds left, before he wound up in a box. But the woman answered her own question. Tuttavia figured Risto had heard something from his clansman, though she hadn't seen Eftah around that night.

"That'll happen." Risto tried to sound like a man of the world. "At a club like that, it's not hard to slip in and out unseen."

The way she waved off his playing detective, she must've known. "*Ragazzo*, look, something else. I have to ask. What does Eftah tell you about my sex life?"

Sticky-fingered, he touched his forehead's sore spot.

"I mean, if he was there that night, and he knew about the movie..."

"Tuttavia, come on. The man's the only family I've got left."

"Risto, truly—I just want to know whether there's talk."

Again he wondered about the white folks nearby. "Talk, eh. No, not..."

"No, sure, that's what I thought. That's what Giussi does for me. The cover he provides, the camouflage—he's the perfect partner in crime."

Lighting a fresh cigarette, Tuttavia moved on into "the other thing I wanted to tell you." The other whopping surprise, she must've thought. "My man, it's time you knew: I do have a sex life."

She was, in fact, "more of a Siren than a nun." As for the shipwrecks at her feet, she'd always been careful to hide those. "But if I'd never been with *anyone*, I mean, what would I have been doing with myself? I've lived down South for, what is it, seven and a half years now?"

She must've thought the news would floor him—while also proving her larger point. "Risto, don't you see, I've always been about the performance? The *persona*? Playing the virgin made for such a fine story."

The Saint Inviolate in the Whorehouse: this proved our heroine's magnum opus. Skillfully she maintained the illusion, taking care that her quarters never served as more than a monk's cell, a space reserved for contemplation and prayer. The libido preferred to go feral, nosing out a lair where you'd least expect one, around this rattletrap of a metropolis. Also the woman observed certain limits; she indulged, if not rarely, not frequently. A Warrior Artist mustn't sink to the level of the profligate, and must never lose sight of the aesthetics. Thus her spasm of ecstasy was always followed by a vicious sneer, and her partners were never permitted to entertain the possibility of lasting affection. *Boyfriend*? The word was anathema, another false idol, and so too *girlfriend*, since when this Valkyrie ushered in the Twilight of the Gods, she didn't hesitate to ravish a few victims born with the same genitals as she. To take another woman in a sybaritic embrace lent still greater explosiveness to her private acts of terror, and anyway what mattered wasn't what a lover had between the legs, a scepter or a purse. What mattered was the terror, smashing every icon in the Temple of Love. The act you might call "love," she never extended beyond the evening in question, and the people you might call "lovers" were never accorded the honor of appearing in a picture.

"Or not till this latest batch," said Tuttavia.

Her smoking was nothing if not stage business, all wands and veils.

"This latest—I mean, who could I tell if not you? This set includes one of the people I've been with. For once I made an exception."

Risto shifted in his seat, cupping his injured foot in one hand.

"But if you think I'll tell you which, *ragazzo*, you haven't been listening."

Some crimes, he reminded himself, lay outside his jurisdiction.

"So I've stunned you into silence? You never saw me this way? You saw a woman with a halo around her head."

"The woman I saw," said Risto, "I called the Italian Mapplethorpe."

"Ah, and that was great to read, my man." Tuttavia kept her smile serious. "But it was years ago, Risto, and for this latest I had to try something new. I had to experiment. That's why I put one of my lovers in the frame."

"Eh. At least it was a man."

Dropping her head, fingering first her gelato cup and then her pack of Luckies, Tuttavia looked like a chess player. She didn't respond to his poke, the suggestion she knew something, speaking instead of how she'd "picked up the bisexual option." She'd been on the road, making her way down from the Baltic, "and it was a hard time. You understand, Risto—the things they make you do."

Her eyes rose to his, almost a glare, and he hoped he showed some kindness in return. "Look," he tried, "a shop like mine—if half the people coming in the door aren't bisexual, I'm out of business."

She snorted and grinned, fishing out a fresh smoke. Okay: "Then there's Giussi," he said. "'Strange bedfellows,' isn't that one of his *Tempest* things?"

If she joined the performer onstage, Risto pointed out, she could count on some of that. "A pantomime fuck, that's practically his stock in trade. Come to think," he added mildly, "I believe Giussi's done porn."

Tuttavia studied her bracelets, making some adjustment in the fit.

"You called him your partner in crime," he continued. "I believe that's what Paola called him too."

"Paola? Talking about me?"

Enough with the pussyfooting around. Briskly Risto revealed what he'd seen, all fifteen slides, and he ID'd the man behind the camera as well. The one detail he left out, for the time being at least, was Eftah's name.

But Tuttavia sagged back unfazed, over a dangling cigarette.

※

So, the night's actual surprise: with Fidel, she'd expected no less. She'd figured he'd get the pictures out, and she'd worked up her story.

The Philistine, the Nemesis—the very magnetized plastic he bran-
dishes in place of cash makes a right-on analogy for his utter lack of
dimension and vacant sheen. Indeed, the name embossed on that card,
that noble patronymic—oughtn't it topple first in any revolution? Was
there any other Golden Calf that bawled so loudly for smashing? Indeed,
the creature's obliteration bore out the nobility of the artist who brought
it down, exposing its hideous bovine lineaments. To kill the beast, however, a hunter had to be cunning, baiting its prey with flattery. As the
Money Monster preened, the saboteur had to murmur sweet nothings,
until at last the dunderhead flaunted his vanity before a multitude and
revealed to the world he was the worst sort of fraud. What higher calling
existed, for the true artist, than to bring the counterfeit to light?

Risto broke in. "You mean to tell me this was some kind of political act?"

"*Amico*, but, haven't you been listening? What I said about the
Ontologic-Hysterics? Or think of Madonna, *la Signore Ciccione*—it's
political every time she takes her clothes off."

She'd worked up her story. Only someone who knew her would
notice how the occasional word veered toward a shriek.

"Madonna, all the skin she's exposed over the years, it was always a
statement. The personal is political. And when Giussi calls me his wife,
Risto, it's not just a joke."

The performance artist, she declared proudly, had come to her as
soon as Fidel made his suggestion. "He knew I'd jump at the opportunity."

To Risto, the opportunity seemed to be Giussi's. The man made
his living pretending, after all, with more than a few stage bits about
love and deceit. Didn't matter what color the other person might be,
or what their politics were. One of the performer's richest riffs took off
from his hookup with a struggling black writer in Paris. *An oppressed
American Negro,* so Giussi described him, *oh la la, one of those who styles
himself a spokesman for the race.* Their hijinks, claimed the Ethiopian,
had provided the basis for a novel. *Except the brother turned me into
a white boy! An Italian waiter!* At that, Giussi dialed up the Flaming
Queen. *I've never been so insulted in my life!*

"Right away," said Tuttavia, "I saw how we'd play this, Giussi and I."

They'd be jesters giving the Queen a tumble, bowling over the Old Regime. Risto strove to look amused. He hadn't forgotten the strangers on all sides, for whom it'd be best if the African and his date came off as sophisticates. A pair of hipsters posed no threat. Besides, Tuttavia had begun to talk like a therapist. Fidel's young wife, she claimed, "could use the self-assertion."

Is that what you'd call it, *amica*? Zelusa had taken the triple-X act more seriously, anyone could see. "She got carried away," said Risto.

"She owned her pleasure. An essential step in coming to own herself."

The language of the coddled North, yes: Tuttavia spoke it fluently. She wore the protective coloration of the bourgeois even when the whole point of her portfolio was épater le bourgeois. The contradictions she lived with, whew. *Il Mattino* had called her "the patron saint of the *clandestini*," and every show drew a reference to Frantz Fanon and *Wretched of the Earth*. Yet here she sat, white as a Lapplander.

Then her tone shifted. "My man," she asked, "I mean, don't you realize what's happening with Fidel? Haven't you noticed he's running out of money?"

Risto's frown poked into his bruises.

"We've noticed, certainly—Giussi and I and all the creatures of the night."

Naturally: if a guy could slip through the Little Window, he could count the cash in a wallet open as often as Fidel's. The goony bird got a shakedown every time he heard of a new playspace. He paid just to get the address. After that, he had to spring for the premium vodka and sit at the high-stakes table. Soon enough the strangers around him knew the truth; they could see it just in the way he fingered his remaining bills. Still, Fidel would go on playing the sugar daddy so long as the bowl held a single snow-white grain. With the person closest to him, his life remained make-believe.

"It's an old story, Risto, isn't it? You've seen the brands he's got that girl wearing. Ha, wearing—and not wearing!"

He remained unsmiling. "I have some idea. Ippolita tells me there's talk."

"And he's still taking her to places like Hermès and Gucci! Where all the shopgirls, think of it, they're the living embodiment of the Fag Hag. They're the myth come to life, and if they've got some juicy gossip, plus a friend like Giussi..."

Lately rumor had it that one of the most prestigious Castelsabbia assets had gone on the market. "That office space in the Galleria? Top story, great light, great location?"

Tonight, he wondered, which of them was getting the spanking? "He put that place on the market?"

"You know Giussi. He's got friends among the suits, too, the bankers."

"You're saying, Tuttavia, you're saying..."

With a slash of her Lucky: "I'm saying the same as always. Our little performance was a political act. That goes for Zelusa too—Zelusa especially, planting a bomb in her Candyman's camera."

"For her too, it was all about taking down the ofay."

"I mean, the big lug showed you the photos, didn't he? The man couldn't help himself. What does that tell you about his stunted imagination?"

Also the show had further drained Fidel's pocketbook. The performers had insisted on top-of-the-line equipment, "nothing you could pick up over in the Forcella," and a studio setting. "That's why he took us up to his space in the Galleria." They'd found the offices barren, without so much as a desk. "And isn't that another of those burning signs in the sky?"

She scribbled in the sky, her arm up, her cleavage. That white shirt might've been another tub of gelato, and it had men to either side ignoring theirs. But then, Risto's client always had guys staring. With her charisma, she'd command a second glance and a third long after that babydoll Zelusa aged into invisibility.

"Anyway, Risto, people've been calling me a voyeur since my first show."

"So, this weekend. You don't mind if there's talk."

His star client might queen it up, here at the gelateria, but it wasn't as if the conversation hadn't taken a toll. Wasn't as if Risto never saw her shake off a chill. Now she returned quietly to Zelusa, wondering how the *Expo* event would feel for that girl. She admitted that Fidel's little trophy had been "eager for corruption. Odd, isn't it, the pleasure in that? The invitation to corrupt?"

But no sooner did she falter than she caught herself. "But then— why give an artist an opposable thumb, if she's not supposed to grope about in the passions?"

He found himself staring at his own thumb, brown over a pink palm. He was the wrong color for this country, and you'd think that alone would be enough of a challenge.

"It's not as if Giussi and I sought to corrupt that child. It's not as if our charade did her no good. Zelusa owned her pleasure."

What's more, while Tuttavia and Giussi had demanded substantial payment, in cash, she'd passed hers along to *'O Pappace*, The Worm in the Apple. This outfit offered whatever it could to the immigrants and *clandestini*. "It could be I paid a month's rent for some brother just off the boat."

Risto went on staring into his hand. "Look—I've been wondering if I ought to cancel the show."

For the first time that night, he heard the nervous rattle of her bracelets.

"*Mais non,*" she said finally, "*jamais, pourquoi fais comme ça?*" Her French had that Conservatory polish. "Risto, I mean, Friday night's important. It marks a boundary."

"For me too, a kind of deadline."

"*Alors, mon vieux, pourquoi?* Truly! You think this would be for *my* benefit?"

"What I think—I think that you and Giussi could matter so much. You two together, you could be the future of the North."

"My man. You're a philosopher. But that sounds to me like all the more reason to hold the show."

When he raised his eyes, she waved away the smoke between them.

"The show's a killer. It's my last flatwork, and I'm going out at the top, *vraiment*. As for the other photos, that klutz Fidel's, they'll dwindle to nothing in no time."

Whatever lift his *limone* had given him was gone now. "Eh, Giussi. Those photos, it was Giussi who sent them around."

The way Tuttavia seized up, you'd think she'd caught something in her throat. But Risto was done with diplomacy: he laid out everything he knew about the slideshow. There was what he'd seen, where he'd seen it, and what his wife had helped him understand. It didn't amount to much, really, a minute of uninterrupted talk, and yet as Risto finished his ears were singing. The blood rush was intense as back in the cave. It rocked him, his plastic chair complaining: the relief of honest dealing at last. As for the eruption across the table, afterwards, he couldn't make out much of it. Tuttavia went straight from gaping to shouting—ululating, the Siren in full cry—but Risto heard nothing but the usual profanity. The worst of it was in the woman's face anyway, pinched in the vise of her hiked-up shoulders. She'd sprung to her feet, the cups and spoons between them jumping.

Still, wasn't this why he'd stopped here? To get closer to the whole truth? As for the tantrum, Paola would've predicted worse.

Neither he nor his wife, however, had figured on an audience. These dozen or fifteen others around Risto had seemed to him, instead, a security measure. All these nice white folks would keep a lid on his Gallery Diva. No such luck, though; she'd gone off as if to start a race war. Now Risto was getting it from all sides, threats from down in the throat, nasty growls. These folks had paid for table service. If any of them spotted his bruises, they figured these were from last night's rape. What else could've set off this lean Nordic looker across the table? Just look at her, spitting imprecations! In another moment a man close by had swung to his feet, and the clatter of plasticware seemed to promise that Risto would get hit again.

But no one sent so much plastic tumbling as his date. Tuttavia grabbed him by the same arm Papers had, making him yelp. How could he not have known she had such a grip? She put her whole body into it, gaining energy from his pain, breaking into a gutty laugh as she yanked the African up and away. Every move made clear she didn't need help. It was a wonder she left the table standing, her free arm waving off interference, her shouting no-nonsense. Maybe these also revealed a note of betrayal, wounding and betrayal, but no one heard it except her hostage. Risto kept his head down and allowed her to roughhouse him all the way back to their Napoli-Ride.

She was still going to drive him home, though he figured this had little to do with any sense of obligation. Her first words, strangling the steering wheel: "The Miss-suss."

"Tuttavia, you chose this. This city, this..." He was worn to gristle.

"And you're telling me he sent the photos just to people of color?"

Risto palmed his scalp, shrugging.

"People of color, and men only—that was the mailing list."

"You knew what you were dealing with. Eh, Giussi. A guy like that, he's a two-edged sword. I'm sure he's told you all my secrets."

Did she need a break? She'd had enough of the She-Monster? Lowering a window, Tuttavia admitted she knew all about "your little game of Clue." With a sigh, she confirmed the latest about the night La Cia was killed: the movie in the back. "As for a snuff film, I mean, that makes as much sense as anything else. That night had an edge on it, Camorra in the crowd, Camorra girls."

"You could tell? In the dark, the confusion?"

"Risto, women like that, they'll talk to me. They'll let me take a shot. Besides, to see the damage they can do, it doesn't take a detective."

He managed a laugh, airless, and then: "The truth is, I'm all through with that. I'm done trying to figure it out."

If the woman was catching a breather, she continued to bristle. "What? Done? *Amico*, till you came along, nobody on the police even knew the victim's name."

"Eh, maybe." But now Homicide was giving the case honest attention, he went on, and as for anything else, "Tuttavia, it's just been a lot of bad comedy."

With each repetition, the decision built up ballast. "Look, I was a kid trying to do the job of a grownup. The real mystery is why I had to get so involved in the first place."

Her shoulders were clenched once more. "*Per carita*, it's one letdown after another tonight."

Risto found himself exasperated. "You're saying Giussi and I, we both hurt you the same?"

She shook her head. "I'm saying you were doing some good, Risto, a bit of good at least for the people I'm trying to help myself. And then you just quit! I mean, I guess that's not so bad as Giussi, all of a sudden my goddamn *pimp*..."

"Tuttavia, I ask you again. Should we cancel Friday?"

She shook her head harder.

"You realize I'll be there as the gallery owner? Not the Protector of the *Clandestini*, not the Conscience of the Police."

White-knuckled, she braked at his front stoop.

"Giussi's going to be there too. The same hot mess as ever."

She wouldn't look at him, rummaging again for a cigarette, muttering. "Lying bastard thinks he *owns* me..."

※

You reach a certain corner, a certain hour, and you wish you could monitor a friend's blood levels—her need-for-blood levels. Does she plan to hurt anybody? Get out the knife? That's the last thing you need, and so you come up with something *simpatico*. You do her a kindness, not exactly a lie, saying you'll pass along her hellos to your wife.

"Hello" was the least of what Risto intended to share, naturally. Even as he climbed to his place, he was weighing how much he could say, in the call to Agropoli. Then once he was out of his death's-head sneakers, the cool marble and ticklish night air had him leaving the lights off, feeling his way toward the phone. He bulled past the pop-up image of his kidnapper, Papers with his head in a corona, and tried to shake off the buzz between his ears. If he'd ever been in such a state, it was back during his nights on the run, poking along some borderlands for an unwatched cranny or cruising a hotel lobby for some guy who wanted a stroke.

Okay, his phone, his own this time, fully recharged. Also his balcony, the wash of streetlight and sea odor, the occasional rising notes of chatter. A family or two was still out on their *passagiata*. As for Risto's family, the "recent calls" readout told him Paola had checked in at just about the time he put Tuttavia's name on the police form. Her voicemail sounded breezy. No need for Risto-ri to call back, his wife said, no blowups over Grandpa or trouble with stinging jellyfish. Risto winced at the reminder. Last August, Rosa had spent three days with her foot in such bad shape, the pediatrician had looked into a seaborne form of rabies.

The husband hit Reply. His son picked up.

"Tonino! *Big* boy!"

He was loud, yet collapsing. Dropping into the lounge, his throat knotted, it took him several moments just to understand that Paola was outside having a cigarette.

"A—a cigarette?" The father faked a cough and, pawing at one eye, stroked a freshly soaked bruise. "You tell her for me she's a wicked woman."

Again he didn't catch Tonino's response, and he choked on his initial attempt at an answer. He wound up telling the boy that he didn't need to fetch his mother. Wasn't it better like this, man to man? And from where Risto lay, wasn't that a good strategy for what, all of sudden, it occurred to him to ask? Insofar as he had a strategy, there with the long day surging through him as if the balcony were full of hash smoke...

The son was answering the father before he realized he'd asked a question.

"...Rosa fell asleep... Mama was in the middle of telling her a story, and...What? Papa, what, when...? Our *babysitter*?"

Risto concentrated. "But Tonino, weren't you the one who told me? Once when our friend Tuttavia was your sitter, she threatened you with a knife."

"Papa, *what*?"

"She threatened you with a knife. Tuttavia, while Mama was out of the house."

"Pa-pa, I don't get it. Tuttavia, she likes to flick water on us. She gets her fingers wet and flicks water on us, yeah. You have to watch her."

"So she never threatened you with a knife?"

"A knife? What game is that?"

The boy's responses kept him in focus, or nearly. At least he could acknowledge his skulking, his crabwise ploy. The older child had his fantasies, his Antonius the Gladiator, but of the kids he was the more straightforward. He had the harder head.

"Papa, what game is that? A knife?"

"You know," the father said, "when Mama was shaken up." Paola was well out of earshot; she snuck her smokes on the other side of the grape arbor. "She got frightened and dropped a bottle of wine."

"Oh, the wine, that was something, yeah. That splashed so much, even the next day I could smell it off my sword."

"The sword? You were playing Gladiator?"

"We had a *game*. I had the sword and Tuttavia was flicking water."

Risto looked up at the spatter of the smogged night sky. Between those stars you had the satellites' ricochet, a wilder spatter, a million million spirits, from aggravation to want. Among them, his son's signal couldn't have come in clearer, now that Pop had stopped crying. The only blade that afternoon, Tonino insisted, had been plastic. As for Mama, she'd just been clumsy.

"She bumped into Tuttavia, like. Or maybe Tuttavia grabbed her."

Tonino did confirm that he and Rosa had been shuttled out of the way, set up in front of a video. "We had to wait in our room. Mama and her, they cleaned up, and then, they did some talking."

"They did some talking?"

"Papa..." Tonino fell into a familiar rant, all about the kind of friends his mother and father had. "When you guys get to talking, it's like the kids aren't even there. Like that Giussi, he's the worst. He struts and he talks, and everybody laughs and talks back—and the whole time, me and Rosa aren't even there."

Tuttavia used to be the same way, the boy went on, but lately she'd changed. Lately, she'd started to play. "All of a sudden she's pretty wild, yeah. She likes to pretend, playing like Medusa and like that."

Risto heaved himself upright on the lounge, working against the bloat inside his head. "Eh, Big Tony. I'm yawning."

"Papa, you need a vacation."

The harder head, the older child. But the boy admitted he'd been half-asleep himself, and you know what he'd really like? Babbo, he'd like a story.

"Mama and Aunt Lucia, there's as bad as all the rest. They talk and talk."

"Oh, Tonino." What sort of *noir* featured a grown man, one who could tell stories in three or four languages, manipulating a child? "All I've got is the story of my life."

"The story of..."

"Story of my life, at this point that's all I've got. Once upon a time, a man grew up hither and yon, he grew up the wrong color and in the wrong places, all around the Mediterranean Sea."

The silence over the phone, the screen's shine in a corner of his eye.

"Now the sea itself, just look at it. It's half-African, like you and your sister. But all around that sea, if anyone's got a better story, they're not African, they're not growing up in Benghazi or Cairo. And this man, in my story, he had to give up everything and cross the sea in rags before he found his true home."

A bicycle sailed along the street below, its reflectors a light show, red-gold.

"This man escaped a place where death lurked on every corner and found one where the streets were paved with gold."

"Pop." Grumpy yet pleased. "Come on."

"Tonino, where I began, where I wound up—it's a miracle. Naples could be the place your grandmother and grandfather always dreamed of. Maybe that's the story I'm telling, about your family out of Africa, educated people, city people. Your grandmother and grandfather, they never stopped believing that they could come home to a place a lot like Naples. Cosmopolitan Mogadishu. The jewel in the Horn of Africa."

Risto's son had heard this before. In a voice thick with sleep, he grumbled that he knew what his father would say: if Babbo's father had been satisfied anywhere else, there was no telling where he, Tonino, might've been born.

"No, that's not it. That's not this story. Tunis, Beirut, Alexandria—none of them would've worked, and none of the others either, not for Antonio Al'Kair. Young Prince Al'Kair, he could only have been born in Naples. His father, that's what this story is about, and it starts in a place of death. A place nothing but smoking ruins, where even God's a lizard. But never mind. The prince should pay attention to where the story *goes*. It introduces the father to a special man, Eftah. It takes him to a university with interesting girls and a gallery run by another very special man. Tonino, he finds himself in an abode of miracles."

Had he actually said that, out loud? Words came hard through the damp clutter of his throat. But if his son gave a peep, it sounded happy. Language out of the ordinary was something else a boy or girl wanted, in a once-upon-a-time, and maybe Risto was after the same. Maybe he needed a glimpse of himself as larger than life.

Nonetheless, during a pause in the Chiaia's traffic rumble, Risto had to raise a warning. Watch out, he told his boy, for the false floors under every happy ending. Watch for the delusions people lived with. "Every brother who ever came North has got some legend he lives by." How else could they survive in midair, above the chasm that'd pitched open in mid-life?

"Tonino, I'm saying, your father may've made it to paradise, but the place has a lot of holes he might still drop through."

The boy took this somewhere else, to the ruins down in Paestum. "In the tomb frescoes, you see it, people who came a long way, posing like heroes."

Risto was left choking again, barely able to praise the boy. "Bravo, the history, always, bravo." Better Tonino's strange turns of mind, he figured, than Paola's. "Except your father's not dead yet."

He waited out another shiver.

"In the frescos," he went on, "you see the legend. But in real life, I never felt like a legend until your mother told me she was pregnant."

There: the moral, one that felt to him genuine. Tonight in the deepening quiet of his balcony it hit home with the same magnitude as the evening Paola had turned up at his original gallery. Risto was alone and he'd needed to unlock the door, though details like that of course didn't interest the young Prince. Nor did Tony need to know that, back on that night, his mother and father weren't yet married. He wouldn't hear any of that, nor how Mamma and Babbo had been getting along famously as scene-makers and rule-breakers. The African *assistente* and his live wire of a girlfriend, they'd played Shock and Awe on the cutting edge, though they'd both wondered at how often, in private, they broke through sophistication to something more intense. Just to get the pregnancy kit, Paola had committed a crime. She'd slipped into Daddy's *studio* and ransacked the cabinets. Robbery felt less dangerous than buying a kit over the counter, where she'd have to stand in line and, among the others waiting, ask out loud.

Still: "Both times I learned your mother was pregnant, it was a wallop."

"A...wallop?"

"Tonino, not like that." He'd begun to tear up again. "We were talking about a legend, my legend. For your father, this is the happy ending."

For other wayfarers out of the old tales, strangers lucky enough to escape the clutches of sea, other stars provide their navigation. For many a fortunate traveler, gold provides the journey's purpose, and beyond a doubt, the gold of the North (itself often camouflaged in other colors, for instance the fey lavender of the 500-Euro bill) mattered to the wet-backed hero out of (most lately) Mogadishu. After all, by and large his way of life had been what's known politely as *shabby genteel*. First with his family and then after they vanished into air, into thin air, he'd mixed refinement with pinching pennies, or pinching piasters, in a dozen or fifteen layovers and with the same number of lovers. Yet in this "New *Polis*" constructed by so many old voyagers, even after the miracles of a bug-free mattress and reliable electricity, after a stable paycheck plus a commission on sales, and after, most spectacularly, a couple of clam- and wine-enriched weekends at the beach with a white doctor's family, nothing so signified Destiny or Redemption or Triumph or *Telos* or Home as the telltale marks on the test strip of a stolen pregnancy kit. The story of those marks became the story of our hero. Alien Hipsters were transformed into Ma and Pa, in the three minutes it took the tale to unfold, and the metamorphosis came over them with such shattering vehemence that, in the next minute, the mother-to-be was left jabbering about, of all things, old-style photography. She spoke of how pictures used to take shape in the developing pan. The incipient father, however, saw the marks on the strip as a shining set of haloes: a covenant which went beyond *Telos* or Triumph or any other name he might give it, every word like a rind too confining for its meat. The immanence suffused both the refugee and the child of privilege; it took them in a family embrace, and for the fellow who'd come to town an orphan it was a family renewed, and one he'd never lose track of again. He'd always have those haloes before him. So too this crescent Gulf of Naples, his jampacked compromise of a home, to the north of the Mediterranean and the south of the white man's continent—his adopted home too underwent a seismic shift into New Atlantis, Utopia, the City of the Sun.

"And that's my story," Risto concluded.

A wordless response, the smack of sleeping lips.

SEVEN

IN FERIE, AS IF "VACATION" were always plural—that was the school-book Italian. In Naples they preferred a single word, *feria*. Shopkeepers spelled it out by hand on a piece of cardboard they taped across their pull-down grates. *Feria*, feh-ree-*ahh*, a loll and a stretch. This morning Risto took a moment for it, finding the cool spots along the sheets. In the shower he lingered till he came out squeaking. The sound brought back the sweetness of giving the babies a bath, finding and losing his grip on two giggling pudgies. After that, back out on the balcony, he rigged up an internal hammock. One end was hooked on espresso, the other on ibuprofen, and once he got the balance right, he could rock away any nightmare that remained.

The street below, however, greeted the middle of the week with such a racket, it called to mind Fidel's check. That too raised a troubling noise, and Risto was intending to call the bank when he discovered Eftah's text.

A text sent in the wee hours, small enough to be picked up by tweezers:

Ari, im OLD skool, sorry. Tonite, sorry, i saw again & Mpris wont work. NEW skool, like u, like Gssi, like Mpris, it wont work, sorry.

He had to count the apologies. One, two, three, from the Black Lord of the No-Account? And just because another boyfriend was history? But then, last night on the drive downhill, Risto had promised Eftah he'd be in touch. The man had saved his life. He'd offered something useful about the hallucinations.

Risto massaged his scalp, slick from shaving. What else did he have on the agenda? Hump day? The major item looked to be the game of

detective—game over—but if anything that reduced his workload. He
no longer had to hustle after his man in Homicide. No doubt Della
Figurazione would follow up on "the operation," sooner or later, but
when he did the C.I. could simply nod along and then shake hands. As
for the big show coming up, and the big check that might be worthless,
those could wait another hour or so. They weren't nearly so pressing
as his clansman's brightly rimmed portraits. The gold in those had recalled Fra Lippi, and even if Eftah weren't at home, the former lodger
could get a look; he still had his keys.

So: first call, Ippolita. She didn't raise a fuss, though he could tell
she wasn't yet out of bed. Any reluctance she might've had disappeared
as soon as the Signore promised again to pay cash. Risto figured he'd
handle it somehow, perhaps even shuttling money out of his personal
account.

The *assistente* did have one concern. "The show," she said, "the pictures—we still haven't gotten them up."

He assured her he had only one stop this morning, "Materdei,
that's it," and he was taking the car. Over at Wind & Confusion, meantime, Ippolita should bring up Tuttavia's pieces. Once Risto joined her,
the hanging wouldn't take long. This wasn't just talk; he'd had things
blocked out in his head for days now, since he'd first spotted La Cia
wearing a halo.

"It's my job," he told her. "My *calling*."

She laughed at that, a bit of hyperbole from the *Manifesto*.

"Look," Risto went on, "be careful on the stepladder. Last night
I took a tumble." The idea had come to him with the last swig of
espresso. This young woman would notice the bruises.

It was past rush hour by the time he hit the road, but Risto took
his time, negotiating the shoals of the road crews. The repairs were good
news; the Camorra might run the union, but the city was getting its
roads back. The thought helped, it cleared away the worst of his dreams.
In one, he'd stood at some viewpoint high above city, and from there he
watched all its haloes disappear, floating off, shriveling as they went…

At one of his last stops he reread Eftah's message. *Sorry, sorry, sorry*,
a cry for help you'd think. Still, he wasn't about to try calling. If his

clansman picked up (itself a low probability), Risto would be in for all sorts of posturing and evasion. He'd have more impact just showing up. Look, your brother's got his head on straight—now how about you? The Black Lord might revel in his bad behavior, in outsmarting the *Guardia di Finanza* or swindling the Camorra, and of course these all had to do with his staunch refusal to live in the closet. Still, the act grew tiresome, in a man pushing fifty. Even Paola had begun to temper her praise. *Him and his anarchy,* she'd say, *always such anarchy, well.*

She ought to see this mess, Wednesday morning in Materdei.

Risto's first glance at Eftah's palazzo made clear that his latest breakup story would be a major soap opera. It'd need a lot of edits, too, before he could bring it up at dinner. Outside the entryway sprawled tangles of clothing, luggage off its hinges, even fractured sticks of furniture. Furniture, really? A chair, brokeback and legs up? A lamp too had gone off the balcony, a perfectly good standing lamp. The affair had ended in an earthquake, plainly, and as Risto climbed away from his car the only sign of restraint he could see was the absence of the boyfriend's manuscripts. You saw books, but no notebooks or printouts.

Next he discovered something out of the portrait gallery, face down. The black backing, buckled, poked out of the picture's frame. Its shattered glass cover rainbowed across the cobblestone.

Risto squatted for look, then hesitated.

"Easy there, cousin." The voice wasn't Eftah's. "Don't want to hurt yourself."

Jabba the Hut lounged against a nearby Smart Car. Could've been Eftah's car, actually, though the shadow of the palazzo was too deep to make out the color. Anyway the vehicle's roof provided the Camorrista with an armrest. Shadow or no shadow, Risto couldn't imagine how he'd failed to notice.

"Cousin, you can see what we've got here. A dick of a comedy."

Risto remained with the photo. It turned out to be one of the shots he'd come to check—the color shot, Eftah and Mepris together. The fall had punched holes through the picture, a corner was torn away, but the heads of both men remained in place, unmarked—unhaloed. Risto found no trace of the bright tiara his clansman had worn just day before yesterday. Going down on one knee, ignoring last night's aches, he turned the photograph. Three o'clock, five o'clock…

Eftah's shaved skull, unadorned, held Risto's gaze even as the Camorrista shuffled closer. The Hut had no reason to mess with him. Besides, for all he knew, the goon worked for one of the co-signers on the gallery's mortgage; he and Risto could be business partners. Still, Risto didn't do anything crazy, or no crazier than crumpling the picture. You'd think it was another of those Get-Out-of-Italy letters. He trashed the thing two-fisted, and flipped the balled photo into the nearest trash pile.

What did he need with the Harbinger of Doom? If his clansman were facing doom, in the first place this might do, the chaos he'd made of his home. In the second—who said Risto should be the prophet? He was a taxpayer and a family man, no longer young and fond of Vesuvian wine, and the last thing he needed was some shaman inheritance from a homeland he'd spent his life trying to escape.

※

Above him, the Camorrista gave a hee-haw. "Yeah, j-just look at it. The dick must've thought he was b-back in Mogadishu."

Slowly Risto straightened up. He felt glad that, getting dressed, he'd done without the jungle fever. He'd gone business casual, blue and gray.

"B-but he, he warned us."

He wasn't some bug-eyed Sambo flailing between tigers.

"He warned us, that ape. It's all turning into a nigger place."

"Nigger place," Risto growled, "and a gay bar."

"That's what the f-faggot said. You're every, everywhere."

"We're everywhere." He raised a hand towards a sore spot, then dropped it. "A thug like you, you aren't the only one who can get around the law."

The man lost his grin, his jowls sagging into the collar of his jogging suit. A plus-size swaddling of glossy polyester, the suit had nothing to do with exercise and was all wrong for the weather. Rather the point was the bulk, the room to hide the hardware. Nonetheless Risto couldn't stop: "If you're an immigrant, Italian law is the worst in Europe. It grabs you by the neck and shoves your faces in the wall."

"Shoves your face in the wall?" said the Camorrista. "Looks like it."

Risto left his bruises alone. "I was downcellar," he said. "On a ladder, eh."

"Oh yeah, faggot?" The Hut stood so close, you could smell the liqueur with which he'd cut his morning coffee. "Sure it wasn't some *thug*?"

Risto dropped his head, once more looking over the mess.

"A thug like me, a cocksucker like you. In a minute I'd put your face in a wall."

The Hut had his Sambuca, that tang of licorice, but Risto had seen how Eftah handled this guy, too. He eyed the mobster mildly, and eventually the Hut broke into another bleak laugh.

"Look," Risto asked, "why don't you just tell me what you're doing here? What do you need with my cousin?"

"B-but, maybe it's him I needed. A Somali p-pirate, right? Comes in handy when you, if you need a p-pirate for the job. A *thug*, that cousin of yours."

The Hut had a lot of flesh around the eyes, the folds of a codger.

"That faggot, he could've given me lessons. He was old school."

Risto found himself scanning his clansman's palazzo. From here he could see the whole length of the roof railing, empty. "And you don't know where he's got to?"

"How should I know? I was about to ask you."

The best response was a shrug. Didn't it figure that Eftah had run off? The litter outside his doorstep could wait; he'd needed some temporary affection.

"What I know," the goon went on, "is where he *used* to be. I know how that nigger used to spend his nights, back before he became Lord of the Manor."

"Look." Risto worked up a cold smile. "I've found what I came here to…"

"He could do the *job*, keep that in mind. The big job, midnight."

He made the gesture, the finger across his throat.

"I was there with him once," the Camorrista went on. "On the job."

His eyes could've been mineral matter, impervious. To him today's visitor was a fugee getting uppity, and if he passed along what he heard, the dick the Hut cared. The dick he cared. "Your cousin's black pirate ass came in handy. It was another *clandestino* he took care of."

The rest of the street, midmorning and midweek, remained deserted.

"Bad news, this *clandestino*. A big swinging dick of a nigger, greedy piece of shit. Greedy and never any letup. But my crew, we couldn't get to him."

An empty street, a car just downhill—why did Risto remain planted? Fifteen years in the white man's country, and still hate like this left him paralyzed.

"But we had our own nigger, see? We had Osama with a knife in his teeth. He could get so close, he could get that black bastard by the dick. And you know why he did it, Mr. Slick?" He jerked his chins up toward Eftah's place. "Because he's a greedy dick himself. He likes to be Lord of the Nigger Manor."

So here was another way Risto had been lucky. All his life up North, he'd known there had to be something like this, behind his clansman's enterprises, but no one had ever opened that filthy bag for a peek.

"See, we knew what our nigger wanted, a castle where he could play the Lord, and we could take care of that. We've got people in real estate, all over town. We had the property, and so that *clandestino*, that greedy piece of shit, he had a date for midnight. The big job. The bastard never saw it coming—or not till I turned up to enjoy the show. Our boy with the knife in his teeth, he put on a *show*."

No one, and certainly not Eftah, for all that he loved to talk.

"He even knew where to dump the body. Your cousin here—he was way smarter than your shit-for-brains art crowd."

Again and again, Risto had been lucky, but he'd known. The palazzo stood five stories tall and went back three hundred years. The man who held title hadn't lacked for signs of remorse, either. Eftah's love life wouldn't have left behind such blasted terrain unless he suffered a bad gnawing within.

"This city's so full of holes, think about all its hiding places."

Last night, the remorse must've torn at Eftah so terribly that, once he got away from Risto and the detective, he had a lot more to say about it. Once he got home, and sat down for a drink with the boyfriend, no doubt he had plenty to say. He wasn't one to beg for forgiveness; rather he'd be all banging and caterwaul, the "overgrown *enfant terrible*." How long would it have taken before the portrait of Eftah and his lover went over the rooftop rail? Risto could see it perfectly, now, thanks to this awful man and his ugly truth. He saw what his clansman had suffered and he couldn't lift a finger to help, and turning to face downhill he tried to gauge the distance between them. No small distance, though Eftah always had more to him than rapacity and striking poses. Still, while the older man had taken Risto in, he'd also given him that fondle, lengthy and frank. While Eftah had found Risto a job, he'd then turned his back. Never mind that the docks had the sort of workplace standards you'd find at Dachau—*zhu ni hao yun*, my brother. The older man had kept himself apart, just as he preferred to stay at a remove from the whole truth. Small wonder Mepris called him on such shit. Small wonder that Risto, born with such a potent gene for fathering, never quite got the man. Eftah Al'Kair, thing of darkness.

"Think about it," said the Hut. "The way I heard it, that job wasn't his only one."

Risto continued facing away, aggravated, confused. As a former lover-for-hire, by what right should he be shocked at the hard choices of another immigrant? Or did he want the last word, after such a heaping helping of racist slurs?

He ventured a shrug. "Whatever. What's up in some cave somewhere..."

"The dick anyone cares, exactly. A nigger in a hole, who cares?"

The Hut went on sneering, his hands on his belly like Buddha in polyester. Between them, at their feet, were more broken leftovers—a good reminder of where kicking up a fuss would get him.

"A piece of shit anyway. Came out of the jungle, wound up in a cave."

Even with the trash at his feet, Risto had to scowl. "As if you have any *idea*. A gorilla like you, as if you have the first clue—"

The blow came fast, a cuff across the ear.

"You calling me names again, faggot? Calling me a *gorilla*?"

The second blow was more of the same, a flick of the wrist, yet his face felt cracked in half.

"You ape, you black-as-shit ape. My neighborhood, you wouldn't last a day."

"We're everywhere." It helped to hear himself speak.

"You're no better than the first ape to wade up out of the water. Ooga-booga."

"I run a business, an honest business. I've got a white girl on the payroll."

"H-honest?" Once more the Camorrista found him laughable. "That p-place?"

This was where they'd begun, the Hut cackling and Risto pretending not to hear.

"H-honest, the crap you're s-s-selling? The n-nerve you have, selling that s-shit. I'm s-surprised you're not p-picking up some of this, this garbage right h-here!" With a toe he poked a broken picture frame. "Put a p-price tag on it and tell those rich morons some f-fucking *fairy tale*!"

At least the laughter allowed Risto to shuttle back a step.

"The art these days? Nigger, just look at it, a swindle, a complete con..."

❖

For the drive back, Risto took the long way, the out-of-the-way. He nosed around the heights, the former farm terraces now paved over, and when the traffic and high-rises relented, he rolled down his window and slowed for the view. The hilltop air alone did him good, but there was better medicine in the sweep of downtown and Gulf. The panorama, late morning, left the islands unmoored. Capri and Ischia might've been a pair of tufted moon rocks in low orbit above a sea of horsefly blue and black.

It did him good, up that way, and down at the gallery Ippolita was ready for him. Beside her, stacked at a slant, stood Tuttavia's photos.

Still, Risto almost reached first for the *assistente*'s iPhone. It caught the eye, another big-city red, maybe Hong Kong Red, and with a touch of the screen he could go on the web. If his thick fingers cooperated, in something like a minute and a half Google would turn up page after page about hallucinations such as his. Visions like the gold that'd lured him up to Materdei this morning must be all over the Internet. More than likely the gallery owner could download a monograph, some piece with a colon in its title. "Mystic Haloes, Ghost Jewelry, and Healing Hands: Paranormal Activity in Recent Diasporic Populations."

That sounded about right. It took him back to the Conservatory, and come to think, wasn't it time he got back to the work he'd trained for?

He turned the sign on the door and pocketed his sunglasses. Ippolita couldn't ignore the bruises, and she said something as Risto was testing the first piece against one wall. He assured her that a show like this was no great strain, and besides, she'd already done the hard part. She'd done the fetch and carry, and she'd come dressed for it too, in jeans. Plenty of decorative stitching and rhinestones, but jeans.

Then Risto was picking up speed, placing a second photo and a third, a fourth and a fifth. The girl might've disappeared into thin air. All the gallery owner could see, as he shuttled back and forth, was his mental sketch of the show.

Last night he could've told Tuttavia: every exhibit was a kind of performance. From his first riffle through this set, he'd seen its blocking, the tension in these black-and-whites and how it could be heightened, pairing two here while separating two there. All of this had been laid out in his mind's eye long before the photographer had delivered her gelateria manifesto. Besides, didn't talk like that give a gallery owner more to work with? If his star client were going nova, didn't that add to the drama? Granted, she might not go through with it, the Renunciation of the Nikon. How would she ever break into performance if she refused to work with Giussi? How seriously did she take herself as some sort of seismograph, the first to register the shifts underfoot? All Risto knew for certain was that Tuttavia herself believed she'd found a new center of gravity, and she'd thrown that oomph into every one of these end-of-summer shots. Readying herself for metamorphosis, the woman had given him more to work with.

Risto's mentor in this business, the American, had spoken of a show as "a dance." He'd gone so far as to name-check Terpsichore. A useful way of thinking, then as now, especially given Risto's own notion that the best art had that baseline roughage and grit. Yes: his job brought together grit and Terpsichore. This month, placement began with the two shots of La Cia. The boy's eyes, two glow-holes beneath the black awning of the Afro, could frighten you regardless of whether you knew they were about to get filleted out of his skull. His stare provided the fulcrum for both those compositions and, at the same time, a natural set of boundaries for the exhibition. Those two went up at either end of Wind & Confusion. You encountered the smaller La Cia alongside the front door, and then went all the way to the back wall to confront the larger, the moneymaker—Fidel's, so long as the check didn't bounce.

The rest took, what, ninety minutes? Between the shots of the doomed young skin-and-bone, the filling in felt contrapuntal, with indications of threat and squalor (the worst always just outside the frame) set off against hints of sweetness or redemption. The gallery owner himself was part of the counterpoint, as his deep dive into the work made him realize how badly he'd doubted himself. He'd worried that he'd thrown off his inner compass irrevocably. But weren't misgivings like that the least he could expect, after his recent knocking around? And couldn't you say he was still knocking around, breakneck, finagling no end with whatever formula he had for his shows (one part uncertainty, two parts vanity, one part "the eye," three parts family lost and found...)? But look, the upshot was worthy of his guru. Better yet, the artist was one Risto himself had discovered and brought along, building up a catalogue they talked about from here to Berlin. He took a moment to bask. A moment when he couldn't care less about the bad guys, whether in Materdei or on the mortgage. They'd been mown down in a withering crossfire out of the bodies and faces that surrounded him. In here, rather than up on some hilltop, he got the healing view.

Ippolita lagged behind, clipping the titles to the walls. Risto went to his desk for the sheet of red dots, the stickies that designated which pictures had sold. As soon as he thumbed Fidel's into place, the girl began complaining.

"That price—honestly, I think that's all that people will notice. I know that's all that matters to Fidel. He might as well hang a sheet of Euros on the wall."

"Ippolita. The idea is, it's the picture that makes someone notice."

"You believe that?"

The girl straightened up sharply. "Oh, signore, so sorry. What an awful thing to say! It's that rich creep, that Castelsabbia—he makes the business feel like such a *fraud*."

The best reassurance he could offer was to keep up the busywork, shrugging amiably. "Ippolita, you should've seen the people the American had to put up with."

"You're telling me there's worse?" Already she was smiling. "More despicable buyers than our so-called comrade? *Per carità*."

"My old boss, himself. Some would say he was worse."

"Perhaps, *signore*, but Castelsabbia's the one I have to deal with. Him and his slave girl. To think that, just night after tomorrow, he's going to come up and *kiss* me!"

Risto went for the mini fridge, a bottle of water. "Well," he said, "we keep the sanitizer in the lav."

Laughing, Ippolita looked prettier than she had all morning. She'd allowed herself makeup and a complicated necklace. This hung in three layers, woven gold and amber, too much really for a girl going up and down a ladder. An imitation antiquity, fake Greco-Roman, it'd first turned up on the roadside prostitutes, the Africans and Filipinos. Now the necklace was everywhere, the season's hot accessory—and so part of the job, for an *assistente*.

※

A *filosofo*, when young, has need of a mentor. Our wandering hero, so fresh out of the South that he remained open to any number of potential Norths, required instruction from a sensibility more or less

the same, nimble and freethinking. Thus the Chiron who settled his
gaze upon our Aristofano: the director of an exhibition space with a
name, Spazio Nova Poli, that itself juggled a couple of languages, if
not three. There an African *immigrato* did more than serve the wine
and cheese; there he was trusted with the Internet login and drew his
pay by direct deposit—a miracle of electronics that likewise justified,
in the eyes of the State, a work visa. Nor did "the American," as this
avatar preferred to be known, dawdle about providing documents for
the pertinent tribunals. From the first, this guru was convinced that he
needed such an *assistente*, of a color most people didn't expect. A young
man out of the South sharpened the profile of the Nova Poli. In return,
to be sure, the job sharpened the former *clandestino*; it awarded the
nigger another library card.

Throughout his first months at the American's gallery, the *nouveau*
Neapolitan passed many a long minute before the lavatory mirror. He
pondered the enigma that stared back, with its workingman's Afro
and schoolboy's pout. A practical interpretation for what he saw there
would hold that these were merely the compromises necessary in order
to keep his skin around his soul. Even "Ahh-ree-STOH-fah-NOH"
was a compromise, for the sake of the clumsy Italian tongue, and
"Risto" still more so. Nevertheless, the word bore the weight of mil-
lennia. Our hero's travels before this had at times occasioned mention
of Aristophanes. Indeed, a former mentor, more specifically a tutor,
during those years when the family Al'Kair was trying its fortunes in
Beirut, used to claim that the Athenian playwright had picked up his
best gimmicks in the dockside theaters of old Phoenicia.

But here in Naples, in the Nova Poli, the old Greek might've been
included in the job description. Every other visitor, sizing up the new
hire, made some reference to *Lysistrata* or *The Symposium*. A number of
these simpering palefaces weren't so clever as they thought; a number
believed that Aristophanes had written *The Symposium*. But then, the
idea that a *nero* might correct a Northerner sent glimmering ripples
across that image in the mirror. It opened up vast new realms of identity, and wasn't that precisely what the young Risto was looking for,
standing there long after he'd pulled his pants back up? Why else was

he going on three hours of sleep here, five hours there, bouncing back and forth between gallery and Conservatory, if not finally to encounter, staring back at him, the New European Citizen? With his American Sage and his Art Society, he might even be rising to that status his parents had talked about, a "citizen of the world."

A status that left him removed, as well, from his former brothers. Down on the docks the coolies passed their days and nights in a city so different from his, they might've gone to China. Up in Materdei his old sachem appeared to take a quiet pride in former ward's rising stature, as this fledgling asserted himself as one of the *fortunati*, and as the *eminence grise* behind the American. In no way did the Black Lord signal, ever, that he took offense. Only, as the separation between him and the younger Somali increased, as Risto began to raid the gallery fridge, preferring a dinner of cheese and ciabatta gone stale to the fresh octopus and greens up on the terrazzo, the Elder would now and again punctuate their diminishing time together with a sigh:

I'm old school.

To a 'Dishu boy who'd quit that school, the act seemed over the top. What did either of them need with hand-wringing, when anyone who could see beyond the color of their skin could see as well that these two occupied separate branches on the evolutionary tree? The one who'd come to function as the American's shadow was the latest adaptation, whereas the one who labored in the shadow, with the tools of a handyman, was a throwback. His efforts deserved a toast, to be sure, since once upon a time he'd had everything to do with launching the new species. Still, his era was past.

So Risto, solidly in place at the most talked-about gallery in town, began to array himself differently, in carnival wraps and a pirate's hoop. The wardrobe of the lawless left him feeling, via some imponderable alchemy, all the more legitimate. A mystery, and it lingered even years further along, even after changing workplaces and becoming twice a father. The younger *immigrato* could comprehend the market benefit of presenting like a Mau Mau, its appeal for the moneyed—but how on Earth did looking like a renegade help him to feel as if he belonged? Yet even during his first weeks in these desperado threads, whenever he paused before the lav mirror, he enjoyed a fresh pleasure. Moreover, he enjoyed the attention from the women of his new community.

For the *assistente* Al'Kair, inevitably, his European dating began with Africans. The sisters too worked odd hours, and even when they came from some far different corner of his home continent, like him they had other languages and, on occasion, a better head than he for the oddities of these southern Northerners. One woman, up from Lagos, had actually completed a degree in European Studies, though she too remained an indenture to the white folks who'd taken her on. The Italians who claimed to "treat the help like family," indeed, made the poor girl's life all the worse. In that unhappy case, a sister could be here today, gone tomorrow: off to serve as nanny up in the Cinque Terre or cleaning woman out on the Eolian Islands.

One evening Risto could lie stroking some "Nubian queen," a sweet nothing they both liked the taste of, either in bed or in some decent facsimile, since around this crowded metropolis they had to make do with whatever shelter they found—and then the very next night, he'd find himself with no better company than a couple of all-caps lines in a goodbye text. The Queen had turned back into a scullery maid, at the whim of her "family," and after a few such pickups and put-downs, is it any wonder that he began to try his luck with white girls? Weren't they a natural extension of everything prior? So long as he was letting this self out of the closet, this clean-shaven, gold-studded Aristo-self out of the Nova Poli water closet, he might as well let it wander.

Even when a date wrapped up with no more a peck on the cheek, he got a better glimpse of the man he was becoming, and he discerned it more clearly still at the first gliding stroke of some woman's astonishing hair. In those cases when the hair came undone, more than once it proved to be a silken blonde, Viking. Whether a hefty Valkyrie or a sylph of the Northern woods, these sun-seekers had a genuine attraction to the city's art, and most of them worked on some project in archeology or restoration, yet the project that mattered more to them turned out to be personal, rambunctious, all about sucking the marrow from a *Wanderjahr*. The Scandinavian girls threw themselves into it, they made a playground of their alternative Latin Lover, and yet ultimately none of that tickle and grind was what drove Risto. For a year there, perhaps fifteen months, any time spent with women remained at heart about understanding what had become of him.

The Europeans had an expression, "respecting boundaries," yet the African felt like he was the one showing respect, when even a Naples date who kept her clothes on could prattle away as if he'd just helped her to a sumptuous orgasm. This out in a piazza, too, where the walls and cobblestones could create an echo chamber. As the woman's confessions resonated, it may have delivered the foundational lesson, the seed and kernel of talking like a white man. Over time, the brown man grasped how the chatter created a comfortable space not simply for sharing, but also for lying. In time he found room for his own most effective fabrications, like the tall tale "Escape from Mogadishu." That went through the iterations necessary to achieve its most perfect rendering, the one in which the older brother is cut down right before the younger's eyes, his head split open by a khat-maddened teenager wielding a machete. Doctored in this way, the tale slipped easily into conversations that roved across the Mediterranean and the Sahara, all while rendering him that much more a man of the North. Eventually the American's *assistente* worked up a line of talk that seemed to meander without a plan and yet maintained strict adherence to a subtle and far-reaching infrastructure, and all this before his first tête-à-tête with the woman he would wind up talking to most, in as close to complete honesty as he could manage: the Neapolitan Paola.

Then Paola came up, interrupting Risto's long thoughts. Ippolita, back at the desk, was asking.

"I mean, if the man who ran that gallery—the American? If he was so bad as all that? Working for him seems like no way to meet your wife."

"Eh, part of what I liked about her." He was still on his feet, doing touch-checks on the work they'd hung. "She wasn't a babe in the woods."

"Just the opposite, signore—Paola is *Napoli D.O.C.*"

"And as for mentors, you do realize the whole point is to leave us behind?"

In Risto's case, he'd simply gone on growing. He'd gotten all he could out of hookups that didn't last beyond the morning cappuccino. By the time the *assistente* had his work visa and direct deposit, he'd begun to distance himself from both his clansman the clubhound and his boss the tomcat.

"You probably know better than I do," Risto told the girl. "It starts to look pointless, all the time chasing the next pretty young thing."

Even as Risto picked up a few moves, he nurtured a different aspiration. He recognized what the impresario brought to the party, the way his cruising disordered the senses. When the younger man began to imagine himself in a gallery of his own, too, no one had encouraged him so much as his boss. But the African had to wonder what had brought him over such an unlikely rainbow to this pot of gold. If the journey amounted to something more than luck, bumping into the right guy at the right time, no way it was just about searching for nookie. For that matter, he couldn't adopt his mentor's notion of art, either. The selection at Nova Poli prized ideas, pieces in which the visual space aspired to be a game board free of human figures. A lot of geometry, a lot of "referencing."

Just looking around, now, Risto got a fresh example of the work that mattered to him. The sponge-print of the actual: the drip of street gunk.

"Signore, what I've heard is, the American knew how to keep people talking. To keep up the buzz. The way he quit, that alone—people are still talking."

"Eh, that. Pulled a fast one on the whole city."

But today it was Risto who'd pulled it off, the show and its "sold" sticker. He knocked back more water, his favorite, the Vera brand. He could taste the snowmelt. Also he reached for the shop's ibuprofen, a strip of pills in the top drawer, next to the thumbnail from Eftah. That mystery, the flash drive—that alone was enough for one detective story. Then as Risto swallowed his painkiller there came a rush of street air. Apparently someone didn't respect the sign on the door: COMING EVENT....

⌗

Della Figurazione might've been on duty, but he took a minute or two with Ippolita. With her he made small talk, clothing talk, or so it seemed. In no time the detective had moved from the shops she preferred to her family's Chiaia church. He'd ferreted out her last name. Risto looked on untroubled. The police needed some background on their informants, and though the officer was flirting as well, today he looked less formal. He did without a jacket, though above his rolled cuffs the watch looked imposing as ever.

He turned to Risto: "How are you feeling?"

Risto waved the strip of pills.

The officer looked solicitous. "Not on an empty stomach, I hope. How about we get some lunch?"

Della Figurazione turned back to the *assistente* and asked if she could "spare this man a while." Ippolita went on playing the coquette, a hand on the faux-antique around her neck, but she had a smile for Risto as well, reassuring. He wondered about the policeman's watch, the alternative timekeeping. Was that past, future, what? One thing for certain: this visit wasn't about the face the man was showing. No way this was about checking his health and taking him to lunch. Not that Risto raised any objections. Just, once he stood out in the diesel and sulfur alongside the detective's car (the badge that hung from the rearview allowed Della Figurazione to park wherever he liked), he wished he'd taken a full 600 milligrams.

Inside, he heard nothing more about lunch. Instead, at the first traffic slowdown: "So, you figured you could catch the man who cut up that *clandestino* last weekend. That's been your plan, yes? Il Signore, he catches the killer himself."

Now, Risto had managed to look Jabba the Hut in the eye…

"The police, they're mongoloids. They don't even know where to *look*."

He made a show of fingering a bruise on the driver side of his face.

"But you, you're the cowboy out of the desert. You'll clean up Dodge City."

"*Per carità!*" Maybe Risto was better off without the extra drugs. "You sound as if you wanted me to get clobbered, last night."

First response, a squeak of the other man's seat vinyl. "Signore Awl Keyer. My sarcasm perhaps was out of line."

"Eh. Don't worry about *my* feelings, Della Figurazione."

"What you and I need is to deal straightforwardly. Without this façade."

"Façade, what a word. I had a choice, very simple. On the one hand, I could forget the young man. Forget him and leave him chopped to bits, along with whatever he might've…"

"Enough, all right? Enough."

"On the *one* hand, I could just go on as if he'd never lived. On the other, I could take some initiative."

"Look, today I've got to talk to you man to man. I can't be talking to some movie poster, the Lone Ranger."

Risto wound up repeating himself, with fresh emphasis on the word "initiative."

"Signore, you make it sound like a work of art."

"Listen to the man. I can't tell him his business, but he can tell me mine."

"Your business. Does that include not telling your wife?" The officer fingered together his open collar. "The police, we do notice some things. We notice the person you put down as a contact."

Out the windows, leaving La Chiaia, things went from pastel to gray.

"Signore, now, both of us, let's stop striking poses."

Della Figurazione explained how he'd put together what was going on. Last night while Risto lay dozing in the clinic downtown, the actual detective had gotten what few clues he'd needed from the talking on the phone with Tuttavia. "Maybe it took me thirty seconds after she picked up. I mean, practically the first thing out of her mouth was a question about your wife."

Risto began to say that a man could have reasons for not wanting his wife to know other than…

"Signore, the police, in this city, we aren't obtuse. Ah, *ka nescunn' e fess'.*"

Another old story, even in a cultivated accent: *Here, ain't nobody stupid.*

"Maybe it took me an entire minute. Before I could get the whole picture, I needed to understand just who she was. This other woman. I needed to establish that you and she weren't, you know."

Risto himself was the old story. Every neighborhood in town must have its version, plus a song that went with it. Some feral creature wandered too freely, it poked its nose where it shouldn't have, and it wound up in a trap. For all Risto knew, it could be that what he'd lately put himself through was just another stage in the assimilation process. He couldn't become a true Neapolitan until he got a song of his own. So he tried to tell himself, anyway, as he sat pawing his head.

Then Della Figurazione slipped a package onto his lap. A package from a café, a *cornetto* wrapped in foil.

"I told you," the officer said. "You ought to eat something."

He raised his eyes. "A snack for an errand boy."

"Signore, I'm doing you a favor. After what you've been through."

"Italy these days, it's like America in the old days. Anyone my color is a child. Lunch—maybe I'll buy for *you*."

But Risto didn't like how he sounded, screechy. He tried again. "Look." He gestured with the bright, floppy package. "I appreciate it, Della Figurazione." The smell in fact was mouth-watering. "But I know what this is about. We're on our way to the station, where you'll ask me to sign a statement. The police aren't obtuse, just as you say. You know when you've put a citizen at risk."

And while they were downtown, Risto went on, he'd be only too happy to share what he'd learned about the murder last weekend. "I've picked up a lot, actually. The kind of information that helped me get Papers for you."

"Ah..." Della Figurazione gave his collar another tug.

"Only, my wife? Let's leave her out of it."

Maybe it was better this way, the drugs light, the emotions near the surface. Maybe this officer had the right idea, tear down the façade.

Della Figurazione remained wordless a while, in the grumble of the Audi's air conditioning. He spoke up only as they reached the precinct house. "About your wife, I understand. In my marriage I was often in a quandary, trying to protect the woman."

"Exactly. It's not as if I didn't realize that this could get dangerous."
"Dangerous, like people getting killed. People close to you."

The grumble of the air, the flat of the man's voice. Risto faced around.

"It's your...cousin," began Della Figurazione. "Your man Eftah."

❋

He wasn't shown the body. Della Figurazione had an explanation; something or other had already been "established." Up in Risto's head, meantime, there screened that crime-show classic, the visit to the morgue, the parents in business dress and the daughter naked above the sheet, her skin color faded like the borders of a Rothko. He understood that this scene too was a fairytale. The TV, the movies, the comic books, they loved going face to face with a corpse. The truth, in a city up North at least, was that the dead remained largely offstage. Their secrets were reserved for the professionals.

In the station house, the detective went on talking. He worked in complaints about the office chaos, chatter that sounded like part of his training, a tactic for handling the bereaved. Still the two of them got a room of their own. The space featured a tarnished mirror across one wall—a window, no doubt, for whoever was on the other side.

Largest thing in the room, a table, and largest thing on it, what appeared to be a compact stereo speaker, a wireless model. The hardware sat inside a clear plastic bag, and this meant it must be evidence, like the assortment beside it. There was a file folder of photos and documents, and another smaller baggie, holding a few bits and pieces, mostly metal. Nothing much, and yet over the last three days Risto had risked his dark hide repeatedly for a peek. One item might even have been left over from the previous murder. Whoever had cut Eftah's bull throat had worn a bracelet, silver. Risto at once recognized the style, the reptilian scales and slits for eyes, even under the smears of blood. Coagulation took place more slowly inside a baggie.

The officer made explanations, saying that "the materials" had to remain "under control," but this was something else that Risto didn't need to hear. For him the evidence was already at a remove.

Everything was no more than a rustle at the fingertips. Even the most shocking details of a photo—the ball gag half drowned in disgorged blood; the shredded flesh at the corners of the eye sockets; the splinters of bone that glistened through the muddy butt of the victim's thumb (the cuts, according to Della Figurazione, "consistent with the use of a serrated blade")—even these bypassed Risto's nervous system. Could last night have burnt him out? Was some new frenzy of grief, of outrage, lying in wait for him yet? In any case the tabletop horrors wound up leaving him exhausted, more than anything else. He fell into the closest chair.

The detective remained on his feet, pointing out that they didn't have a murder weapon. The C.I., his voice flat, suggested that Eftah himself might've brought the tool that killed him.

"Signore, seriously? A knife such as this…"

"Think of the work he did. Everyday equipment."

"Actually, ah. That's something we haven't quite got straight, the work he did."

Risto shrugged and began to talk about it, how his clansman had made a living. Before long, it turned out that Eftah's wheeling and dealing hadn't gone unnoticed. The police had occasionally collared an illegal doing the Black Lord's grunt work, and these laborers had swapped information in return for being let out. The cops hadn't yet put together a case, they hadn't bothered, but the detective had only been pretending not to know. Another interrogation tactic, sure. When Della Figurazione himself brought up Eftah's Posillipo project, Risto shrugged again. He moved on to the victim's private life, speaking of the broken flotsam outside the Materdei palazzo. He brought up this morning's text and, meantime, tried to recall what he knew about shock. How had that one book put it: "the psyche erecting a wall"? But didn't a man's wall go only so high?

Still he kept on placidly, amid scuffed and uncomfortable furnishings, an arm's length from tooth-and-claw barbarity. Only his mind's eye had more going on. It put up a weather-beaten old print of his brother Ti'aba, his head split open. Risto had imagined it a thousand times, three thousand.

"As for the bracelet," interrupted Della Figurazione. "There is an inscription on the inside, the word 'Mexico.' Not much to go on."

Risto recalled the rattle across the gelateria table.

"Not much at all, Signore Elk A-whir. Plenty of women wearing them."

"Yes. For instance my client, Tuttavia."

The detective had been moving around the photos, the paperwork out of the folder, arranging a display. Now he drew up straight. "The woman from last night?"

"She's pretty high strung. Between her and Eftah, there was no love lost."

"Ah, no?"

"She hated what he stood for. A brother who took advantage of his own kind."

He might've been translating a complicated joke from another language.

"Do you, do you know what you're saying? You want us to look at this woman?"

At least the question cleared Risto's interior screening room. Still, he was so slow about shaking his head, Della Figurazione kept on eyeing him. No doubt he had the attention of anyone on the other side of the mirror, too.

"She's high strung," he said finally, "but the only person she'd hurt is herself."

A less-than-straight answer—maybe the only kind you hear, at a homicide lunch. Maybe full honesty had gotten snagged down in the same place as high feelings, so that when one got the least bit of wiggle room, the other kicked up as well. Risto came out of his chair gasping, pawing his face. Insofar as he could look at anything on the table, it was the handcuffs. They appeared too small for the man whose blood was all over them.

"Horrible," he managed. "The bastards took him apart."

He knew better, the limits on Eftah's mutilation, the same as Friday night. The murderer had contented himself or herself with the eyes and one thumb. Taken apart, torn to pieces—that was Risto, all of a sudden. Yelping, snuffling, he staggered into the mirrored wall. He sagged into his own swollen reflection as the officer came out with sympathies. Apologies: *So sorry, but, ah, the sooner we do this, the better. The first day on such a case, the first day and a half...*

How long did it take, half a minute? How little time, before his next level breath? Half a minute, give or take, while Della Figurazione stayed put across the room, allowing him space. Then Risto was upright again and frowning at himself. Scolding himself, silently: the precinct house was the last place a man from the South ought to lose control. Worse, there was probably a woman watching. On the other side of the one-way glass, the detective had probably posted his partner, the former nun. Whoever, whatever, spasms of grief did no one any good. Neither Eftah nor La Cia got anything out of his blubbering, and the same went for any brothers still in jeopardy.

Hadn't Risto suffered some similar bad moment recently? Sometime during these past few days, a squall of tears, like a flick of water off someone's fingers?

"Did you get a look at these Earthquake I.D.?"

Risto had turned from the mirror, a hand extended to the papers. Della Figurazione kept his distance.

"The I.D.," repeated Risto, "there's not a mark on them. I'm saying, they couldn't have been anywhere near the body."

"We did wonder about that. That they should be left behind like that."

The false documents had lain pinned beneath the speaker unit, the only piece of furniture on the crime scene besides the sopping mattress. Apparently there'd been dancing. Not that the cops who responded to the call (an anonymous tip, what else?) had found much besides what was on the table. By this time, the lab had gotten to work as well, putting its instruments to the corpse and mattress. They too had turned up little, a woman's partial shoeprint and shards of Nastro Azurro. Still, a person didn't need a microscope to see that Eftah had bled to death at a party. The evidence yielded an obvious storyline to a man who'd got himself back under control. Risto declared that this couldn't have happened in a club, not even one of the irregular places.

Della Figurazione, likewise businesslike, assured his CI that all the precincts had begun coordinating their efforts against venues like La Fenestrella. The officer had seen the paperwork himself. The police would reach out to more *clandestini* and pay better attention to word on the street.

As for last night, the Black Lord's last boogie, that had been private. Another penthouse affair, but downscale: the rooftop sprouted valerian flowers and slum trees. The building had been condemned for nearly a decade, since the city's last decent campaign of renewal. In those years, the authorities had cracked the garbage problem, or they'd given it a substantial dent, and they'd served papers on building code violations previously let slide. Many a palazzo had an illegal rental perched up top, a shed the landlord had slapped together overnight. Up there, water and electricity were items for negotiation, and yet all over town, the rooftop hovels claimed paying tenants: a celestial city composed of hellholes. When the authorities at last went after the problem, they'd taken stronger measures than pinning up strips of orange plastic. In a few cases, the entire building was shuttered and locked.

So, the scene of the crime: a ramshackle setup from years back, on the roof of a palazzo deemed unfit for habitation. In other words, Eftah couldn't blame his destruction entirely on the sirens who'd led him astray. At least one of them, some friend of friend, must've been suspiciously jumbo, Jabba-jumbo. Also the Black Lord had known the neighborhood, the Sanità, where the System was almost as pernicious as in the Forcello. Most likely the chill of a threat held some appeal for the man, late last night. He had plenty of cash. He found himself lonely.

The cash had disappeared, naturally. When it came to the contraband I.D., though, the police theory just didn't hold up. When Della Figurazione suggested that "the documents played some part in luring the victim in…" Risto waved him quiet.

"I.D. like these, eh. Eftah never had eyes for these."

It took a moment, watching the officer draw up straight, to notice the expression he'd used. "Eftah never needed such stuff," Risto went on evenly. "He made his own arrangements."

"We're looking into his legal status." He fingered a cuff. "The speculation is that the papers were intended for his friend."

"I don't believe it."

"You mean, not when he sent you such a text. Not when you found such a disaster outside his building."

"Look, last time I was in here you gave me this song and dance about terrorists. But in Naples, the closest thing to terrorists I ever saw were Eftah and his boyfriends. This latest kid, just the other day, he gave Eftah such a slap, I saw it..."

"A slap, you're saying. You were a witness to physical violence."

Risto thumbed his damaged lip, but if anything had started to ooze, it was within. Trying to respond, the very word "personal" had him faltering. He fell back on generalities. "Look, some people aren't cut out for commitment. I mean, just wait till your crew up there sees what happened to the photo of him and Mepris."

"You may be sure we're searching the premises."

"Whoever's up there, they'll see. Commitment went sailing off the roof."

Della Figurazione, staring hard, kept his tone matter of fact. He thanked his C.I. for the suggestion about the knife. Certainly the unit in Materdei would take special care with any tools they turned up, as well as anything the clansman might've used as I.D. Risto confined his responses to half a nod, keeping the lid on. He couldn't let another tantrum interfere with what he had to say about the business on the table.

Finally he pointed at the contraband papers. "Don't you see it?"

"Signore Auk War..."

"These aren't the good ones," Risto said. "The quality I.D., like we found last night, up by—by *the other* dead brother."

The officer frowned. "Now, I brought you in on this. I took full responsibility."

"Just look at them." This time he pointed with his chin.

Wordlessly, the other man drew closer.

"You see it, the weight of the bond? The watermark, that's shoddy work."

"Signore. You've got the eye."

The problem lay with the material, the paper itself. Today's contraband couldn't compete with what Papers had. It lacked the NATO ragstock and the currency-style threading. The legal boilerplate, as for that, was in place. Della Figurazione's own diploma must bear some similar script. But the difference in the paper, the weight and weave of the bond—that's what the officer had missed. That's what set apart the good fakes. No doubt he'd have noticed on another day, a better day, when he hadn't been confronted with horror shows back to back. Risto could grant the man that much. He could keep his tone respectful as he pointed out more flaws in the counterfeits: here a smudged signature box, there a Gothic capital with a thread through its base.

This drew another compliment, a warm murmur, and within, Risto's latest agitation settled down. In the photographs, the torn face could've been anyone's. The goo alongside might've been from raspberries. Meantime, he wondered about the same thing as the police: why had the documents been left behind? These forgeries might not "convince Caravaggio," as Risto put it, but they could well fool some weary border agent. They could take a Libyan or an Iraqi all the way to a new life. Then there was the speaker, a perfectly good piece of equipment, left to serve as a paperweight. In more than one way, it'd kept the papers from harm.

"The evidence may not be trustworthy," was how Della Figurazione put it. "Tampering appears more likely, given what you've told us."

Risto didn't miss the note of gratitude.

"So, Signore Owl Cure. Anything else?"

He took a moment with the mirror, the reflection murky at best. "Look, Della Figurazione." He rolled the *l* and *r*. "It's time you stopped butchering my name."

"Ah."

"My name, and the name of my, my 'cousin' here. One of his names, anyway."

The officer began to gather the materials on the table.

"Al'Kair, Detective."

Give the man credit, he left off fussing.

"Al'Kair, let me hear it."

"Yaw Le Car."

Risto, taking care with his smile, suggested the detective try both names.

"Aristofano Hulkier."

"Aristofano, and also Eftah. Al'Kair."

That time Della Figurazione came distinctly closer, vocalizing the hiccup. Risto gave him an approving noise, almost an *Om*.

Then: "Aristofano and Eftah Al'Kair."

The white man repeated both, just about spot on.

"Yes. *Per carità*. Yes, now just the last name. Al'Kair."

"Al'Kair."

"Al'Kair."

"Al'Kair."

They went through additional repetitions, call and response, an echo that created, in so barren a space, echoes of its own.

⁜

Later, when Risto began bawling to his wife, streaking his phone's screenshot, at least he'd found peace and quiet. Insofar as it was possible in this city, he'd gotten off by himself. Well up above street level, his crying and moaning were lost in the general Neapolitan rumble. The sun up here also helped with the chill of the officer's goodbyes.

Della Figurazione shook off whatever camaraderie he and Risto had built up. Sternly, citing yesterday's contract, he repeated his warning: not a word. His own suggestion was that Risto get out of town for a couple of days.

"If I had a wife down in Agropoli," he said, "I'd go stay with her till the Expo."

Della Figurazione hadn't spent his entire time in Wind & Confusion staring at Ippolita. He hadn't failed to notice the dead man on the wall. And though he admitted he couldn't stop the show (a freedom-of-speech headache was the last thing any of them needed), the detective pointed out that his C.I. had "no idea the toll it takes, spending day after day with the picture of a murder victim."

What unsettled Risto most, though, was the man's stare. Della Figurazione posed before him flatmouthed and crossarmed, Mr. Charlie himself, but what was that in his gaze? What oozing stump?

Risto wanted no part of another ride. Rather he scuttled off on foot, and he couldn't have said where he was headed. He walked unseen blocks, maybe twenty maybe thirty, then stumbled upon a hash of construction. Scaffolding, wiring, coils of cable. He'd reached the Galleria.

Was this what he'd been looking for? A racket of lunching and hustling, amid the storefronts' glitz? Surely not, especially now that it came to him he needed to make a call. A private call, personal, and more than likely it would go on a while. Now it came to him: the Galleria had a roof. Five stories up, above the shopping, the complications of the *Expo*, you could wander as freely as a desert nomad. From down here the exposed girders could suggest the charred remains of a bonfire; up top, you thought of a dinosaur graveyard in the Gobi.

Around the dome, even when there wasn't a problem like quake repair, things needed the occasional fix. The glass in the ceiling, though thick as the stuff in a rocket capsule and reinforced with wire, needed replacement from time to time. It got regular scrubbing as well. The steel ribbing went through adjustments and retrofits. For all this as for the quake repair, the city had contractors, and among those this summer had been Risto's husband-and-wife team, Cops & Robbers. The two miniaturists got the job through some connection or other, some old parish acquaintance. The arrangement could be dismissed with a wisecrack, *one hand washes another*, except this hand was right for the job. Cops & Robbers remembered their trigonometry, and they could handle a rivet gun. Also they had less tangible qualifications, decent hearts and good heads on their shoulders. A citizen like Risto could appreciate that. Every now and again his adopted hometown actually rewarded folks who deserved it.

What's more, he'd gotten to watch them work. As Cops & Robbers made their repairs, he'd clambered over the dome's exoskeleton. When was it, seven weeks ago, eight? They'd invited their gallery owner up. He'd toured the catwalks, crawling out onto dictionary-thick glass, getting an angel's view of the hustle. Seeking a summer outfit? Opera tickets, a cappuccino, a stolen kiss? It was impossible to tell, three hundred feet above the action, through the distortion of a heavy industrial skylight.

Today a visit to the roof struck Risto as just the getaway he needed. The door to the stairs looked as unpromising as before, as if you were stepping into a broom closet. As for security, Galleria management doled out the midweek assignment to a brother from Eritrea. The guard spoke excellent Italian, though he wasn't yet a citizen (when two Africans started talking, this question tended to get settled in the first minute and a half). Still, Risto knew better than to insult him with the offer of a few Euros. Rather he agreed to get coffee after he returned downstairs.

His first time, he'd been surprised by the stairs, set in a tight spiral. You'd think you were climbing a lighthouse. Then out at the top, at the base of the dome, the first breeze-buffed view seemed to reveal a hub-and-spoke pattern. As you got your bearings, though, you noticed how none of the hubs amounted to more than half a wheel. In every direction lay smaller semicircles swallowed by larger. The smaller domes of the churches nearby were each only half a sphere, and it looked like you could tuck them all under the immense bulge of steel and glass to your back. The turrets of Castel Nuovo, the curved embrace of the Piazza Plebiscito, likewise suggested preparatory sketches, more than half erased by the vast, winking, blue-black oblong of the Gulf. All of Naples appeared to have achieved, at best, only a partial geometry.

The phone, Risto. The call that brought you up here.

He caught Paola at the beach, taking lunch under the family umbrella. She enjoyed the same sea breeze as he did, up on this roof, but with her so close to the water, the connection proved patchy. No more than a word or three came through at a time, in either direction. At first his wife didn't understand that he'd started crying.

"...Risto-ri? ...tell me anything? ... but...?"

And after she'd at last got the news: "Awful... your only family... awful..."

The problem wasn't just how the sand and water played havoc with the signal but the storm of interference set loose inside Risto's head. His voice catching, his words shrinking to sobs, he collapsed against the railing. Below, the view made even less sense than before, the parabolas mantis jaws about to bite. The icons right here in his hand, onscreen, went blurry—but what was he doing looking at his screen? What, with his head and shoulders out over the railing?

"Horrible." He tottered backwards and sank to his seat. "They tore him apart."

Paola did seem to be saying the right things. She made an offer to come back to the city tonight, and after that the same suggestion as the detective. "…Agropoli, why not, a couple of days…Rosa and To… arbor's fixed…"

Saying the right things, moving to where they'd have better reception. Risto pictured his wife ducking out from under the umbrella and wheeling toward the clubhouse. As she trotted along the slatted lido walkway, she'd have her chin up, addressing the phone's receiver as if it were a slice of pizza. In her favorite one-piece, she'd be showing dusky cleavage.

"There, *caro*, I'm up by the bar. Is that better? Can you hear me?"

He could see her, the face and phone coming together into an embrace. And where was his embrace, soothing his bruises and split lip? His face ached in new ways, stretching, wrinkling, as once more he took Paola through his terrible morning. His butt grew painful too; the dome girders were no good as a chair.

"Risto-ri. Those lights in the photos, his photos, those strange lights, haloes you called them—those lights you saw—do you think I've forgotten?"

Just like that.

"Risto-ri, do you think I can't imagine, the way it must feel?"

He sat three hours north of her, and five stories above sea level, but in no time Paola had found his own private evidence bag and slipped her thumbnail under the seal. Risto rocked and groaned.

"Do you need me to say it?"

A halo showed up every time he blinked, a trick of sun and tears.

"What happened, it's a terrible business, but it's nothing to do with you." Giving absolution, Paola kept the tone priestly; she and Risto had both grown sick of the tendency to shout, over the *telefonino*.

"*Caro*, how can it matter, what you saw in a couple of pictures? Whatever. How could you have done any different?"

So long as she didn't shout, the husband realized, she could speak freely. At this hour on a weekday, the only person in the lido clubhouse would be a dozing cashier. He'd begun to think again, yes, to come out of the murk.

"Whatever," he said. "Whatever it was I saw."

※

Risto turned to hard data, Della Figurazione and his dismal bits and pieces. With each detail he gained more control. He could talk about the bracelet. He could reconnect with his anger. "Look at it, a second murder, and look, all of a sudden the police are just *jumping* on it. All of a sudden it's, it's…"

"It's a flower behind the ear." The real Neapolitan had the expression at the tip of her tongue. "A serial killer, that gets their attention, doesn't it?"

"The detective, the man, the man who called me in—you ought to see him. The way he dresses for work, he puts up quite a front."

"And isn't this his opportunity to shine? To go on camera and play the hero? This is a great story."

"It's a story with a moral."

"He can say the police are here for everyone."

"Doesn't matter if your skin's the wrong color of olive oil."

"Doesn't matter if you can't vote. Oh, my poor, benighted children! Even the least among you are safe in our hands."

His wife had a dozen ways for giving Risto heart. A dozen, if not fifteen, and he regretted that he had to rein her in. "A serial killer," he said, "eh. Look, I have to tell you, I told the detective too, Eftah doesn't fit the case."

Now what? What, was his voice breaking? Risto clutched at the rail overhead and yanked himself back to his feet. The air off the Tyrrhenian cleansed even the muggy approach of August, and the hullabaloo off the boulevards swaddled him in white noise. He gave a cough, lamely. He spelled out the murder's more questionable details.

"In particular the I.D.," said the husband. "Like somebody didn't want to waste the good paperwork."

"The good paperwork? But, by this time, isn't the Earthquake I.D. starting to lose value? All it ever was was a stopgap."

"I, the way I heard it…" Another cough. "There might still be some excellent forgeries in circulation."

"And then there's Mepris. These papers, good or bad or whatever, couldn't they have been for him? Or are you saying you don't believe that?"

"I can't believe it."

He paced the catwalk, his voice rising. He reminded her of his clansman's final text. "I don't read any farewell gifts into that, Paola. Plus there's Mepris, such a powder keg. The way he can go off about *integrity*—fake I.D. is the last thing you'd give him. Eftah had already gotten slapped once."

Besides, the Black Lord would've known lousy goods when he'd seen them. "He can spot a, he could, he—he was never one to go for garbage."

Stumbling, Risto had to catch himself against the rail. His missed what his wife said, though he got the tone, the agitation. Was she repeating herself? Something about their daughter?

"She's waving, Risto," Paola said, "our Rosanina."

Their youngest had come out from under the umbrella, and overhead she was waving one of her flip-flops, an impossible Smurf blue. When Mama had run off, she'd been the lone adult on duty. "The *riposo*," Paola reminded him. "My sister, you know her, she's back at the house and out like a light."

"Rosa's waving," said Risto.

His wife mentioned the family under the next umbrella over; she reminded him that they could keep up via text.

He put his back to the city. Before him rose the dinosaur's rib cage, the girders and dome. Over the phone, on the lido walkway, Paola was getting patchy: "…you rattling around up there…honestly…."

With that came the grief again, here in his peculiar place for a *riposo*. The wind snatched away Risto's sobs, and at his first stagger the rail bit his hips, but his vision blurred so badly he saw the Galleria as his own shaved, aching head. A glimpse was all it took, a blink of a vision. With that, the difficult moment drained away. He struck a better balance on the walkway, cooling, going dry. The change was so complete, so sudden, it felt as if he'd suffered his last bad spell. He'd weathered the worst, and when the duomo before him came back into focus, what he had in mind was a kind of joke. Cops & Robbers had told him the rooftop was perfect for the final showdown in a spy thriller. You could see Jason Bourne up here.

His phone went off again, a roundelay of cheesy electronica. For texts, Risto had never figured out how to use his Masekela download.

Her first message reiterated that he ought to come down. The husband assured her he'd thought about it, then added that there were plenty of trains back to the city as well: *15 a day.* Next, what about the kids? *A squabble,* she wrote. *A few €. A fruit ice.* Then Paola sent the name of the murdered clansman, followed by a question mark. Risto again found a seat, a more comfortable V of girders, and reminded his wife that he'd begun to pull away from Eftah long ago. *Yrs now, closer to ppl like Gssi.*

But Giussi and today's victim had shared the demimonde. Paola reminded Risto that the performance artist had come up with the "Black Lord" business. *Made u believe E wd always land on his ft.*

Risto could only parrot his clansman: *He was old school.* Not much of an elegy, a stencil on an eggshell, but didn't they have plenty of time for better? They'd return to this lost brother again and again, rethinking what he'd meant.

Paola: *Howd E ever get himself in such a situ?*

In shorthand, the crime scene looked that much more dubious. Whether the cutting tool had been the landlord's own made no difference. Paola tapped in an observation about the fishermen down her way: every one of them carried a serrated blade. *As for bracelet, rlly, 1000s.* You could buy them on the beach: *Same salesmen towels & toys.*

Risto suggested the obvious: *The breakup. E was needy, wasnt thinkg.* Yet he could see Paola's objection before the text came in. Eftah's emotional state only explained why he'd gone out again, on a *rough night.* (Rough? The wife had no idea.) Eftah was the kind to go out, she went on: *Never a man for TV & Nutella.* Risto had to grin at that, and wonder too about his own grief therapy, up here above the downtown. How did a man pull himself together by risking a fall that would break him to bits? Whatever the answer, it wasn't Eftah's. For the Black Lord, only fresh hugging and kissing could soothe him.

He needed a party, wrote Paola.

Yes, and he'd go for a party out of bounds, yowling with the alley cats. But since when had Eftah fussed with cuffs and a ball gag? *Since when did he play w/knives?*

The husband didn't know how much he could share, how much he had strength for, and he left his keypad alone until Paola asked about the Camorra.

Yes, he answered, *ystrdy & again this AM. In Matrdi, Camrr @ his bldg.*

His bldg? she asked. *When the mob held the mortgage? R, rlly - I bet the body was found in whole other pt of town.*

He was surprised he hadn't yet shared this detail, and as soon as he did, he was surprised again.

Sanita? The response came so fast, it laid Risto back against the dome. *& Cmrr @ the apt? Do the math - its Systm, mob bsnss.*

The husband reread this a time or three, belly-up on the glass. He grew aware of what a mess he was, his good shirt untucked and speckled with rooftop dust, even steel dust. He let the phone drop to his chest and studied the hot blue overhead, smudged here and there with afflatus from a grumbly volcano. He and Paola might've been holding this conversation between smoldering pots of soothsayer's herbs.

The phone went off again, his wife repeating herself, making sure he'd got the picture. The killing must've been some arrangement between Eftah's crooks and the one who ran the Sanità. The motive must've been real estate. The Black Lord had the Black Hand as his co-owner, anyone could see that. Anyone could see the property value, walking distance from city center, rich in history and now fully updated. Full ownership was only a matter of the right signature, the kind of respectable front the Camorra could always bring to the table. First, though, something had to be done about the squatter in the pent-house—and then had come the uproar last night, the furniture flying off the roof. The opportunity.

Look @ my Paola, Risto replied at last. *Solves a murder via text.*

Up and back between earth and moon, a smaller sphere ricocheted: ☺.

Risto didn't know how to send the same in return. He'd never learned the emoticons, and anyway he was done with this, his midair spin and rinse. He was back on his feet, dizzy but frowning, brushing himself off. By the time Paola brought up the thug outside Eftah's, this morning, Risto was ahead of her. He replied that Jabba the Hut must've had a reason for visiting.

Xactly. Planting evdnce? Knew police wld search.

Im on it. Police, Homicide, Im on it, right now.

Risto had brought up his Contacts, Della Figurazione, when his wife's final message reached him. It stopped him for a moment, at the top of the Galleria stairs. He'd been working up to the call, telling himself the detective should've known. Follow the money—he should've known. But then arrived Paola's last text, unlike her, oddly formal. *I imagine you have a lot to talk about with the police.*

※

Fifteen minutes later, he'd gotten no farther than one of the best bars on Via Toledo. He stood with the brother out of Eritrea, over an empty espresso cup and water glass, nibbling at an olive and talking about art.

"My friend," said the security guard, "there is one new painting I like. There is one, a nutty painting, and it's got a big number five, bright yellow."

"*The Figure Five in Gold.*" Nutty, Risto thought, just like this conversation. "That's not so new."

The gallery owner passed along the date of the New York piece, almost a hundred years back by now, and the name of the artist. This in turn recalled more recent struggles, the grind of his exams, up early and up late. Italian higher education offered several arts-related certificates, *laurea*, and by the time Paola was pregnant with Rosa, Risto had earned three. Wind & Confusion would have more behind it than the owner's taste and the in-law's money.

Anyway, Risto was in for a more demanding give and take soon enough, back at the gallery. His man in Homicide had said he'd stop by at three. Della Figurazione had been about to call, it turned out; he had new business "best discussed face to face." For the moment, Risto might as well take time with a semblance of nourishment and another sort of police. The security guard had asked to be called Konan, *Kuh-NAHN*. He worked on the last of his panino and, between chews, tried his luck with the name "Charles Demuth." After the third attempt, he grinned.

"I do like that one. That's how I dream of New York, you know?"

Might as well smile back. "My guess is, that's just what the painter would say. He'd say that nobody understands him so well as Konan the Eritrean."

"My friend, let's not kid each other. The truth is, most of the things you put on the walls, over at your gallery, I don't understand them at all."

"You don't understand? I ought to show you the—" Risto lost his smile "—the photos I have sometimes."

The guard swallowed and nodded. "Sure, the photos, black and white, the clubs and the squats. You've got a batch going up for the Expo, now."

"Yes." Risto fingered where his hairline would be. "Those."

"Sure, the photos I understand—except, what's there to understand? That white woman, her work, it's just our people, the hardships we face every day."

Lugubrious talk, Konan. Yet as the guard polished off his sandwich, you could see why this was the price he'd named, in exchange for roof access. A lunch date with the owner of *Vento e Confuso* did him far more good than a few Euros. Side by side at the bar, one brother a fireplug and the other a giraffe, didn't they prove something to the Italians at the cash register and the espresso machine? Weren't they the shape and color of the future? They wore professional clothing (Risto had put himself back together in a Galleria restroom) and made intelligent conversation.

"But, art," continued the guard, "that's your decision, what's art."

"My decision, eh. You must've noticed what I'm trying to represent, over there."

"Okay, but let's not kid each other. The reason those photos get so much attention is because it's a good-looking white woman taking them."

Konan, declared Risto, ought to write for the arts blogs. "One of those rich kids on the web—he says that what Tuttavia does is '*clandestini* porn.'" Nor was that insult the nastiest, he continued. More than once now, the photographer and her gallery owner had asked themselves whether she ought to show her face at the receptions. "As it is, every reception, four out of five people there, they can't see past her face. For her, every reception's a performance."

"My friend. You're not saying I should feel sorry for her?" Konan must've worked on that look, the lifted eyebrow and bent smile. "That woman—Lady Di didn't get such pampering. Whatever she wants, somebody else pays for it."

"I'm saying you need to see past the pretty white face and take another look at the photos. If you really take a look, you'll see it's nothing like porn."

"I'll tell you, I've heard talk. Last Friday night, I was at a party, and she was there too, and the talk was all over the room."

"You were—you were at the club? The club, later they found that brother..."

Both he and Konan fell into a studied casualness, both facing the street door with an elbow propped on the bar. Risto's voice hadn't dropped to a whisper, exactly, but he hadn't finished his sentence either.

"All over the room, talk about the worst kind of porn. Rape and murder."

Risto couldn't handle eye contact. "A, a snuff film. You heard this."

"Oh, I left. I'm not looking for any trouble. But your girl with the camera, she stayed. Also that big silly white man, the moneybags with his pretty young thing."

Hiding behind his cup, he tried to recall if anyone else had put Fidel at the scene.

"The clumsy bastard had a camera too. But any pictures you get from that night, they won't show you the city of brotherly love."

"Brotherly...?" Risto doubted he had the strength to talk about either kind of film work. "Look, Konan. Tuttavia's pictures, they do the Africans some good." He couldn't risk another olive, not when it might make him tear up. "Up North, she's one of our angels. But that's not why you need to come back to Wind & Confusion."

The name of the shop, yes. Konan grinned to hear him work it in.

"What you need to see is how a person imagines themselves into a different life. Into a different person, entirely."

"Oh, now this, I should've expected this—you believe anything is possible."

"But look at you and me, what we're doing here. Look at you, a cop in Europe. Keeping the bling safe for the white folks. You're a different person entirely."

"Oh, so I'm the same as the items up on your wall? Get a whiff of this uniform, you'll see I'm flesh and blood."

"But that's just what she puts in every shot, stinking humanity."

"As if a piece of pastry like that has any idea."

Risto actually raised a finger, professorial. He wasn't talking about the artist. "That woman, eh. I could tell you stories." But Tuttavia's work...

The Eritrean lost interest. His only response was a jerk of his head, leading Risto back out in the afternoon. The crowd had thinned and a number of shops had pulled down their grates, but these blocks always had some rhubarb going. The Expo work crews kept up their noise, piecing together the bleachers and stage.

Konan didn't have to go far in order to ask about Earthquake I.D.

"I heard you were looking," murmured the security guard. "And a man in your position, why would you go up to the roof just to make a phone call?"

The men from the South had shared a meal and the Citizen had shown he could be trusted. He wasn't a police stoolie. Risto, throwing in a nod or two, could only wonder at how easily he'd proven himself.

Could the man have read something into how quietly he'd taken that Friday-night rumor? The ugly talk of a murder on camera? Anyway Risto kept nodding, going with it, and when Konan said the documents weren't for him, they were for a friend—what could a guy do but take it straight-faced?

They stood surrounded by buying and selling, after all. Brand names and discount offers flagged the boulevard, Via Toledo, *Tuleda*, in the songs. On some maps the name was still Via Roma, and the packed quarters surrounding the street had undergone a lot more makeovers than that, trashings and renewals, and a few of the improvements had managed to last. At this hour on a Wednesday, with the sun so high, it could've been a Hopper painting. The shadows set sharp, tight frames.

Konan, bending over him, appeared more the giraffe than ever. Risto, low-voiced, agreed to try. It wasn't as if he was lying whole cloth. For starters, he admitted he didn't have any I.D. "Yesterday," he said, "didn't work out the way I'd hoped."

It wasn't as if he was lying, or wished the man harm.

❋

If Risto had stayed away from the shop any longer, quipped the *assistente*, she'd have started to think she'd inherited the place. Her boss, still grappling with a decision he'd made on his way over, had no comeback other than a weak smile. He'd made up his mind, but he still fretted over how he'd handle it. Wind & Confusion, however, showed him something else again: a seduction in progress. Della Figurazione had a haunch on the desk, a perch like a bird of prey. Down in the chair, meantime, Ippolita swiveled from side to side indulgently. She knew just what she was showing him. Her wisecrack about the shop was more of the same.

The man from Homicide struck a more serious tone. "As a detective, one always has to improvise and to experiment. One works like an artist."

The girl had a couple of fingers in her hair, twirling: "But, really, don't you think I've heard that one before?"

"Oh, you meet a lot of men on the force?"

"Oh, never, truly."

Della Figurazione gave a tepid laugh.

"I mean the idea," she went on, "what you said, the detective as artist. I heard that my first year at university. For a course on *film noir*, I mean—the professor posted it at the top of his website."

At that the officer turned to Risto. Della Figurazione swung out of his perch, glowering, looking a little like Konan. Again he said he had news, adding that he'd heard from the unit in Materdei. Now if he and Risto might have a moment alone...but Risto cut in: "You found his knife."

The man was stumped again.

"The knife that belonged to my so-called cousin. Serrated blade and all."

"Signore?" asked Ippolita.

"Your people, they found it. Standard handyman equipment."

"Are you—signore, are you talking about your clansman Eftah?"

"You found it, but it was clean. Wiped completely clean."

"Your clansman? His knife? Oh, Madonn', did he get into it with Tuttavia?"

Both men looked to the *assistente*, sitting up in her chair. Sitting up, breasts up, she set Risto thinking about Paola. His wife had shown the same alacrity, in her texts from the beach—but then, he'd already been thinking of the beach, or at least of getting out of the city. He'd made a decision.

The detective loomed closer. All he'd say about the "site of the crime" was that a search had "proven fruitful." What had brought him to the gallery, rather, was "another matter," something to do with "the Moroccan friend."

Risto ground a knuckle where one sideburn would be. He'd been intending to send Ippolita home anyway, he said—just, give the two of them a minute, please. Once the officer had withdrawn across the exhibition space, Risto bent over his keyboard and pulled up the gallery's accounts online. The figures looked as bad as he'd expected, but he could do this.

The *assistente* wouldn't be needed tomorrow either, Risto told her. "Wind & Confusion is closed till Friday. The morning of the show, I'll call you."

Della Figurazione had retreated to the farthest wall, by the larger La Cia. He wasn't too far off to hear Risto's announcement, however, and while Ippolita's mouth went prettily ajar, their visitor gave a murmur of approval loud enough to echo. The *assistente* got the message, and swiftly became bland and agreeable. When her boss went on to say he had "a family issue," and he might cut back on his August hours as well, she waved this away.

Whatever the signore likes, she declared. With a shrug, she added: "August."

Risto brought up the painter out of Libya. "Yebleh," he said, "I'll put him on the payroll for a couple of weeks. He's always asking about this end of the business."

Ippolita allowed her eyes to widen. She knew a thing or two about the watercolorist.

"He could use the structure," Risto went on. "If I put him on payroll, he won't have so much free time on his hands."

First a glance over her shoulder, then: whatever the signore likes. She slipped out of the chair and let Risto take over the computer, where he set up the transfer for her overtime payment. He made sure Ippolita saw the figure. At that, at last, she risked an indiscretion. The *assistente* bent to his ear and whispered, never mind what the cop across the room might think.

"Oh, signore, listen. The bank returned his check. Castelsabbia."

Risto's first thought was of the ibuprofen in his desk.

"Non-sufficient funds," Ippolita continued. "The creep lost track. Taking out a fresh line of credit every time he bought his little doll another miniskirt...."

"Some of those banks, eh."

"I did try calling, I mean the bank, but I couldn't get past the switchboard."

"The switchboard?" Risto kept his own voice conversational. "*Per carità*, that's not even in town. You could've been talking to Atlanta. New Delhi, maybe."

By now she'd quit whispering too. Upright beside him again, she agreed that details could be put off till Friday. If anyone deserved a day out of the city, it was the signore. And such a lovely surprise for the wife and children!

Actually Risto had somewhere else in mind, but Ippolita didn't need to know that. He assured her he'd clear things up with Fidel, and while he was at it, Yebleh. It wasn't as if her boss were going to China.

Also he had other thoughts, meantime, about pornography and what it paid. Even poorly done—if it left a corpse, wasn't that worth more?

※

Della Figurazione had more news from Materdei. The unit on the scene didn't just have a possible murder weapon; also they'd come across a person of interest.

How much of this gobbledygook would Risto have to listen to?

"He walked right in," continued the detective. "Three of our men in the place, turning it inside out, and the boyfriend, he walks right in."

Ex-boyfriend, the Moroccan had insisted. Mepris was claiming that he'd come back to collect a few things, and this was also why he'd brought along a large friend.

"One *immense* African," said the detective. "The kind that makes you think of diamond mines."

No it doesn't, thought Risto. The diamonds are down south, the former lands of the Dutch, the Brits, the Portuguese.

"Anyway," Della Figurazione was saying, "that's how it was reported to me. The crew up in the apartment thought of a diamond miner."

"What, not a basketball player? Not Big Shaq?"

The detective fingered his watch. Even a white man, he said, could see that the pretty boy wasn't telling the whole truth. "He'd brought his friend for protection."

"Protection, possibly. But I bet neither of them had the knife."

No, and whoever had used the thing last had cleaned it thoroughly, with oil. "Just as you suspected, signore. Signore Al'Kair."

Risto, still in his chair, lifted his chin. Della Figurazione went on to explain that more than the weapon itself, what seemed telling was where it turned up. "Our people found it in a file of papers. Like a bookmark, deep in the middle."

It took the police a while to make sense of all the paper. Mepris had to dig out a poem he'd published in a magazine from Prague. "Published in Prague, but written in some street patois out of, I don't know, perhaps Casablanca. The only word I recognized was *labyrinth*."

The sign on the gallery door, Risto reminded himself, was turned out.

"Even now," continued Della Figurazione, "we're going over these materials in the lab. The knife in particular."

"Sure. You've got one of those lights, sure."

The officer adjusted his lapels.

"Those supernatural lights, C.S.I. You can see the aura of anyone who... "

"Signore, I heard you tell your young woman that you were closing shop. You're taking a day out of town, I heard."

Risto pinched his lip, the fat spot. His visitor added that, earlier, the gallery owner had sounded "quite determined about leaving police work to the police."

Risto couldn't help himself: "Look, what kind of a murderer hides his weapon in the victim's apartment? And then comes back the next morning?"

"Ah, except this was an act of passion. This, logic was out the window." Della Figurazione gestured to the photos as if they offered some corroboration. "But then, you're the informant. You tell me." He strained for conviviality. "Tell me about this 'Mepris,' signore. That remarkable alias, for instance."

"Give the boy credit. For him, it's about the writing."

"A boy, ah. That's him, yes, isn't it, an excitable boy."

Risto tried his tongue on his lip.

"Signore Al'Kair—" Again careful with the name. "—we understand there was an altercation. Just recently, this Mepris and your, your clansman, they came to blows."

Hadn't Risto already defended his friends to this guy? Or had he tumbled into one of Paola's fairy tales, some story of infernal reiteration? He got out of the chair and put his back to the officer, busying himself with a photograph.

"Our sources tell us," concluded Della Figurazione, "that you were at the scene."

At the scene? Today, if Risto had arrived in Materdei half an hour later, he'd have been the African to stumble in on the police.

Della Figurazione pressed. Was the information correct? Had the signore been present at the Moroccan's assault?

"Assault. That's your word, Off-i-cer."

"You told me yourself that they fought. According to witnesses, the morning before last this Mepris was threatening worse."

"But, what is this?" Risto met the man's gaze. "First the photographer's the murderer, and now it's the writer?"

Drily the detective pointed out that he hadn't been the one to bring up Tuttavia. "Insofar as that woman interests the police, it's thanks to, ah, an informant."

As for the fireworks in the Camorra bar, Risto had a different interpretation.

"It was about the *opposite* of killing anyone. About trying to fix things." The witty Mepris had been at wit's end; to salvage the romance, all he could think of was to make a scene.

"An act of passion, eh." Risto was sitting again, hands folded. "Look, that was it, that one single act, Monday morning in the bar. One hard slap." Della Figurazione needed to understand: the madness had worked. "After Mepris made a spectacle of himself, those two made up. They got a couple more good days."

"You're saying, after the trouble in the bar?"

"No more than an hour after. Eftah and his pretty Moroccan, I'm a witness. They were back in each other's arms."

The man's look lightened a bit. "This Mepris sounds like an Italian girl."

Risto cracked a smile, but Della Figurazione once more turned ominous. He knew his game, Good-Cop-Bad-Cop all in one package, and grimly he pointed out that wild swings of feeling tended to get wilder. Mepris would hardly be the first angry lover who graduated from hand to blade.

And the C.I., what was his game? "Look, let me spell it out for you. My clansman, last night, over in the Sanità—that was business."

He spelled it out, his theory of the crime, or his wife's. It felt no less solid than earlier, every connection tucking into place, even his run-in outside Eftah's this morning. What could that goon have been doing there, if not planting evidence that would implicate the remaining tenant? The mob preferred a clean sweep, with no one left to interfere. Down at the bar in the piazza, likewise, it could only have been the *malavita* who'd made certain that the police heard about Monday's fight. Jabba the Hut himself might've told them. He'd known the cops were coming and he'd have been more than happy to slander a couple of nigger f-f-faggots.

Paola's solution to the murder fit together so snugly that, when her husband let a phrase dangle, the detective finished it. It got Risto up and pacing. "The motive was real estate. As for the means, in the System they've always got the means..."

"But the opportunity, you're saying. They lacked the opportunity. Then all at once, right before their eyes, they had the incident in the bar, and this on top of what'd happened over the weekend. The first ugly business."

Risto, unsettled as he was, had to smile. *The means*: one name the Hut had never been called. He'd earned it, though, the waddling obscenity, and the gallery owner didn't hesitate to bring him up.

"Ask whoever you've got in Materdei," he suggested. "A type like that, he must be the neighborhood nightmare."

Risto saw no special risk in this. Della Figurazione's precinct no doubt had a man who passed information to the Camorra, but it also must've had a thick file on the Hut. The creep probably sat in that bar and bragged about his file. One allegation more or less wouldn't matter much to him, and as Risto spoke of the mobster, he worried more about the detective, his narrowing stare.

But the officer liked what he was hearing. He actually squeezed Risto's bicep.

"Most civilians," he said between thank-yous, "have little or no conception what an investigating officer might deem useful."

Since the quake, he went on, the interference from the public had gotten worse. "We've had those pests coming out of the woodwork."

He dropped into Risto's chair, and the way he sighed, even a *clandestino* could tell that Della Figurazione was letting his hair down. He'd had a long night, a long summer, and slumping in his seat, he brought up a recent case of civilians getting in the way. "An American woman, an unhappy wife." The family had come to work with the quake relief....

"An unhappy wife," he repeated suddenly, gloomily. "Signore, I was quite unprepared for the calamity."

He sank still lower, spread-legged. Risto waited against the doorjamb.

When Della Figurazione again found his voice, he'd abandoned his story. In a lighter tone, he reflected that in times of crisis a person fell into unusual collaborations. "A street salesman might wind up in bed with the local kingpin."

If the detective had become a brother, it was a fraternity brother. He wore a keg-o-beer smile, admitting that this latest homicide could prove a terrific boon for his career. "It's a copy, but that adds something, it makes the first one matter, that someone cared enough to copy. This latest, whoever makes the arrest, it's, ah."

"This one's a flower behind the ear," said Risto. "The first, that was only another *clandestino*."

The visitor's smile gave a turn.

"It was a mess, sure, the kind of awful mess that makes the mayor pick a fight with the governor, but it was only a..."

"Signore, you're the one doing business with Castelsabbia. You think I didn't hear? You two do regular business. You and the wicked white man."

Risto fingered his crown.

"Police like me, you know as well as I do. We're only one number in a very long and complicated equation."

Now Risto used his knuckles. "Look, I was never trying to change the whole city. Eh, might as well try and change all of Europe."

Della Figurazione gave another of those sighs: June, July, and August. The best he could promise was that both investigations would expand. "Now one of the murders appears to involve organized crime," he said, "one at least. But signore, that possibility, you do realize, some of us on the force were already looking into it."

Much as the officer was grateful for Risto's contributions—"genuinely useful"—chances were he'd only helped speed up standard police procedure. "The *malavita*, 'the state within the state,' it's into everything, you know as well as I do. Any housewife watching TV, she knows."

Risto had a comeback ready: *Yes, and a housewife would've been quicker about it*. Leaving his head alone, he confined himself to observing they'd most likely find no connection between today's discoveries and La Cia's murder. "Your people in the lab, they won't be any help with the first brother."

The officer was out of the chair, straightening his outfit. The investigations would expand, he repeated, and checked his watch.

Risto let his head alone. "Della Figurazione, wait. Please, what about Mepris?"

"Ah. As I say, he's a person of interest."

"You mean you're holding him. You're, you've got him under questioning."

"Signore, you told me you were through with this. Your efforts in Homicide."

"Look, you can't believe it was that *kid*. He's no more the murderer than—than one of these jihadis you're so frightened of."

"Frightened." A Tuscan chill bore down on the word. "Frightened, isn't that interesting. After all, you're the one who nearly had his head split open last night. You're the one who any doctor in Italy would say is still in shock."

The man's face was in shadow, between Risto and the street windows.

"Signore Al'Kair. Truly. You go to any doctor, his wall full of degrees. He'd say you still haven't come back to your right mind."

He had a halo, but it was nothing more than the sun behind him.

EIGHT

O N THE ISLAND FERRY, THE upper deck, Risto had a bench to himself. It was therapy, alone in a breeze full of salt and fermentation. For this trip he preferred the slow boat, a fat old *traghetto*. The low-slung hydrofoils made for a shorter journey, but they didn't have the deck space. If you did find a seat outside, you risked getting your phone doused by spray. The gallery owner intended to use his phone. The calls, just a couple, shouldn't be too hard on him, but till now he'd put them off. They hadn't seemed reason enough to stop moving. He'd skipped swinging by the apartment too, driven to get some distance, some perspective. At his back, besides, he had the detective, a man still under the shadow of his ex and now, out of nowhere, with the opportunity to change his life. Della Figurazione had some powerful dreams going about this case, maybe a transfer to Milan, and the last thing he wanted was some hyperactive *nero* in the way. But then Risto himself was sick of his hyperactivity—his "experiments," to use the language of the dead. The getaway mattered more than a change of shirt and underwear.

Topside on a ferry, for some reason, you caught the communications boomerang better than on a beach. Risto got a connection clear as a bell on his first call, the one out to the island. In no time he confirmed that he was welcome and, therefore, in his right mind. His man on Capri remained the same as ever: sharing the house with a "lady friend." She wasn't one of those who preferred to go unseen, either, and for Risto they would pull together a party. At this, the man who'd just invited himself over had no choice but to sound pleased. Maybe he was, anyway; maybe island-style debauchery, more understated than the city version, would be good for him. After all, the ride across the Gulf looked like forty-five minutes of solo meditation.

Before the second call, he tried to force down one of the shipboard panini. Bad idea: the sandwich might've dated back to the Crusaders. Marauding knights like those who'd put up Castel Dell'Ovo, the hulking waterfront keep—you got a great view as the ferry pulled away, and come to think, that castle had a lot in common with Risto's attempt at lunch. It had a color you might call Desiccated Bread, if not Ham Past Expiration. Worse, the humpbacked medieval warren was a drain on the city. Every administration tried out something new: last year an arts venue, this summer a prison. Dell'Ovo had been the only place the police could find for locking away some immigrant protestor, a West African who'd gone through bewildering cycles of arrest and release. You wondered how the case turned out, and whether it might somehow help Mepris.

Anyway, somewhere amid Dell'Ovo's decaying brick, undoubtedly there lay the fossilized remains of the other panini put together the same day as this one. *Per carità*, the Crusaders had no idea about food to begin with. What did they eat, bones and mead? They'd been boat people, pirates, yet they'd had the nerve to claim Naples as Northern and white.

Risto fought down a couple of bites and half an Orangina. The next call was to Paola, and once he'd given up on the *panino* he needed only a moment more, a scroll through his photos. When a stranger took him by surprise, an African woman sliding in beside him, she had no need for black folks' radar to see she wasn't interrupting.

She noticed the photos too, the kids mostly, grinning hugely. With their complexions, the smile could've been a halo slid down to the middle of the face.

The woman nodded and cooed. "Aren't you the lucky father!"

Her Italian, husky, passable, could've come from half a dozen countries on the other side of the Mediterranean.

"Why, they're dolls, just perfect *dolls*." Risto didn't so much as raise his eyes, but she kept on. "You ought to thank your lucky stars! One day soon, you mark my words, those two will make you rich."

Maybe she had some radar after all.

"They'll make millions for you in the fashion magazines."

Dubious as Risto found the compliments, he made a note to share them with Paola. He hid behind his Orangina and took in his uninvited guest. A woman no longer young, but slender and flexible and fresh from a shower. Her dress was a wraparound, its colors a match for one of his splashiest shirts.

Okay, benefit of the doubt: "The fashion magazines."

"Oh sir. You must've noticed. They're all the rage, these days, mulattos."

Wherever she'd gotten the dress, she'd been careful to choose a forgiving fit. Her chest was so flat that you thought of drought in the Sudan. The woman's hair, though, was a showpiece, a sunset-gold pageboy that fell across one eye. With a wig like that, her actual hair must be cropped as close as a man's.

Risto thumbed through another few shots. Eftah came up, blowing a kiss goodbye. Next was Giussi, striking a pose, arms akimbo.

"My my my."

Even at phone size, the man looked like a star, Jamie Foxx of the fleas.

"One after another, just look, such a handsome array of colored folk."

With a woman like this around, who needed a sandwich? Her energy had Risto noticing something new about his photo scrapbook. Other than Paola, he didn't have any white folks. He'd even left out Tuttavia.

"Oh la la," the stranger continued. "*Comme ces sont beaux, les Africains comme ca, le sang mixte.*" The language was the least of what had changed; the voice had dropped a good octave. "Small wonder Benetton can't get enough of them, the tawny pelts, United Colors."

Risto almost lost hold of his soda.

"The ads, Benetton, they're the opposite of the old story. Where's it from, that story, the *Thousand and One Nights*? Or was it Kipling, his Hindu act, *Just So*? The one about the leopard that can't change his spots—why, that's the *opposite* of what those ads are selling. They're telling you, wear our clothes and you're pretty as we are, in whatever color you'd care to become. The right clothes and, scrub-a-dub-dub, who says you're just a spotted old jungle cat?"

Risto had the hiccups. "Gi-Giussi!"

The performer tossed back his hair. A few colored sticks, an ointment or two, and he had a whole new face. When he laughed, he sounded a dozen years Risto's junior.

"So fetching a frock," he said, "you understand, I simply had to. You of all people, patron of the arts, philosopher of happiness. You know I had to *try.*"

"You had to try the...the frock?"

"Oh la, have you forgotten I'm a 'featured performer' with *Expo in Città?* Risto, the event just begs for something fresh, *n'est-ce pas?* One can't restore the city's cultural credibility in the sort of drab threads you'd see on Madame Mayor."

Giussi would have three-quarters of an hour, on the stage alongside the Galleria. The booking loomed large for him, naturally, a refugee song-and-dance man who would never play the Opera House. Nonetheless, the Expo offered a stage sanctioned by the city and *Regione.* It was a show that ought to lead to better, and why not better legal standing as well? Was that so inconceivable? Up in Rome this summer, there'd been talk of a saner immigration policy...and look at that, a wild notion, brought to mind by seeing his friend in drag. Look what the performance artist set him thinking.

Risto knew himself, his densely populated head. These last days he'd had worse of a crowd than usual, up there—yet here this Pulcinello out of Ethiopia, a man who took fiendish glee at warping the squares, had teased out stranger thoughts. He'd made his ferry audience aware of how, from time to time in this country, the earth could move. Up in Rome they were talking. Berlusconi was in exile.

"Giussi," he said, "you're amazing."

"Dear boy, frankly, you have no idea."

Anyway, continued the performer, wasn't it fitting that they find themselves "in the same boat?" Wasn't his citizen brother also traveling in disguise?

"As for me, you know what they say, the clothes unmake the man. This thing of colors I acknowledge mine. It's what I do, after all—but then there's you."

A Gulf breeze snatched away what there was of Risto's laugh.

"This wig, this frock, they're nothing much. They're but the outward show. And yet, you know, they help me to predict the future."

The performer covered his eyes (the nail polish, Risto noticed, matched the eye shadow), meantime extending the other thin arm. Reaching toward, what, the first black Prime Minister of Italy?

"Ss-spir-rits," he moaned, "*mesdames, messieurs! Réveillez votre mystère*, yes, let your marionettes take their places on the stage, yes, that's us too, this philosopher detective and I. Let us take our places.

"Yes-s-s...yes I see...tonight we dine at the American's!"

Risto got a hand on the outstretched arm, but by then Giussi was letting it drop. Neither of them wanted to risk the attention, and both had the same friend on Capri.

"My dear Aristofano, this visit, I made the arrangements ages ago. Ages ago last week. My business, this visit, is show business."

With a gesture at his bodice, his vacant bodice, Giussi reiterated that his weekend performance included new material. "Now, *mon vieux*, I imagine that you imagine that a talent such as I has no need of rehearsal..." But Giussi needed to glean for inspiration like everyone else, combing again and again over the performance field. He needed space to workshop, far from prying eyes.

"And for this, a rehearsal getaway, I must thank your former employer."

The American's setup wasn't so lavish—hardly a *villa*, as one of the papers had put it. There'd been a number of articles after the man had emerged from hiding. Still, for Giussi the island house and grounds served perfectly. "And I must tell you, for our friend too, the arrangement has its advantages. Should he have a guest or two, should he have three, they won't lack for entertainment. Ooh la la."

Much as Giussi loved *The Tempest*, he'd never been one to remain long marooned. Yet with his next breath, he quit sounding like a party boy.

"But you know, if I hadn't been there, the man's last couple of parties would've felt rather lonesome and meager."

Lonesome and meager? The American?

The Ethiopian let his pageboy head sink between his hands. "*Helàs*, I can't offer the man much by way of company. Not while I'm lost amid the baseless fabric of my visions." He straightened up, his gaze serious. "But then, tonight's host will hardly be alone, in contending with tragedy."

Risto should've known: by this time news of Eftah had seeped into the city's cracks. The performer began to offer sympathies.

Your last family, your last living link back South, I'm just sick about it...

Giussi would've swiftly discerned his friend's state, bruised and searching his phone for a bit of cheer. He would've got it at once and figured he had just the remedy. But now: *And to end the way he did, and him such a strutting, proud brother....I'm just sick about it. You know those police in Materdei, poking around, you'd think they wanted to slander the man.....*

"It seems the mob put out the word too," Giussi added.

Risto managed a nod. He noticed his sandals, dress sandals, in keeping with the morning's buiness casual. At least he'd tossed the skull-spotted slip-ons.

"The bad boys," Giussi said. "They put out the word, I mean, I heard it where I buy my hashish. One suspects they have an interest in that palace on the hill."

Risto got his damaged foot in one hand. At his grimace, Giussi began again.

"My brother, Aristofano, do you want an apology? Honestly, I thought you'd see the benefit in a game of pretend, a game between adults—"

"What?" Risto snapped. "Are you looking for a *review*?"

His Mr. Bones took this unfazed. "On the other hand," said Giussi, "why not, after all? We find ourselves both in the same boat. Why not play pretend?"

His gesture, rolling over, took in the entire Gulf. "We find ourselves here rather than, oh just for example, on the train down to join the wife and the wee ones."

Risto gave himself to the throb of the ferry engine, a kind of massage.

"Dear boy, Paola and the children, can't you handle them just yet? You'd still prefer, shall we say, a private workshop of your own?"

"Listen, Giussi." Risto sat up formally. "There's something else."

He found the words to address the gruesome news out of the Sanità, and to accept his friend's apology. "This stunt," Risto said, "making the crossing in drag. Eh, could be it did me some good. " It only seemed as if everyone was trying to play Detective, he thought; the game they really enjoyed was Doctor. "Anyway, you're right about Paola and the kids. I'm just not up to them yet. While I'm at it—you're right about the *malavita* too. They've had their eyes on Eftah's place for years."

The performer took this with an affable pout.

"But, Giussi. Something else."

※

The triple-X jpegs, for Tuttavia, amounted to a space worth saving out of her own inferno. A space on which she might construct a new city of the arts. But then there was her gallery owner, with no such stake in the work. It wasn't his face and genitals. Now, as for that, the nakedness and folderol itself, he had no serious objection. Risto went ahead and said it: *consenting adults.*

As for the artistic possibilities, he could make out, dimly, how the material might amount to something. God knows he'd sat through his share of stage nudity; back before the marriage, Paola herself had taken her shirt off for one of those Theater-of-Outrage things. For all he knew, given the right workup and the right trio, an ideal version of this performance would turn white male power inside out. Or expose black male self-loathing, or explore new frontiers of women's sexuality: whatever. He could take it like a philosopher. But the way the slideshow had come to his attention, via a mailing list that was Africans only—that changed everything.

Giussi fluttered his lashes. Risto's mouth ticked, unsmiling.

"Look, a trick like this, a dirty trick, I couldn't even figure it out on my own. I had to have Paola explain it."

"Oh Paola-la-la."

"You don't deny it. The photos, the recipients, you don't deny any of it, even when there's no one in Naples who Tuttavia trusts like she trusts—"

"Oh please. No one the woman trusts more? You yourself, she's trusted you with every piece she's ever done, and then there's your saint of a wife."

That irked, but Risto kept pressing. "Oh la," Giussi sighed, "I sent to a select few only, I assure you. The gentlemen I consider my core audience." But this didn't just sound familiar, it sounded flimsy. Since when did Giussi get defensive? He'd built a career on other people's secrets. Risto tried saying so, seeing where flattery would get him. Around the Naples honeycomb, he told the performer, there was no one better at interpreting the dance of the bees.

"Onstage, you've always got the dirt. Back last winter, that one riff? That riff about the governor's Nigerian whores? That was weeks ahead of *Il Mattino*." Any other time, Risto would've loved another round of icon-smashing. "Castelsabbia, I mean, such a fraud, 'Fi-del.' Paola and I both would love to see him taken down."

But this time, the target was closer to home.

"Giussi, she's one of your own. On top of that, you're hurting the gallery."

"Oh, listen to you, 'hurting the gallery.' Now who's talking like one of the elite? You've nothing against a *ménage a trois*, not even on camera, but you can't have anything that might embarrass the firm."

"Giussi, this isn't you. You're smarter than this."

"My dearest friend, even if people talk, you know what my brother Andy used to say. He never read the reviews, he said....'"

Risto's frown put pressure on a bruise, against the stem of his sunglasses.

"Well, our Brother Andy, I'm sure he loved to measure the inches."

"Giussi, if you could've heard Tuttavia. If you could've heard how she went off, when she learned who you'd been sending to."

No one rolls their eyes quite like a cross-dresser.

"Look, I realize she's Ivana Drama. But she was talking bloody murder."

"But what about the white, white, *white* man who took the pictures?" Growling, Giussi sounded closer to his real age. "That wife of his, you know she's more than half out of her mind over his money, and I'd say she was the life of the party. Am I to assume you've had this conversation with him?"

"Fidel, but…"

"'But…' oh *naturellement*, we can't piss on our Sandcastle."

"Look, Fidel's got nowhere near the same risk."

The sour set of the performer's mouth was utterly a guy thing.

"Giussi, she's an immigrant too. A person like her, outspoken like her, all that anger—she could wind up in cuffs."

"Yes, and it would be quite the eye-opener for a white girl."

Risto reached for his sunglasses and discovered he'd already taken them off.

"A *person like her*," Giussi went on.

It was as if the man had come out from under a tarp. The synthetic hair and the greasepaint somehow enhanced the honesty, the should've-seen-it-coming ferocity, enough to set Giussi baring his teeth. Risto was left wondering how he looked. Dumbfounded? Unable to get his friend's latest act, intense, convoluted, crossing some new threshold of irony? He felt as if he'd crossed a threshold himself, in the last spot he'd expected to find it, and wound up hip to hip with pure Extract of Enmity. Every response that came to mind sounded phony. *Giussi, I thought you were her friend*—could he say that? Or, *She trusted you?* He had nothing to match this edge, here at his hip.

"You hate her," he said.

"Aristofano, oh la, don't exaggerate."

"A woman like that, with her success."

"'A woman like that'? Is there no end to your euphemisms? Won't you speak with me man to man?"

"A white woman. A white woman, getting famous for pictures of our people."

Giussi shed the worst of his antagonism, giving a pout. "I can see what they put in the program, you know, for the Expo. I can see it as well as anyone. That shot of her face, who'd they get for that, the Modigliani of Photoshop?"

"They made her look like a model. They included half her résumé."

"*Eh bien, c'est vrai, je suis jaloux.*" The French helped, supple, as
if he'd relaxed. "Jealous, honestly, how could I feel otherwise? Someone who looks like a model." He went vogue, his hands a frame.
"Someone who steals all my best lines. You're so concerned about
how artistic property circulates, Risto, I do hope you've noticed *that*.
The interview with *Cultura*, as God is my witness, she took all my
best lines."

Risto could've used some way to check his own face.

"And white, oh la la—as white as the severed bones poking out of
our two recently murdered brothers."

From where he sat, Risto could take in his whole afternoon's journey. Ahead lay the island, like a hunk of prosciutto left out too long,
the meat gone brown and green; in the other direction, the city yawned
like the melon that went with the prosciutto, a slice worked over by
ants. He figured it was time again for a hard word.

"You hate her."

"Oh, but that simply won't do, that word. Not for a case like this.
Rather I was thinking how all of us out of the South, even our esteemed
Aristofano, we've had to sell our bodies."

If an African wasn't selling his aching back on the docks or in the
orchards. then he was selling his black ass outside the Galleria. "Our
poor friend La Cia, he wound up selling his own butchered corpse."

"You're sure of that? There was a movie, him getting killed?"

Giussi gave an agitated nod, rushing on. "But I'm talking about
earlier, when Fidel showed up with his latest toy, dreaming that he
might break into the market."

Risto was wondering about another market. How much money
could there be in such a film? As for Friday night's, come to think—
where was it?

"Child's play," Giussi was saying. "Utter child's play, to turn his
nitwit notion to my own ends, and it earned a far more satisfying pay-
back." He'd brought in the cover girl for the *Expo*. "High time she
learned what it feels like to wear a price tag."

As he'd gone on, Risto had sunk lower in his chair. "Giussi, I think
she knew already. I think you've heard her story."

"*Ah oui, quelle dommage*—the travails of a white girl fresh out of Conservatory!"

Frowning again, Risto roused himself.

"Oh la, whatever she suffered, I'm not without sympathy. I know the woman's heart so well that I can see our naked frolic through her eyes. For Tuttavia, it meant freedom to play, a return to innocence. If you were an artist you'd understand."

Why give an artist an opposable thumb, Giussi asked, if he's not supposed to grope about in the passions?

Good line, thought Risto, no matter which of them came up with it.

"Think of my brother Pedro, his *Woman on the Verge of a Nervous Breakdown*—isn't that always the case? On the verge, teetering, always? Or think of my brother Walt and his barbaric *yawp*."

A brother, Risto reflected, but another white boy. And Almadovar came from Spanish farm people and Warhol had been whiter than Tuttavia. But if he were to cut in on Giussi, to argue, the artist he'd bring up would be Degas. Degas had been aristocracy, with a family in the same upper echelons as Fidel's. Yet the painter hadn't needed a full cavity search of his own worst impulses. He hadn't needed a nervous breakdown. Still, Risto held his peace. The lean Ethiopian had been caught out, claws bared; he needed to talk, to get the stage patter rolling and pull his disguise back together.

"Do you know how I envy old Walt? With his yawp across wide-open America, the wide-open skies of Brokeback Mountain, oh say can you see?"

The sea air, Risto noticed, had pitted Giussi's makeup.

"Oh la la, Brokeback Mountain, Jack and Ennis. Those two lions lay down among the lambs…"

✳

Paola didn't hear his voice, it turned out, till he was at the American's. She and Risto spoke over a landline, the phone on a cord in an alcove in the foyer. The host liked it that way. The setting put constraints on any conversation, and in this case, when the call came in from Risto's wife, there was a show about to start.

A command performance: Giussi wouldn't take no for an answer, when it came to his rehearsal. *Critical mass*, he kept saying. Friday in Naples, he insisted, he needed to explode—*and how can I do that without critical mass?* He was a regular carnival barker, Giussi, hollering as if he wanted Paola to hear him on her end of the line. He realized that, should she and Risto talk for more than a couple of minutes, they could go for hours.

On top of that, down in Agropoli, the woman had Tonino and Rosa tugging at her. It was late by then, past dinner, and Mama couldn't neglect the kids two nights in a row. Risto had to wonder whether the one-man circus, out here on the island, weren't part of a wider rowdiness breaking loose up and down the coast.

Paola left him with a warning. "Risto-ri, I've got to run back up to Naples, it sounds like. If I don't, honestly, I shudder to think. You could be on the next flight down to Mogadishu."

"Mogadishu?" He'd been playing catch-up since he'd taken the phone. "I like it here."

"Yes yes yes. Hasn't my husband found Paradise, here in 'the North,' as they say? Hasn't he seen the figure five in gold?"

"Paola..."

"Risto. One ugly item on the news, really, is that all it takes? One ugly item and you forget you have a *family?*"

"Paola."

"A brother, you call him, that poor child cut to ribbons."

He rubbed the phone against his face, his bristles.

"Do you understand that I'm sorry about that child? Do you? But this little game of yours—well, it's no help to *him*, certainly."

Out back of the cottage, Giussi went on bellowing: showtime! Over the line came the fainter clamor of Tonino and Rosa.

"Just the opposite! Your little game only brings the ugly stuff closer to home. Now have I got to run back up to Naples?"

Risto had been playing catch-up, but he ought to have seen this coming. His wife knew he'd been playing detective. She'd come up with something clever in order to find out. But then, it'd been pretty clever of her just to track him down, here.

He'd never told her he would be at his old employer's. Back on the *traghetto*, Risto might've made sure his friend in the dress had seen Paola on the screensaver, but she never heard from him. She never heard his voice. The first person he had called, after he'd stepped away to the ferry railing, was his watercolorist Yebleh. And wouldn't you know it, the young Benghazi sounded a lot like an irritated spouse.

Yebleh took offense at being put on staff, even short term. He took it like some sort of demotion. Didn't Signore Al'Kair have the "Libyan O'Keefe" under contract for *painting*? The boy only simmered down after Risto asked if there were changes he'd like to see in the shop. At that, Yebleh started to sound executive. He'd believed for some time that Wind & Confusion needed a better presence among the city's marginal populations. The Africans knew the place, granted, or the average brother anyway. But what about the Bosnians, the Syrians, the Pakistanis?

Eh, admitted the gallery owner. Fair enough. Better outreach.

The watercolorist, mollified, agreed to try the desk job for a few days. "Ippolita," he asked, "she'll be there, right?"

Risto rang off having gotten no further. Really, he had little idea what he'd do about Wind & Confusion, after the *Expo*. Nor could he say why, though he'd pulled up Paola's number on the screen, he couldn't hit "Call." He sent a text. He told her he loved her but included only a single scrap of information: *Capri*. After that he powered down, reducing his phone to pocket ballast, as if he were an old man carrying a box of pills. He concentrated on the rituals of island socializing, the stories at dinner and the *passeggiata* to help digest. At the American's, these demanded a lot of attention. Every guest was expected to be some kind of performer.

Nevertheless, in the time it took for dinner and a walk, Paola had found him. Either she'd had the cottage number or she'd worked some Capri connection of her own. She'd claimed her moment, and after she'd let Risto know what she knew, all she knew, the roar of the old-style dial tone in his ear seemed the most unnerving distraction anywhere around the Gulf.

Then the American was squatting beside him, pulling the plug. The man could hardly manage, as he went down and up you almost heard the wine slosh, but tonight, his backyard was an arts venue. The space was too small to leave the phone on.

Four odd-lot rooms made up the cottage, though there was also a terrazzo, up under one of those domes the tour guides liked to call "Saracen." Quadrilangular bide-a-wees such as this, stucco and brick, had multiplied across the island, what, a century back? A century and a half? Whenever Capri became the place for the more paleface Europeans to carry on their own experiments. Whenever the moneyed Aryan freaks like Friederich Krupp had started trolling for dusky island boys. More recently, over in Naples, Risto's old boss had done his bit for the area's reputation. He too had played the sybarite—hetero, thank you. But though he'd run the only gallery in the south that could attract "Establishment clientele," the deep pockets from Milan or even Berlin, the man's own getaway didn't include much artwork. A few pieces had come over on the ferry, and these Risto knew well, Neo-Geo, the Nova Poli paradigm. For the island, though, the former tastemaker had limited himself to softer angles and pastel hues.

Actually, his most prominent display wasn't what you'd call art. On one sideboard, the American had laid out an array of antique knives. The collection had been smaller over in Naples, where the Somali *assistente* had been one of the few to see it. It had started to come together, his employer explained, back during his days on Manhattan's Lower East Side. Here on Capri, tonight, Risto counted fifteen. Three of the knives were the sort that people used to turn up all over the Gulf, Roman or Greek. Where you could still make out the decorations, you saw mazelike spirals or squares, and one bore legible script: *Imperium I.C.*

The oldest of the tools, though, set a person thinking of Noah. Now there was a boat person, Noah, praying the whole way, his passage arranged in a rush and without papers. No sooner had the man made it to shore than he'd hogtied an animal (which could he spare, you wonder?) and made sacrifice to his God. For that, he could well have used this piece on the American's sideboard. Its blade was veined as if with seaweed and the shredded handle could've been an atoll eroding.

"All right," Risto said finally. "I think we can rule out any of these."

The host came close to a smile, his mouth stretching. News of the crimes hadn't taken the same slow boat as the guests. Out on the cottage stoop, the American had showered his former assistant with condolences, kisses, rubs of the head. The man kept repeating that he understood. A night away from the madness, he *understood*, nothing so good for a fellow. By the time Risto made it inside, the knives came as a relief. He took time for another of the set, fashioned like a snake, Incan or Aztec or whatever. Actually he preferred it to his host's calculating tease of a smile.

He'd gotten enough of such double messages, double or triple, back at the Nova Poli. At the gallery, when newcomers got their first look at the proprietor, with his cheekbones and eyes at the angle of a martini glass, generally they took him for Japanese. They asked about tsunami damage or manga comics. The questions left Risto's mentor looking all the slyer. After a moment, with a diplomat's politesse, he'd explain that he'd been born in Saigon.

How many times had Risto seen it? White embarrassment, easy to read.

The American could rub it in, too. *In point of fact,* he might add, *Saigon doesn't exist anymore.* His native city, he'd remind them, was no longer a capital, and besides that named after its conqueror.

I think of myself, he'd conclude, *as an American.*

❊

This evening, once the host was done with his ceremonies of welcome, he sprang a prettier surprise. He produced a conversation piece, a pitcher of rococo hand-tooled ceramics, gussied up with vines and leaves and grapes. The glaze was beaded from the ice wine within, a whiff alone cleared the head, and the American had long since served his other two guests. As for himself and his girlfriend, his current girlfriend, they'd started earlier still. Risto's sensei had become a citizen of Capri. On his calendar, the only dates that mattered anymore were those that let you know which seafood was in season.

So too, the American out of Saigon had little to do with the other Asians snatching up island properties. These were the Chinese again, clumsy new money. Tonight's host, on the other hand, could get the party started just by bringing out a pitcher. To pay for the piece, probably he'd needed no more than a loaded remark.

As Risto worked through these ceremonies, he couldn't shake the sense that his butchered clansman had joined the party. It was as if the host's kisses and sympathy had summoned the ghost. Both he and Eftah were older and knowing, though neither was much of a father figure; between them, in any case, the younger 'Dishu boy had practically gotten the world on a platter. Yet now the loss took hold, the gloom. Struggling to shake it, Risto noted the differences between the Black Lord and the American. The latter barely came up to his chin, and though he'd lately put on boozer's jowls, otherwise he remained yoga-lithe. The guy wasn't about to start shaving his head, either, not with that spill of black straw. Back at the Nova Poli, it had occurred to the assistant that, if he'd been white, anyone coming in for the first time would've assumed he was the one in charge.

But then, he'd never have come up with so cagey a name for the space. The phonemes could be read so many ways, they triggered speculation in the press, but no one ever wrested an explanation from the proprietor. As for Risto, he'd always imagined that the point was to keep people guessing. One of the first things that impressed him about Paola was that she felt the same, enjoying the trickery.

"New Police, New City, *Exploding*," she used to say. "Signifiers without end."

Dinner unwound thorough a fourth course, a fifth, and the filigreed decanter seemed bottomless. Risto came to think he was doing Paola a favor, leaving his phone off; she would've been sorry to hear what she was missing. The host had arranged a caterer, though the menu was hardly a stretch. Linguine and clams, tomato and mozzarella, dishes the girlfriend no doubt could've pulled together for free. She looked old enough to know her way around the island's galley kitchens, and she wore low-cut summer yellow, her tanned *abbondanza* heaping. The American went in for fleshpots, an ectomorph's compensation. This latest had an old-fashioned mouthful of a name, Berenice, and as for the relationship, Risto's host proved (no surprise) evasive. He mentioned an evening of song in the Capri Town piazza.

The other two guests, you had to figure, were the reason for the quality of tonight's ingredients. Tonight wasn't about the old cronies from the city, but the young couple descended from Valhalla. They could've learned to pout from an angel. Their golden hair hung in bangs—low-slung haloes—and the boy's was even silkier than the girl's. A not-atypical pair of island strays, a couple breezing through their *wanderjahr*, and anyone hip to high-season Capri could understand that this wasn't their first free meal. Even when they said *grazie*, they sounded entitled.

Risto forgot the kids' names half a minute after he'd been introduced. He concentrated instead on the host's stories, dinnertime entertainment. The former *assistente* would be needed on the punch lines. The girlfriend wouldn't know the repertoire, and as for Giussi, he'd withdrawn. He'd changed back to original gender, black jeans and white T, and right through the pastry course, he took no more than a finger of wine. He was gathering himself, up in some mental studio, and insofar as he joined the banter, it was for the sake of strapping young Beowulf.

The kid in hiking shorts found himself in the chair alongside Giussi's, and once at least Risto spotted a dark sub-Saharan hand on a thigh that deserved its own variety of white, beyond even "zinc white." Risto wondered how the encounter might play onstage. Caliban rapes Miranda, maybe? For now, though, as their host trotted out his anecdotes, Giussi kept his contributions to a word here and there.

The inevitable story, the centerpiece, featured the other African at the table. Risto had a major role, and as the American began, he broke into an outright smile.

"Let's call this," he said, "*The Joker's Greatest Triumph.*"

The eye candy, Dutch perhaps, appeared comfortable with the English.

"Quite a triumph, yes." The American was back in Italian. "The gallery never had a better quarter than after I faked my own death."

Risto wasn't the only one in on the scheme, but there'd been no one closer. It was he who'd come up with the McGuffin, and it was he who'd yoked in Paola as an accomplice. Together they'd run up north of Naples on a stormy spring night. Together, they worked out where to plant the evidence. A few bits and pieces, well selected and well placed, were all it took to make it look as if the proprietor of Nova Poli had drowned. So too, tonight on Capri, Risto was the one who noticed that young White and Bright didn't know the context.

North of the city, explained the former *assistente*, lay more volcanic fields. He threw in some of the drama you found in guidebooks: "In legend, these were the entrance to Hell." The landforms posed a bad risk, calcareous and unstable. The cliffs along the shore were flagged with warning buoys, their inlets briar patches of rock. Under the water, fresh fissures opened unpredictably. Walking the coastal trails, you saw lost netting and boat scrap. Every year, there turned up a couple of corpses.

Fine drama, and for Risto the most fun he'd had all day.

"That's why the story fooled everyone," he said. "The entire arts crowd."

Risto and his girlfriend hadn't even needed the man's passport, nothing so valuable. Paola beat up one of his NPS shirts, the mongram on display at every opening, and the assistant got the boss to give up one of his favorite Converse sneakers. The shoe, also trashed and soaked, was left on a flat spot in the cove. Nearby the couple tossed a cheap personal agenda, and in its cover pocket they wedged a couple of receipts dated that day: one for boat rental, another for a bottle of what Neapolitans claimed was the true Falanghina, Grotta del Sole. As for the wallet, eh. Wallets were always disappearing, around a Gulf that was nearly fished out. Whichever *pescatoro* had first spotted the half-sunk craft, he'd have snitched anything valuable.

Before all that, going back a good nine months, the Nova Poli owner and his assistant had weighed the pros and cons of various untimely ends. Drowning had come up early, Risto's idea, but still, you had to talk about these things. Meanwhile a bank account was set up over on Capri. As for the name on the account, that was the same and yet different. The man had crossed the world's two largest oceans and he held three passports, each with its own riddles of spelling and pronunciation. Still, as the Somali worked with the island bank, he'd prickled with gratification to see the name of his boss at last—and in it, another name as well: Pô Li Navô.

Over time, Risto and Paola had learned that words in Vietnamese contained a range of meanings. The intonation made all the difference, and the *assistente* had never followed up. Paola tried, though only once or twice, when the American's guard appeared to be down. Sharply she'd spoken up: *Fo? Li?*

At most, the man cocked an eyebrow.

Tonight, over his last tangles of pasta, the host took over the story. "Now, I should point out that the woman I was seeing at the time happened to be a lawyer." His mouth stretched but didn't bend. "Oh yes." The American had taken his time with the relationship, staying well past the point at which he usually grew bored. After all, he'd been an *immigrato*. More than that, he hadn't wanted any protracted legal wrangle making a mess of the way he quit the business.

"The one work of art of my life," declared the American.

At that Giussi came to life, grinning. "A counterfeit death, *chapeau, mon vieux*."

The performer's change of clothes had turned him macho, Idris Elba. "What does your little *jeu* enact, after all, if not the flim-flam game that is artistic 'success'?"

Risto didn't know about that, but he wouldn't argue about the success. Before the Nova Poli owner went missing, he'd announced he was closing. "Nothing left to accomplish," he told the media, and he pulled together a finale full of blacks and grays and tombstone uprights: "Dead/Undead: The Next City." Then a week before the opening, Risto and Paola made their night journey to the Mouth of Hell, and with that the songlines of the art world began to trill. The opening brought in the kind of sophisticates who made their selections with their chins. One piece went to Venice, another out to some city in the Chinese iron ranges—and this before the American strolled in. He turned up in blue Armani and yellow Converse, a party boy fashionably late.

Nova Poli wound up enjoying a bump in sales bigger even than the *assistente*'s estimate. He'd been happy to make a projection, going all in. By that time he had a trial balloon in the air himself—he'd put down the deposit on the original *Wind & Confusion*—and by the end of the opening he could see he'd bet a winner. The gallery would keep a tidy

profit even after the settlement, quiet, out-of-court. The stunt proved
the capper on the venue's prestige, as well, landing a glossy spread in a
London magazine (with a title only Giussi could explain: "Fib-a-notch
à Napoli"). The proprietor looked like a voyaging visionary, one who'd
created new markets at every port of call. Also his exit raised a question:
if he'd let go of the cultural switch, the on-off for the arts buzz, who
had hold of it now? Could it be the young man out of the South, rising to the challenge? That was the question for Risto—or it had been,
every other time he'd helped to tell the tale. Tonight, as the pastries and
limoncello went around, he found himself thinking about the star, the
Joker. This Fo or Li or whoever he'd been back home.

Risto declined an after-dinner drink. The pastry alone was a lot
to deal with, the powdered sugar spotting his hands as if he were Michael Jackson. Meantime, the hands of his former boss revealed liver
spots. The signs of age, thought Risto, had begun to show up years ago.
"The Next City"? In dreaming up the show, the American had already
moved on, though back then Risto had failed to notice. He'd heard
little beyond the usual enthusiasm for Neo-Geo, this time in the colors
and shapes of the grave. Yet even then, the *assistente* had worked in
the midst of decay. His boss had been another proud baronial palazzo
starting to flake and show spots.

Once during Nova Poli's final year, in a desk drawer, Risto had
come across a "Traveler's Companion" for Capri. The book compiled
observations from people like Henry James. An entire page was dedi-
cated to the ruined Imperial palace of Tiberius, and on this he found
hand-drawn stars, oriental in their delicacy. He should've been able to
read those stars. The traveling salesman was looking to settle down with
the Emperor.

※

Around the table now, it was Giussi who supplied the energy. The
way he carried on about the host's "farewell performance," he set the
Teuton youngsters laughing till they spluttered. Those two might've
put away a pitcherful each. The girl had trouble just keeping her bangs
out of her eyes, but she tried to come across like a lawyer. The Ameri-

can's stunt, she argued, had been a con game without a victim. Giussi shrugged and nodded, refreshing her glass and her boyfriend's. Himself, he reiterated, he had to pass on the drinks, *aimé*. He'd so love to "get gay" with them. But they'd have lots of fun and games, oh la la, if they stuck around for the rehearsal.

Again his hand fell on the boy's toned thigh. "Fun and games?"

Oh la—no. The kids started making excuses before they'd knocked back their latest round. The boy recalled "a thing," down in Capri Town.

"Ohhh." Giussi played it crestfallen. "Had enough, have you, here at the Villa of Mysteries? A peek in the windows was enough?"

Risto's own *passegiata*, while the performer prepared his stage, took him in the other direction. Alongside the American, he climbed away from town, toward the ravaged clifftop Palace. He wanted that, drawing closer to the host and getting farther from the phone, the landline in the foyer. Throughout dinner the thing kept catching his eye. Risto preferred the man at his side: the go-getter at twilight. He managed most of the climb without a stagger, though the route petered out in a dirt trail. At the other end of the island, Mt. Solara, you got a better sunset, but here the light suggested goldflake scattered on the breeze. The tourists tended to stay down in Capri Town, so you heard nothing but the rustle of pine and jasmine, the scuttle of lizards.

"Your ladyfriend?" Risto tried.

Berenice had grumbled that she had no interest in "that pile of rubble on the hill." Now her boyfriend, her old-man-friend, said only that she'd joined him once for a picnic up at the top, the Emperor's Leap.

"And she swears that if you take her again, she'll throw herself off?"

In this light, he couldn't read the American's smile. The man's choice of lovers had never revealed much about his soul, and he didn't appear to be doing much thinking anyway. He'd marinated pretty thoroughly in alcohol, and Risto figured their *passegiata* ought to stop short of the cliff's edge. He kept up his patter, pointing out that way he'd heard it, Tiberius hadn't actually disposed of his enemies up there. The Leap was a fairytale, a bit of slander concocted by a later regime. Nonetheless, the drop was terrifying, wasn't it? The worst on the island, no? Come to think, maybe Risto and his old boss ought to stop at the base of the ruins, what used to be the slave quarters.

The shorter man remained wordless as underfoot the tarmac gave way to dirt. Risto, to his ear, sounded as phony as some stale Hollywood title badly dubbed into Italian. Could that be the insecurity of the underling, back for an evening's visit? By the time he brought up Fidel's photos, the threesome, it felt as if he were grasping at straws.

The American, it turned out, had been forwarded the set days ago. "Bound to happen sooner or later, Little One." An old joke, the name. "This or something like it, bound to happen. One artist takes down another—it's an occupational hazard."

In Risto's shop, he added, the problem was exacerbated. "On top of the jealousy, you've got race. Outsiders of all kinds. Actually, I'm surprised that someone didn't erupt before this."

Out on Capri, in the email with the "performance," the American had no trouble spotting the recipients list or figuring out their color. Risto tried to sigh, but again the sound betrayed him. It came out pinched, and he had to admit he hadn't expected this, "such drama." He worried about both the artists.

"Eftah's show is right downtown, Maestro." Two could play at the name game. "A big crowd, mixed crowd. I can see it turning ugly."

"Hm. Aristofano, horseman of the Apocalypse?"

They'd reached the end of the trail, the base of the palace stairs. Risto felt the cracked stone for a place to sit.

"Little One, I could tell you stories..."

"Mother*fucker*! Another story, that's the *last* thing I want!"

The American had stayed on his feet, and at this angle Risto could make out his face: never further from a smile.

"That's not why I came here," he went on. "That's not it at all."

Up the ancient stairs, behind him, he heard the scree of some animal ducking into a hole. His host turned away; he didn't need a cliff in order to stare off into eternity.

"Look," Risto tried, "you could be right. Okay, it was bound to erupt sometime. But with everything that's gone on—it makes me think of that old Eastern emperor. The one who kept a sword hanging over his head."

That brought his companion around, a quarter-step anyway.

"I came to here to get out from under that sword. Get some sea air and a fresh perspective."

Another quarter-step. "Well, if you're sick of old stories, Aristofano, I'm afraid that's all I've got. I'm a wreck."

"A wreck? You've got an Earth Mother for a ladyfriend."

"I'm quite the wreck, believe me."

"Not tonight. Not around the dinner table."

"You don't have to mollify me, Risto. When you said 'motherfucker,' that wasn't my first time. I'm telling you, what I've got going on up in here?" The man's face was so close that when he pointed at his head, he could've been indicating them both. "More often than not, the scene's Gran Guignol."

Risto rocked back, figuring his grin was still visible. "Maestro. Maybe when we get back, I'll take a closer look at those knives."

This elicited a chuckle, and as the two started downhill again, their give and take had lost its imbalance, master-pupil or sponsor-addict. When the American asked about Tuttavia, Risto replied that he'd been the one to tell the woman, sparing none of the bad news. If he could handle her at a time like that...

The older man hmm'd.

"Tuttavia, eh. She can get pretty scary, banging on the table."

"Sounds familiar, I must say. The problem comes when they take the Temperament too far, the wrong corner and the wrong hour."

"*Per carità*. That does sound like Gran Guignol."

The American asked if Risto realized how the photos would be taken, as they spread across the Internet. Did he know that the high-end prostitutes, the call girls—this was how they advertised? "It's quite the high-tech operation, these days. Anymore, they don't hang out in hotel lobbies."

Risto turned, lowering his big head. "You're saying what Giussi's done, it makes Tuttavia look like a whore?"

"Dirty pictures on the Internet, that's money. That's how most people would—"

"Please, give it a rest. One bumbling detective is enough for this trip."

They took a moment listening to the footfalls. "Actually," said the American, "Giussi tells me you did some good. You got the police involved."

"Eh. Inspector Clouseau did some good."

"He says even the bastards behind La Fenestrella are feeling the heat."

Risto figured that, if he couldn't truly escape the bedlam, he might as well bring up the latest. He asked if his host remembered Mepris. Eftah had brought the Moroccan out at least once, and he'd used the visit to make a statement. He'd booked the two Africans into one of the old English-lily hotels. When he and the Moroccan headed for the cottage, they arranged the ritziest taxi on the island.

"But this morning," Risto said, "they got the boy. He's in custody."

"In custody? Didn't you tell me Eftah was a Camorra contract?"

"The murder's just the excuse. While they're at it, you know? But Mepris, I doubt he's got his papers in order. He could be looking at deportation."

Risto fingered his crown. "I did what I could."

He gave the American the thumbnail version, his man in Homicide. "If that cowboy can keep Mepris from getting ground up in the system—that could justify my game of Detective."

"Well, I wouldn't be surprised. Just look at your track record."

Risto wound up telling the American about the time—two days ago? three?—he'd needed to double-check his own date of birth. "I couldn't believe," he said, "it was so many years back."

The other man laughed, but somehow this rankled. "Look, sometimes it feels like I've done nothing but fake my way. Like nothing but luck."

"Luck? Signore Al'Kair, you always had the eye."

"My eye, eh. I think of those explorers, out after the City of Gold..."

But he didn't complete the thought, seeing how the smaller man had shrunk further. Earlier his old mentor had called himself a wreck, and now he was even out of sweettalk. Risto hadn't left the city, or taken this *passagiata*, just to end up once more talking to himself. He got enough of that, steeping in cogitation. For the final stretch, he made an effort to re-engage the party engines. He made a fuss over tonight's wine, repeating the name, pointing out how well it went with both the caprese and the clams. And what was that scent, along the road here? Was that myrtle?

Then, down at the cottage: Paola's phone call.

"Risto-ri, honestly, you think I didn't know?"

He thought of euphemisms for what he'd been up to, catchy brand names—but this was his wife.

"You think you can take truth and justice into your own hands, *Aristofano Impero,* and I'm not going to know?"

Out back on the terrazzo, they were dragging furniture into place. The iron feet of the chairs, grating across the brick, sounded better than Risto's apologies.

"You think I can't read what's on my own husband's computer? Have you forgotten about the History?"

Last Sunday, he'd worried her. Last Sunday, before he'd thought to clear his History, she'd stolen a minute with his laptop.

"And you know, *amore,* a part of me was relieved? A part of me was worried I'd find another sort of website, one of those with dirty pictures, with a number to call."

But what she'd found was bad enough. Later that day, she'd kept an eye on her husband's after-dinner conference with Giussi. "When you were out on the balcony, honestly, didn't you think I could see you seething? All that righteous anger? Just to remember it makes me think I should get the next train to Naples."

Also she'd read between the lines the following afternoon. "First it's Eftah and Mepris at each other's throats, and then it's the spooky business, the haloes of death. You think I couldn't see through it? I ask you, really, just whose life is at risk?"

The wife waited out his fumbling, and at least he knew better than to push back. He didn't challenge her about Tuttavia and the kids, the knife that never was. Rather he went on apologizing till her tone softened, and she pointed out she'd held her peace for some time now. "A night, a few nights," said Paola, "I could give you that. I'm Italian enough for that. I'll give a man room to work the fantasy out of his system."

Also she couldn't miss Giussi's barking, on Risto's end of the line: *Critical mass!* Meanwhile, on hers, she had Rosa and Tonino.

"Lover," she said finally, "honestly, I had to track down this number. The friends I've got on the island, I didn't mind telling them—I've got a man in trouble. I've got a man who needs someone to take his head in their arms."

※

Was it that he'd heard from his Sybil, wreathed in oracular smoke? Between her and his sundown up-and-back, did he feel more grounded, somehow? Risto couldn't say, but as he settled in for Giussi's "workshop," he refused more wine. The girlfriend didn't bother with a pitcher, uncorking a Lacrima Christi, mainland stuff, and setting it down on the terrazzo's brick floor. Glasses? You were on your own. The American brought out limoncello as well, a bottle with a label. Store-bought, yes, they'd stooped to that, and to a cream-orange option, touristy meloncello. The former *assistente*, however, waved it all away. He found the mineral water where he'd expected, the tall bottles stacked sideways in the fridge.

The cottage did have a room Giussi might've used, the dining room, but he preferred the scrap of a yard. Out back lay a one-man amphitheater, spiced by the basil alongside the deck. Out farther stood wind-wrangled trees, citrus of some kind. In daylight the view took in the Gulf, but at this hour all you saw were trunks and branches, leached white by the houselights. A chalk scrawl at the back of the stage.

Risto, the last one out, didn't get a chair. Rather he had an arrangement of sofa cushions, tossed together by the boy handling setup—the cold-water surfer boy, it turned out. The trekker was back from town and under Giussi's direction. The girl too had returned, but she sat out the stage prep. She'd claimed a comfortable chair, woven wicker, and thrown one of her own fine legs over the arm. A dissolute Heidi, she had a spliff going, tobacco and hash, and she wasn't offering it around. Even the host could only get a toke in exchange for a shot of meloncello. The boyfriend too had to ask, and as he stood over his girl, they shared a look.

Risto turned away. Tonight's entertainment was sure to spread enough smut, all on its own. No need to top things off with backstage gossip, and anyway he had a job to do, here on the sofa cushions. He had his usual job, looking, judging. *Bidding and forbidding, like a potentate of old,* wasn't that the line? Besides, he might see something he could use next time he sat down with Tuttavia. And what was the alternative? Holing up in his room and replaying the phone call from Paola, with an anti-mosquito coil stinking by the bed? More smoke in his head was the last thing Risto needed. Far better to watch his ectomorph friend leap and caw.

Just sitting there drinking his mineral water, he learned something. He picked up the name of the stagehand. This was Ludwig, a name Giussi could sink his teeth into. He went Nazi on that *d* and *v,* and then on the *oy* of "my Best Boy."

As a final touch, the performer had Loodd-vvig set out a waist-high lamp table, not quite at center stage. On this went a pitcher and cup, the pitcher the same as at dinner, the baroque local ceramic. The cup however came from the far side of the world. It was decorated with a pair of fat koi and pinched at the waist, under a glaze like crusted snow. Japanese, surely, and yet its purples and greens matched those of the pitcher. A nifty juxtaposition, a Giussi juxtaposition—a jolt. Kyoto and Capri, together at last, and Risto tried to recall if he'd seen the goblet before. For all he knew, his former employer had smuggled the thing out of Saigon (though the Vietnamese glaze, wasn't that muddier?).

The Best Boy was off the stage now. Ah-one, ah-two: Giussi went into a dance.

The music was his own loping outcry, a Senegal blues, but the movements smacked of the North. Risto found himself thinking again of Michael Jackson. "Billie Jean" had been around for, what, going on half a century? The song might be older than Giussi, yet the moves still felt fresh, the shimmy and tap that'd defined the Motown pervert, somehow both robotic and seductive. Then next thing Risto know, he was watching a jeté and spin as if someone from south of the Sahara had turned up in the Moscow ballet. Except this performer worked barefoot, beginning at the edges of the table, skipping away and then back. He defined his space, corner to corner, with articulations of his pink soles. At the same time he somehow kindled the stage lighting, two gooseneck lamps manipulated by Ludwig. These brought out the blush and lipstick, refreshed to the intensity they'd had back on the boat, almost a *Cabaret* contrast with the man's severe jacket. The black three-button might suggest an undertaker. Giussi must've had it in the purse.

Then the man planted himself center-stage, a kangaroo transformed to a signpost. From his pockets, from somewhere, he'd come up with signs. A pair of documents, they gleamed too brightly to read as the lights came together.

"What have we here?" Giussi often began in this voice, a network announcer. "What, what, what? These things of whiteness I acknowledge mine."

Despite the glare, already Risto had recognized the papers. How the performer held them up, two documents facing front and framing his head and shoulders, that was the mystery. You couldn't see a thumb or fingertip poking around the edges.

"But what else could they be, I ask you, except the lash and the caress?"

A terrific new trick, especially when Giussi gave each paper a different rattle.

"The lash!" He snapped the right-hand piece. "And then, ahh, then this." The left: more a flutter, a stroke. "Thahhh caresssss."

The TV in Giussi's throat kept changing channel. One moment he cooed like a starlet hawking perfume, the next he declaimed like a rebel on a street corner.

"Oh the *North*, you dirty, dirty old man! Old white man! You miss no opportunity to corrupt us." He swooped the two pieces of paper together and rubbed them face against face before his narrow chest. "Out of the South extends your shadow, ourselves, your shadow, and you like to watch as we writhe, as we lose all cun-cunt-roll…"

Nothing like sex to get everyone's attention, especially in the first minute. The voice alone was a ménage a trois.

"You push us to the *edge*..." In a new burst of dance he was up at the stage edge, fluttering along the deck. As his pink soles flashed, above them his white papers remained somehow stable.

"You like to watch. Watch us writhe." He twisted as he pranced, the papers too snaking back together. "Whatever it takes, you know, to stay in our skin."

Abruptly he slipped backward, out of his skin. By the time Ludwig caught up with the lights, the man was once more the signpost, bracketing his face with his magic sticky paper. Just turning his head toward one, he called attention to the contrast, his painted face alongside the black-and-white, the printed doc. "Behold," he declared, in full Prospero, "the filthy-minded thing to this side, the whip-side?" He swept that document forward, a wing in slow motion. "Behold this scrawl at the bottom, like the lips of an old roué, his lecherous pout. But then, my children, do you see what's over on *this* side?" The first retreated, the other fluttered up. "Do you see these grim lines, these letterheads, frowning in stern judgment?"

The physical business was arresting enough, even the pose. To the front-right of the lamp table, Giussi had found the two-thirds point, showing off his compositional skills. Something else he had in common with his former missus. More compelling, though, was the mystery. Where was the man going? So far, the one element Risto could be sure of was the paper itself. Giussi's lead document, the first he'd waved at his audience, was one of those letters that ordered you out of the country in three days. A kind of whip, yes, though the sting wasn't too serious. You'd find its welts on most of the brothers in Italy. As for the signatures at the bottom, now that Giussi mentioned it, those did look like the paired wrinkles of two old men's lips. A puckered scribble at the bottom of a square and bloodless face: just what you'd expect from a bureaucrat with decades at the desk. The performer had an impressively clean printing, too, no blurry third- or fifth-generation copy. Come to think, his collection of get-lost letters would have to be one of the largest in the demimonde.

Still, the other document was cleaner. A "thing of whiteness," maybe, but actually the paper was eggshell, quality stock. Afloat in the makeshift spotlights, its "frowning letterheads" appeared free of smudges. A cherry Earthquake I.D.

※

Performance like Giussi's didn't have a Fourth Wall, or not that Aristophanes would recognize. Now the supple Ethiopian stepped out of Primetime a moment, instead talking shop. He let his arms relax and provided a clarification for the handful on the deck. In the piazza downtown, Giussi said, the difference between his two props would stand out as clearly as in tonight's "teacup." Outside the Galleria, the documents would be projected brightly on a screen behind him, looming twice his size.

"Twice my size," he said, "the lash and the caress, bad news good news."

Risto felt glad he was watching on the small screen. Not long ago he'd had the A-grade paperwork right under his nose, though the man who'd brandished that I.D. now wore his as a toe tag. Risto didn't need the reminder, and when someone's phone went off, he flinched. A punk-metal ringtone, a guitar taking abuse, and it would be the drunken Valkyrie, wouldn't it? The girl didn't show any embarrassment. Just the opposite, she made everyone look, reaching for phone and purse by thrusting up crotch and midsection. She bucked up, exposing navel and ribs, so that her hand could flop across the bricks after her bag. Yet with all that, Risto realized, Heidi was just getting started. The show she had in mind would come after Giussi's ended.

The man out under the trees lost no time snatching back the attention. All at once, magically, his hands were empty. He cupped one to his ear while the other gestured at the girl, enthusiastic. *Bring it on*, he said, or his hand did.

"Oh la, oh yes, sweet interruption!" Enthusiastic. "Cell phone, Blackberry, pager! Whatever you're packing, *mesdames et messieurs*, please do leave it on."

The girl, phone in hand, collapsed back into her seat.

"Can't you leave it on, my child, and up at full volume too? Oh do, please, as loud as if you're out in the very moil of downtown."

She'd already killed the call, Mom maybe.

"Let's have the traffic in here. The babble of the *agora* in the temple of the arts. Don't you see that I'm a messenger between worlds, a changeling who's escaped the Pit, and tonight I'm bringing the Fallen the news out of Heaven?"

He'd brought out his paperwork once more, two rectangles gleaming on the air, against the pale wisps of the trees. This time the performer played up the Earthquake I.D. His voice a girl's, exaggerated, Betty Boop, he gushed about his "fav'wit card in Monopoly, Get Out of Jail F-*wee!*" Certainly his eyes could be Betty's, or maybe a cartoon cannibal's. In the very next moment, though, they began to blaze like Isaiah's. The transformation moved on down the body, as he shrank from a spread-eagle showman to a figure at prayer. The papers disappeared (did Risto glimpse another jacket hideaway?), and somehow the performer signaled the boy on the lights, so that the makeshift spots swirled down with him as he sank to one knee, arms tucked, the face nothing but eyes. You'd think he perched before a ritual fire. The man's voice quieted as well, but you couldn't call that a "stage whisper," not when he had a prophet's stare and used a magician's line: *Vanished into air, into thin air...*

Giussi was talking trash about his own props. The two documents with which he'd begun, he insisted, weren't so different after all.

"Whether the cops whip you out of house and home, or NATO and the UN gift-wrap you in a fine, fresh identity—in either case, my children, what've you got?"

Weaving finger-shadows before his face, he erased his own features.

"What've you got with either of these? No more than a veil, a shred, a baseless fabric. Another few months and even the Earthquake I.D. will be worthless!"

With a shift in posture, he gestured to take in the Galleria and downtown.

"Our new home, our place in the North—all vanished into air."

Was that a laugh line? Why should Risto chuckle? In any case Giussi was rising again, weaving up, a lava-lamp of a man even as his voice went ordinary. Briskly he explained that, Friday, he'd have occasional music, "just a touch." Yet even as he spoke his arms spread wide and once more sprouted their rectangular flowers. He burst into a juggling act, the documents somehow cooperating. Did the stickum add weight? Whatever: the pages flashed white then dark, switching from hand to hand as he fluttered all over the yard, buoyant amid a swirl of light. The lamps even added a soundtrack, their old necks creaking. One moment the performer seemed sure to send the cup and pitcher flying, the next he all but sailed off over the Gulf. Even his shirt was part of the effect, a loose T that ballooned as if to carry him.

"Oh la la, these papers—nothing but the funny papers! One the Bogeyman and the other the Fairy Godmother! How they keep us hopping!"

On the last word, the man planted himself back center stage. The juggling ended, the documents disappearing and, with them, the hands. Armless, ramrod, Giussi once more intensified his stare. His voice sank to gravitas.

"No more, my children, no longer. No more of these flimsy delusions. We are millions now."

Risto sat up on his cushions.

"We deserve a more durable token, a true and lasting I.D., we the refugee. Yes, my children, yes at last. Don't we deserve this city?"

Others to either side grew alert, even the Scandinavian floozy.

"Don't we deserve this and more, an earthquake all our own, shaking off old Europe? Get a new master, yes, be a new man! 'Ban, 'Ban, Caliban!'"

The girl gave a laugh, a kind of laugh, betraying nerves. Naturally everyone on the patio suffered some version of the same bad dream, *Darkies in Revolt*. Risto too smothered his nerves with a brittle laugh. But the performer was playing it straight, or as straight as he got—going for chills. He had his crowd on edge, now as he dropped again to one knee and fished elaborately in a jacket pocket.

A gun, a grenade? Giussi came up with a golden ring, glinting in the lights.

"A more durable token." As straight as he got. "Made to see and hold, a blade to sink in the earth, and so anchor a wandering brother. An artifact impossible to ignore."

He rolled the ring along the tops of his fingers, the trick you usually saw with a coin. Every end-over-end shot out a glimmer. On the screen downtown, the day after tomorrow, the flash would play beautifully.

"That's the new home we need, durable as gold, perfect as a ring."

Then a moment of song, bawling song, still on one knee with arms extended. "Full fathom *five*, the boat people lie, their flesh un-*an*-chored *ev*-er." Was this what the Americans called "minstrel," where even blacks performed in blackface?

"But our mooring's *here*, our harbor, in the sea change of *mar*-riage, *mar*-riage, rich and *stra-a-ange*."

Giussi settled back into proposal posture, though his smile remained a showpiece, just this side of wicked.

"Of course in most marriages," he said, "after a few years, you might as well be wearing a hunk of metal over your privates."

Now that was a laugh line. He milked it, too: "You realize, a wedding band, it's recyclable? The shops on Spaccanapoli, the goldsmiths and jewelers, that's half their business." The performer was up again, on the boulevard, walking and moonwalking. "You hand the smith a ring and, half an hour later, he hands you back a chastity belt."

Oh la, the band of gold had its sorrows, didn't it? Still, for Giussi's brothers and sisters it offered a better way to live than any paperwork. Yes, and everyone knew what he was getting at. "For someone such as I, a wary itinerant, at the center of the ring there's a loophole. You duck through and wind up in a recycling unit. A place where a refugee might recycle *himself.*"

Once more he was down for a wedding proposal, stage front. The ring gleaming between thumb and forefinger, he extended it toward the last person you'd expect.

"Marry me," he asked the girl with her shirt half off.

And went on, after a moment: "When I marry the Old Regime I am renewed. I remake my Afro-self in its Aristo-image. Marry me, my own—my Europa."

Heidi or whoever weighed the offer with a smirk.

"Oh the suspense, the suspense, how we suffer."

When she flung herself up to take the ring, however, Giussi kept hold. Together they rose into a seamless shared rhythm. The girl came out of the chair as if hooked, the willowy African backed away, and then the two moved in time, she on barefoot tiptoe and he in the undertaker's outfit, waltzing to the table and its setup. Risto had to envy the youngster's flexibility, her zero-gravity glide. Still, Giussi—how did he *do* it?

Eventually they stood at the two-thirds point, facing front with arms up, the ring between them. They might've been a pair from the funny papers, Blondie and the Chameleon, but the music was Shakespeare again. Not that Risto knew the song, but he knew Giussi, the ethereal tone he struck for the Elizabethan numbers. Also he got how this latest stage business must've been set up beforehand. While Risto and the host were out of the house, the performer had been busy. The two comely hitchhikers probably hadn't even have made it out to the road. The performer had offered better: a chance to join the show.

At the last minute, after all, he'd needed to make a cast replacement.

"Oh the suspense," he was saying. "You know, just this morning, I asked another woman. She blew up like one of those IEDs."

Risto got this as well. This morning Giussi must've tracked her down, Tuttavia. He must've made some apology, some appeal. Most likely they'd had a plan to rehearse.

"Like a backpack filled with nails!" the performer cried. "The way she exploded, the iron flying everywhere—have mercy!"

Risto, putting it together, needed the last of his mineral water. Back on the ferry, sitting elbow to elbow, the Trickster had kept one of his masks in place. He'd never mentioned this latest run-in. Under Risto's third degree, he'd had enough aggravation.

In performance, meanwhile, the IED business helped to ease the tension; it turned terrorism to a joke. Then Giussi began to speak of love.

To gain a wife of this color—"Paris white, Olso white, quite the *right* white"—prompted a spin move, James Brown or Prince, with air guitar from the girl. Yet Giussi came out of this looking like some medieval *Melancholia*, wrist to forehead and mouth ajar. He moaned

that, *hélas*, a Euro bride would never grasp how much of the relationship remained mere paperwork, "for a poor 'fugee such as myself." He
confessed that he'd never been much for love.

"Never," he declared, "and my children, I don't see that I'm missing
much. Love, oh la la, no. This rough magic I here abjure."

This sequence lacked for showbiz. The man appeared to be feeling
his way, tossing in a recollection of his first affair. "Think of it, me a
street thief, him the king of the local silk trade. I mean, is this what the
anthropologists have in mind, when they speak of the 'pair-bond'? A
form of commodities trading?"

Not bad, but meantime the girl had nothing to do. If Risto were
a dramaturge, he'd be making notes. But he sat there more concerned
with a player inside his head, still the same, Tuttavia. Wasn't she too
one of those who lacked whatever it takes to love? Whatever needs to
engage, brain and nerves? For her as for the man who used to be her
closest friend, the paradise of intimacy looked as fake as Disneyland.

"Worse," announced the performer, "*Euro* Disney!"

He suggested, trying to put it in body language, that the same held
true for most of the hustlers around La Fenestrella. Granted, a *clandestino* might still keep, folded in one pocket, a map to love's invisible city.
A boat person might still dream of some partner...

"Oh la!" Giussi returned to full roar. "Enough talk! Let me show you!"

He sent a jolt through the show by leaving it, ducking into the
dark stage right while his "bride" spread her ring hand flat before her,
the gold band over her upstuck thumb. She wasn't alone long; the performer needed hardly a beat before he came flouncing back in drag, the
dress and wig from the boat.

"Love," he was saying, "you see what you're in for, with *love?*"

He fed off the renewed energy, his sneer stretching. He found a
higher gear for a quip about gay marriage: "Nowadays, if you're gay
and single, you're the pariah. You're Mohammed Attah!" Love, too,
came in for fresh zingers. "Yes, we've found each other, my girl and I,"
Giussi declared, grasping the other's upraised hand and shuffling left
and right, soft-shoe. "Yes, we've come back from the dead—but then
what? Even Lazarus had to go out and make a living!"

For Risto, the glow of the pageboy suggested a halo. He settled against the wall and began to lose track of Giussi's hijinks. Something else felt ticklish. Last Friday night, yes, still ticklish: the irregular venue with a clientele that'd included a razor-toting Camorra whore or two. The girls had even scared off Konan, and after all the guard from the Galleria gone out looking for a girl. Love was what had lured him into La Fenestrella—or what passed for love. Konan too would never understand "troubles" such as Risto's and Paola's. The wife was a handful, he could see that. But Paola hadn't threatened to leave or otherwise cast a shadow over Risto's legal status. She hadn't stopped cooking him dinner. So then, Konan would ask: what was the 'Dishu boy so upset about? What, a fall-off in "closeness"?

Risto could've provided answers, or tried to, sketching a security too vast for any security guard. He could've talked about a wealth never stable and yet wholly authentic, about a thoroughgoing ecstasy, familiar yet full of discovery, the shivers branching ever more deeply. He could even have reached back to the multilingual joshing and sighing of his Maman and Papà, spreading its betterment throughout the smaller places they'd lived in....But he doubted he'd have sold the argument, even out on romantic Capri. He was the exception among the boat people. In by far the majority of cases, inoculation against love came with booking passage. You tended instead to trust in hard goods—and to fear hard people, like whores who carried a weapon.

※

Now what had he missed, on stage?

Had there been some sappy ballad, sung as though gargled, the performer's mouth full of water? Risto recalled a bit of slapstick too, or near-slapstick, with the cross-cultural pitcher and cup. At some point the pretty Scandinavian had returned to her chair, and Risto could no longer find the ring. Now the drag queen had his back to his audience, one hand overhead with a cell phone, framing some sort of mass selfie. Now he shot one side of the terrazzo, now the other.

"It's not love," he was saying, "it's *art*, bringing us together." He'd gotten loud, declamatory, working toward climax. "Art, my children, and you're all in the selfie with me. Vogue, vogue, oh la la!"

A Fellini finish, sure, a group hug under the Big Top.

"Men, women, white or black? My children, we've gotten beyond all that, all in the same picture! Isn't that what why we've come here, into the rough and tumble, the moil of downtown?"

A final exhortation—though only when the performer again whipped out his two documents did Risto grasp that he was still in a dress. Where had he hidden the things?

"Cutting edge!" cried Giussi. "We're all on art's cutting edge! Cutting through every limit, every border, every color!"

The documents came apart in his hands—you'd think they'd been perforated—and he became less Astaire, more Shiva. The shadows of his arms multiplied against the ghost branches. The paper, gone to strips, fluttered like snow.

Risto joined in the applause. Privately he'd worked out something else altogether, but he'd followed the show enough to see that Giussi had a show that could reset a viewer's internal GPS. The bedlam had everything to do with the satisfaction, in this act, though it might have struck home with Risto in a way it didn't for the others, considering that he was the African in the audience. He might be the only one to realize how, even as this magic brother appeared to break free of gravity, he'd remained tethered to his own ambivalence about the cast member who'd just dropped out. Tuttavia and Giussi might've had a different plan for tonight. They might've intended to work through the show together, here on the island. That last couple days would've changed all that, and Giussi couldn't help but suffer the absence. Even poking fun at "the pair bond," he must've felt a pang at losing his. The performer might not know love, but he knew companionship, and now he'd lost it. The silence weighed on him as the applause died down. At least, that's how it appeared to his fellow *immigrato*. For others Gussi might be the Night Crier, but Risto noticed the quieter work: an act of contrition. The performer, in the clothes of his victim, strove to comprehend, to justify, and even to make amends.

And what about Paola? How would she have enjoyed the night's entertainment? She would've used that word *friend*, Risto figured.

She'd have spoken warmly: *Giussi and Tuttavia, your slippery old boss too, these are your friends, your life...*

At the center of the cottage crowd, meantime, the performer stood talking business and fielding compliments. Risto too gave a smile, another *bravo*, but he ducked inside for more water. He would've stayed in, too, if Giussi hadn't called. He wanted Risto's *telefonino*; the camera app was far better than his own.

Risto was surprised he still had the strength. When he switched the thing on, the screen lit up with notifications, but he could ignore those. He handed the phone to Ludwig and took his Vera water up to his room. It wasn't as if he had to unpack, but stuffy and small as the space was, a closet with a porthole, it offered a better opportunity to be alone with his thoughts than on the unlit road. Out there, he'd been risking his ankles, plus the island police. A *nero* at large! With an *earring*!

When Giussi showed up, he was out of the wig but still in the dress. Making sure he had Risto's eye, he used the same word Paola would: *friend*. Weren't the two of them still friends? Couldn't the performer still count on Risto to say what he thought? "Man to man," he said.

"You got a picture, right?" Risto asked, taking back the phone.

"But of course. A couple of photos, *Aristofano*, and..."

"In full drag, or with the wig off?"

"The wig off, with the dress—that stops 'em in their tracks."

Vigorously Risto nodded. The outfit, he said, had a lot to do with how well the night came off. Once more he offered his congratulations: "You've got a winner. A lot of ideas in the air, like always, but *per carità*, the physical business!" The kicker was when he'd shown up in a dress. If tonight's photos included a keeper, Giussi ought to post it on every kind of media out there. The right pic on the right screen, and day after tomorrow he'd find himself playing to his biggest audience ever.

As Risto said this, though, he ignored the photos. With a swab of his face, another of his screen, he checked his messages. His reluctance earlier rankled him: such a wimp! As if Giussi didn't know his heartache already! Three times, Paola had tried him, and she'd left one message in voicemail, another in text. There was Yebleh too, but the watercolorist had only left a number.

The performer's mind was still onstage. He had a question about a slow moment, maybe halfway along. Risto cut in: "So, that night. Last Friday night."

The other man blinked, making an adjustment at his bodice.

"There were bad guys in the crowd. Women, but bad guys, and word was, in the back they were shooting a dirty movie."

"Oh la, what's this, my brother? Still on the hunt?"

He powered down his phone. "And in the crowd, some scary people."

Giussi gave the dress another tug and touched a pinky to a corner of his lipstick. "It did appear," he said, "they intended to get into rough stuff."

"Rough. As in, more than just—"

"Too rough for *me*, my friend, how's that? It did appear that way to some of us. To some, not to all, alas."

"You mean La Cia. How about others, though?"

Giussi cocked his head.

"Tuttavia." And her bracelet, Risto thought. "She'd come there with you, right? But you thought this might go very bad, it might turn into a—a *snuff film*, and you left. But did she stay? Or Fidel?"

"Oh, Fidel, honestly? The big lummox was simply clueless as ever. Now, again I must ask, do you intend to—"

He'd had far too long a day to bother with explanations. "Did either of them go in the back? For photos, for some wild notion?"

The skinny frame before him straightened up, a plumb bob hung in the center of the bedroom door. Insofar as the man could speak without dissembling, he was doing so: admitting he didn't know. Friday night he'd lost track of both his former missus and the doofus with the new camera. Five nights later, Giussi still hadn't realized what Risto had, during the show. La Cia's killer could only have been some burnout on the Camorra's payroll. A woman like that wouldn't have minded the camera rolling, and she wore so many scars herself, she'd have been glad to hack away at someone else. Perhaps she'd had a partner, too, another old hand with the blade. But Giussi didn't get that. He couldn't tell Risto anything about just how the awful business had unfolded, and what if anything Tuttavia or Fidel had to do with it.

"Honestly, Risto, I imagine Tuttavia simply went home. That's what I did. And isn't it the reasonable assumption—reasonable, you know?"

But Risto was done, turning away, plugging in his dark phone.

NINE

YOU REACH ANOTHER CORNER OF the city, so quiet and distant and easy that it's hardly city at all, though in getting here you've had rough trade and long travel, and it's something else again. It's something new; it's taking your ease. The bed's too narrow, the porthole opens no more than a finger, yet here you lie, profoundly asleep. Not entirely comfortable, no, naked and sweating and bumping the wall, but nonetheless it comes together as healing. You know yourself and your rhythms, the nightmares that ought to follow a turbulent day, the locker room visited by a pillar of fire, of blood and grease and fire. Yet now you've got sweet dreams, falling back into embraces you'd forgotten, better stirrings right through the night and long into the morning, here where the dream-maps put the border of city and not-city. The thread of air through the window lends its flavors, jasmine, pine, myrtle, and later the kitchen sends up odors of espresso and marmalade, but these too merely melt in among the others, like the faint laughter, the good mornings and goodbyes. When at last you wake, you truly wake, it's all of a piece with the healing, and no more nor less than what you had in mind when you caught the ferry: the miracle of rest. When you're up and massaging your head, even the stubble's something else, feathery and provocative.

The cottage has excellent water pressure for Capri, and yesterday's clothes have gotten an airing. Finally you sit and grin across a fresh *macchinetta* of coffee, across the last pastry in the box, and you take your ribbing like a man. The joke about Rip Van Winkle, for instance, the New Yorker who overslept so badly he found himself in another country—not much of a joke, but no bother either, since across the table there's only your host, never quite smiling. The old man's alone by this time, and as for his checklist about the others, no need. What difference did the ferry schedule make? You'll catch one of those boats soon enough. But none of your obligations, not even the call to Homicide, feel particularly pressing at this hour on a Thursday morning. You can leave the phone charging and accept the invitation of one more stroll up to the Villa of Tiberius, one more righteous airing out. The man across the table doesn't want to sit and listen to the laundry, and he made your coffee this morning and your career before that.

Up top, across the pitted remains of marble flooring and front steps—toward the Leap—the American reveals his plan to jump off.

※

Risto almost lost his own footing. At least they weren't at the precipice. They'd come onto a sort of front lawn. Underfoot was scrubby, stumbly; the man who'd spoken of suicide remained unsmiling.

"A new world," Risto tried. "I get it. The Maestro's got himself a new stage. He's got a famous setting. For a disappearing act, it's perfect."

The cliff top offered a breeze, but he couldn't miss the Sambucca on his host's breath. *Caffè corretto* for breakfast: he'd whiffed it first on the Villa's back stairs.

"Tiberius's Leap," he went on. "Even a bigger story than last time."

The American allowed his dimples to deepen. He and Risto both checked the tourists, three dawdling old white women. What was that chatter, Greek? All three looked frail, hard of hearing, and one appeared oblivious to everything except her extended iPhone. What'd she have in mind, suicide by selfie? Still, Risto's host wanted more distance between those three and the two of them. He retreated from the cliff, back to what'd once been the most intimidating front stoop in the world.

"Good eye, Aristofano Al'Kair."

Good accent, Pô Li Navô. Risto found a half-intact cornerstone. "'Good eye?' What's that got to do with anything?"

The American pulled at his mouth, an old man who wanted a drink.

"Look, you better not have brought me up here to talk in circles again. You say you intend to *jump off*?"

He didn't worry about getting loud. Their only company tottered around as if deaf. High season always saw more beach action, but it surprised him to find the place so empty. This had been a city unto itself, both the seat of power and Party Central. The sex shows mixed men, women, animals, and gods, and for a special treat, they'd throw some *persona non grata* off the cliff. Extremes like that lurked yet, across these ruins; the stones' notches and divots in might be millennial Braille, spelling out wild yarns. A day-tripper could draw the moral. They too were a patrician elite, at their leisure.

"Out here," the American was saying, "what good would a stunt like that do me? Another stunt like in Naples." He spoke so quietly, it was hard not to think they were hatching a new plot. "Out on this island, it wouldn't do a thing for me."

"Eh, it's only the richest island in the Mediterranean. There's probably a Hollywood producer in town right now, eager to hear your pitch."

"Oh, you know how to make a Hollywood pitch? The immigrant dream…"

"I'll tell you what I know. You're never going to jump off."

"Little One, can't you understand?" The man sat up as if to lecture. "Some of us were never invested in that dream."

Risto's head-stubble felt differently, prickly, as his host went on. "You see yourself as a figure in Caravaggio, an old man in a pool of divine light. An old man basking in esteem, his grandchildren at his feet." Up in the American's head, you'd find no such picture. He'd had something else in mind from the first. "Make my pile and climb on top, that was my masterpiece. Climb up among the rich, on their island. Around here they came through the quake without a scratch."

Pausing, he flexed back and shoulders. Risto used to see a lot more of that. Prowling the Spazio Nova Poli, his boss could call to mind one of Mao's gymnasts.

"You and me," he continued, "as transplants we're opposites. Mirror images." If Risto didn't yet get it, he would soon. "You just watch me, my friend. One day soon, while I've still got the money. It'll be a great party. Champagne empties on the floor and a pretty girl in my bed. A white girl, sleeping it off. In my purse, she'll have my last three hundred-Euro bills."

He might've been mulling over a recipe.

"A grand finale. Pretty little blonde like the one last night, while I can still handle her. I'll have to handle her and then these stairs. I'll have to get up here early, when there won't be anyone to interfere."

Risto was leaving his head alone, up and pacing, but the American kept on with his list of to-dos. He claimed that if anyone deserved to hear "the whole song and dance," it was the man who'd learned his name. "You learned one of them, at least." In the process, his former *assistente* had made this possible, his "initial leap" across the Gulf. That deserved special consideration, and yet at the same time, Risto needed to understand how the move to Capri had been predicated on self-destruction. "From the first," declared the American. "I've had this trajectory in mind. Little One, it's been my gold ring."

"Don't call me that."

"Aristofano, then. Signore. You watch for what turns up at the foot of this cliff. It won't be one of your stage props." He counted on the discovery, too. "That's rather the point, showing them all."

"Showing them a wreck," said Risto. "A mess of bloody broken bones..."

"You saw me on the stairs. I'm already a wreck."

The three oldtimers by cliff's edge, he noticed, appeared to have just spotted him, his color. If anything they were paying even less attention to where they put their feet. Risto didn't want to risk a smile; he didn't want to startle anybody. Turning back to the American, he brought up the previous suicide. "After that, I saw what kind of a final quarter Nova Poli had. I saw the books. Both sets of books."

His host stared back mildly.

"You were rich. Rich and free, with the cottage here."

"Yesh indeed." The man had relaxed to the point of slurring, now and then. "For a while there, ah yes." Once more he complimented his former *assistente*, so smart—

"I heard this already."

The older man gave another upper-body flex. "My friend. My *guest*. Maybe I'm tryna helpya, sharing this. Maybe I'm the one worried about a friend."

The American realized what he sounded like, "with, ah, such a goal." But the way he saw it, he'd never have come to Naples if it weren't for the end he had in mind. "Back in New York, you know, I looked into it, the same big finish." But the cost and speed of that city, its constant turnover, had robbed his plan of its impact. "There, I'd just be more of the turnover. Another of the shem, the semi-famous, semi-rish, here and gone. I'd never make a *statement*." But the first time he'd seen Naples, he knew it was perfect. "The decay everywhere, even in the better neighborhoods. The highsh, the heights on all sides, too—*memento mori.* "

To him the city recalled the ghost towns on the South China Sea. "Some old French quayside, never so attractive as when it sat decaying."

"I've *heard* this. Last night, didn't we both hear it? The next earthquake, it's going to take down all of Europe! And that's a good thing, utter destruction!"

"Yes, and you sat there listening. At the end, you shouted *bravo.*"

Risto scratched where a sideburn would be, checking on their little audience.

"I do hope you *were* listening, Risto. You're the *Filosh,* the *Filosofo.*"

The Greek hags were nowhere in sight. What on earth? "Lately," Risto said slowly, "Giussi hasn't been the only one trying to convince me. Telling me there's nothing better than to see it all destroyed."

"This empire will fall to smish, smithereens. A million desperate refugees, that's not the only threat. There's the ice melt, the poisons. One day soon…" Better to leap into that void, the American concluded, than get thrown off with the rest.

Risto responded more quietly. "I've been flirting with bad trouble myself. Some of the things I've gotten up to—I don't see what I hoped to accomplish."

"My friend, precisely. And do you understand how, for years now, for decades, I've seen my own purpose with exquisite clarity."

Risto dropped his head, running a hand over the hashed palace stone, the millennial Braille. "I have to say this too," he replied. "To live well, live and be loving, right down to the grandchildren at your feet—that doesn't mean you live oblivious."

He stood again, finding his footing around some stubborn protuberance, a root or, for all he knew, one of the million million Neapolitan bones underfoot.

"Perhaps. But you've shee, seen—I'm a wreck, hardly living at all."

"Eh," Risto said. "Sounds like every time you come here, the edge gets closer."

Once they were down off the stairs, a workout that could only have helped clear his host's head, Risto brought up the drinking.

"Even this morning, I notice. *Caffè corretto.*"

"Risto, please. If I've been so assiduous about emptying my bank account, wouldn't I do the same with the liquor cabinet?"

At least, with the effort of climbing, the effort or something else, the man had lost his eerie calm. "You know," Risto tried, "you sound like a teenager? Like a kid who wants to go out in a blaze of glory."

The way the American grumbled didn't sound particularly adult either.

"What I've heard this morning—that's not my mentor. That's not the guy who brought in buyers from Berlin."

"This is the immigrant dream again. You think I had some *vision*, and that this struck a chord all across Europe."

"Neo-Geo, down in Naples! And in Italy we aren't supposed to do geometry. We're supposed to be all about the body. The Michelangelo twist."

"I had a good run," the American admitted. "Over here too, I've shown these old snoots a thing or two. I've shown some taste, no easy thing at these prices. These Capri girls, their idea of a threesome is with Dolce & Gabbana."

Risto pulled up, giving a laugh. A laugh ought to help, right?

"*Per carità.*" The American was grinning back. "It's a miracle I didn't go broke as fast as Fidel."

What? "Fidel?"

"Me, at least I've got enough pride that I'll fall on my own sword. *Il Signore* Castelsabbia, he's going to make the girl do it for him."

Enough. "Look, don't you see how you're coming across? Out here in the sunshine? You're talking shop, not missing a trick. This is the man I know."

The American wheeled downhill, setting a good pace.

"This is the *mentor*." Risto lost a bit of breath catching up. "But what I heard earlier, that was a kid trying to duck out of work."

This sudden hurry had shaken loose his sense of betrayal. Betrayal, yes: no point putting it in makeup and a wig. The man who'd taught him the ropes had cut them all away. Even when the two of them shared a laugh, it was part of the scam, the delusion of achieving status. What status? For the older immigrant, the only true success lay in a spectacular dying fall.

"Like a *kid*," he repeated.

He had to get a yoke over the anger. He had to understand, to imagine the man's trauma, most likely back before he'd become an American. Something must've slashed major ligatures and left awful scars. All Risto had heard of his past took place after the fall of Saigon. As a refugee, his former boss had spent time in a California neighborhood known as Garden Grove. "A lot of Vietnamese in Hollywood" had been his closest thing to self-disclosure. Yet today, for the second day in a row, he'd wanted a walk with Risto. His closest thing to a friend.

As they reached the pavement, the American missed a step, and Risto steadied him with a hand. Once more he brought up the drinking. "You know, even on Capri they've got A.A."

As for betrayal, eh. Most brothers would be glad to suffer far worse, if it turned them into citizens and business owners.

"They've got meetings," he went on. "Usually it's a church space."

No reply, and the smaller man pulled his arm free. Still, he must've realized his case was a classic. Closing a business and falling into the bottle—a real philosopher would call that an historical inevitability. Worse, the American lacked for companionship, other than his various moochers. Three hundred Euros for a pretty face.

Was that all they'd been talking about? Loneliness, lack of direction? "Working through the Steps," Risto tried. "It'd be like having a
job again."

Or was this just another case of someone who didn't get love? The
man had shared his strangest, dearest dream, and it had nothing to do
with love. More like a secret handshake. Now with the cottage walk
in sight, the bricks peeking out at the foot of flowering hedges, Risto
felt like he could use some wine. How about a good, deep pour of that
island white?

"Tiberius' Leap," he growled. "Another fraud."

The American blinked up at him.

"Another *lie*. Someone just made it up, so-called 'history.'"

"Well, people do leap. I won't be the first."

"Eh, I bet they've all got their songs too. Love songs."

"Quite the love songs. Over in the States, they'd call the Leap a
brand."

"Over in the States, Capri, Naples, it's all a brand."

The other man had quit blinking, at least. "Risto, what are you
talking about?"

Hotly he erupted, as they crossed into the yard: "I believed in you.
I *believed* in you, making over the whole Naples scene." He had his
oversized hands in the air. "The way you made the place sexy, I always
figured you were seducing all of Europe! But now you tell me it was the
other way around."

Glaring at the man, Risto was startled to see he might be doing
some good. The last thing he'd expected—the American appeared to
be growing a spine. He flexed body-length, like the old days, like an
athlete.

Not that Risto could quit: "For you, I reinvented myself! I arrived
at Nova Poli and I said, 'This.' This is the better place. It's the better
man!"

When his host got a word in, he raised a warning about the neigh-
bors. "Aristo-fano, don't forget. Around here, we're the wrong color."

"Yes, and that's just the problem! The new man is nothing!" All
of Risto's study and argument, archetype vs. astonishment, Euro vs.

Afro—it was all for nothing but a few years' supply of booze? And a spectacular final dive?

"My friend, really, I must ask, who made you the arbiter of all that's good and just? Supreme Advisor to the Khan?"

Risto gave a loud exhale, scrubbing his face. His rage had begun to feel lumpy.

"Getting all holy on me. Risto, you're the one who married a girl with mob connections."

Within, Risto had more going on than he could handle. He shook his head and made for the cottage. The American followed him in, and there the tufa walls put them in another world, cool and dark. It soothed him just to stand and let his eyes adjust, while the other man paused over his knives. The next they spoke, they were conversational.

"At least talk to someone," Risto said. "All that wine and limoncello last night. *Melon*cello, ugh! Then more this morning, Sambuca."

"Risto, I took you up there. I took you up and I told you."

"Okay, but try sharing it in a meeting. You'll find plenty of company."

Risto had lost all interest in wine. He went for his *telefonino*.

"My friend," said his former boss, "you tell me you believed in me. But you don't seem to understand—I believed in you."

On screen, Risto found a text from Paola and another page from Yebleh.

"I knew what I was, quite the Dionysus. I knew I'd dance and dance and then die. But it felt good to have Apollo alongside me. You understand? "

"Maestro," Risto said.

"Apollo the wise, there in my dark rooms with me."

"Eh, I think the wise one was Athena."

"Risto. I'm talking about what you stood for. I was just there for the party, but you showed up with something better."

Across the room, the American had again grown difficult to read. His features were so small, his tan the dark of country mustard. Risto still suffered his resentment, that lump in his feelings. He took care to sound mild: "Are you playing the cheerleader? Bucking me up before I head back to Naples?"

His host shrugged. "I get enough people stomping out of here hurt and angry."

Did that mean he might go on living a while? Play host another time? Risto couldn't be sure, but he couldn't go on ignoring his phone either. "You know La Cia's murder? Last night I figured something out."

"You figured it out? You came to Capri and solved a murder over in Naples?"

Risto gave a hollow laugh. "*Solved*, eh." He shared what he knew. The talk of a movie luring the young wannabe into the back of the club, a kid who hadn't paid enough attention to the crowd that night. "Some very dangerous people in the crowd."

The American cocked his head. "This was mob business?"

"It has to be. God knows why, to them a movie's just pin money, but the way they cut up La Cia—the work of professionals."

"But then there'd be a movie. What happened to that?"

Risto clicked open his photos, visual comfort food. "My friend, an excellent question. All I can say is, God alone—"

Down on the screen, the last picture taken was the first one up. Giussi at midnight, out back, square-shouldered and grinning. The performer was queening it up, and you noticed the bodice on the dress, how tightly it was wired. The wig, though, didn't look right. It wasn't the blonde flip Risto recalled, but rather a hard yellow wildman's mane, flaring wide. It wasn't the wig at all, come to think; Giussi himself had told him. Rather what Risto saw, in both photos, was a halo in glittering Renaissance gold.

Back across the Gulf, downtown, his searching came with a bad earworm about Tuttavia. Questions about the woman burrowed and squirmed, in there: how crazy was she? How bad might she get? Last night, Giussi's show had seemed most real when it came to the photographer's explosiveness. The IED spitting nails, yes, that corroborated the story put together by Inspector Al'Kair.

As he hunted across the lower city. Tuttavia troubled him the same way as his former boss, ever closer to the edge. Last weekend she'd already caught the stench of blood, nearer to La Cia's destruction than Risto would like to think, perhaps a witness. Chances were she had the inside word concerning the backers on the project. Murder on film had to be a specialty item, high-ticket but low-volume—beneath the mob's interest you'd think. Tuttavia however could talk to the Camorra women. They might even have explained the bizarre business of cutting out both eyes but taking only one thumb.

In any case, she'd known what was going on, and she'd stuck around. No one remembered seeing her leave, and she herself, over gelato, had ducked the question. On top of that, now Risto knew about her own bad wounds and how she'd taken revenge. Paola might've fabricated some part of her pillow talk, the other day, but she'd never have made up the whole drama. He knew his wife better than that. Besides, they'd sort it out soon; he'd seen her text, with the time her train would arrive.

On the ferry over, the only person he spoke with was his man in Homicide. This time he'd found a seat inside, a row otherwise empty. He'd tried both Tuttavia and Giussi. Just hearing the performer's voice would've put his mind at rest, for the moment at least, but in both cases, Risto wound up in voicemail. He'd followed up with texts, to be sure, but by the time he called Della Figurazione, he'd figured this too would get nowhere. He was calculating how much he could say into the officer's machine.

But: "Signore Al'Kair!" Every syllable correct. "*Citizen* Al'Kair, most worthy!"

What? "You sound as if you're celebrating."

Della Figurazione didn't mind saying he was. "Signore, you know, lately, I've practically had to move my bed into the office. But sometimes even in Naples, we police put the cuffs on, ah, on a worthless oaf we've been after for a while."

Risto set aside the reason he'd called. "You're saying, up in Materdei, that monster, you're saying you've got him?"

"Sometimes, even in Naples. The file we had on this hooligan, *per carità!* To put a lout like that in cuffs—we're celebrating. Better yet, my name's on the arrest sheet as lead officer."

Was that a whoop on the other end of the line? The ferry engines had grown louder, gearing down for final approach, and Risto put his face to the ferry window. He had to catch up, join the party, but at the same time make sure no one overheard.

"Della Figurazione, this is probably just the beginning for you. I expect this man's got all sorts of stories to tell."

The officer grew sober. "You understand that there are limits to what I can say."

"But he must be eager to talk. A bad guy like that, he'll give you as much as he can without getting his own throat cut."

"Signore..."

"Detective. Last weekend, that ugly business? The reason I got in touch with you in the first place? Now, look."

Speaking into the window, the dockside chop beyond, Risto began to reveal what he'd come up with. No sooner had he brought up the film than the officer cut in.

"The earlier homicide has turned yellow."

Risto sat back, trying to frame a question.

"On our list, on the board. This case number is shaded in yellow, indicating we've identified a suspect and have a warrant for arrest."

"You know the killer?"

"I've seen the woman."

The detective began to reiterate that he had limits, but in another moment his C.I. had again brought up the movie.

"It's—it's in circulation?"

"Streaming on all the *malavita* networks, signore. The hooligan we brought in yesterday, he had it on his phone."

The Hut had pulled up the video, a key piece in his negotiations. He had a name for the murderer, too, "one of those System nicknames." This Della Figurazione couldn't share, but he saw no harm in confirming that she was a prostitute. "Eager to move up the ladder, obviously. The woman showed herself adept with that razor."

The film itself, on the other hand, was incompetent work. "Ninety seconds in, they had blood splatter across the lens!" If the suspect didn't have such a distinctive tattoo, Homicide would've had trouble getting a warrant. "Signore, you recall the bracelet? Mexican more or less?" The best the police could tell from the video was that the killer had worn something similar.

"The focus was that bad?" asked Risto. "The framing?"

"*Framing*, that's your gallery talk. For myself, I'll just say that the bad guys would be lucky to make so much as a Euro off this piece of malarkey."

"Eh, you wonder why they got involved in the first place." Risto was past his shock; Della Figurazione had only told him what he'd suspected, anyway. "Have you looked into that, the question of—"

Coldly the other man broke back in. The case had turned *yellow*, he said. As for the Camorra's involvement, that'd been one of the lines of investigation from the first. "Now, Signore…" he began.

Listening, slipping in the occasional word of agreement, Risto worked up some warmth. No, the Naples police weren't "the Keystone Kops." Yes, he ought to "take an indefinite sabbatical from crime-fighting." Risto even offered a kind of apology. The last thing he'd wanted, he said, was to make the detective worry about what he was sharing. Pretty much everything he'd told Risto, after all, would soon turn up in the news.

"And it's good news," Risto went on, "worth celebrating."

It was the whole reason he'd started poking into the city's uglier nooks and crannies. He'd wanted to find that butcher—and now look! Risto ventured a little whoop himself, and in another minute was off the phone without damaging the other man's goodwill. Tuttavia was Risto's problem anyway, at this point nothing but a bad hunch. He could find another time to ask about Mepris.

✖

Over the next couple of hours, as he hiked around asking after Tuttavia and Giussi, he didn't bother trying anyone's phone. The performer's would be powered down anyway. Giussi might like his audience wired up, an incoming call might inspire a fresh riff, but he went off the grid whenever he was about to give a show. Today, besides, he had his new Valkyrie to break in. Oh la. As for the man's former Valkyrie, she didn't mind staying connected; she'd check her screen. Rushing to reply, however, wasn't her thing at all. Hers was the haughty remove. As Risto came off the ferry, onto the docks at the foot of the downtown castle, he wished he could climb one of the turrets for a look around. The barons were getting unruly; he needed to check the shifting clan borders. As for the photographer, he knew where she lived, her pretense of a monk's cell. She'd tucked into one of the better old-city pockets, where at this hour on a Thursday the shops had reopened after *riposo*.

His star client had her own pre-show ritual. Her hauteur had its limits, actually; she liked to get out and get busy. Risto soon learned she'd been gone all day. The old woman on the next balcony had long since gotten used to Africans stopping by.

After all, Tuttavia was a refugee herself. Otherwise she'd never have been so vulnerable to the Ethiopian. She'd believed the two of them had founded a city of their own, Artsotopia, a place above the banal. Above envy, above schadenfreude and every other septic stink. Eh, a fine fairytale. An immigrant dream in black and white—yet the same as continued to unfold on the streets where Risto did most of his searching. The *quadri neri*, the black blocks: where else was he likely to find the photographer? In these marketplaces, legal and otherwise, she'd long searched for models, and today, could be, she was looking for real trouble. Could be.

The earworm kept turning, as Risto poked around, stepping under the awning of a stall run by Moroccans or dawdling before a pair of Angolans with a sidewalk spread of goods. Millions now—Libyans wrecked by war, Rwandan Tutsi scared to return, Nigerians threatened by Boko Haram. All those and more had set up some makeshift, but nothing he came across revealed a hiding place for Giussi or Tuttavia. After a while Risto's lack of success started to look like karma. It looked like just desserts, especially when, at a stall in the Forcella, he ignored the latest call from his wife.

As Paola left a voicemail, Risto suffered shame enough to plunk down thirty Euro, tourist prices, for a necklace in ebony and pine. The colors were used for alternating animal heads, antelope and cheetah, and in fact on Paola the piece might look good. Then once he'd arranged delivery, Risto found a protected spot by some repair scaffolding; he gave a listen. His wife, it turned out, was back on their Chiaia balcony. She had blood oranges for him, plus prosciutto and tart cheese, caciocavallo. She'd been worried about his diet, she confessed, soft-voiced. Yet Risto, shrinking into the scaffolding, still couldn't respond. Her number was the first up on speed dial, but he couldn't. He didn't get back to Ippolita either, after his Gal Friday dinged him with a page. By then he'd pushed on to the next market and once more pulled up his phone's photos. He'd gone back to his last shot of Giussi, the halo still burning at center screen. After that, he couldn't be bothered with some quibble over at Wind & Confusion, no doubt the same as Yebleh's. As for his wife, once she and Risto started to talk, they'd keep it up right through August.

Better to go on hoofing it. Better that than the scenes in the back of his brain, like Tuttavia in an unlit corner, gasping and sticky with blood. He raised her name in hub after hub, along with Giussi's, letting word travel out along the spokes. The *centro storico*, underfoot, seemed to work better than the communication satellites overhead. Risto never hesitated to give his own name either, and whenever he was recognized, whenever somebody wanted to salute his good fortune, he took a moment for it, the nod, the clutch-and-shake. *A'salam alekom*. He hoped again that he'd made a difference. He hoped that, around his gallery as around some Duomo, a hub had taken shape, and that from it extended a few better avenues.

As he circled back toward the docks, he got something.

"Giussi, man." A young Sudanese, strapping, his face finely angled. "Sure, an hour ago. Maybe less, Giussi, with a couple of white folks."

The kid had spread his mat of goods on the widest sidewalk in this part of town. The spot appeared to be his usual.

"All friends, man. A couple of white folks, and one, like, pretty."

Pretty himself, with not just great bones but also a baby's wide eyes, this was just the sort of hawker Giussi would get to know. Risto pretended interest in the girl.

"Like, *white* white. Pretty girl. Giussi say they got business at the Galleria."

A couple of hours' hike, and then in thirty seconds he had what he needed. Still, Risto could hardly rush off. He couldn't neglect the vendor's display: animal totems, wood and bronze. Always plenty of

artwork, among these bits and pieces. Always the jewelwork and statu-
ettes, the beaded webs in which to snare a dream.

If Risto and his gallery did offer a hub, a navigational star for the
brothers still adrift, it had something to do with this: the Naples-wide
reliance on the ornamental and intriguingly made. What this young
man offered was the sort of thing he'd seen, what, three thousand
times? The spiky ears, the missile breasts? The eyes and mouths showed
careful detail, though, and the wood had been treated to last. The kid
had better in his duffel, too, a specialty item. For the signore he came
up with, of all things, the reptile god out of the Bakool Hills. As close
a likeness as Risto had seen in fifteen years: his namesake polymorph,
sometimes a lizard and sometimes, who could say?

Mixed in with the sales pitch, the Sudanese had news. "Man, you
hear about the brother, police got him in custody, and he come out all
beat up?"

Risto kept his eyes on the shape-shifter in his hands.

"Moroccan brother, educated. Gay boy, you know?"

Risto dropped onto one knee, seeing if the piece would stand upright.

"Police got him, man. Time he come out, somebody thump him
good."

The beating, however, wasn't what had the black blocks talking.
Plenty of *clandestini* came out of a holding cell in worse shape than
when they went in.

"But this boy, they cut him loose the same day. Man, ever think
you see?"

Mepris had been let go before nightfall. Sure, the hours inside had
gone hard on him—if it wasn't the free-handed police, it was the bad
guys making a point—but in most cases the paperwork stretched out
to three days, five days. The ex-boyfriend of Risto's murdered clansman,
however, had been sprung in time to pick up some ibuprofen. He could
pay for it, too. When he'd retrieved his wallet, it still held all its cash.

"He have some writings too. Like, his own writings? Man, the cops
give 'em right over. All the money and all the writings!"

Along with his manuscript, Mepris did get served with one of
those letters. Three days to get out of Italy, the letter said. But then,

so slender and flexible a creature as he could easily slip back in one of the country's little windows. Circumstances, in fact, suggested that the authorities would prefer he did just that. Better for all concerned if the Moroccan simply laid low. Yet he'd spent today, the first of his three days, raising a ruckus against the Powers That Be. Mepris had taken his case to the Immigrant Council. He'd found a reporter who'd listen.

"A reporter, man. Brother get picked up, beat up, same old story— but this boy like to go Hollywood."

Risto, getting to his feet, wondered about his own bruises. He wondered if Mepris had any idea who'd stepped up for him. But he himself had to step up now, and as for this vendor, the gallery owner found a business card. Another artifact from a distant world. He said that this last item, this reptile thing, held a certain interest.

※

To get oriented, Risto looked for a glow overhead: the reflection of the slow-setting sun off the repaired Galleria dome. Down that way, on lower Toledo, stood better properties, taller and with roof gardens. To reach the mall you descended into shade, and in the deepening cool Risto noticed the funk he'd raised, hustling around in yesterday's clothes. He imagined the shape of the sweat across his back, a map of Africa, wide at the armpits and funneling down the spine. After today, the shirt ought to go in the rag pile—even if it wasn't soaked in blood.

Outside the Galleria, in the piazza, tomorrow's stage setup loomed. It framed the sea glitter beyond and, to this side, the dark of a crowd coming together. A far bigger crowd than the usual evening wave, a throng, largely indifferent to the SALE signs and window displays. Nobody cared about Risto's shirt either, and the party drew him in, centripetal. He had to scuttle sideways and beg *scusa*, working through an energy that felt young.

The mob included a number of Africans, but these didn't give Risto a second glance. Their faces bore no ritual scars, and their Italian came out in an easy flow, no matter the color of the listener: black, white, or in between. All appeared to live in neighborhoods nothing like those he'd just been turning inside out, and he doubted

any of them ever worked on the docks or carried a duffel. Before
Risto called one of them "brother," he needed to understand that
they subscribed to a different, more comfortable model of transplantation. The Facebook model, or was it Twitter now? In any case they
set Risto thinking again of Yebleh. Like most of these brown and
black children, he had some college and was in Italy by choice. He'd
lost both his parents— and this had everything to do with his hunger
for pills—but the remaining family had given their blessing for the
trip North.

Risto left his phone alone, working his way down past the Galleria
entrances. The stage should tell him something, and it turned out that
the city had come through with a sturdy job, a tic-tac-toe of steel and
planking. The performance space had no-nonsense curtains and the
sound booth, walled off by plywood, faced it from across the piazza.
The cables underfoot were duct-taped to the paving stones and covered
by mats. The whole shebang had been thrown together in about thirty
hours, midweek. Yesterday, Risto had barely noticed as he'd made for
the docks; now he caught sight of a sandwich board:

Tonight! Start your Expo early! DJ Monte Zu @ 7:30!

Start early, of course. If you're seeking to get your city born again,
first you get the young up and dancing. The scene would have Giussi
feeling right at home, and for that matter his former missus. It wasn't
just a celebration, but a tribute, one that honored the children, their
sinuosity and flirting. The hope was that this would charm the years
to come, that Rosa and Tonino, to name two, would enjoy a gentler
time of things. The tectonics underfoot would hold their peace, the
metropolis would pull out a few more wins, and this evening's energy
would carry over into an untroubled future, with the opportunities
even-steven all across Southern Italy. A lovely promise, though empty
of course. Now as the DJ onstage tried out a trance groove, the bass
understated, Risto couldn't help but think of those Somali tribesman
who'd danced all night, feeling bulletproof, and then charged half-na-
ked into colonial Gatling guns.

Nevertheless, neverthe-what-on-earth?—he found himself slipping
into the evening's spirit. He found the groove irresistible. A rousing, a

boost, it had him slinging his hips around as he shuffled to the front of the dance floor.

The boy on the decks had the touch. Close enough for a look, amid the already tightening crowd down front, Risto discovered that the artist was the same as at La Fenestrella. The white boy in dreads, nodding over a rack that could slip in a backpack, and apparently the hookah was a signature. He'd got it smoking, the apple scent unmistakable. Nor had the uniform changed for DJ Monte Zu, though tonight's djellabah had more color, rocking zany for the pre-Expo. Still, he'd stayed with the brand. He must've met Tuttavia and Giussi too, or at least he'd know who they were. Risto only needed to get the kid's attention, calling and waving, meantime feeling every minute of his age. The DJ's eyes flicked over him as if they were still on some creaky rooftop.

But then, with a flip of his dreads, Monte Zu grasped that this wasn't some clueless old pudge. As soon as the turntable lamp caught Risto's face, he was a VIP with table service. The boy slipped off a headphone, his eyes so wide you could see he was sober. He offered a compliment on Wind & Confusion.

The DJ, it turned out, followed the arts blogs. Risto indulged a brief give-and-take, talk about the "outsider perspective." Then, speaking of outsiders...

"Juice?" asked Monte Zu. "Jews?"

The name had often provided the performer with stage business. At times he worked in the lost Jewish tribe of ancient Abyssinia.

"Oh," the DJ was saying, "him. Very femme when he's out on the floor. Always that white girl with him, too. That Tuttavia, one of your people."

Monte Zu hadn't told him anything yet, but Risto found himself grinning.

"Not tonight. Not yet." The white boy grinned back. "Tuttavia, though, she's around. No camera, though. No taking pictures. I mean, you almost don't recognize..."

A cluster of girls rushed between them. One had her hands in the air, bopping with the conga and bass, and Risto turned away with a raised-thumb salute. The Afro-*falso* onstage dialed in a wailing reed, almost Bedouin.

The kid might only have spotted Tuttavia, but no question Giussi too was part of this. Here between a Greco-Roman downtown and a stage intended to kick off the next Renaissance, both would be in their element. They'd quicken at the nubile oomph. The performer might be passing out flyers, maybe with one of Risto's photos from last night. As for Tuttavia, ordinarily she'd be hustling around with a camera. She'd frame tonight's racial mix as a gauntlet thrown down to the rest of Europe.

But what was she doing without a camera? Risto looked round for the cops, as he worked upslope from the stage. The police wagon was the lone vehicle in the piazza, a mini-bus corded off from the gathering crowd. Next to it extended a tent space for anyone who might party too hard. A field hospital, this was flagged with a green pharmacy cross, and out front a man in a smock busied himself over a reception table. Brochures, a clipboard, water bottles. The doctor looked too old for night duty. Portly, he had a lot of white in his goatee, a beard all Afro-Neapolitan bristle. At the open collar of his smock, you could see wattles, bunched together under a formal tie.

Risto couldn't say why he drew close—did he want distance from the police?—but soon enough he recognized the doctor. The man ran the rehab clinic down by the water, in the rattletrap palazzo. The program you could count on not to blab.

"Ah, Signore Owl Car."

DiPio, that was the name. Despite his old-school ways, the pronunciation and the outfit, the man wasn't fussy. As soon as Risto began to speak of "a performance artist, slender and full of zip," the doctor understood. Giussi, *si si*: DiPio had seen him with a white couple. They'd been checking out the performance space, back when the crowd was smaller. There'd been no mistaking the Ethiopian, hot for the stage.

Now it was the doctor's turn: had the signore seen Yebleh? "The boy called to schedule a session. Therapy, you understand."

Risto nodded, he wasn't surprised.

"Yebleh tells me," said the old man, quietly, "that his crisis is political."

Risto rolled his eyes. He pointed out that the painter always had some rationale. "With him, every excuse contains another. A Chinese box."

The doctor picked at his beard, using some small silver piece on a chain around his neck, a crucifix or saint's medallion.

"He made me come to the phone," DiPio said. "He wanted to talk about another African. A young man who ran afoul of the police."

Risto had to wonder how he'd been left with so little energy for either Yebleh or Mepris. He couldn't be bothered. Even as he acknowledged he'd heard about "this young unfortunate," the sound of his disconnect set off a shiver.

"Signore?" asked the doctor.

But why wouldn't he shiver, after he'd worked up such a sweat? Really, it wasn't as if he wished a brother any harm. If he and Yebleh crossed paths, Risto assured the *medico*, he'd send the young man to the green cross. Likewise, should DiPio get the chance, Risto would appreciate having Giussi directed his way. Or Tuttavia, the photographer, her as well, please? Please and thank you, and as he double-checked the limber youngsters around him, Risto took inventory within. A man could only handle one refugee crisis at a time, right? And Mepris or Yebleh, they other resources, AA and the Immigrant Council. It wasn't as if he'd gone all let-them-eat-cake.

But the performance artist, his gilded headgear, he was Risto's problem alone. With that thought, there at a still point amid the boogaloo, he had a better idea.

For a moment his mind's eye held all the haunted pictures of this week: La Cia, Eftah, and Giussi, two each. A moment, and then he'd got it. He knew how to confound the haloes. The Crown of Doom might yet be snatched off its latest wearer, and if Risto managed that, if he saved just one guy—if the warning at last did some good—then he'd be done seeing things. The first killing he prevented, he'd be rid of the mystic Photoshop forever. He'd got it, he could feel it, as clearly as the bass that rumbled in the cobblestones. He had an end to the madness, up ahead.

⊠

Also Konan, up ahead. No sooner had Risto gotten moving again, crossing one of the mats over the sound system's wiring, then he spotted the security guard. The man had his elegant neck extended full length, keeping an eye on the gallery owner. Now what might Konan think he was seeing? Documents of identification? From his post at one of the Galleria entrances, the Eritrean gave a showy wave. Risto swung his way, and at once stumbled into Ippolita.

He couldn't miss her perfume, a French accent, and the girl's hair too had made a quick roundtrip to Paris. She'd come to shimmy.

"Tuttavia?" she replied. "Haven't seen her, no." But she was glad to have bumped into the signore. He appeared better for the time off—as if he had the strength for, "ah, a strange message from Yebleh, troubling I'd say. A text about noon."

This far from the stage, Risto could keep his voice down.

"No, the shop stayed closed, just as you wanted. Still he had to write to me, and it looked troubling, truly. *I can no longer ignore what they make us do.*"

Risto fingered a bruise, putting this together with what he'd just heard from the doctor. "Ippolita, I think I understand."

"Would you like me to pull up the text?"

No thanks; he'd had enough of screens. "I know what this is about. Yebleh's told me some things." As Risto gave his assurances, though, he wondered if he'd ever get through to his fragile client. The notion that any two Africans would just naturally click was a routine fallacy, up North.

The girl was thanking him. "You know," she added, "when I saw him tonight, it actually gave me a chill."

"Tonight? He's here, Yebleh?"

Ippolita recovered her smile. Picking up the rhythm once more, she told him they had friends all over the piazza. "It's a Wind & Confusion crowd!" As for the painter from Libya, she'd spotted him first, and she'd been able to keep her distance. "But that Fidel and his Russian doll, ugh—I wasn't so lucky that time."

You could find anyone, hitting these streets. "Giussi's here as well, I imagine."

Even the girl's frown looked amiable. "Yes, I think that was him, here outside the Galleria. Here in the doorway."

She indicated Konan's entrance. Giussi she'd known by his outfit, "as if he's in rehearsal for his own funeral," but she'd never seen his face. He'd been talking with someone inside, and then Fidel and Zelusa had surprised her.

"The creep. Naturally he kissed me, *both* cheeks, oh ugh, and then his girl took her turn, you know, with The Master looking on."

She'd had half a mind to bring up the returned check. But meanwhile Giussi, "or the one I believe was Giussi," disappeared into the Galleria. "And Fidel and Zelusa went on in too. No doubt they're planning some little tryst. The office up there, you know, that's still in his name."

She shrugged, it was part of her dance, and as she moved off Risto caught Konan's eye. Mall security ought to be part of this investigation. More than likely the guard had spotted one of the suspects on the scene—perhaps even Mepris. The pre-party had just the kind of energy the banged-up Moroccan could use. The smell of pot alone would help stoke his outrage. In any case combustible materials lay everywhere, tonight, and with that thought Risto had to signal the lanky Eritrean guard to wait a minute more. He ducked into one of the cornices around the Galleria walls, out of the music and jabber. Just bringing out his phone prompted another look at his latest photos, where the gold remained in place. Risto, studying the shot, might've been in drag himself: a Gypsy woman bent over some sucker's palm. But this hoodoo, this *kuragura*, he believed in. This told him his friend was still among the living, and he should call Homicide.

The officer was quick as ever to pick up. Brushing aside Risto's apology, Della Figurazione said he'd been expecting the call. "In my postion, I could hardly miss the fuss kicked up by your friend from Tunisia."

Against the stone, Risto gave his back a bear's scratch. "Mepris, you mean."

"That's not the name on his visa. But yes, him. The one whose release I arranged, on my own authority. With, I might add, all his cash, all his—"

"Mepris, from *Morocco*. He came out pretty banged up."

Even the man's silence seemed formal. "The police can hardly guarantee the safety of everyone in our custody. A person such as your friend, your Moroccan friend, signore—the police can hardly be responsible."

Naturally, Mepris had the same right to complain as anyone else. In a free society, the detective pointed out, the police were there to *protect* a man's right…

"Look," said Risto, "I appreciate what you did."

On the other end, there was an audible sip. Risto swabbed his face.

"Ah, well," said Della Figurazione. "You did warn me that the fellow was volatile." Anyway, he continued, "the arrest that mattered" was the one this morning. "Putting the cuffs on that scoundrel up in Materdei."

None of this was why Risto had called. The detective needed to know where he was, and who else was nearby. Once he'd revealed that much, he needed to slow down, picking his way carefully. The haloes of course had no place in his warnings, and for the *ménage à trois* he could use a euphemism, "embarrassing photos." Still, Risto came across seriously. He pointed out that he'd heard threats, disrupting a gelato stop on a quiet evening. He'd witnessed an angry public scene. More than that, Della Figurazione should think about race. Wasn't it about race, if something should explode tonight? Wasn't that the fission core?

The other man cut in. "Do you mean to say I should arrest someone?"

Risto slipped his free hand over his mouth.

"Ah, do you mean to say that a police officer should act like one of the Camorra? If he doesn't like someone, he should simply yank them off the streets?"

An angry thought: *Wouldn't be the first time.* But as Risto held his tongue, the detective lost the chip on his shoulder. "I could alert the units on the scene."

"I saw the van. You must have plainclothes, too."

Della Figurazione took more information. Tuttavia he'd heard of; he'd seen the notices. It wouldn't be difficult to find her photo or, now that he thought about it, one of the performer either. A man whose problems with the police became part of a stage act—his mug shot must be somewhere in the precinct house.

"A bit of coffee," said Della Figurazione, "and I'll track down good pictures for both." After that, he'd carry them over to the Galleria. "Do it myself, yes. After all, it's not as if your friend on the police has a wife and a family."

Risto hadn't even expected the man to pick up the phone.

"It's not as if the squad on duty will turn down an extra hand tonight."

"Della Figurazione..."

"Signore, let me tell you." Another sip. "They had me on a paper chase. Earthquake I.D., quite the odious task. The documents started to look like the manuscripts of your Moroccan friend, all typescript and scribble..."

"Look, you were weeding out the fakes. Important work."

"Ah, to me it felt odious. I've had such crazy energy since Serena left, there's no telling the trouble I'd have gotten into if you hadn't called."

It sounded as if Della Figurazione was putting away his glass and bottle. He made sure his CI had the cell number—and no delusions about "playing the cowboy"—while Risto confined himself to thanks. Honest thanks: he'd gotten more out of the call than he had any right to expect. Also, knowing he had police backup helped him ignore his Favorites list, the next thing up his screen after Della Fiugrazione rang off. His Favorites, with Paola at the top.

Risto put away the phone and fixed up a smile for Konan. The security guard wasn't about to bring up the contraband, he figured, though he muttered a warning about officers in plainclothes. *We don't want to give them any excuse.*

But it turned out the Eritrean had seen Giussi. Konan didn't know the name, but he made the connection as soon as Risto began to describe the performer.

"Skinny freak? Black jacket?"

He jerked a thumb toward the stairwell door.

"A smart mouth on that man," Konan went on. "Give me some clever talk, get me to let him upstairs. Him and his boyfriend."

Risto staggered as if he were shouting.

"Man, I thought you'd know him. Thought you'd like to find him."

So Giussi had the surfer boy to himself. For the getaway, though, he'd chosen a dangerous place.

"Skinny freak with a smart mouth, looking for a party. Plenty of cash, too."

Risto got out his own wallet. To pay the man felt better than leading him on, making vague promises about good I.D. Swiftly then the tight spiral stairs carried him up and out into something else altogether: a skeleton picked clean, in the sea breeze under a bright low sun. He was steeling himself for the kind of thing he'd stumbled on in Alexandria, a couple of men naked and busy. But it wasn't Giussi he found, at the base of the dome. It was another skinny freak, Mepris. He still had his pants on, and so did Yebleh. The two young Africans sat rigging a bomb.

❇

"*Per carità.*" Risto didn't think he'd ever felt the expression, so. *Mercy.*

Mepris made no bones about it, confirming almost casually that the two ciabatta-sized packages to either side of Risto's feet were powerful plastic explosives. Two loafs of gray meat, each had been laid on the milky reinforced glass inside a V of curving girder at the base of the rooftop bulge. Risto wound up tiptoeing between the two, trying to make sense. A wired chip, a small moth on a long pin, poked out the upper end of each. Some sort of detonator, must be, though he knew next to nothing about such contraptions. Mepris, glaring up from his perch on the catwalk, was the one to identify the stuff: "C-4, straight off the NATO base." Then there was that chip Yebleh was struggling to slip into the back of a cell phone, hunched over as if huddling against his fellow bomber. Risto had only seen such stuff in the movies. But then, hadn't the Galleria stairs, their claustrophobic spiral—hadn't they ushered him into a movie? There was even a soundtrack, the low threat of the faraway bass. As for these two, young men he'd thought of now as friends, now as annoyances, they too might've shrunk to sheer skin, that lighter North Saharan skin. The Moroccan had pulled off his jacket, a black jacket though not Giussi's, and his arms were the color of the foam on an espresso. Risto, over them, was the black wet dregs.

"You want me to make up a story?" Mepris was asking. "Tell you it's performance art?"

"*Per carità*. And you two got all the way up here with..." Risto waved at the meaty clumps at his feet.

"Who thinks twice about a couple of *neri* with a duffel bag?"

Maybe Konan, thought Risto. Down at the door, the guard must've asked more than his usual ten Euros. He wouldn't have raised questions about the fat lip, the cut cheek, the black eye. Eftah's ex was calling attention to his eyes, grotesquely, with a clown's heavy shadow, coral blue. But Konan wouldn't have mentioned it, as he took perhaps fifteen apiece. Not a word to Risto, either. What'd mattered more to the security guard was fixing the position of these two young blacks in the old white man's city. On the margins, that's where he would've put them, which meant that Konan had the advantage and could demand a higher fee. He'd probably also picked up on Yebleh's extra-legal jitters.

The kid couldn't keep his hands steady. You'd think his hair felt too tight, in its tortured bebop straightening. When at last Yebleh uncoupled from Mepris, he scooted only so far as the outer edge of the catwalk and then slipped one leg under the bottom rail. He let the foot dangle out of sight. The perch must've been frightening, but it created a workspace for the phone, with its recalcitrant chip.

Wasn't that Mepris's job? And couldn't Risto talk to these two? It came to him that, if he got them to unstrap their suicide vests, he might also knock off Giussi's Death Hat. Giussi could still be in the mall underfoot. The place had more than one entrance and any number of places to hide.

Risto swabbed his face. "Look, I'm up here. I heard some things and I came up."

"Whatever you heard," said Mepris, "you'd never understand. Your charming life—it's all Babylon. Your children are the color of caffè latté."

This was useful, resentment. Risto raised one arm and got a pinch of flesh.

"Skin color, Morocco? Really?"

Under the makeup, the younger man's glare was a terrible thing. Risto kept on: "You know, down in Mogadishu? Down *South*? We had no end of ruined buildings. I saw enough to last the rest of my life."

"*Mon vieux*, Naples is Mogadishu."

"*Mais, vraiment?* I thought you just said it was Babylon."

Mepris was always, at some level, working the street. He was forever alert to the shadows, the baser motives in play. As for Yebleh, he was born to be the accomplice. Most nights, Yebleh would be taking his aggravations out on himself. Both the young men at Risto's feet were showing what made them tick.

"Look," he tried, "never mind the city. Let's talk about the piazza." He gestured at the scrum below. "The piazza right down there, full of young people. Young white and black both, right down there in, in—"

"Inside the blast radius," said Mepris. "That's the expression."

They shared a moment of frosty eye contact.

"Down there," continued Mepris, "all they care about is their boogie-woogie." He shimmied from waist up. "A dance on the broken backs of our brothers."

"Look, I saw our brothers down there."

The Moroccan bent over some preparations Risto hadn't noticed before, something like a pillbox with wires.

"Any time before yesterday, you would've been in the piazza yourself. You would've been dancing. And if I asked, you'd have told me you feel right at home."

The younger man kept his head in his wiring. Risto tried arguing that Naples in this century could be for the Africans what New York had once been for the Italians.

"Ah, Si-gnore Aristo-fano." Mepris spoke in time with the DJ's mix. "We've all gotten new names, but only you turned out a philosopher."

"Come on. Just the other day the police had their hands on me."

"The police?" Mepris put a finger to one cheek, denting a bruise. "You think this is their work? The cops know better, *mon vieux*. All they do is pick the holding cell."

"You're saying, they put you in with a bad crowd."

"Bad, *caro mio*? That's one word for it, as well as, say—densely populated. Just crammed with so-called brothers. Millions, it felt like."

Yebleh meantime clung to his perch, halfway to freefall. At least he'd quit wrestling with the detonator, sitting glumly over the chip and phone, looking to his leader. Mepris however got to his feet, wheeling toward the rail.

"Look at them," he said, "all cramming themselves into the nooks and crannies of the Old Regime."

The boy had hit the rail with such momentum that Risto started to cry out, yet in the next moment Mepris had gone still. He settled on his elbows.

"They've come for the money of course," he went on, looking off towards the sea. "Yet it's the witch's weed, that money. Circe, you know? The first handful of Euros she gives a brother, it turns him to a rabid dog."

"Mepris. Talk like that, the poetry—that's the better man in you."

"Aristofano. Tireless champion of the arts."

Risto scowled. "You're the one playing terrorist and wearing eyeliner."

The young man's smile took him by surprise. "Speaking of poetry, *mon vieux*."

What was that? Softening? Risto recalled the scene on Eftah's rooftop Monday, how swiftly the boyfriend had lost his rage. But Mepris got back to money.

"The whole city's rabid for it. The Galleria itself could eat you alive."

This too seemed like something Risto could work with. These two hadn't imagined just any catastrophe, flying debris and shrieking crowds, but they'd targeted a specific place, the shoppers' Duomo. Here the rococo on the walls might well have included a detail off an old-fangled cash register, a number five in gold. The mall was the closest that a crumbling city came to swank and entitlement.

"A showplace," Risto said, "the white man at his worst. I get it."

Mepris folded himself back down alongside one of the loaves of *plastique*, taking up the pieces of IED. Risto wondered about Fidel, his Galleria office space. He wondered if a rooftop blast would take out the entire top story, or just this section. Come to think, how much did these two know about the damage they'd do?

He couldn't ask. He studied the Moroccan's hands, scuffed and bandaged, then tried again to say that Naples had done them all good. "Even today, I heard you made a sweet connection."

It might help, Risto thought, if the setting weren't so dramatic. You could see Jason Bourne up here, grappling across the steel and glass.

"You found a reporter, I heard."

"Found and lost." Mepris sighed hugely, nothing like Bourne. "It appears I'm not much of a story."

"Come on. Immigrants in trouble, that's the biggest story in the North."

"Not this brother. I'm just a whore who fell into the wrong hands."

"So this is what you give them, instead? Raining down fire and brimstone?"

Mepris cracked a nasty smile. "You remember Warhol, his advice? Don't read what they say—"

"*I know the line!*" Why shouldn't Risto get loud? "The last man who told me, I think he's here in your 'radius.'" And why not let them know about Giussi? "If he's not up here, he's got to be close. In one of the offices, I'm thinking."

Somehow that brought Yebleh to life. Groaning, careful about the chip, the painter extricated his leg from under the rail. Risto tried to gear down, to come across like a meeting facilitator: *Think about this… innocent people, even friends of ours…*

"Listen," Yebleh said. "Those people, it's nothing to do with them."

Again the Libyan didn't get to his feet, scooting past. His gallery owner extended a hand, but Yebleh ducked it.

"It's destruction, that's all. Destruction—there's nothing more real."

Risto felt like he needed to get off his feet himself. He felt as if the potent smoke below had reached him, undoing any notion that he might get somewhere with these two. He gave his crown a knuckle-scrub and offered the lame reminder that Mepris had gotten his manuscripts back.

"Oh, my work." With that grimace, the Moroccan could've been showing off his damage. "As if!"

Risto stared, trying for sympathy.

"None of you ever had a clue. Every word I wrote was sheer *fury*."

A better brand of fury than this, Risto thought. Aloud, he brought up the arrest of Eftah's killer. "He's in cuffs, that piece of shit."

The clansman's ex budged over so that Yebleh could settle in. "Do you mean to suggest we've won a sort of victory? Because one cruel and usurious system got the better of another? *Mon vieux, c'est a rire!* The truth, the better word—you heard that from my boy here, my partner in anarchy."

Risto looked elsewhere, the lower city, the filthy meander to the sea.

"To blow the whole charade to pieces, that's the better word."

How many times did he have to hear this, in a single week?

"*L'acropole officielle outre les conceptions de la barbarie moderne....*"

"Mepris, cut it *out*. Cut it out and get a look at yourself. You sit there quoting Rimbaud—right? Rimbaud, when you've set up some rinky-dink 9/11!" Someone started to respond, but Risto couldn't be bothered. "9/11, eh. Why don't you ask yourself, did it make any damn difference?"

At his feet Mepris and Yebleh sat up wide-eyed, two startled schoolkids.

"A bunch of crazy brown bothers killed a mixed batch of folks a bit better off. Then a week later, business as usual."

"Um..." This sounded like the most humane thing out of either of them yet.

"After all that noise and dying. Business as *usual*."

"You know," Mepris said, "I've got a couple of friends in New York."

"I've got a few myself. Friends in Iraq too, Bagdad. Either way, they can make a money transfer. Either way, they go through the same banks as before. The World Trade Center, it's still right where it was on September tenth."

Mepris had let his wires drop. "Signore Al'Kair, did you ever share this line of thinking with the Immigrant Council?"

"Oh yes, my honored imams. Grooming me for the Pashtun caliphate."

"You understand, Yebleh and I, we couldn't care less about the Koran or—"

"Mepris, just get a look at them. The Immigrant Council! They didn't come for any caliphate, they came for *Europe*. The work, the laws, the banks, the trains. Look, you're the one reciting French. You're the one who lived with Eftah."

"Um, I did, yes…"

Risto was rocked briefly by the impression that he made no more sense than the cawing nearby gulls. "I'm saying, Eftah would be the first to tell you. The whole point is to stay in your own skin!"

Risto's listeners drew closer together, their arms around each other.

"Just the *opposite* of what you're doing! And when I think of how you could *matter*, you two, brothers with talent and smarts—when I think!"

Shaking his head, he glimpsed Mepris and Yebleh as a comedy act: fat and thin. The elbow of one hooked like a broken stick around the other's thick neck. With that, Risto's rant ran out of steam. He stood stumped. Then the door behind him creaked and his wife Paola emerged, with a stair-climber's exhale.

❋

Honestly, did her husband mean to stand there and call her a *sorceress*?

Paola's grin alone seemed to sweep away everything he'd been dealing with. The crowd below, she said, posed no challenge for her "detective skills." Before that, all she'd needed was another call to his former employer, over on the island, and then a quick stop at the gallery.

"I must say," she added, "it's a good idea, staying closed till the Expo."

To hear her, you'd think they'd all gotten together over linguine and octopus—though Risto wasn't knocked so far sideways that he didn't notice when she gave him a sting. "A good idea," his wife repeated, "if for no other reason than to make sure we all remain in our right minds."

A sting, but immediately afterward came a small stroke, as she ran a finger along a shaved sideburn. The husband tumbled back into a wooze from which everything else disappeared. The young men disappeared, along with their tools of violence—and why not? One miracle after another, why not?

Paola, meantime, argued for common sense. "Risto-ri, down in the piazza, it's a Wind & Confusion crowd." She'd run into plenty of friends, and then at the foot of the Galleria stairs, the security guard had recognized her. The wife of the gallery owner.

"Honestly," she chided him, "if you call a man a 'brother,' don't you think he'll notice you've got a white sister?"

Besides, when she'd approached the guard she'd had Tuttavia with her. "Every immigrant in town, it would seem, knows that woman—"

"Tuttavia?"

He'd hardly gotten loud, but at this Paola's hand dropped. Risto returned to the moment, his high-diver's insanity. His wife needed to be warned. Paola, however, already understood. She made a face at the other two and their apparatus.

"*Per carità!*" When she said it, the expression didn't sound so hapless. "What have we here, Barbary pirates, thirsty for blood?"

Everything was out in the open, even Yebleh's phone, its back off.

"Goods like those," she went on, "they're stolen from the Americans, yes? The base up at Aversa? As for the rest, what, you learned it off YouTube?"

But the terror they hoped to rain down remained ill-defined.

"Enough for them to *feel* it," Mepris insisted, over Risto's follow-up. "For once in their fat and oblivious lives, they'll know how easily their world can shatter."

Paola didn't want to hear it. She made another face, as if the catwalk had brought her to a mad dog. As if she might clamber away over the girders, and Risto actually gave a laugh, the last thing he'd have expected. But no sooner did he himself try for a lighter touch, groping once more after sanity, than Mepris cut him off again. "Oh yes, it's all

world without end for our Risto. The brothers may die and the Towers
may fall, but it's all forever and ever amen."

"What's this now?" asked Paola. "Towers? Naples doesn't have
towers."

She wasn't looking at the Moroccan, however. Her arms akimbo
and eyes narrow, she studied Yebleh. The Benghazi had gone silent,
shrunk over his cupped hands like a boy over a broken toy. He huddled
more tightly against his companion.

Risto changed his tone: "Mepris, come on. It's over."

There was that tarted-up glare again.

"Look, there's two of us now. Two witnesses, two citizens. Now
really, what are you going to do? It's *over*."

Maybe the pair at Risto's feet were a comedy duo after all. The
fat one was moping and the skinny one ready to fight. His banged-up
hands were in fists.

"Risto-ri," put in his wife. "Don't you see what we have here? Don't
you recall the dizzying effects of love in its first days?"

Still staring at Yebleh, she didn't quite smile. Risto, following her
gaze, at first saw nothing beyond the painter's yearning to cleanse his
soul in fire. The kid had chosen a different drug this time, C-4, but
the goal was the same: an all-consuming blaze. Then Risto was struck
differently. He realized that Yebleh and Mepris had sought to be alone.
Anyone else looking to blast a hole in tonight's party would never have
taken the tools of destruction up to the Galleria dome. The setting
these two had chosen, come to think, worked better as a symbol than
a weapon. The most likely victims were a few high-end shops. With
that—all of a sudden Risto couldn't help but notice—he sensed the
balance of power between the two. The need for support, no matter
how it looked, wasn't all on one side. The Moroccan was lost without
his sidekick.

Paola kept on: "I've always said, you know, that our friend Mepris
is a boyfriend of quality. A splendid choice. And in your case, Yebleh,
I doubt he's your first."

How had Risto been so slow to catch on? His painter's first experi-
ences of sex must've been with boys. In Quadaffi's schools, never much

about learning anyway, he must've stumbled across the same grunts and shudders as Risto had. Also Risto recalled that his brother, insofar as he'd gotten to explore his sexuality at all, had gone further. Once or twice, Ti'aba had indulged in flirting. If Yebleh had enjoyed the same, over in Benghazi, wouldn't an encounter in Naples fit the troubled pattern? Wasn't it a kind of relapse? On top of that, the painter was pushing thirty. He was old enough to have started yearning for more; he could even be one of those up to the challenge of love. In that case, any throb of comfort he'd felt with Mepris must've rankled. Any promise it held seemed certain to collapse.

"That dizzy first day or so," Paola was saying.

Yebleh met her gaze frankly. He'd straightened up, and meanwhile the young man beside him softened, turning to the painter with a sloppy grin. Mepris had never been one to stay long in the closet.

"Paola, you know something?" Risto touched his wife's shoulder. "You know Yebleh was just saying, the only thing real in this world is destruction?"

She broke into a real smile. "*Amore,* honestly, he said that? Oh now, Yebleh—we can do better than that. Have you forgotten the immigrant dream?"

In the silence, you noticed the party's music. Had the DJ worked in some James Brown? Did Risto, out of nowhere, see the four of them up and dancing?

He didn't raise his voice. "Mepris?"

Looking livelier than he had all evening, with a flourish like a card sharp, Yebleh tossed the chip at Risto's feet.

❈

Mepris still did most of the talking. *Okay, we went about it all wrong, but we won't be the last Africans in Europe to…*Risto couldn't follow. He was more concerned about the detonator chip, scooping the thing up and sailing it out over the piazza, all in a single wheeling motion that left him braced at the rail. Below, the street wouldn't stop whirling. Miraculous, it seemed, the stonework and the swarming crowd. Then he needed to he get hold of his wife, cupping her head in both hands. Rowdy, this hair between his spread fingers, full of kinks and all over the place in this breeze. The woman seemed made to spend her life tiptoeing along some high Neapolitan ledge.

Now what was she saying? Something about "goo-goo eyes"?

By the time he got his bearings, Mepris was done rationalizing. Paola had assured the Moroccan they wouldn't breathe a word. She'd brought up some fairytale, something about a secret word that brings down a kingdom. Risto helped Yebleh toss scraps of hardware after the chip, between the outer railings, and then held the duffel bag open for the claylike explosive. Also he asked for the phone.

The Moroccan had got back some of his swagger. "You don't believe that's an instrument of murder? Fist, stick, knife—and then *telefonino?*"

But it wasn't his phone, nor Yebleh's either, just a street pickup quickly smashed and sent flying. Even Mepris smiled to see the bits and pieces tumble away.

"Risto," he asked, "you do realize this wasn't just about the two of us? Yebleh and me, you do realize…"

Paola, however, could field that one. Risto turned to his painter, once more avoiding everyone's eyes, struggling with a throat full of phlegm.

"Yebleh, that's all right. How about if I take you over to Capri?"

The younger man's eyes were spongy too.

"Look, you're one of my artists. It's high time I took you to Capri."

Yebleh pursed his lips, blinking. Could he be calculating how many times Tuttavia had been to the island?

"You know I have a friend over there. You and he, you need to talk." Risto still felt a few degrees apart from himself, but on this he trusted the impulse. Group therapy seemed indicated, for both the Vietnamese New Yorker and the Benghazi O'Keefe. Nobody could help an abuser like another abuser, wasn't that the idea? In any case, the offer had Yebleh pulling himself together. He touched his hair, a jazzbo making sure he looked good.

Paola, meanwhile, had gotten around to the contents of the duffel bag. "Mepris, honestly, Risto and I ought to take that off your hands. If the cost is an issue…"

"Cost?' asked the Moroccan. "You think we had to pay for it?"

She smirked. "My friend, you said it yourself—you won't be the last."

When Risto caught his wife's eye, Mepris didn't fail to notice. "So now you're a team? Working together to rid Gotham of evil?"

Risto allowed himself a chuckle, holding out his hand. "Let's just say we know exactly which cliff to throw it off."

The Moroccan's shrug, his quick handoff, seemed surprising. Then, however, Risto felt the weight of the stuff. He required both big hands just to hook the bag over a shoulder, and he didn't catch the man's next question.

"Oh, La Cia," responded Paola, "that poor child."

Also the way the two younger men sprang up, Mepris whipping his jacket back on, seemed to add to Risto's burden.

"Just awful, how that boy died, but naturally I've picked up a detail or two."

"Naturally. Never mind that your husband insisted this was hush-hush."

"Mepris, honestly, what did you expect? Did you think Risto would keep it from me for long? Even now, after you leave, I expect he'll have more to share."

How had Risto's spirits fallen so fast? He'd disarmed a bomb and saved the city—and yet a heavy bag and a minute's chatter left him sunk in gloom. It set him growling. *Eh, we've got lots to talk about…*

Then, however, his eyes fell on Yebleh. A sensitive kid, the watercolorist. His gallery owner had barely uttered an unhappy word when Yebleh's look began growing heavier, his eyes rounder. He looked as if he was about to collapse again into a heap.

Risto got him by a bicep, the way he used to do with Eftah. "Just get back to the studio, Yebleh. Have faith in the work and don't do anything crazy."

On their way out, Mepris and Yebleh gave no show of affection. No holding hands on the catwalk, no hug at the door. Their hookup could've been a mere field dressing, of course; the wound would need further treatment. Certainly the wounds between Risto and Paola continued to nag. Once they were alone, she spoke up first.

"*Amore*, tell me, what on earth brought you up here?"

She wondered if he'd had some inkling of the madness being hatched by the other two. The idea was laughable, though Risto only managed a snort. But then, this was the one person he could tell the truth: his iPhone had shown him a vision of death.

"You can see the picture if you like," he said.

Actually she would, and he supposed it was time he had another look. The menacing capper remained in place. To see it set off such a shiver that Paola had to steady Risto's hand, and then with his guidance she finger-sketched the thing.

"So, there's still time, isn't there?"

"If either of us had a clue where to find him." He was growling, toughening. "Maybe we should ask Tuttavia."

She let go, backing off.

"You two arranged a meeting."

She never broke eye contact, though one hand grew unsteady, rising and falling. "I made a phone call, yes, though of course she was already headed for the piazza."

No doubt the photographer picked up right away, too.

"Risto, you know as well as I do, that woman loves a scene like this."

He eyed the stairwell door—could Tuttavia be next?—then looked past it to the city's rising tenement cliffs. "Paola," he said, "all your little nooks and crannies…"

Now she had her phone out. "Would you prefer to text?"

He slung off the heavy bag, with a showy sigh. The evening odor surprised him, though; the air carried no trace of sulfur. The stink had been inescapable, the first weeks following the quake.

He said so. "Naples is smelling better."

If she responded, he didn't catch it.

"It smells better," he repeated, "and tomorrow there's the Expo. Better yet."

"What on earth?" That, he heard. "We're alone at last and you talk about civic renewal? Risto, if you intend to be the first African to run for mayor, you'd better first come clean with your wife."

"Please, just give me this. Some things get better." Was his voice breaking?

"*Amore*, honestly, when haven't I given you this? When have I interfered with your cheerleading?" She spoke in a rush, yet the words had a melody. "Brothers, onward—by now it's practically the family anthem."

Paola Paolissima, she had her ways.

"Brothers, follow the arrow shot out of Mogadishu, straight on to Xanadu."

"Paola, I wish it were so simple." His voice was breaking. "Back in 'Dishu, the way I got out was nothing like an arrow."

She'd drawn closer, but he didn't want the old condolences.

"It was on the run, that's all. A blur, so fast I never found out what happened."

"Well, that morning, with your brother."

"With my brother, it was never so simple. There was never a…a Parable of the Machete. He went to speak with the goons. Me, I was on the run."

"You're saying you didn't see what they did to him?"

"Maybe it means nothing."

"You're saying, you went one way, him the other?"

Risto could understand his blubbering again. But why should it hit him here, back up above the downtown?

"And Ti'aba was the last family you saw alive."

He swabbed his face and kept forcing up the words, letting her know just what had happened, back in the workers' squat above the goons' city. The lie itself might've been puny, but after all this time in his craw, it'd metastasized awfully. It'd become a desecration of his brother's memory, and the man who'd dreamed it up a fraud. This evening at last he'd be rid of the malignancy, in a splutter under his wife's gaze. He said his piece and she closed in with hugs and kisses.

But he didn't want the old condolences, her sighing *Risto-ri*,

Wobbling against the rail, for a moment he feared they'd pitch over—a nightmare all too familiar by now. A thrill that seemed cheap, though he sensed as well how much it meant to the woman with him. Teetering at the verge helped to define his wife; it heightened her contrasts. She liked both to purr and to bristle. Still, if now she and Risto understood each other better, that was all the more reason for straight talk. He gave her a final peck and slid away. With a grunt he stepped off the catwalk and sank onto one of the girders, the dome's sun-warmed steel corset.

He had only to mention Tuttavia.

"I kissed her," said Paola.

"You didn't even want me to talk to her. You're having an affair."

"I kissed her and I regret it."

"A, a *kiss...*"

"Risto, honestly, a kiss and a bit of fondling."

He gave a lurch, starting to stand, but what good would that do, all up in her face?

"A moment of weakness, that's all, against the wall of the dining room."

"A moment of weakness." The girder made a poor seat, but he was far too worn out. "You didn't even want me to talk to her."

In the gathering dusk, in her gypsy skirt, her legs had fused into a mermaid's tail. Her uneasy gestures could be keeping her afloat. But Paola's gaze never wavered as, quietly, she repeated that she was sorry. "And I haven't had her in the house since." When the husband's only reply was a grumble, she added that it was one thing to invent a fantasy about a knife and quite another to go up against an actual weapon of murder.

He remained dry-eyed. "What? Who told you that?"

In her silence, the gulls seemed to time their cries to the dance beat.

"Eh," he said, "it's like I'm no longer comfortable in my own skin." Reeling, he clung to the notion of straight talk. "Paola, yes. I've been—reckless."

Regardless of what she knew, he could own up to the worst. He could do it without his voice catching, getting at the truth even when he fell back on the counselor's euphemism, "acting out." Every apology seemed to engage his entire nervous system. Now and again Paola made some reply, something he didn't fully hear but which got across the change in tone, the deepening sympathy.

But when he'd finished, she turned conversational. "So what've you found out?"

He rocked back in his perch, coming up against a fat rivet.

"Isn't that part of the therapy? Closing the case like a proper detective? Besides, frankly, by now I'd like to know."

The rivet helped. Risto could nudge the steel plug, now and again, getting a good back-straightening jolt as he spelled out what he'd learned. "The woman who actually cut him up, over in Homicide they've got a good lead. She was just a tool of course, another victim." The larger questions concerned the video. "Whoever was the cameraman, apparently he made a mess of it." But even a professional job, a decent recording of a terrible act—even that should've been of no interest to the *malavita*.

"Why would they arrange the room? Why send one of their slave girls?"

Even in the dark, Paola's frown was visible. She agreed that the motive was hard to figure and asked if the police were investigating.

"One of them is, anyway. The officer I found, I was lucky." *Aristofano fortunato.*

"Well," said Paola, "if the people doing the killing are the same as ever, then it's got to be for the same reasons as ever."

This sent him back into the rivet.

"Murder in this city, it's always the Camorra, isn't it?" She may have smiled. "And they're always after the same thing. The same as with poor Eftah."

"Real estate?"

"One way or another, *amore*, it's got to be about territory."

Good thinking, Paola. Yet as she unpacked the idea, Risto suffered another imbalance. A different concern took shape, as he looked over the last week or so. He had to bring it up, to interrupt, thinking aloud about the time sequence. First his wife had grappled with the photographer, he pointed out, and then came his own wild nights.

"It must've been days earlier, when you and Tuttavia, when you…it could've been a week or more before I charged off to La Fenestrella."

She was giving another half-gesture. "Risto-ri."

He'd gathered himself, once more ready to leap up.

"You said it yourself, *amore*—you wish it were so simple."

"First you started to stray and then I began to go nuts." Still Risto stayed put.

"Oh so simple. A simple tit for tat, and it all starts with one wickedness, one Original Sin. All you need to do is find it and fix it."

"Paola Paolissima." Sagging, he spoke to her knees. "Have we done so badly?"

His throat remained clear, but he didn't like the sound of his voice. "So, so badly," he said. "Our whole life in Naples a sham."

"*Amore*, honestly, you go to such extremes!"

When she dropped her hands, she could've been some piece of classical statuary, eroded yet monumental.

"Our life in Europe, our life with Rosa and Tonino, did I say it was a sham?"

If he'd come close to crying, no longer.

"Even my father, his wicked deeds, and the monsters on the mortgage. We've got a handle on all that. Risto, what, now it's my turn to be the cheerleader?"

"Paola, you said it's not just one thing. As if we'd done terribly."

"Perhaps you're expecting some state of marriage in perfect balance? One that's never doing at all badly? The temple of Flawless Matrimony?"

Below, the volume had picked up—just ahead of the church bells, starting to toll across the downtown. Plainly the DJ was watching the time.

"Where's the Duomo?" asked Risto.

"Exactly." You'd think she'd been with him, up on Eftah's terrazzo. "I must say, I've never found such a sanctuary, and lately I've been chasing my husband all over the Gulf. Perhaps the best we can hope for is the occasional glimpse."

He massaged his face. "It's like I haven't been comfortable in my own skin."

"And then there's me, *per carità*, knocked off my feet in my own home."

Tonino, Risto reminded himself, hadn't seen anything. "I wonder," he said, "if all I need is another trip back South. Maybe Addis Ababa, this time."

He could see her smile; the other two had left on the light in the stairwell. "And where should I visit, *amore*, the land of the Amazons?"

"Paola, at least we've gotten though this. We've got a handle on it."

"This isn't going to fester and gnaw? You're not going to run off and found a commune? Or, the worst, contact a lawyer?"

"Oh, a lawyer." As for his smile, surely she could see it. "Better I should just go cut my throat."

"*Amore*, it's still Italy, isn't it?" Now the light set her hair aglow. "In court especially. You'll never find a judge to rule against *La Mamma Santissima*."

"I don't even want to think about it. I spend enough time in my head as it is."

What then could the Savior of Gotham do except take up his Best Beloved in another embrace? Striking a more careful balance this time, athwart a girder? Too, this time, their renewed kiss and murmur kept a sensible distance from the echoing abyss, echoing and, what's more, fragrant with intoxicants, the smoke rising from small fires that glimmered all across the deeps. But they kept their wits and kept their distance, coming together on the lowest slope of the Galleria dome with one knee bent each, statuesque, as if that very night they'd been memorialized as founding father and mother of some city not yet visible but taking shape atop the old. This new *Polis* stood fully formed already in their recommitted hearts, where too the charter had been drawn up, between apology and canoodle. First came the solemn vow, *the secrets have got to stop*, then the sober compromise, *time to talk with someone*. The evening's hero indeed recalled a clinic that could be counted on for discretion, a place not far from their airy perch, and yet even as they spoke of their present city, the couple felt swept on into the next, their future abode insofar as they could cobble it together.

So too the helpmeet at his side began joshing. She wondered if her man had been affected by the ascending fumes. What *were* they smoking, the revelers below, with their hookahs and chillums? Whatever its name, whatever the herb or rosin, it came out of Africa. Few immigrants, she teased, could match the success story of hashish, its connections all across the North—and yet even in this raillery, in comic performance, the woman struck an ineffable balance between storytime and bedside prayer.

"And as for getting back to the South," Paola added, "you realize we'd never be able to stop the children, if they want to go?"

Freeing one arm, he fingered his scalp.

"You realize it's probably one of them who'll get down to Mogadishu?"

"First generation born abroad..."

"Exactly," she said. "Aren't they the ones who have to return? Who can't resist the lure of the Old Country?"

The husband went on nodding, but he lost his grin as he turned toward the exit door. The stairwell had gotten noisy, and Risto thought first of the duffel bag. But this was only Mepris, his eyes swollen with worry.

"Police, down there."

※

Paola insisted on taking the duffel. Heavy as it was, yes; a white woman's bag would draw less attention. Mepris agreed, though distractedly, gabbling on about what he and Yebleh had found just one spiral down. As they'd reached the office level, they'd spied a nest of cops. Three cops, five? He didn't know. He'd tried to wait them out, hunkering down with the Libyan, but finally he'd come creeping back.

Once everyone was under the stairwell light, you could see that Eftah's ex had swabbed off his blush and eye shadow. He'd made himself over, adaptive coloration, switching from hothouse hues to rainwashed simplicity. Mepris remained jittery, too, taking the stairs one slow step at a time. In a whisper, he explained that he and Yebleh had found a utility closet.

"*Les flics* had a man by the door," he said. "He ought to've spotted us, really. But they had some trouble down the hall, a ruckus. We had a moment to hide."

"A ruckus?" asked Risto. "Paola and I were right upstairs."

"But, *mon vieux*, surely you realize, one story down is a world apart."

Besides, it wasn't as if he'd stumbled upon gunplay. "Just banging, just shouting. Though we did hear about a knife."

Risto caught the Moroccan's eye.

"Heard it distinctly," said Mepris. "A cop, '*Drop the knife!*'"

"But, Yebleh?" The Libyan had a visa, to be sure, but if the police were in a lather, who could say?

"Hm." Mepris gave a smirk. "That boy came out of the closet."

Yebleh had recognized one of the voices in the office corridor. The security guard, Konan, had come upstairs with the cops. "Once the scuffle died down, you could hear him clearly, the Eritrean. The brother wasn't in cuffs, get the picture?"

Mepris, as if it hung on the wall of the Uffizi. The Libyan hadn't wanted to scurry back to Papa. He'd developed some spine, after the day he'd had, and then he heard another African up on the office level. With that, he'd made a run for it. By now Yebleh was out in the piazza.

Risto, just over the younger man's shoulder, wished they could move faster. "What about a woman's voice?" he asked.

"Hm, could've been. Could've..."

"Look, you'd know the voice."

The younger man paused to shrug.

"Mepris, I'm asking about Tuttavia."

"Tuttavia?" This was Paola, a step behind.

Down at office level, the Moroccan let them pass, crouching on a step above the door. Risto had already fished out his card from Det. Della Figurazione, flashing it at Paola over one shoulder. Then once the two of them were into the hallway, the open office with a cop at the door, there could be no mistaking the photographer. If the evening had been a bumpy ride, Tuttavia loomed up like Queen of the Rodeo. Her mouth and fingertips royal red and the rest black and white, she flashed the silver at her wrists like a scepter. Around her the men looked ordinary, even in uniform. They gave the impression that the worst was past. All that mattered was Tuttavia and the girl at her feet.

A girl, her short skirt spangly and long hair streaked, down in a limp party bundle. Beyond this heap of bright rags and the Goth icon over her, Risto at first couldn't see much. To one side stood cluster of men and farther in lay another fallen figure. But Tuttavia, here before him—could she be talking to the disarray at her feet? If so, what was that language? Even the woman's tone came across strangely, almost motherly. Then, however, the photographer spotted Risto and his wife. She fell silent.

Paola rushed by. "Girl, honestly, what've you got me into now?"

Tuttavia's hands dropped, her fingers fluttering.

"Such wild scenes, why—it's Sodom and Gomorrah!"

Risto left them to it. He needed to study the rest of the wreckage.

You reach a certain corner, a certain hour…but tonight had brought Tuttavia and her gallery owner full circle from last Sunday. Up in La Fenestrella she'd come between him and a murderer, and here in the Galleria it was his turn. Risto had got his man from Homicide involved, and the officer had put a stop to Fidel's and Zelusa's violent games. That was Zelusa on the floor, yes, with a wide slash of blood down her one exposed arm. She was hiding her face, moaning in that unknown language. What tongue should he expect from a broken sex toy? And what repairs could she expect from her Daddy? Fidel was under interrogation, face to face with Della Figurazione. The questions appeared to bewilder Risto's buyer, as did the cop at either arm. One of these had Castelsabbia's build, thick through chest and belly, but the other was slender and tall. This officer's uniform was lighter, his skin darker: it was Konan, deputized. The brother had known a special opportunity when it turned up at his door. No I.D. in Italy was worth so much as friends on the police.

But the goony bird with the head of an ox—he'd never looked so animal. His smile seemed a spasm, a rictus.

"She gets carried *away*," he was saying. "I've seen her get carried away."

The voice too was hard to take, blithering.

"If it was she, killing that proud nigger with the big mouth! People would pay good money to see that."

Risto looked to Giussi. Surely he was the farther heap, Giussi, the rumple on the floor of the inner office. Risto only needed to slide sideways to make him out—and to know his friend was still alive. The lights on Giussi were powerful, gilding his narrow head, but this was no halo. More than that, the performer was stirring, his back flexing under his thin suit jacket. Otherwise he remained in a close tuck, massaging his jaw and wrists, and Risto may've spotted a fleck of blood on one black sleeve. But the man could've been Nijinsky, *Afternoon of a Faun.* The mat on which he lay was industrial, easy to wash. It was just the thing for a bloodletting. Risto didn't spot the hardware, the ball-gag and cuffs, but the willowy Ethiopian couldn't have taken long to subdue. One swift kick from those Doc Martens would've done the job.

He thought back further as well, picturing Giussi at the door to the Galleria stairs, alongside Fidel and his Ukrainian doll. Those two were the white couple he'd been seen with, first by the handsome street-salesman and then the Eritrean at the door. As for the Nordic beauties from Capri, they were off duty till tomorrow. They'd probably hit the dance floor by the time Risto had gotten to Konan. The man working security had the wrong white folks, and he himself had the wrong floor.

He could sort it all out with a single look. Fidel must've lured the performer with talk of another quick porn payoff. Wrestling him into cuffs was just part of his job, the goony gaffer, the whole crew.

The setup remained in place, the mat on the floor, the lights and camera on their stands. Fidel's Canon was of course multi-function, yet another burden on the man's fraying finances. Far cheaper was the essential prop, the serrated fisherman's knife. No doubt the cops had it in a baggie, but earlier, with Giussi trussed and down, Fidel would've handed the weapon to the pretty young thing he'd wanted as his star. He'd counted on her changing his luck. The stills, the threesome, hadn't made him a penny. When he'd stepped up to live action, last Friday night, he'd botched it. He'd messed up even with a helping hand from the Camorra. But if tonight he could manage the job, if he could make a movie that people wanted to watch, that would at last justify the way he'd whittled down the family accounts. After all, the deepest cuts had to do with Zelusa. If she didn't need a passport, she needed a corset from La Perla, and by now the man's only chance for a return on his investment was to whip her into some sort of freak.

"Good money," Fidel repeated, between Konan and the cop "Think of the money the Americans made, with their *Girls Gone Wild*."

Yet the intended victim, over in the next room, looked little the worse for wear. Giussi rolled over and stretched with a big, blinking yawn. The cops hadn't bothered to keep a man on him, and they hadn't sent for anyone from the green cross. They were making this up as they went along, the police. This duty roster for the evening would've made no mention of Tuttavia, but she was the reason Della Figurazione and a couple of uniforms had wound up this far above street level. Whether the man from Homicide had spotted her first, or the other way around, once the detective brought up the threat to Giussi, she'd thought again about what she and Paola had heard from the Galleria security guard. Then Tuttavia had gone back to Konan, this time with the cops, and unlike her gallery owner she'd gotten the facts straight. Thanks to her own session in front of Fidel's camera, she'd known where tonight's threesome was headed. As for the man who'd called her "missus," maybe Tuttavia didn't want anyone else to kill him, or maybe she didn't want him dead at all.

Risto could sort it out, even the thick stink of hash and the half-empty bottle of pink vodka. The filmmaker had thrown a party, using every trick he could to blow his baby's mind. He'd plied her with smoke and liquor, no doubt encouraging her as well to sample some X or the like. Giussi no doubt had joined in the whoop-dee-doo, until they'd got him hogtied. After that: another Cosmo, honey?

Yet Zelusa hadn't gone through with it. She hadn't gotten carried away. Before the police burst in, the only person she'd cut was herself.

By then Risto had company, the detective. "The *man*," said Della Figurazione. "The name all over the piazza."

Signore Al'Kair might've missed what happened, claimed the officer, but he was the one who'd made it happen. Without him, the police would never have found "this little apocalypse." They'd have had to put it on the caseboard at Homicide.

When Risto didn't quite manage a nod, the other man reined himself in.

"Ah, surely the signore is cognizant of the Department's other sources. Our mutual friend over at the *Guardia Finanzaria*, in particular."

Nardo there, amid his spreadsheets and extension cords, had been following Fidel's money for a while now. "A lifelong desk jockey like that, he's only too happy to track the fall of his playboy cousin." Between what Nardo had told him earlier and what Risto had told him this afternoon, Della Figurazione had known what was up as soon as he'd stumbled upon this bedlam. If you asked him, Fidel's latest scheme proved he was crazier than his girlfriend.

"*Per carità*! Trying to recoup his losses with a, what's the word? A 'snuff film'? In the first place, there can't be much money in it, and in the second he'd have to do business with some vicious desperados indeed."

Now Risto was nodding. Vicious, he thought, and always with the same goal...

He looked to the women, drawn into a cluster. Fidel's wasted plaything sat up, the photographer was down on one knee, and Risto's wife, the duffel at her feet, stood in prayer posture. Zelusa raised one spread hand, revealing how she'd mutilated herself, an ugly crescent from her wrist almost to her elbow. After a moment Tuttavia closed her own hand around the gash, so that the blood seeping through her grip outlined her knuckles, making their bulge all the more powerful. Both she and Paola began asking questions, neither much above a whisper, and the Ukrainian was likewise subdued in her answers. Still, Risto got it: he wasn't alone in trying to make sense of this.

Tuttavia, he expected, also had to recognize how she'd contributed to the damage. Her recent shenanigans, the listless pornography and groper's adultery—all the flailing of a creative spirit that's lost faith—this too had left its fragments amid the debris. Tuttavia's stagger and fall was far from the worst, of course; see Rothko, see Caravaggio. Still, as she held the murmuring Ukranian, she could've been thinking how much she owed the girl. Zelusa too hadn't wanted him dead, their dancing Ethiopian.

As for Paola, she was back to basics, a hand on the wounded girl's cheek.

Risto too could offer comfort. "Paola Paolissima," he said, "look around."

His first complete sentence since leaving the roof, it even had Zelusa staring.

"Look at this real estate, *bella*," he went on. "Historic real estate, top story."

Della Figurazione drew closer. "Signore, what?"

Paola had given him only a glimmer, a hint of a smile and nod, but with that Risto could turn to the detective. Mildly he asked if he might see "the weapon." The ranking officer on the scene had found no better place for the evidence bag than his jacket pocket, and as for the knife, eh. The kind of tool you'd find in a lot of homes around Naples. Risto wound up wondering more about the detective's home. How often did this man think of the happiness he'd lost? Even if it were a dream, the wife docile, the pasta steaming? The ache of a vanished life—I know it well, my brother. It can make you believe you've got shake the whole thing off its foundations.

Della Figurazione, at least, had something to show for going rogue. He could have the coup that made his career, the perp and his accessory and more. He pointed to the second item in the baggie, another bracelet, pseudo-Aztec. The jewelry, he explained, was merely supporting evidence.

"Every investigation," he said, "turns up some such flotsam and jetsam."

Nonetheless, the cheap piece helped Della Figurazione understand something about last Friday. As he put the bag away, he brought out his other hand, its thumb extended, wagging back and forth. Some sort of pantomime? The detective told Risto to think of a phone, the swipe and touch with which a man selected a pretty face.

"Signore, the mutilation? Think about it. Isn't it the thumb that takes a man from picture to picture, on a sex site? The thumb and the eyes?"

Risto stared down into his own hand, fingers spread.

"You understand, Signore Al'Kair? One expects a girl would grow sick of it, all these men ogling her online."

"She took his tools of power. A ritual humiliation."

When the other man rolled his eyes, you saw how little sleep he'd been getting. "Please. This is police work, not anthropology. Now, I ask you again. What are you telling me, when you bring up real estate?"

Risto checked the women, but they'd gathered closer, murmuring, intent.

"Look, a place like this is top of the market. It couldn't be more exclusive, a legacy property." Fidel's office presented no end of possibilities for the *malavita*. If the shop girls of La Chiaia knew the family credit had worn threadbare, then the mob for damn sure knew. "They had the cash. They even had a girl who'd cut somebody's throat on camera." One hand washes the other; before long the goony bird would be so deep in the Camorra's pocket, he'd have no choice but to give them title. Come to think, the Castelsabbia heir would himself be a part of the deal, a throw-in.

"They can always use a front," said Risto. "A man of impeccable character."

Della Figurazione had drawn himself up, fingering together the front of his jacket. Risto knew the look well, he'd seen it so often around the gallery. *Great show, you goddamn gifted bastard.*

⌗

So far as Risto could see, scrubbing his scalp, the only questions remaining concerned Giussi. How about that bright, strange shadow, the golden headdress in last night's photo? Risto brought out his phone—the detective had returned to his prisoner—and then the man himself was at his side.

Even a performance artist needed a break from those bright lights. Giussi had broken a terrible sweat, worse than you'd expect from someone out of the sub-Sahara. Risto ought to have whiffed him coming. Still, nothing mattered more than the photo, and with Giussi at his elbow, Risto worked his thumb. Once the shot came up, he did a double take, triple, making certain that they both saw the same. Unhaloed.

Giussi pursed his lips, finicky. "I decided not to use that one."

Risto was just the opposite, a guppy.

"Oh la, my prince, oh wizard of the black arts. I do so hate to disappoint you. But a photo such as that, to my eye, it's better suited for a person's I.D."

Risto gripped the performer's worn black lapel, the one without the bloodstain. Gently, he butted the man's sweat-soaked chest. "Giussi."

"Risto. A soul such as mine, so teeming and full of tricks, they could never destroy it. Not in three thousand years."

Gently: "These will hardly be the last white folks to try."

"Hardly the last, indeed, but at least we've got this one in cuffs. The Philistine Fidel. And isn't our life here, in the North—isn't it all a high-wire act?"

"High-wire act." He tucked away his unmagick'd phone. "Just tonight, I've seen more than one way it could all come tumbling down."

Giussi struck a pose, terrified. "Captain, we split, we split!"

"*Per carità*. Our revels now are ended, is that it?"

"Oh la la. My fans anticipate my every move. At any event, Risto, look at how handsomely the White Devil pays."

The performer fished out his advance, a clip of Euros, but the defiant gesture wasn't quite intact. His grip trembled. Risto, still smiling, laid a hand against the taller man's cheek.

Elsewhere, the cops were taking over. Someone carried a walkie-talkie, and Della Figurazione had taken this, loudly making arrangements with the paddy wagon and the hospital tent. He was coming with "rather a caravan," he said, "a mixed group, two whites in custody and two foreigners with the police." He needed everyone he could get on this. They had to cross an unpredictable stretch of city, riddled with impedimentia and rocking with smoke and lights, hue and cry.

ACKNOWLEDGMENTS

An EXCERPT, ADAPTED TO STAND alone, appeared in *Web del Sol: The Del Sol Review.* Thanks to the editors, in particular Linda Lappin. Deepest thanks to everyone at Dzanc Books.

Among my early readers, none mattered so much as Lettie Prell.

Financial support came from the Iowa Artist Fellowship Program, the Northwestern University Center for Writing Arts, and elsewhere.

The many strata of Naples yield many literary gems, live and kicking even in dead languages. What's more, as I pulled my Naples work together, fresh treasures turned up, like Elena Ferrante. Rather than list them all, I'll just offer blanket gratitude, and add that this book also owes a great deal to the city's magnificent abundance in the visual arts. In particular I'm grateful to the wizardly Oni Wong, and her salon ArteStesa.